THE MARINES OF AUTUMN

THE
MARINES
OF
AUTUMN

A NOVEL OF THE KOREAN WAR

JAMES BRADY

THOMAS DUNNE BOOKS

ST. MARTIN'S PRESS ❧ NEW YORK

THOMAS DUNNE BOOKS.
An imprint of St. Martin's Press.

Book design by Clair Moritz

Library of Congress Cataloging-in-Publication Data

Brady, James.
    The Marines of autumn : a novel of the Korean War / James Brady.—1st ed.
    p.cm.
    ISBN: 0-312-26200-0
    1. Korean War, 1950–1953—Fiction. 2. United States. Marine Corps—Fiction.
    I. Title.

PS3552.R243 M37 2000
813'.54—dc21   00–025472

First Edition: June 2000

10   9   8   7   6   5   4   3   2   1

DEDICATION TO "THE CHOSIN FEW"

This book is dedicated to the Marines and others, American and Allied, who fought and defeated the Chinese army in the autumn of 1950 in the mountains of North Korea near the Chosin Reservoir, those who ever since have called themselves, with a rare humor, the Chosin Few. It was my honor to serve with some of them.

Acknowledgments

I fought as a Marine officer in the Taebaek Mountains of North Korea from Thanksgiving weekend of 1951 through that autumn and winter into the spring of 1952, first as a rifle platoon leader in Dog Company of the Seventh Marines, then as Dog Company's executive officer, finally as battalion intelligence officer. This area of operations was just south of where the Chosin Reservoir fighting took place exactly a year earlier, in the autumn of 1950.

In writing fictionally about the 1950 campaign I have drawn on conversations and correspondences with men who were there and on articles in general magazines and newspapers as well as such specialized publications as *Leatherneck* magazine, *The Old Breed News,* and the newsletter of the Chosin Few organization.

Books on which I've drawn include:

U. S. Marine Operations in Korea, 1950–1953, volume 3: *The Chosin Reservoir Campaign,* by Lynn Montross and Captain Nicholas A. Canzona, USMC; reprinted by R. J. Speights, Austin, Texas, 1990.

Korea, the Untold Story of the War, by Joseph Goulden; Times Books, New York, 1982.

This Is War, by David Douglas Duncan; Harper & Brothers, New York, 1951.

Marine! The Life of Chesty Puller, by Burke Davis; Bantam Books, New York, 1962.

Colder Than Hell, A Marine Rifle Company at Chosin Reservoir, by Joseph R. Owen; Naval Institute Press, Annapolis, Maryland, 1996.

Retreat, Hell! by Jim Wilson; William Morrow, New York, 1988.

Triumph on 1240, The Story of Dog Company Seventh Marines in Korea, by R. D. Humphreys; Professional Press, Chapel Hill, NC, 1998.

Korean War Almanac, by Harry G. Summers, Jr.; Facts on File, New York, 1990.

Breakout, by Martin Russ; Fromm International, New York, 1999.

Witness to War, Korea, by Rod Paschall; Berkley Publishing, New York, 1995.

Truman, by David McCullough; Simon & Schuster, New York, 1992.

American Caesar (a biography of Douglas MacArthur), by William Manchester.

And for general information about Korea, *A Handbook of Korea,* published in 1988 by Seoul International Publishing House for the Korean Overseas Information Service.

We'll be home for Christmas,
The kids never missed us.
So cheer up, my lads,
Bless 'em all.

—*Polite variant on a Marine ditty,*
North Korea, Autumn 1950

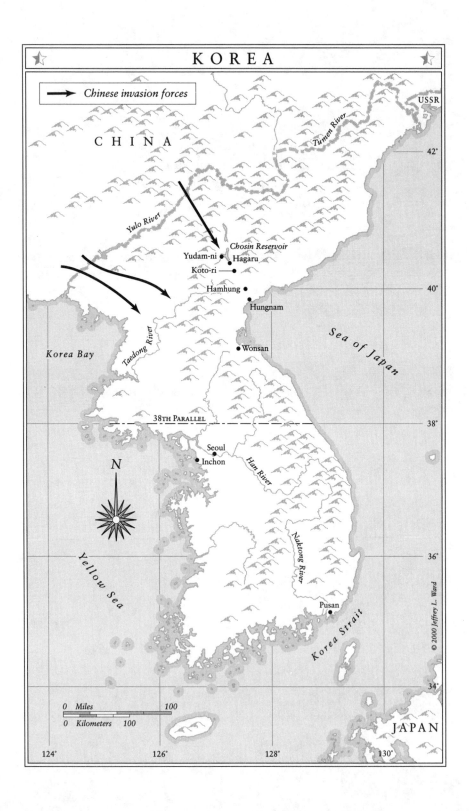

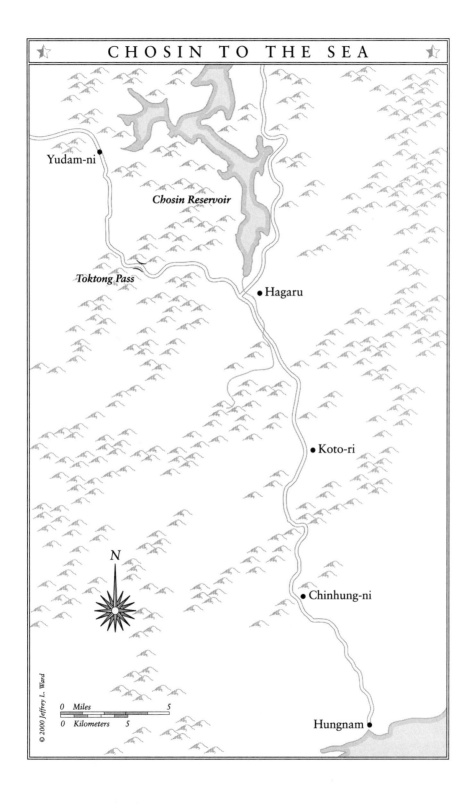

CHOSIN TO THE SEA

Yudam-ni

Chosin Reservoir

Toktong Pass

• Hagaru

• Koto-ri

N

• Chinhung-ni

© 2000 Jeffrey L. Ward

0 Miles 5
0 Kilometers 5

Hungnam

PROLOGUE

*This was mountain country, beautiful and terrible, and it was a
country that had been at war almost four months, but with no
fighting this far north.*

There were still tigers in these mountains and it was natural
for the smallish deer, tawny with white markings, to move
cautiously when it came down to drink on an autumn
morning from the big lake that served as a reservoir and for the
hydroelectric power system. The deer's caution was normal and
instinctive and had nothing to do with the country being at war.
What was not normal, the morning's cold.

Winter was fierce in this place, the wind out of Siberia crossing a
brief corner of Manchuria and heavy snow coming off the Sea of
Japan, the two combining to bury the Taebaek Mountains of
North Korea for five or six months of every year. November could
be very cold, and true calendar winter, when it came, would fasten
its chill grip on people and mountains until late April and into
May. There were few gentle months in the Taebaeks.

But this cold in early October?

The deer, which of course had no knowledge of dates or fron-
tiers, knew only it was strange to find skim ice at the edge of the
lake so soon after the summer's heat. The ice was barely there and
no obstacle to drinking, and the deer pawed it away easily with a

hoof before bending its neck to drink. If there were a tiger about, now was its moment. But no tiger sprang and the deer drank its fill before moving back up the slope of the hill and away from the water. Beyond these low hills sloping upward from the natural bowl of the lake were real hills, mountains of twenty-five thousand meters or more, eight or nine thousand feet in height, with snow cresting their summits, even in autumn.

This was mountain country, beautiful and terrible, slimly forested by fir and pine, spruce and cedar, with small, swift streams of pure water racing through narrow gorges that divided the steep hills, and it was a country that had been now at war almost four months but with no fighting this far north. Not even the dull pounding of distant guns or the rumor of war to disturb its calm.

The lake at which the deer drank and where skim ice formed in the shallows was called Changjin. But on the maps, which were mostly in Japanese from forty years of occupation, this lake was marked down as the Chosin Reservoir rather than its proper, Korean name. And it was at the Chosin that two opposing armies would soon meet. Though in early October, with great China not yet in the war and Gen. Douglas MacArthur declaring the conflict almost won, no one knew this.

Now a pinecone fell noisily and the deer, in some alarm, scampered from the lake into the shelter of trees.

In the district of Georgetown, Washington it still felt like summer, hot and humid, and Tom Verity was promising his daughter Kate a Christmas in Paris.

"Madame told me so much," the little girl said, "about places she lived when she was young."

"I know a few places myself, Kate," her father said, remembering a wedding trip, "places even Madame doesn't know," "Madame" being the French nanny.

"Oh, good!" Kate exclaimed, clapping her hands, enjoying conspiracy.

"And we'll practice our French with cabbies and waiters," Verity said, "and you'll help me with my verbs. And we'll walk across bridges over the Seine."

"*Bien sur, Papa,*" the child said, in an accent not at all bad for her age and for someone who lived not in France but in Washington, D. C.

Father and daughter pored over a book of pictures of bridges and churches and sidewalk cafés and formal gardens where little boys in short pants sailed boats on ancient ponds, and the two made plans for things they would do and marvels they would see in Paris that winter.

Then the call came from Arlington, Virginia, where the Marine Corps had its headquarters, asking Tom Verity to come by on a matter of some importance.

CHAPTER ONE

"MacArthur will be sprinting north. You know how he is; you know about the ego."

The Marines, hard men and realists, had never heard of the Chosin Reservoir, but they did not believe the war was over. Not yet. Nor did they truly trust MacArthur.

When they "liberated" (a headline writer's word no Marine ever used) Seoul, the South Korean capital, MacArthur flew in for ceremonies with that old fart Syngman Rhee, accompanied by honor guards of spit-and-polish South Korean troops who had run away and hadn't fought. MacArthur and President Rhee accepted the city as explorers returning from the South Pole once had received the keys of New York from Mayor La Guardia.

It was all bullshit. In the two or three days after MacArthur and Rhee took the salute, another two hundred Marines were killed in the house-to-house fighting that continued after Seoul was "liberated."

Within a few weeks MacArthur would be announcing that "the boys," his phrase, might be "home for Christmas."

In the early autumn of 1950 MacArthur's image had rarely shone as brightly. At his vice-regal headquarters in Tokyo he could look back on the extraordinary events of September, when a battered American and South Korean army pulled itself together at Pusan, swept ashore at Inchon, recaptured Seoul, and burst north to the Thirty-eighth Parallel toward victory. MacArthur had never gone back to America after defeating the Japanese, and if he could win this new war swiftly, he would at last come home and on a giddy wave of popularity. The *Chicago Tribune* and the *Hearst* papers were already pushing his cause for the 1952 Republican nomination for president. If he could beat out colorless Senator Taft and the politically equivocal, naive Eisenhower, well, who knew? But he had to win this latest war first, and quickly, settling the affair before winter closed down. Even the general, with a solemn regard for his own divinity, knew you could not fight a modern war in the mountains during a north Asian winter.

As his troops crossed the Parallel into North Korea there were warnings, diplomatic and military, that Communist China would not idly permit its Korean ally to be crushed or tolerate a UN, largely American, army installed on China's border at the Yalu River. MacArthur, out of pride or ambition (who knew which dominated?), ignored the warnings and at the end of September divided his triumphant army and ordered it to push rapidly north, one column to the east, the other column to the west of a spine of mountains through which there were no roads, only trails and footpaths.

He did not know that in what was then called Peking, on October 4, Mao Tse-tung ordered Chinese Communist Forces (CCF) to intervene, secretly at first, filtering across the Yalu by night and hiding in the North Korean hills until sufficient force had built up, out of sight of marauding American planes (each man carried a sort of bedsheet as camouflage in the snow), to fall upon and destroy MacArthur's two armies fatally divided by mountains. There were rules about splitting your army in two like this, with mountains or swamps or deserts separating one column from the other. But Douglas MacArthur or, "The General," as Jean MacArthur invariably called her husband, was an officer whose legend was founded on broken rules.

The First Marine Division was to spearhead the eastern half of the UN army, what was called X Corps, in its sprint to the Yalu River and to China.

Perhaps Omar Bradley should have spoken up. Later (but only later) he said of MacArthur's plan to divide the army, "To me it doesn't make sense . . . the enemy himself could not have concocted a more diabolical scheme. . . ." Bradley was chairman of the Joint Chiefs.

Joe Collins, "Lightning Joe," admitted he was "worried." He was army Chief of Staff. But as Matt Ridgway said later: "No one was questioning the judgment of the man who had just worked a military miracle," at Inchon, where the Joint Chiefs had registered doubt and had been proven wrong.

Nor were *any* of Truman's chieftains willing to argue the toss with MacArthur.

Captain Verity didn't want to be in Korea in the autumn of 1950. Of course, what American did except a few crazy regulars like Col. Chesty Puller and maybe MacArthur himself, hungry even at age seventy for a military encore after five years of playing shogun to the Japanese? Verity had a specific reason for wanting to stay home. A child to whom he was both mother and father. The war began in Korea in June, and thousands of Marine officers and enlisted reservists had been called back. Even Ted Williams of the Red Sox. Verity had not. He was still living and working in Washington, still a civilian.

Verity's home was on P Street, just west of Wisconsin Avenue. It was a narrow house on a narrow plot on a leafy, cobbled street with trolley tracks, a five-minute stroll from Georgetown University, where he worked.

Verity was a disciplined sort who ran three mornings a week before changing to stroll over to Georgetown, where he taught Chinese history as an adjunct professor and, in addition, helped out at the School of Foreign Service with the translation of sticky bits in a dialect none of the resident scholars understood. In this, Verity was something of a freak. Few Americans spoke Chinese at all; almost none, even the scholars, could handle more than several dialects. Tom Verity, it was said, could speak and read a half-dozen.

And now, on this morning, when he got back to the house, sweatshirt soaked and shorts hanging baggy and damp on his mid-size frame, the olive drab sedan with Marine Corps plates was parked out front.

"You were granted compassionate relief from active duty when the reserves were mobilized in July, then, Captain?"

"Yes, I requested compassionate and it came through."

"Your wife—"

"She died last winter. We have a small child, a daughter, almost three."

The colonel asking these questions knew all this. But he was a regular and they like to establish the line. The two men sat across the desk from each other in an office in Henderson Hall, the Marine Corps headquarters over the Potomac from Washington in Arlington, close by the cemetery. Sun streamed in the windows behind the colonel, and he was still dressed in summer khakis. Verity wore a navy poplin suit. There was no air-conditioning and both men sat easy as they spoke, conserving energy in the heat.

"And you have qualified help at home, for the child?"

"I hired a full-time child's nanny, through a French placement firm. She's been very satisfactory, very professional."

The colonel also knew Verity had money.

"And your daughter likes her?"

"Kate likes her very much, yes." He wondered where this was going and worried that he already knew.

"Now about China," the colonel said, "you were born there."

"I lived in China pretty much all my life until age fifteen."

"Your parents were missionaries?" The colonel knew that they weren't.

"No, my father worked for GM and then went off on his own, building and selling light trucks to the Chinese. He made a very good living off it until the Japanese came. Then we got out. I was already in the States at school and my parents came back in '38 and bought a place in Grosse Pointe. During the War he did things for GM."

His father had been more than a businessman and China more than a market, but Verity let it drop there. He was not accustomed to providing justifications. The thing spoke for itself, as lawyers say.

"And you went back after the War."

"After the Japanese surrendered I went up to Tsingtao with the First Marine Division as a rifle company commander. After about six months I came back to the States and got out."

"And in North China those six months . . . ?"

"We accepted the surrender of local Japanese units, kept the rails open, fought bandits and occasionally dickered with local Communist Red Army units, and tried to keep from freezing."

Then the colonel stopped fencing and began to talk about why Verity was in the office.

His old uniforms from five years ago, the forest green worsted wool of winter and the khaki gabardine of summer, lay creased and flat and smelling of mothballs and locker boxes.

"We could have them cleaned and pressed, Tommie," his wife had suggested, "put them in garment bags, as women do with furs. They're beautiful uniforms. Keep them nice."

"No need, Elizabeth. They're only relics never to be worn again."

Now he pulled them out. Early autumn. Well, they'd be out of khaki any day now and into the forest green, and he was damned if he was going to carry two sets of uniforms. So he chose the forest green bought almost seven years ago from that tailor in the town of Quantico, down the street that ended at the river. Italian fellow. Good tailor.

"Nell?"

Nell was the maid. "Take this to the dry cleaner on Wisconsin, please, and tell him I need it back tomorrow."

"Yes, Mr. Verity."

As he handed it over he stopped. Wait a moment. He'd better try on the jacket. Elizabeth kept after him about that, about putting on weight. It was fine. He looked at himself in the mirror. "OK, Nell, you can take it. Not the ribbons." You didn't send them to the cleaner.

There were ribbons in the locker box as well, and the rule was that you wore your ribbons. But no captain's bars, no silver railroad tracks, only the old single silver bars of first lieutenant. The captaincy had come by mail. And without bars. Well, he supposed there were still PXs that sold such things.

He'd not looked into mirrors while trying on the uniform jacket, and he wondered if he'd looked as strange as he felt.

Like Henry Luce, another old China hand, when he got back to the States Tom Verity was enrolled first in Hotchkiss, then at Yale. At Hotchkiss, like Luce, he'd immediately been nicknamed Chink, in consequence of which he never used the word as slang, even later and among Marines. He was a senior at New Haven, majoring in Chinese history, when Pearl Harbor was attacked, and with several classmates he went downtown and enlisted in the Marine Corps.

His father, and other prudent people, said they should have waited, that as Yale graduates the following spring they'd be assured of commissions. Instead, Verity was run through boot camp at Parris Island and in August, as a Marine private, found himself fighting the Japanese on Guadalcanal.

Guadalcanal was the worst, Marines said then and some still say. Steamy tropical swamp and jungle surrounded rugged, chill mountains. Some of the natives were cannibals. The Japanese fought with a medieval savagery. One night five Allied cruisers, American and Australian, were sunk by the Japanese in a single disastrous battle.

"There weren't many sailors that got to the beaches," the Marines reported. "The sharks ate them."

When the 'Canal fell Verity was a private first class and ticketed for an officer candidate program back in the States. He wrote his father in some glee: "So, you see, a Yale education, even short of a degree, has worth after all."

He came out of Guadalcanal with malaria and the usual skin infections from the heat and the swamp and sailed through OCS. In 1944 he was in Australia, and the following year, as a second lieutenant, he commanded a rifle platoon on Okinawa, winning a Silver Star and promotion to first lieutenant. When the war ended they shipped the First Division to North China, to Tientsin. Verity now had a company and with his fluency in the language was pressed into service negotiating with the local warlords and the Eighth Chinese Route Army, Mao Tse-tung's people. He was twenty-five years old and for the first time back home.

"You know, it even smells the same," he told fellow officers.

"Yeah, Tom, it stinks."

"No," he said happily, "no, it doesn't."

They didn't understand this was really home; this was what he knew. And loved. Even the familiar, sweetly reeking smell of it.

After you have been in hard fighting, garrison duty is both welcome and boring, and Tom was glad to be seconded into liaison work. The warlords were easy to handle: A combination bribe and threat was usually sufficient. The Communists, like religious zealots, were tougher. Stubborn, repetitive, endlessly patient, anything to win an argument, achieve an end. Other American officers, who didn't know the Orient, lost their temper and pounded tables and cursed. Verity sipped tea and called everyone Comrade and was deferential to the older Chinese officers. He was relatively successful in getting what the Marines wanted, whether it was a rail line opened or a straggler returned or swapping canned goods for fresh turnips.

"Tom, you understand these people and I don't," a fellow officer might say. "You like this country and I hate it. You don't even seem anxious to get home, and I sure as hell am."

Verity just grinned. He'd had some close calls on Guadalcanal and more on Okinawa and understood how fortunate he was to be alive and unhurt, and it would take more than China to depress him. And, as he sometimes said, "Guys, I grew up here. I *am* home."

In the spring of '46 he was released and returned to the States the other way round, through southern Asia (carefully skirting a suddenly surly Soviet Union) and Europe, sailing to New York on the recently refurbished *Queen Mary*, in a first-class stateroom, which was not how most GIs came back. He'd already been accepted in the graduate program at Harvard, and a day trip to New Haven assured him his work in North China qualified for something or other and they would send his bachelor's degree along in due course.

The Marine Corps promoted him to captain by mail, the passage of time in grade being what it was, and then, on a football weekend in November of '46, he met Elizabeth Jeffs.

"... Now that we've taken Seoul," the headquarters colonel at Arlington was saying, "UN forces, specifically the ROKs [Republic of Korea units], will be crossing the Thirty-eighth Parallel into North Korea."

"I didn't know that," Verity said.

"Not in the papers yet, Captain, a political decision, not a military one. Crossing an invisible line doesn't mean a damned thing to most of the soldiers on either side. The North Koreans seem to be beaten. In any event, they're running. The UN troops report very little organized resistance. So crossing the Thirty-eighth Parallel is militarily insignificant. But it could be very important to the Chinese."

Verity exhaled. He suspected where all this was leading.

"To the Chinese," he said numbly, aware of the repetition.

"They've been sending strong messages, both directly and through their Indian mouthpiece at the UN, Krishna Menon, that for us to cross the Parallel would be considered a hostile act toward China. Washington isn't sure. MacArthur assures everyone there's nothing scary going on north of the Yalu—"

"The Yalu?"

"Border river, divides North Korea and China."

"So nothing's going on."

"So MacArthur says. Here at HQ Marine Corps, we're not all that sure."

Verity sat there hoping he wasn't going to hear what he was going to hear.

"Captain," the colonel said, leaning forward on both elbows, "we'd like you to go over there and do some listening. Just listen."

"In Korea." Verity wanted to be sure. Maybe they wanted him in New York, at the UN. Small chance.

"In Korea," the colonel said. He was very reasonable. Amused, even. Easygoing.

But he could see the alarm in Verity's face and tried to reassure him.

"Look, we've got enough company commanders in the pipeline. No one's sending you over there to command troops. We need an intelligent man who's seen combat and who knows Chinese."

"Colonel, the Marine Corps gave me a compassionate pass on Korea. I asked for one; they gave it. I'm trying to raise a kid without a mother."

"It might come to nothing. This could all be political posturing by the Chinks. Who the hell knows?"

"You said MacArthur does."

The colonel was less amused. Losing patience, perhaps.

"Headquarters Marine Corps wants its own assessment. A second opinion, so to speak. You know, is this appendectomy really necessary?"

This was pointless. Why should Verity be arguing the merits of the case? He was a civilian. Well, not quite. He was still a captain in the reserve. Truman had authorized calling up the reserves. He didn't want to get into the subtleties of that argument.

So instead he said, "Colonel, I'm not your man. Get someone else who speaks Chinese." (He was going to say "Chink," but the sarcasm might irritate the colonel. Captains don't irritate colonels.)

The colonel didn't take offense, despite having been told no.

"Verity, reserve officers activated so far are in for the duration. Six months or six years, however long it lasts. Could be over by Christmas, could still be going in 1955. Nobody really knows for sure, not even MacArthur. I'm authorized to offer you a deal:

"Go over there, monitor this Chinese 'intervention', try to ascertain if it's just sabre rattling or something substantive, make a report, and come home. We won't keep you in. You'll spend a month, maybe less, maybe a little more, depending.

"We're not satisfied, Verity, with the intelligence we're getting from Eighth Army. MacArthur's top intelligence guy is Willoughby. He hates Marines. Don't know why, but he does. Some sour experience from the War probably. So we're not confident the First Marine Division is getting the dope it needs. We want our own man."

"I'm not intelligence, Colonel. I've had a rifle platoon, a rifle company. Never even worked as a battalion-2." A battalion-2 was a low-level intelligence officer.

"Verity, you speak Chinese." *Jesus*, the colonel thought, *we're beginning to go round in circles.*

"There are others who do. I could supply you a few. . . ."

The colonel tried one more approach.

"Captain, now that we've crossed the Thirty-eighth Parallel there's nothing between us and China but a dozen or so badly hurt North Korean divisions. If the politicians don't put a hold order on him, MacArthur will be sprinting north. You know how he is; you know about the ego. And he'll be doing what he did at Inchon. He'll have the Marines going for China. Around here we're edgy. We don't want fifteen thousand Marines out there like raw meat on the end of a stick with a million Chinamen waiting around just north of the Yalu."

Verity said nothing but must have looked gloomy.

"That's the job, Verity. Find out if the Chinese are coming in, find out if the Chinese are going to fight, and then come home and tell us."

"Hello," she had said, "I'm Elizabeth Jeffs. You're not a professor or anything important, are you?"

This was November of Verity's year in the master's program at Harvard, a football Saturday, with all variety of cocktail parties and mixers and dinners in and about Cambridge, and here comes this tall girl on someone else's arm to an apartment Verity shared with three other graduate students in one of the narrow streets between Harvard Square and the river.

"No, nothing as grand as that. A graduate student. And you?"

"Oh, I'm a child. A freshman at Wellesley up quite past my bedtime."

"It's only six."

"Is it?" she said. "Then I can stay awhile."

Harvard lost that afternoon, but gallantly, as Harvard customarily did, and people had wandered back across the river from Soldier Field to console themselves or celebrate. (There were, after all, men who'd done their undergraduate work at Yale and elsewhere and had other loyalties.) Verity was drinking a beer, and when he asked this girl what she wanted she said, "A martini, please, straight up with an olive."

She had long straight brown hair and a broad, placid, very beautiful face, and she certainly was tall, maybe five-nine or -ten, and with swimmer's shoulders. When people told her she was beautiful she tossed her hair as if to say, "Yes, I know, but can't you say anything clever?" and went on to dismiss beauty: "It's the accident of birth. Mixed blood. My mother was a Dutch Presbyterian and a nurse, and my father's a Jew who muscles people in Wall Street. The genes work out perfectly."

Verity asked her out for dinner, but she wouldn't go. "Not fair to the man who brought me," she said. "He's besotted with passion, as any fool can plainly see." (The man in question was across the room vigorously debating Harvard's offensive strategies with two other men.)

"Then tomorrow. Lunch."

"Yes," she said, "I'd like that."

The brattiness was a pose, a defense mechanism. At that age it usually is. She was seventeen and Verity twenty-six. He was going on to become a teacher; she was bored with college already. His family had money; hers had a lot. Jailbait was his nickname for her; she liked it. They saw each other almost every weekend through that winter and into the spring. This was 1947 and it took that long for them to sleep together.

"My gosh!" Elizabeth said. "That was terrific. Let's do *that* again."

They married in May, spent three days in New York at the Plaza listening to Peggy Lee sing "Bye-bye, Blackbird," and then took the *Queen Mary* to Southhampton. In London it was the Connaught and the car dealer's where they bought an MG roadster in British racing green, spent a couple of weeks speeding about England and then France, and sailed back home again on the *Mary*. In September he began teaching at Georgetown, and Elizabeth had baby Kate in November.

"Premature," they explained, if anyone asked.

By spring Elizabeth had her figure back and was the bane of faculty wives.

"She plays tennis without a bra."

It was true.

"I am bouncy," she admitted, "but Tommie likes me that way, don't you, darling?"

That was true, too.

A fundamentally serious man who could have become ponderous found himself dizzyingly in love.

"You'll keep me young."

"Of course I will," she said, "and must. You know, Tommie, you have a frightening potential for 'stuffy.' And I absolutely refuse to let you lapse into it."

That was also true. And he knew it.

She drove the little MG with its steering wheel on the wrong side onto the campus to pick him up after class, hitting the brakes hard and skidding to stops, alarming Jesuits and delighting undergraduates. She was not yet twenty and married to a "prof," and Verity's reputation among the students soared. Some knew he had been a Marine officer; now here was this sex-bomb wife zooming around in her sports car.

"Wow!" teenage boys marveled. "I want to grow up to be

Thomas Verity." Just imagine, a "nice" girl, already a mother, who looked and acted like this. There was fevered speculation about just how Verity, at his age, could satisfy such an obviously randy younger woman.

He was not yet thirty.

Elizabeth became pregnant again in the late summer of '49. She died the following February, the child born dead.

Verity, maddened, cried out, "But nobody *dies* in childbirth anymore! Nobody!"

The Jesuits, who recognized a good man when they had one, gathered about supportively. They and his daughter, who didn't entirely understand, pulled him through.

"Poor little poppy," Kate said when she caught him staring into nothing. She was not yet three.

The Korean War began that June, and the Marine Corps called him back in late September.

Verity phoned Elizabeth's married sister in Philadelphia to tell her where he was going. She was a reliable, responsible woman, and she promised to keep in touch with Madame. When Verity thanked her, he wondered how he was going to tell Kate.

Putting it off, he packed a few things. They'd issue him fresh fatigues in Korea, he supposed. And web gear. And a tin hat. There was an old down jacket he'd worn that winter in North China, bulky but light, and feeling foolish in the heat of Georgetown, he decided to take it along. Plus a couple of good wool sweaters and some long johns. He put in his L. L. Bean hunting boots as well. Not that he ever hunted, but still . . .

Last of all, self-conscious about it, he packed his .38, the Smith & Wesson Military and Police Special revolver with a four-inch barrel, the blue steel worn smooth, the old leather holster soft and easy as he slid the weapon in and out a few times.

Verity packed that, too. In a war, you never know.

CHAPTER TWO

What was surprising, Captain Verity thought, was how pleasant the war had been so far. If it doesn't get any worse than this, he told himself, it's a stroll. And this was enemy country.

It took three days to fly Verity from Washington to Tokyo, where he reported in at Far East Command to the ranking Marine on MacArthur's staff, a full colonel, who endorsed his orders and sent him on.

"The Mikado himself is in the building, so keep an eye out," the colonel said. "If you witness officers prostrating themselves and elderly Japanese gentlemen practicing disembowelment, you'll know you've seen General MacArthur pass."

No such wonders occurred and Verity got himself and his one piece of luggage, an antique valpack, into a Tokyo taxicab and sufficiently well understood to reach Haneda Airport. There was an army transport laid on, and he sat up front with the pilots. It took only an hour and a half and then they were over Kimpo, the big airfield nearest Seoul, some of the runways still cratered from shell fire, with burned-out planes, most of them North Korean, littering the margins of the tarmac, bodily shoved out of the way by bulldozers.

"Couple weeks ago this was all gook!" the pilot shouted.

"Plenty of guerrillas still around, they say, shooting at planes as they land!"

This was cheering news. They came in smoothly and there was a Marine gunnery sergeant waiting for Verity on the ground, reporting to Verity and welcoming him to Korea, introducing himself as Sergeant Tate.

"Thanks, Gunny. Where's the division?"

"Well, that's the thing of it, Captain. They went back to Inchon to board ship. You missed 'em."

That's typical! Verity thought sourly but didn't say so. He didn't know this Sergeant Tate and you don't rip the brass in front of enlisted men you don't know, not even gunnery sergeants. Tate understood this and went on to explain.

"I was left behind to meet you and fill you in, sir."

"I'm listening."

It was apparently another MacArthur brainstorm. While the American army and the ROKs pushed north by land, the Marines would sail all the way around the bottom of Korea from west coast to east, to be landed far north of the Thirty-eighth Parallel along the east coast of North Korea at the big port of Wonsan, catching what was left of the North Korean army in a giant pincer.

"MacArthur pulled it off once at Inchon," Tate concluded. "Why not twice . . . ?"

"I'm sure," Verity said, not accustomed to dealing with such global strategies only a week out of a Jesuit classroom. It was odd, too, being back in uniform and saluting people and being saluted. Even the old Smith & Wesson .38 hanging on his right hip felt strange. He'd worn side arms nearly four years in the War, which was what they called World War II, and still it felt strange. That's how quickly a man becomes a civilian again.

Tate had been in all the fighting from the very beginning with the Marine Provisional Brigade down south in the Pusan perimeter and then with the division when it came ashore at Inchon. He was cool and seasoned and he was a good radioman. That was part of the deal: Verity was to listen to the radio as they moved north, trying to pick up Chinese radio traffic if there was any and to make sense of it.

It turned out Tate was not only a radioman; he was a radioman who spoke some Chinese.

"Before the War," he said, "I was Fourth Marines at Shanghai and later spent time in a Jap POW camp in China. Got to patter the lingo a bit."

"Good," Verity said. He'd try Tate out later, to see just how much of the "lingo" he had. But anything was a bonus. They could share the monitoring.

"And now, what about a driver?"

One of them listening to the radio, the other riding shotgun, watching the country, watching for hostiles—they needed a third man at the wheel.

"I'm not much of a driver," Verity admitted. Elizabeth drove in their family; she just loved that little MG.

He didn't say that, of course.

Tate was reassuring. "We'll get a driver, Captain. One with savvy. Up ahead. This kind of disorganized grab ass with one army falling apart and the other army chasing, you come across all variety of unexpected and talented people. Rough diamonds of every sort. You'll see."

The army that Verity was joining wasn't one that sang when it marched, not much anyway. But that didn't mean it wasn't cheerful.

The hard fighting in the Pusan perimeter down south was behind them. And the seawall at Inchon. And the tough house-to-house combat in Seoul that had killed so many. Now the North Koreans were whipped, well and truly, an army just falling apart.

This wasn't a retreat; it was a rout.

"Nothing between here and China but hills and rice paddies." That was how one Marine saw it.

Most of the company grade officers saw it the same way. By now they knew themselves. They knew their men, what they could do. The men were good, the weapons, the air support. Maybe this was the best infantry division there ever was. People said that; you heard it. Three rifle regiments, the First, the Fifth, and the Seventh; the artillery men of the Eleventh Marines; an additional regiment of Korean Marines ("Hell, they're almost as good as us, and why not? Didn't we train 'em?"). The usual division had maybe fifteen thousand men. The First Marine Division, even after taking casualties in September, numbered more than twenty-two thousand in October as it moved north. And that didn't count its own air wing. No army division had an air wing; that wasn't how the army did things. This was a big, powerful, and very dangerous division of hardened, seasoned combat veterans that was heading north toward China.

Kate liked it when her father took her down Wisconsin Avenue to the old C.&O. Canal where donkeys (or were they mules? Verity was never sure of the difference) pulled canal barges from a path paralleling the canal. Kate loved the donkeys. You could rent those barges, for cocktails or a wedding reception, and in the spring and fall and even in the steamy summer there always seemed to be a pleasant breeze under the big trees, weeping willows and elms and cherry and oak and trees Verity did not know or even suspect.

"Daddy! Look!"

She was always seeing something. Elizabeth had been like that, curious about the world, enjoying every new sight, each fresh sensation.

A donkey regarded them. And brayed. Kate clapped her hands and squealed. Verity had always considered a donkey's bray shrill and off-key, a rude, ugly sound. No more, not when it could make a child squeal and clap.

Coming back up the slope from the canal, he carried her on his shoulders, legs around in front of him, his hands grasping her ankles. It was a long walk for a child, and by then she was ready for a ride. Sometimes he took her into Billy Martin's at the corner of N Street. She liked their lemonade and he would have a beer as they sat in a booth in the cool gloom of the bar on a summer afternoon and Kate informed him all over again of the wonders they'd seen on their walk. The same accounts would of course later be narrated to Madame, who, being French, occasionally lapsed into chauvinism:

"Ah, Kate, but you must see one day the canals of France."

"I shall, Madame. Daddy will take us there." She had no idea what or where France was.

Most nights they ate dinner together, the three of them, Madame and Kate and Tom Verity. Kate had recently graduated from a high chair to what they called a youth chair, higher but without its own tray.

"Will I cut my meat when I'm three?" she inquired.

"It's quite possible," her father told her.

"I want to, you know."

She even sounded like Elizabeth, arch yet confiding.

Bedtime was the best time, when he read to Kate. One story a night, or one chapter of a book. He self-censored, skipping over some of the more gruesome details of the Brothers Grimm where it seemed to him appropriate, playing down some of the hardships meted out in *Black Beauty*. He thought his daughter was just about ready for *Hans Brinker and the Silver Skates*, though not where poor, mad Mr. Brinker lurched around the cottage and set it afire. He was sure she'd love the part where the boys, including pudgy little Voostenwalbert Schimmelpennick, set off to skate to the Hague. Voostenwalbert's name alone would set her laughing. She liked odd sounds, including names, as much as she enjoyed new sights.

Another few years and she'd be ready for *Huckleberry Finn*. His own father, a long time before and in another country, had read that to him, and Verity had loved it since.

She asked about her mother, where she was, and why. These were the hard questions. Compared to these, the Brothers Grimm were simple. But Verity tried. Without a real anchor of religion or alternate theory, it was very difficult to tell a child why her mother was dead. And what dead meant. Verity had his own problems with such questions. Why the hell was his twenty-one-year-old wife dead and why did he have to explain that to anyone—stranger or municipal authority, or a little girl?

Or to himself, for he had no answers.

Soon Kate would be old enough to understand and to accept such things, and he would be long home by then. A couple of weeks, a couple of months of listening to the Chinese on radios, that was all. That was what the Marine Corps said, a month or two and out. He didn't know quite how to explain this to Kate, and in a war, of course, one never really knew.

* * *

Verity's orders were simple enough, once you fought through the official forms and poetry about "duty beyond the seas" and joining "Fleet Marine Force, Pacific, with all expedition."

He was supposed to report in to Gen. Oliver P. Smith as soon as he could. Except that General Smith was on board a ship rounding the Korean peninsula a few hundred miles at sea. Verity slid one haunch onto the jeep's fender and pulled out a folded small-scale map of Korea he'd brought from Washington and had studied on and off inside the plane. Gunnery Sergeant Tate, as was right and proper, stood a few paces away, not at attention or anything, waiting.

"Wonsan?" Verity finally said, wanting to be sure he'd understood Tate's account of the fleet's destination.

"Yessir, Wonsan. Up there on the east coast of North Korea."

It was clear enough on the map, which was little more than a Texaco road map. Maybe one hundred and fifty, one hundred and sixty miles north, north by northeast more precisely, from here on the west coast to Wonsan on the east. There were roads showing on the map; how good, it didn't indicate.

"Too bad they didn't issue you a driver coming over, Gunny."

"They did, sir. Had one who wasn't very good and then he got shot."

Tate didn't look distressed about the driver having been shot, so he must not have been very good. Gunnies were notoriously difficult to please.

Tate added, not as if it was important, "They said he'd live."

Verity was about to inquire who'd shot the driver, "us" or "them," but bit it off. He didn't know this Tate yet, not enough to try wit. Instead, he asked, "That radio of yours work at sea?"

"No better than on land, Captain."

"OK, then," Verity said, a finger tracing the route from Inchon to Wonsan on the spread map, "we'll get up there by car and meet the navy coming in."

"Yes, sir," Tate said, "like bar girls in Subic Bay welcoming the fleet."

Verity must have looked stern, because Tate rolled a tongue around in his mouth as if regretting humor.

The two Marines were still feeling each other out. Officer and NCO. It was Verity who decided to bridge the distance between them before it became an obstacle. They would, after all, be working together. He didn't need antagonism.

"Well," he said with a small grin, "I don't know about you, Gunny, but I'm getting a bit old to be a very successful tart."

It wasn't much of a joke, but it relaxed Tate. And that is what bad jokes are for, aren't they?

"Yes, sir," Tate said, not attempting to top Verity. Gunnery sergeants know where to draw the line.

While the two men talked, all around them was hubbub and expedition, much energy and some work, as a Casual Company left behind by Division finished dismantling what had days earlier been a promising small city. The Marines now taking it down and stowing it away for erection elsewhere were more carpenters and riggers and electricians than anything else, construction workers who happened to carry weapons. Four huskies at a time took hold of a neatly folded tent, a big package of green canvas weighing a few hundred pounds, and slung it into the bed of a six-by truck.

"These trucks going by sea, too?" Verity asked.

"No, sir, I believe they'll move overland, meeting the division at Wonsan."

"Well, if they can do it we can."

Tate patted the radio paternally. "Would the captain like to put on the headset and start listening now? Try it out?"

"What kind is this, Gunny?"

"This is the best field radio we have, Captain. An SFR two-forty. Fine piece of equipment, single-sideband and amplification, sending and receiving, of course, and pretty good range. Only trouble is the weight. A man couldn't carry it in combat."

"Heavy, is it?"

"About ninety pounds. Just fine for the backseat of a jeep. Want to give her a try?"

The gunnery sergeant beamed, proud of the radio, pleased that this new captain they'd imposed on his good nature would have the best equipment to work with, relieved that he wouldn't have to apologize for the hardware the way Marine NCOs so often did what with the antiquated rebuilt junk they had, bought secondhand from the army.

"Well, Gunny, the fact is I don't know anything about radio. Don't even know how to turn it on." Verity smiled pleasantly at the gunnery sergeant. It was worth it to see Tate's face.

"Well, yessir, I must have gotten the wrong impression. I was told to come down here and wait for a Captain Verity that was going to monitor radio while we traveled about, seeing the country, so to speak, and listening in."

"That's just what we're going to do, Gunny. So tune in and I'll start listening while we drive and you can sort of teach me how to run her as we go along. . . ."

"Yessir." Tate was back in control; it takes a lot to unsettle a Marine gunny. "Except there are a lot of bandits out there. . . ."

Verity, remembering North China in '45, took him literally. "You mean real bandits?"

"Nosir, guerrilla bands some, but mainly broken North Korean units, battalions, and regiments wandering around out there after being whipped, trying to get home. Couple of Marines in a jeep driving through run into a regiment, doesn't matter how beat up the regiment is; it wins. Pitches a shutout."

Tate was like that, sensible, competent. Did things well. In that, the gunny reminded Verity of his wife.

"Is there anything you can't do?" he asked Elizabeth.

"Can't dance. I'm a klutz."

But she was fluent in French.

"I attended a French boarding school for the unruly children of the rich," Elizabeth said.

And in consequence, she sang to Kate this little song:

"Sur le pont d'Avignon,
  On la danse, on la danse.
  Sur le pont d'Avignon,
  On la danse, tout en coup."

Once when they were in Paris and Kate was just a year old, Tom and Elizabeth, having dined well, actually did dance on one of the Seine bridges by midnight.

"We're not exactly Fred and Ginger," she admitted, laughing, and he agreed, "Yes, Jailbait, you are a klutz."

After she died he took up the practice of singing "Sur le pont d'Avignon" to his daughter Kate and promising one day he would dance with her on Paris bridges.

They came across their driver late that same day. In an army brig.

The provost told Captain Verity and Gunny Tate they'd caught a Marine stealing.

"They call a brig a prison," the prisoner complained. "No wonder the army is so screwed up, Captain, sir."

His name was Izzo.

"Important people in South Philadelphia," he said, "a respected family. We had a barbershop, a beauty salon. The bus for the racetrack left every day from our front door. Civic responsibility, pillars of the community. I had a cousin became a priest. Didn't work out. He chased skirts and left after a few years. But the good intentions were there. You can tell people from their good intentions, Captain."

"I'm sure," Verity said, measuring the man.

Izzo was a reservist called back into the Corps in July from a pleasant and constructive (he said) civilian life.

"I myself, Captain, independent of family connections, have a career marketing previously owned automobiles—"

"You sell used cars," Tate interposed.

"—at fair market value with all warranties in order, working on pure commission at rates previously and amiably agreed upon by management and me. The neighborhood could vouch; they could give testimonials. If Izzo sells it, the car runs." He never dealt a car that wasn't "glorioso."

The army said Izzo stole a jeep.

"It was there, Captain, abandoned, key in the ignition. All about me roving bands of North Korean soldiers in headlong retreat north, plus guerrillas and irregulars. I am to leave a taxpayer asset like this where the enemy steals it? I was looking for its rightful owners when the MPs came upon me."

"You a good driver?" Tate asked.

Izzo looked pained even to be asked. "Gunny, any year now they will invite me to drive the pace car at Indianapolis. Briefly as a lad I got in with bad company in South Philadelphia and drove for evil companions. I was in several major stickups, highly publicized in both the *Inquirer* and *Bulletin*, as wheelman. It was how I got to join the Marine Corps in the first place back in '42. It was that or serve time. I was seventeen and wise beyond my years, so I enlisted in the Corps. After Peleliu I knew I'd make a mistake; I should have gone to friggin' jail for life."

Izzo was small and skinny and said his nickname was Mouse.

"Mouse. That's what they call me, being small."

Ferret, Verity thought, more vicious than a mouse. Mice were soft and gray and issued little warning squeaks. This Izzo was neither soft nor colorless; all sinew and bone, no bulk. Cunning was his muscle.

Well, they were going to the wars. "Can you fix it, Gunny?" Verity asked.

"We'll try, sir."

Tate arranged things with an army master sergeant, a fifth of Verity's scotch and some of Verity's cigars changing hands, and they had Izzo released into Captain Verity's custody.

"I was in the first wave at Inchon," Izzo claimed as he got into the driver's seat, running hands admiringly over the care-polished wheel.

"What outfit?" Tate inquired.

Izzo was somewhat vague about that and noisily ran through the various gears, trying them out. Changing the subject. "Want to be sure you've got a good vehicle here, Captain."

"I'll remember you said that, Izzo," Verity replied.

He knew about shifty-eyed enlisted men. It was funny, how quickly being a Marine officer came back.

"All right," Tate growled, "let's move it."

The new driver no sooner had the jeep rolling when he reached into a field jacket to pull out a pair of silver-mirrored aviator glasses, which he hooked on his ears before squaring away his fatigue cap.

Tate, in the backseat, tapped him on the shoulder. "You see with those things?"

"See great, Gunny; they cut down the glare. Very restful on the eyes. Glorioso for distance vision. They—"

"All right, Izzo, all right. I'm not pricing them, just asking if you can see."

"Just fine, Gunny."

Verity, amused, said nothing. You let senior NCOs chivy enlisted men and didn't get into it yourself, not if you were smart. An officer lost authority that way, picking at every little thing and nagging.

Izzo turned the engine over smoothly and drove the jeep slowly out of the army compound, resisting the temptation to burn rubber and showboat.

"Where to, Captain?" he asked, polite as prep schools.

Well, Verity thought, *we've got ourselves a driver. Let's hope he's a good one.*

Izzo drove well but talked endlessly. Free association. About playing baseball in the Southern Association as a Phillies farmhand, selling cars, racing midget autos at the track at Upper Marlboro, Maryland. Verity marveled at the man's imagination.

"Begging the captain's pardon," Tate said, "there's imagination and there's lies. This boy lies like a newspaper."

The next time Izzo began his spiel, Tate cut him off.

"What I'm interested in, Izzo, is a little more about your military experience, not how you pitched no-hitters or broke into movies."

Izzo looked hurt. He was about five-four, maybe one hundred and thirty pounds, but he made up in brass what he lacked in heft. And he'd go at you.

"Anything you want to know, Gunny. You want fitness reports, I'm your man."

"In the War, Izzo. What'd you do in the War?"

"Oh, yeah. Absolutely, Gunny. I carried a Browning Automatic

Rifle on Peleliu. General Geiger himself noticed me. 'Smallest BAR man we have,' the general said. Proud about it. Bragged on me, he did."

"When did you make corporal?"

"Well, that's complicated, Gunny. I made corporal twice. Busted back once. A first sergeant had it in for me. Didn't like Italians. 'Wops,' in his words. I don't usually take offense, but who needs that? I don't need being called wops or similar names." He looked over brightly at Verity. "Right, Captain? Nobody needs that crap. Not even from top soldiers."

"You talk to me, Izzo," Tate said. "Captain has other things on his mind. You address me."

"Absolutely, Gunny."

"Good. Now listen up, Corporal."

Izzo listened to instructions and swung the wheel right, sun glittering off the shades, his eyes invisible, impossible to read. *Do you think he rally drove for holdup men?* Verity asked himself. *Or was that, too, a lie?*

On the day they found Izzo, October 4, though Verity didn't know it (neither did Douglas MacArthur), Mao Tse-tung in Peking made his decision to intervene militarily in the war on the side of North Korea and gave orders for units of the CCF to cross the Yalu River and move south by night, hiding by day.

Of course there was bitterness.

They'd given Verity compassionate. His wife was dead; there was a small child. Then they'd taken it away, much as a cutpurse might steal a wallet. It was ludicrous to believe he was the only Chinese language expert they had. Surely at the CIA or at Naval Intelligence, if not in the Corps, there were such people. He wondered how far he would have gotten away with it back there in Washington if he'd simply refused to go. Not very far, he guessed. The Marine Corps had its ways. During the War he knew a professional football player, a running back named McHenry, who refused to play for the base team at San Diego.

"I didn't join the Marines to play football," Mac said.

They sent him instead to the Sixth Division as a rifle platoon leader, and he died in the push on Naha during the Okinawa fighting, legs blown off by a mine.

Verity remembered McHenry running through broken fields in the National Football League, long legs churning. And when he died, he had no legs.

So you played the game, you went along, you snapped off a salute and an "aye-aye" and did the job.

As he was doing it now.

But it *was* unfair. After the War thousands of Marines had gone into the active reserve, attending armory meetings and drills Thursday nights, spending two weeks every summer at Camp Lejeune or Camp Pendleton, running field problems and taking courses and getting paid for it. Others, like Verity, were in the inactive reserve, carried on the rolls and answering their mail but nothing beyond that, nothing. No armory drills, no summer maneuvers, no pay. Yet now that a war was again on, the inactives had been recalled but not all the active units.

"We've called the specialists we need," the Marine Corps said, justified and pious.

"You called who you friggin' wanted," Marines responded.

And what they wanted were infantrymen and fighter pilots and, on rare occasions, Marines who spoke a half-dozen Chinese dialects.

Verity realized there was a tinge of paranoia in how he felt. Elizabeth had died; he was left alone to raise Kate. Now a war was on, aimed personally at him, and by the accident of his knowing a little Chinese, he was someone they thought they needed.

Jesus, what else could happen?

Like most intelligent, informed people, Verity had followed the progress (or lack of same) of the war in its early months. He kept up with the fighting as best he could through the newspapers and radio and TV. There was a woman sending back some of the best reporting, a correspondent named Marguerite Higgins. She worked for the *New York Herald Tribune*, but her stuff was syndicated and he followed it in the *Washington Post*. Her pieces were a bit heavy on the human-interest angle, some of the soldiers' quotes sounding suspiciously literate and portentous, but she had a way of setting the scene that rang true, of conveying swift violence and grinding fear.

Maggie Higgins. America had had war heroines before but rarely a woman journalist. Verity was tempted to dismiss her as a press agent's invention except that, when he thought about the possibilities, it came to him that if Elizabeth had been a reporter she might have done an equivalent job. Even the photos of Miss Higgins were suspect, portraying her, in helmet and field shoes and fatigues, as reasonably attractive. Verity had never seen a woman at war you would want to look at a second time. Bar nurses.

Damned newspapers.

The jeep hit a bad rut and tossed him heavily against the dash, eliciting a muttered curse and raising a bruise on his cheek.

"I thought you were a driver," he said, surly.

"Yessir," Izzo said. "Sorry about that, sir."

The road was crapola, Izzo thought, *and blaming him was crapola, too.*

"Just watch the road," Tate said. He knew it wasn't Izzo's fault, but you do not argue with a captain with a sore face.

"Right, Gunny," Izzo said. "Right you are." He knew the position Tate was in and swallowed justifiable resentment.

Verity knew he had been unfair. So to Tate, though not to Izzo, he now said, "Hell of a road, Gunny. It's a miracle anyone can drive it." Officers apologized, if they did, by indirection.

"Yessir, it is that."

Well, Izzo thought, *maybe he's human after all.*

Verity recalled roads he'd driven with Elizabeth, she behind the wheel, and how close to disaster they'd brushed.

"Well done, Izzo, good job," he murmured finally.

So he was OK, after all.

Izzo did not know Verity used to fight with his wife over her fast driving. Or that he even had a wife, now dead at twenty-one.

Nor did Verity enlighten him. Or do so with Tate, a more responsible man.

Douglas MacArthur, our most brilliant general since Lee (also a West Point legend and not nearly as successful), sat on his ass (as the irreverent had it) in his Tokyo palace, the American embassy he'd requisitioned, running the war at long distance and contemplating his own greatness.

The General had only rarely felt as smug.

It was one thing to win a war as Ike had done in Europe five years earlier, smashing a drained, defeated enemy fighting on two fronts and losing on both; quite another matter to salvage a smallish army from the lip of disaster and, in a few weeks, turn a war around. It was, the general told himself, rather enjoying the parallel, as if Marshal Ney had abruptly at Smolensk wheeled his frozen and retreating French to smash the pursuing Russians snapping at Napoléon's rear and head back to take Moscow all over again.

Few of his aides, the smart, tailored young ones, had ever seen MacArthur as crisply confident. He had two splendid victorious armies racing north, straight for China and the Yalu, the war's finishing tape. The MacArthur who conquered the Empire of Japan would now turn back Communism and cow great China. A sprint north, before winter, and at the end of it victory and, just maybe, the presidency of the United States! Already the phone calls and adulatory letters from Washington poured in, the confidential communications from Henry Luce, the praise even from Senator Taft, the *Hearst* headlines, wires from corporate chairmen and the smooth men of Wall Street.

In October of 1950 Douglas MacArthur was quite sure of himself and his destiny.

What was surprising, Captain Verity thought, was how pleasant the war had been so far. *If it doesn't get any worse than this*, he told himself, *it's a stroll.* And this was enemy country.

He and Tate and the driver had left in warm sunshine already hazed over from the dust lifted by trucks and tanks and other transport clogging the dirt roads, the usual traffic you see in the van of armies. Near Seoul the country was badly beaten up, buildings burned and blown, roads pitted, and trees and wires down. That was what house-to-house fighting did to you. The city hadn't been secured until September 29, and not much worked, not yet. But Verity saw some old friends, men he'd not seen in five years, men left to tidy up after the division sailed.

"Heard about your wife, Tom. Sorry."

"Gracious of you. Thanks."

The Marine Corps is so small you know just about everyone else. Or if you don't, you know someone who knows him. Especially officers. Captain Verity had been a Marine in the War, and these were friends he knew from back then. It was like that with senior noncommissioned officers as well. Master sergeants knew other master sergeants, or, if they didn't, had heard of them. One master sergeant would know if another drank or played a good hand of poker or chased skirts or ran a good organization. Most of all, he usually knew if the other master sergeant could fight.

Not that first sergeants are in the normal course supposed to be out there getting into firefights and shooting people, not men as distinguished as that.

"What's the country like north of here?" Captain Verity asked a major he knew.

"Nice country, Tom. Low hills and rolling. Roads not worth a damn. They say farther north it's like the Alps up there, ten-thousand-foot mountains with snow, even this early, even now. You going far, Tom?"

Verity shrugged. "Hope not. I'm supposed to catch up with the division."

"Yeah, Tom, well you take care. Regards to the missus."

This was a man who didn't know Verity's wife was dead, and he saw no need to tell him. So he said thanks. And the next morning he and Tate were off north in the jeep, Izzo driving and Tate sitting in the back with a BAR, scanning the roadside and the near hills.

The country north of Seoul was less beat-up. There hadn't been the same fighting here. According to the people in Seoul, after the city fell the North Koreans seemed to lose stomach for it.

"They ran, Tom. May still be running. You're gonna have to drive fast to catch up with this war."

Tate was a very senior NCO and a regular, a tall, long-jawed man, very lean and hard, and neither he nor Verity took such counsel entirely to heart. Once the armies crossed over the Parallel into North Korea, they would be fighting on the enemy's ground. Verity understood the difference, as did Tate.

"Like Lee in Virginia, Captain; in Virginia Lee was tougher to lick than he was up in Pennsylvania." Tate was Kansan and had read some in military history.

The road north of Seoul was being worked over by an army engineer battalion with Korean civilians, some of them women, doing most of the labor. At the Imjin River, the bridges had been blown, "by us or by them" Verity didn't know, and it didn't matter. They crossed by pontoon bridge, an army MP officiously waving them on after careful scrutiny.

"I guess he thought we might be escaping North Koreans, sir," Izzo said, and all three men laughed, Tate blond and Verity brown-haired and green-eyed. Izzo noticed the highly polished black jump boots on the MP, tied with white silk laces.

"They steal them laces from parachutes, Captain. Parachutes are in short supply. But they steal them anyways. They like the effect."

They stopped to eat tinned rations on the hood of the jeep at noon and then drove for another four hours heading vaguely north, as if heading out of Washington for Philadelphia or New York. And it *was* nice country, as the major said, but for the occasional smashed house or downed high-tension tower. There were civilians, mostly dressed in white, but they were nervous, staying out of the way and pretty much off the road. Which was not surprising. This ground had already been fought over twice since June.

According to the map, they crossed the Thirty-eighth Parallel in midafternoon near a town called Yonch'on.

"I'd keep an eye peeled along here, Gunny," Verity told Sergeant Tate. "We're in their country now."

But nothing happened and they spent the night sleeping out in their sleeping bags on the ground next to the jeep, near where an Australian brigade was momentarily encamped.

"I'd sure like to go over there and see them Aussies, Captain, maybe trade for stuff," the driver said.

"You stay right here," Tate said, answering for Verity. The sergeant didn't know this Izzo they had for a driver yet and didn't want him causing trouble with foreign troops. You never knew about foreign troops, not until you fought alongside them for a bit.

He had flown to Detroit and taken a cab to Grosse Pointe.

"Well, she's very beautiful, Tommie," his mother said, "if this picture is anything to go by. A very beautiful girl."

"Jeffs?" His father said. "There's a Jeffs in Wall Street, Arthur Jeffs."

"She's his daughter, yes."

"Then she's a Jew."

"Well, I don't know. Her father's Jewish; her mother's Presbyterian or something. What does it matter?"

"I guess it doesn't," Mr. Verity said. "I simply remarked on it."

Mrs. Verity looked again at the photo of Elizabeth, the girl her son was going to marry. "When can we meet her, Tommie? She *is* lovely."

Even his father conceded that.

They parked the jeep at the edge of the place, and Tate went in on foot, cradling the BAR in his arms as a bird shooter might carry a Purdey shotgun.

"You never know," he said. "I'll just take a look-see."

He was back in twenty minutes.

"Raw, Captain, it's raw. But no trouble I can see."

Just bodies.

"Jeez, look at them," Izzo said.

"Yeah," Thomas Verity agreed.

A retreating North Korean regiment had come through here two days before, the Americans and the ROKs hard after them, and it was the ROKs got there first. The North Koreans pretty much wiped out the village, and then the ROKs caught them at it and, in an almost casual cruelty, fought it out with them here. Ruin upon ruin, the dying among the dead. Why would North Koreans destroy their own village? Had someone put out a premature ROK flag of welcome? That's all it took in a war.

"Raw," was how Tate had described it. "Fierce," said Izzo, "friggin' fierce."

They filled with water at that town and got out in a hurry. It was a hot day and the bodies, especially those gutted and lying open in the sun, had swollen and were starting to smell. There were still some people around who weren't dead or too badly hurt, but they seemed incapable of burying their neighbors or kin or doing much of anything. It was as if the violence had shocked them mute, had drained them, and they watched the Marines at the town pump without saying anything or doing much.

"Not much heart nor soul left in that place, Captain."

"No, Tate," Verity agreed, "nor much of anything else." They were across the Thirty-eighth Parallel now, the border with North Korea, and he wondered if that's how it was going to be here.

Whatever men tell you, when they set off to war there is always the consideration they may not come back.

Verity had been to war before and had no neurotic or irrational fear of death, was not even all that afraid of dying. It was different this time, though, because Kate would be left alone. First her mother, now her father? That didn't seem fair to a child not yet three years old who had never done anything to anyone and deserved better.

But even a less intelligent man than Verity could figure out the logic. If he died, Kate would be alone. There was the syllogism.

So it was one and the same thing, and for the first time in his life he was frightened of death.

Not for himself, but for her.

He kept this information to himself, of course.

* * *

Early on the second day Verity and his two Marines drove up to a sort of stockade set up in a farm village. There were plenty of ROK troops about, and Verity wanted to check road conditions ahead if they could find someone who spoke English. It was ROKs who'd captured this place, apparently after a hard fight, if you could tell from the several burned-out tanks and damage to residential and farm buildings and smashed and flattened fencing.

"Looka that, Captain," Izzo said, pulling off the road to a bumpy stop in a rice paddy, partially fenced by farmers, the rest in barbed wire, where perhaps a thousand men were sitting on the ground or lying flat, docile and not sufficiently curious even to look around.

"North Koreans," Tate said, "prisoners."

Good, Verity thought. *That's a thousand of them we won't have to fight.*

"Yeah! And looka that," said Izzo, his voice low and husky, conspiratorial.

ROK officers and armed guards strolled unafraid among the seated or squatted POWs within the compound, looking down at men's faces or scrutinizing uniforms for badges of rank and occasionally throwing a fist at a man's head or kicking him in the thigh or knee or rear end. A long table, the length and shape of a dining-room table but quite flimsy, was set up by the gate of the stockade with ROK officers seated behind it on camp chairs, conducting interrogations.

Then Tate spoke. "Over there, Captain," he said, the flat, nasal Kansas voice lower than usual but urgent.

Verity saw what he meant.

A half-dozen stout posts had been driven into the ground, and from them hung North Koreans, men evidently executed by the ROKs after they took this town. Several of the dead men, officers probably, were naked and showed signs of beatings and deeper wounds, the sort bayonets might make. Now they just slumped there, tied with ropes, hanging on the posts like rag dolls, left to dry in the autumn sun. There were still other posts prepared and ready, to which no one had yet been tied. That must be the purpose of the interrogations now going on.

Verity was still looking at the dead prisoners when an ROK officer, noticing their jeep, got up from the table and headed for them.

"Get it in gear, Izzo," Verity said. "Let's get out of here. This isn't our affair."

The ROK officer was closer now, and Verity tossed him a salute and Izzo had the jeep moving before the ROK officer had a chance to return it.

Who knew what happened in this town before and during the fighting? Or what happened to ROK prisoners?

Neither side had a corner on cruelty.

The skim ice of early October on the Chosin had been freakish and soon melted as the country slipped back into what we call Indian summer and the first snows vanished and ran off the lower slopes into the creeks and small streams that led to rivers and eventually to the Sea of Japan. There were birds of all sort and red fox and deer, but because most of the trees were conifers, no leaves turned golden and fell.

"Not much like China, is it?" Verity said, and Tate, also the old China hand, agreed.

"Not much. The trees, for one. . . ."

And they drove north through strange country, closer to China with every mile.

CHAPTER THREE

Enemy advancing, we retreat; enemy entrenched, we harass;
enemy exhausted, we attack; enemy retreating, we pursue.
                              —*Chairman Mao's military dictum.*

N ight's best," Tate said.
     "Why's that?"
     "Signal carries better. Bounces off something up
there called the Heaviside layer, and it's why back home you can
sometimes pick up a baseball game late at night from a ballpark a
long way off. The signal's clearer and travels farther after dark."

"Oh," Verity said. He was notoriously unmechanical.

From then on he stayed with the radio from six until midnight
or so, which was when most of the traffic died. Tate showed him
how the controls worked, how he could fiddle with various knobs
and dials to provide a clearer signal and eliminate static, or at least
some of it, how to use the antenna directionally to bring in a better
sound. It amused Gunnery Sergeant Tate that they had sent him an
"expert" whose entire assignment consisted of listening to a radio
but who knew nothing of the Heaviside layer or even how to turn
the dial. "The Marine Corps," Tate told himself, a mix of love and
wonder in his voice.

From their first night on the drive north there was plenty of Chinese on the air. They camped by the side of the road; the whole

column they'd joined did, not wanting to drive with the lights on in case of enemy planes, and the road too narrow and rough to drive it safely in the dark. None of the Chinese seemed especially important to Verity, but there was a lot of it and he found himself enjoying the sound, listening to it as he had every single day of the first fifteen years of his life, when Chinese was as much his native tongue as was English.

It wasn't cold, and while Tate and Izzo slept in the small nylon pyramidal tent they carried, Verity sat outside playing with the radio, sitting in the jeep smoking a good cigar and looking up at the stars. This night was clear, no wind. He jotted down the occasional note when a word or phrase caught at him and seemed to connote something. Nothing dramatic. He liked the Korean night sky, that at least reminding him of China, except that here the hills pressed in closer and you didn't get that vast expanse of black. As black as the sky was, the hills were blacker. Once your eyes became accustomed to the dark and night vision took over, it was amazing how much you could see, and how clearly, without artificial light. There was no moon, but that only made the starlight brighter. Once your eyes adjusted you could read newspaper headlines with illumination from the stars alone.

He picked up several names that had a familiar sound and that were repeated. Peng. Lin Piao. Common-enough names. There'd been a Peng in North China in '45 that he dealt with, a major in the Communist Fourth Field Army. He couldn't recall the rest of his name. Polite fellow and, if you could believe the stories, a veteran of the famous Long March of six thousand miles in the 1930s when Mao took his people north and then east to get away from Chiang Kai-shek and conserve men and resources until they were strong enough to fight back with a chance of winning. Lin Piao was a colonel in the Fourth. A Chinese field army under the Communist setup was equivalent to an American army corps with three infantry divisions each of about ten thousand men, a regiment of cavalry, and two or three regiments of artillery. Verity got along with Peng and had him to dinner at the officers' mess a couple of times, where he demonstrated a fondness for bourbon. Old

Forester, as Verity recalled. And, like Verity, he preferred coffee to tea, the ceremonial beverage.

It would be funny if it was old Peng up there commanding the Chinese. Or even Lin. If it was one of them, he hoped it would be Peng. Maybe he and Verity could meet under a flag of truce and chat a bit, about old times, maybe pour a little Old Forester over ice. As he monitored the radio and listened to the sound of Chinese coming in over the static and tried to make something of it, that was how a man's mind wandered; that was toward midnight, when Verity understood he was tired and should cut his losses and turn in.

The big radio clicked into silence, and, with a final long look upward at the autumn stars, he got down on his hands and knees and crawled into the pyramidal tent, trying not to disturb Izzo or Tate en route to his own sleeping bag, where he dreamed of other late nights.

Elizabeth liked a weekend in New York. They went up on the train and stayed at the Plaza or the Pierre and hit the clubs, 21 and El Morocco and the Stork. They weren't regulars, but they had money and wore the right clothes and looked the part and she was undeniably beautiful and so they got good tables. Billingsley, who ran the Stork, was a shit to his employees and a phony in general, but he played up to the people he thought decorated the room and might be important.

One night Hemingway and his current girl (or wife) were there, looking the way you hoped Hemingway and his girl would look, handsome, competent, assured people.

Billingsley went to their table to chat. And then to Verity's.

"Nice to have you here again," he said, not quite sure who they were but remembering the faces.

"We always drop by en route to the house at Cap Ferrat," Elizabeth replied, feigning languor. "It's so restful before the parties begin."

"Oh, yes, the parties," Billingsley said, not sure which parties.

"The parties, the endless parties," Elizabeth went on, overcome apparently by a fashionable ennui.

"Yes, yes, quite," Billingsley said, out of his snobbish depth and retreating to Winchell's table.

"Who are they?" Winchell inquired.

"Cap Ferrat. South of France. Lots of money. Oil money, I think. Name of Verity. The wife's rich as Croesus."

They danced until the band quit or the joints closed and then hailed cabs and drove around before returning to the hotel, where each time Elizabeth would astonish her husband with an imaginative lust good girls weren't supposed to demonstrate and few wives could.

Later, as they lay there spent and slick, he muttered, "Cap Ferrat, indeed."

"Why not admit it's one of our playgrounds?"

"Because it isn't, brat. And you've never been there."

"Have too, have too."

She lied incorrigibly. Except about important things.

He propped himself on one elbow. "Just when were you in Cap Ferrat, Elizabeth?"

"In *Tender Is the Night*. Fitzgerald stole me for a terrific scene in chapter five."

"Come here," Thomas Verity said. "I'm going to spank you."

She licked ripe lips.

"Oh, good," she said, tossing the bedsheet away.

On Monday, as they rode the train back home to Tom's job teaching college boys, their names appeared in Winchell's column as en route to their château in the South of France and they read it aloud and giggled about it almost all the way to Baltimore.

There were plenty of ROK troops rolling north, and sometimes they traveled with them. Not that ROK troops were any good; most of them weren't, Tate said, but three Marines in a jeep couldn't just go joyriding through North Korea alone. The towns and villages they passed through were pretty much untouched, nothing like the wreckage Verity had seen in just a few days down near the Parallel. The people, the civilians, made themselves scarce. But any one of the villages could have concealed a company of North Korean regulars. For three Marines, a company of North Korean regulars could be somewhat embarrassing.

So they traveled with the ROKs and from time to time an American outfit.

"Hey, Marines, what the hell you doing here?"

"Out for a drive!" Izzo shouted. "A friggin' Sunday drive!"

They got the finger for their trouble and some cheerful obscenity. The soldiers knew what the Marines had done at Inchon and in taking Seoul, so it wasn't that tough. These men were part of the Eighth Army. The Marine division would be part of X Corps in a few days when it got to Wonsan. Both arms of the UN army would then push north, toward the Yalu River, toward China.

That, at least, was the idea.

Mouse Izzo was a good driver. On that he hadn't lied. As for the rest of his story, and cautioned by Tate, Verity continued to reserve judgment.

"I got separated from my unit, Seventh Marines, in the fighting north of Seoul. I ran into some North Koreans and offered to take them prisoner—you know, Captain, put in a good word for them. Instead they put a gun on me, and since there was maybe a dozen of them and one of me, I was reasonable; I didn't make life difficult and I went along. I was with them two days. Then they joined up with some other NK and I guess they heard how bad things was going and they gave me back half my cigarettes and turned me loose.

" 'Hey,' I said, 'my weapon. I'm not touring Korea without a weapon, not with all the shit and chaos going on.' So they gave me back my M-1. Amazing thing. I think if I'd had time to stand around bargaining with those guys I would have ended up owning them. Near glorioso it was. But I didn't have time and I took off, heading south. That's when I found the jeep and attempted to return it to the rightful owner."

He remained vague as to how he'd gotten separated from the Seventh Marines and precisely what outfit he'd been in.

The country was changing again now. In ways it was like northern New England—short, steep hills, narrow valleys with water, six-foot streams and thirty-yard rivers running through the bottoms, and the hillsides covered with firs and spruce and pine and other conifers Tom didn't know. Nothing Asian or exotic. It could be the country between White River Junction and Stowe, Vermont. He didn't like the Japanese very much and had fought against them, but no one could argue with reforestation in a country this poor. If the country was pleasant, give some credit to the Japanese, damn them! No, take that back. The War was five years ago. He no longer hated except for the thing that had killed his wife.

No one died in childbirth anymore. Not in the States. Not in a great city. Not when the mother-to-be was educated, had money and the best doctors, and was intelligent and knew about exercises and diet and all the rubbish that was supposed to make us safe, immune to tragedy. And, in this instance, had not.

The road now ran almost straight north to Wonsan.

"That's where you'll find the division, Tom. Or should." That's what he'd been told before he and Tate left Kimpo.

Now, with the division still at sea aboard troopships, the ROKs had captured Wonsan without much of a fight. The port city was one hundred and ten miles north of the Thirty-eighth Parallel. That's how fast the war was moving when even ROKs went a hundred miles in a few days; that's how completely the North Korean army had fallen apart.

"Wonsan coming up, Captain," Izzo announced. He drove with a map folded on his lap and knew how to read it.

"Noted," Verity said, charm exhausted elsewhere, thought elsewhere.

They rolled into Wonsan at midafternoon, drawing salutes and impressed stares from ROK troops and one or two Americans along for the ride as advisers.

"Make way for the First Marine Division!" Izzo shouted. "General officer coming! . . ."

Men stood in the dust they raised, straightening their caps and preparing to salute.

Down by the wharves Izzo asked directions and was given them.

"Good drive, Izzo," Verity said.

"Why, thank you, Captain, very generous of the captain to say so."

Maybe he wasn't all that surly. Maybe the man had suffered. Izzo was always ready to give an officer a chance. It could always pay dividends.

He was respectful, too, of senior NCOs like Tate. But didn't give them an entirely free ride.

Tate came from a place called Engine, Kansas, which drove Izzo near to distraction.

"What the hell kind of name is that for a town? Engine! Jeez, Gunny, you got to be kidding."

For all his cool, Tate was sensitive. You could get to him. And while he would never agree aloud, he knew Engine was some name for your hometown.

"It was a railhead, Izzo," he said patiently, "on one of the early transcontinental routes to the Pacific, the Union Pacific or Northern Pacific, one of them. Engine was where they repaired locomotives, did boiler work and the like. There was a big roundhouse. I remember seeing it as a kid, a big red-brick building that—"

"Jeez, Gunny, I used to think Philadelphia sounded like a stupid place to be from. But, Engine? . . ."

"Just watch your mouth, Izzo," Tate said, turning crisp, "and while you're at it, get under the jeep and see if you can find that rattle. No reason we got to have a rattle interfering with radio monitoring all the way to the Yalu."

"No, Gunny."

The ground was wet and muddy and Izzo knew he was being punished. And unfairly.

But what the hell did you expect from people that lived in a shit place like Engine, Kansas?

Chairman Mao had long ago shaped his military philosophy, one that still directed the strategic and tactical thought of his generals.

"Enemy advancing, we retreat; enemy entrenched, we harass; enemy exhausted, we attack; enemy retreating, we pursue."

Both Lin Piao and Peng Teh-huai, Mao's leading generals in North Korea, held fiercely to his way, though both men were nimble thinkers who knew how to improvise. Variations on a theme. Peng also knew the Marines. Some of their young officers had impressed him in North China in the winter of '45–'46, after the Japanese surrender, when the country was in chaos with bandits and not yet disarmed Japanese troops and Kuomintang forces and Communist units wandering the land and engaging in pitched battles until the Marines came in to establish some variety of crude order.

Peng wished he were assigned the sector west of the Taebaek Mountains, where the American army and the ROKs were advancing, and not here in the east near the Chosin, where, when the word came to attack, his command would meet the First Marine Division.

He wondered if any of the Marines he'd met five years ago at Tsingtao and Tientsin were still serving. And would they recall him?

By October 20, though no one on the Allied side could yet know this, four Chinese armies numbering about thirty thousand men each and under the command of Communist veteran soldier Peng Teh-huai, had crossed the border into Korea. Three of the four armies lurked in the hills north of the Eighth Army; the Fourth was positioned opposite X Corps in eastern North Korea in the mountain territory roughly encircling the Chosin Reservoir. By the end of October two additional Chinese field armies would join them. On October 15 President Truman and General MacArthur held their summit conference on Wake Island. MacArthur assured the president there was little danger of Chinese intervention.

According to Truman, "He [MacArthur] said the Chinese Commies would not attack, that we had won the war, and that we could send a division from Korea to Europe in January."

As for rumblings back home that MacArthur had his eye on a

run for the White House two years from then, the General said politicians had made "a chump" of him in 1948 and he assured the president "it would not happen again."

Said MacArthur, he "had no political ambitions."

As for Korea, there were "a few loose ends," but the General told Truman, "Formal resistance will end throughout North and South Korea by Thanksgiving."

Their conference lasted just ninety-six minutes.

At the time of the Wake Island meeting (October 15), Lin Piao's Fourth Army was well into North Korea. By the end of October he would have six armies comprising eighteen divisions in North Korea. Also much of the Third Field Army based in Shantung was aboard trains heading for or already in Manchuria, ready to cross the border, another three armies of twelve more divisions.

The total Chinese deployment ordered in mid-October, when MacArthur was assuring Truman no substantial intervention was coming, was nine CCF armies totaling about two hundred and seventy thousand men.

As "Lightning Joe" Collins said of General MacArthur that autumn, "He was like a Greek hero of old marching to an unkind and inexorable fate."

CHAPTER FOUR

*I've been doing this since 1941. March Field, California. I did a
radio show for Pepsodent and one night we went down there to
do the show for a bunch of kids just drafted. The war wasn't on
yet and they laughed and cheered and stamped their feet and
whistled. . . . The producer said, "Hey, . . . we got something here.
You're going back . . . every week." So it wasn't anything
patriotic at the start, just a comedy hour in search of laughs.*

—*Bob Hope*

Verity and Tate and their driver weren't the only
Marines in Wonsan. The division itself might still be at
sea, puking up its guts and raging at MacArthur and
the Russian mines, but the advance parties and air wing were
already here. So, too, the USO troupe. Bob Hope and Marilyn
Maxwell were en route, it was widely (and accurately) reported.
Verity was admitted to the presence of one of Oliver Smith's staff.

"Verity, you're supposed to be our Chinese expert."

"I'm not, Colonel, you know. I speak the language, know the
country. But not much about their army."

"Well, you know more than I do. Or General Smith does. So
you're it."

"Yessir." You never got anywhere arguing with rank.

"Now, General MacArthur pulled off a brilliant stroke at
Inchon. Give him credit, an imaginative and subtle plan. Mar-
velously carried out by the Marine Corps. Give us a little credit,
too. But now he's done an odd thing. He's separated his army. We
and two army divisions and a ragbag of other units, all of them
gallant and so on, I'm quite sure, comprise the X Corps. We're

here [he poked a finger at maps] in the east of North Korea up against the Sea of Japan. To our immediate west is a range of mountains running north and south the length of the peninsula. Four thousand, six thousand, eight thousand feet, most of the passes already closed by snow. The middle of October and there's snow up there a couple of feet deep. The other side of that mountain range is the Eighth Army, the other half of MacArthur's command. We can't get to them; they can't get to us. Oh, maybe a small unit could make it up and over the mountains, traveling light. You couldn't move armor or artillery or heavy units. So in effect, MacArthur's army is split in two until spring. And we have all these rumors about the Chinese. You were briefed on that."

"Yessir, in Washington."

"So you know why you're here."

"To assess the Chinese threat and to report directly to General Smith and his staff on what I hear, what I find out, what I even suspect. Yessir."

"Find out anything yet, Verity?"

"Not much. I have a good radio and a gunny who knows radio. We're picking up plenty of Chinese traffic—"

"Traffic?"

"Conversation over the air. Transmissions. But the Chinese border isn't two hundred miles from here. Without a lot of triangulation you can't tell if what I hear is north of the Yalu in Manchuria or south of the line inside Korea. Or a bit of both."

"If you went farther north, would you learn more? Better reception, that sort of thing?"

"Sure. A lot of this traffic is low-power stuff. The closer I get, the better the read." That was what Tate had assured Verity, as he, shamelessly, now assured the colonel.

"Well then, when the rifle regiments finally get off those damned transports and start north, you go along."

"With which regiment?"

"I don't know what General Smith wants yet. You've got Litzenberg's Seventh Marines, Murray's Fifth, and Chesty Puller's First. Whichever is the point regiment, I'd think."

"And can I see General Smith?"

"Soon as he gets here, Verity. Headquarters Marine Corps seems to think you're something special."

"Yessir."

Verity and Tate requisitioned an abandoned Wonsan house that was almost clean.

"I looked pretty close, Captain. Don't want us to get lousy."

They'd not yet decided whether to keep Izzo as a driver.

"I might get us a better," Tate said, "young man with a bit less personality. When the division disembarks, this town will be a-crawl with promising young men eager to establish reputations and make a career for themselves. Then again, Izzo reads a good map, drives a good car."

Verity took his time deciding about enlisted men, even gunnery sergeants, but he was starting to enjoy Tate. He knew his work and did it and had a sense of humor left over, a muted realization life was absurd and its comedy ought to be enjoyed. And he didn't press Verity for family anecdotes or intimate details, the things old-timers often did to ingratiate themselves with an officer. Verity saw early on through that brand of bullshit. Izzo had tried it on Verity and been shot down.

It was taking the First Marine Division so long to get into Wonsan harbor (some thirty thousand mines had been laid, it was said), the town was crawling with journalists who'd flown in.

"There's Maggie Higgins of the *Herald Tribune*," an impressed lieutenant told Verity. "She's pretty cute, for an older woman."

Miss Higgins was in her thirties.

On October 24 Bob Hope and Miss Maxwell put on their show. The Marines didn't land until the next day and were the butt of jokes. Verity had been invited, but he sent Tate instead.

"You go, Gunny. May be the last laugh you'll have for a time."

"Yessir, I will go," Tate said, "and thank you."

He didn't know much about Verity as yet, but he knew the man wasn't a big laugher. And, like most of us, had secrets and held them close.

* * *

Gunnery Sergeant Tate had never married. Nor did he think he ever would. And unlike most senior NCOs he knew in the Corps, many of them assertive and cocky men, he was awkward around women. Not so with other men. And he was very much at ease in all other ways, including with superior officers. So much so that he'd put in three years as a drill instructor at San Diego, at the Marine Corps Recruit Depot, where DIs fashioned raw boots into proper Marines and where only the finest sergeants and exceptional corporals drew duty as DIs.

Women, well, they were another quantity entirely. And although he rarely spoke of it, he'd pondered long and hard and thought he understood why. Japanese prison camp in China during the War.

When they are sent to prison and spend almost four of their formative years (Tate went behind the barbed wire at twenty) entirely among men and are beaten and humiliated and shamed, helpless to strike back, even the strongest men are unmanned. Even now, more than six years after his release and in the midst of a new and different war, Tate carried the weight of a guilt unearned, but no less real.

He handled men because he understood them. But he was nervous and fearful with women, sure they saw through his crisp, efficient exterior and to the shame and guilt inside.

Women were cleverer than men; he couldn't kid them about his failures and his past.

And so he maintained a prudent distance and when friends proposed a social occasion where he might meet this splendid young woman or that, he invented reasons not to do so and went to a ball game or a movie or tugged from his footlocker a volume of *Lee's Lieutenants* or an old and well-thumbed life of Cromwell.

"This is a small, odd country," Verity wrote Kate in a letter Madame would read to her, "with big hills that already have some snow up high. Do you remember the snow on P Street last year when I pulled you on the sled? The people live in small, funny houses and everything smells like the Chinese food we buy on Wisconsin Avenue. Or wet laundry. It is a smell I remember as a boy in China, and I find it pleasant."

"Madame, is Daddy in France now?" the child asked.

"*Non,* Kate, in France there are lovely smells of flowers and wine and the sea. Mr. Verity is in Asia, in a place called Korea."

"Oh."

Later, in such letters, Verity would not write as nostalgically of the snow.

At Bob Hope's USO show for the troops at Wonsan, Gunny Tate sat well back in the audience of mostly GIs, trying to be inconspicuous, enjoying Marilyn Maxwell, leggy and blond, and Mr. Hope's anti-Marine wit and double entendres. There were some ROKs in the audience as well, officers, who did not seem to understand just who Bob Hope was and why everyone laughed so heartily. Various celebrities in the audience were introduced and stood in acknowledgment, one of them Marguerite Higgins.

"She was banging some hotshot army general down at Pusan," Izzo remarked the next day.

"There are no hotshot army generals," Tate said rather stiffly. "Nearest thing they had to a hotshot was General Dean, and he was so dumb he got himself captured."

"Well, it was a colonel, maybe, she was banging."

"You don't know, Izzo, and I don't want to hear general officers or colonels being accused of consorting. Even if they are army."

"It's just what I heard, Gunny. No offense. Just what I read somewhere in the newspapers."

There were no newspapers. Izzo didn't really need any. He was one of those people to whom gossip and rumor gravitated like iron filings to a magnet.

"Our Walter Winchell," Verity said.

"Why, thanks, Captain," Izzo said, pleased. He knew Winchell was a famous columnist and broadcaster.

"Think nothing of of it," Verity said.

That evening there was a reception in what passed for an officers' mess and he met both Hope and Miss Higgins. By now there were more Marines, liaison officers off the first ships, landed early to prepare the way for the entire division. Hope was less comic in person than he was in movies or on the radio, rather elegant in a well-cut double-breasted gray business suit. He'd flown in with Miss Maxwell and a small troupe at some risk and seemed ready to be away, having done his show. But he chatted easily with the officers, signed a few autographs, promised to make the odd phone call to wife and family when he got back to the States.

"You look very much at ease with the troops," someone remarked.

"I am," Hope said. "I've been doing this since 1941. March Field, California. I did a radio show for Pepsodent and one night we went down there to do the show for a bunch of kids just drafted. The war wasn't on yet and they were just kids and homesick and they laughed and cheered and stamped their feet and whistled and applauded and the producer said, 'Hey, just wait a minute. We got something here. You're going back there every week.' So it wasn't anything patriotic at the start, just a comedy hour in search of laughs."

Most of the younger officers clustered around Miss Maxwell. She'd been the blonde in a big movie the year before, *Champion*, with Kirk Douglas, and they all wanted to meet her. Verity found himself talking to Marguerite Higgins. By the time she got to him the evening was nearly wasted.

"Hello. I'm Maggie Higgins." She wore a light, fresh perfume.

"Verity. Thomas Verity."

"And where are you from and what do you do, Captain?"

She knew rank.

"Oh, a place out in the country. We take a newspaper, but I regret to say it isn't yours."

"You win some, you lose some. And are you on General Smith's staff?"

"No, I'm in communications. I work with radios."

It was only a half-lie. He wasn't going to get her started asking why a Chinese expert was up here in North Korea with the Marine division.

She asked, ready to move on to more promising material, "And what are the big radio programs this season in Korea?"

"Oh, lot of stuff no one understands." Then, brighter, as though he didn't want her to think him a total bore, he said, "But sometimes at night, very late, if you twist the dial, you pick up dance music, American bands, from a long way off."

"Oh? You can?"

"Yes, it's something called the Heaviside layer," he said, cribbing from Tate. "It's an effect that fetches radio waves from a long way off. Perth, Australia, Honolulu, I've picked them up. And one night San Francisco. An orchestra playing at the St. Francis Hotel in San Francisco. . . ."

"Dance music."

"Yes, dance music."

She took his hand and shook it. "Thank you, Captain, for reminding me. It would be nice to hear dance music again some night."

"I'll try to let you know, Miss Higgins, the next time it comes through."

"The Heaviside layer?"

"Yes, the Heaviside layer."

A light colonel made his way over. "What was that all about, Tom? You seemed to have fascinated *la belle* Higgins."

"Dull dog like me?"

But he grinned as he said it. And when he went back to the house he shared with Tate and Izzo he was still grinning.

"Anything interesting on the air, Gunny?"

"No, sir. Not much. A little music came in for a few minutes. Tinny and lots of static. But it was American music."

"You turn in," Verity said. "I'll listen for a while."

He wasn't sleepy and stayed with the radio until 2:00 A.M. but didn't get much, and there was no more music that night. He wondered what perfume Maggie Higgins had been wearing and whether there had really been an army general down at Pusan and disliked himself for wondering.

He'd not made love to a woman since Elizabeth.

There were chaplains, of course, traveling with the army and praying over the men. Verity, who did not attend church in peacetime, wondered about their value; didn't all this piety cause men to ponder and, perhaps, reduce the thirst for battle?

Regardless of denomination, every chaplain was called Padre. Even the rabbi.

Izzo, who was forever looking for an edge, attended services regularly, whatever the sect or theology. "Look, Gunny, who knows what's gonna happen? You get ready; you make friends in high places, right?" And during the singing, if he knew the words, he shouted the hymns with enormous fervor.

He also kept close watch for when, before a Catholic mass, the priest would offer the men general absolution. "You can save up the sins and then get rid of them all at once without saying nothing. You know, 'Bless me, Father, for I have sinned. I got laid twice; I whacked off three times; I got drunk once.' Who needs that when you can be just as sorry without blabbing it out?"

Izzo said sinners were also expected to resolve not to commit the same offenses again.

"But you always do, don't you?" Tate inquired.

"Yeah, Gunny, but I always promise not to. Otherwise it's negative thinking, ya know?"

Tate, a Presbyterian, limited himself at times of stress to the quiet recitation of Scottish psalms.

Tom Verity wished he were able to share their faith. It seemed such a consolation. And as Izzo remarked on leaving a Jewish service, "Ya can't be too careful, Captain."

There was plenty of gossip that did not involve Marguerite Higgins. Except in the military it was called rumor.

The war was nearly over. No, it wasn't; the Chinese were coming in. Not only the Chinese, the Russians. No, they weren't. A deal had been worked out at the UN, brokered by the Indians. The French. By the king of Denmark. By Emperor Hirohito. Half a million Chiang Kai-shek regulars were on ships heading for Wonsan and would take over. The Marines would be back at Camp Pendleton before Christmas. Before Thanksgiving. Before Election Day.

"Tom? Tom Verity?"

It was Bjornsen, whom he'd known in the War, a career forest ranger from Nevada up near the California line above Reno.

"What do you hear, Bob?"

"War's about over is what they're saying. And I keep saying, then why are we pouring this division and a hell of a lot more into a two-bit port like this one?"

"I dunno. They don't consult me."

"Say, weren't you some sort of China watcher? Born there or something?"

"Born and raised, Bob." He let it go at that, sure of Bjornsen as he wasn't of Miss Higgins but figuring the less said the better. He'd always had his taciturn side; Elizabeth's death made silence a refuge within which he did not make a fool of himself, blubbering sadness and loss.

Bjornsen had a rifle company in Murray's regiment.

"Good man. And at my age I sure don't need Chesty Puller running me about, thank you ma'am."

Bjornsen was thirty-three, six-foot-four, blond, resembling the actor Sterling Hayden, and built like a redwood tree. Yet he didn't want any part of Chesty Puller.

"How's the company?" Verity asked, glad to be talking about Bjornsen's work and not his own.

"Good. Almost all regulars. I took over toward the end of the Pusan fighting when they lost their captain. Tough boys. We'll do OK up north."

Bob Bjornsen was what they called a mustang, an enlisted man who'd become an officer who hadn't gone to college. There was always a residual snobbery. But not with Verity, who remembered Bjornsen as a platoon leader on Okinawa five years before.

"Well, I've got to see to the company, Tom."

"Sure."

"We'll get together later. I guess we're all going north together."

"I guess so, Bob."

"I wonder if we are going to fight the Chinese, Tom."

"Guess that depends on them," Verity said, shaking Bjornsen's hand and sending him on his way.

In the morning Verity was to see General Smith, and he supposed then he'd find out. That was, if MacArthur wasn't keeping it to himself and had briefed Smith.

MacArthur.

Even among the Marines who claimed to despise, and certainly among army officers who both revered and feared, the General, they were obsessed by him.

"You ever met him, Verity?"

"Never even saw him. Not in the War, not out here."

"Too bad; he's something to see."

"Oh, where did you get to know him?"

"Never laid eyes on the man. But I feel like I know him. He's all anyone bloody well talks about. Like as if he were God. And Satan at the same time. Some people claim he's a nutcase; others say he walks on water. The Japs worship the son of a bitch; hell, they liked Tōjō, too."

Tom Verity made sure he was down at the waterfront to see the Marines come ashore from the troopships, reeking after ten days at sea.

"I haven't seen Marines in any number since '46 in North China," he told Tate. "I want to be there to see them."

He was not quite sure why. Maybe a bonding process, the need to reassure himself he belonged, that he was again a part of the glorious whole, even as a most reluctant warrior.

The Marine reserve system worked. Oh, there were inequities, sure. But it was admirably pragmatic, calling up the men it needed to feed the war.

What bothered Verity was a schizoid aspect to being a reserve. Was he at bottom an academician who taught college boys? Or was he again a professional soldier, the trained killer he had been for nearly four years of his life?

Do we really shed civilization quite that easily? You put the uniform back on and you slip automatically into the skin of a man who kills for a living?

What an odd thing.

Izzo was off scrounging with the jeep, and so Verity walked down through the town toward the piers and quays and the handful of small coasters and fishing boats and lighters. There were plenty of Koreans about, but they were still shy of Americans and scuttled away. *Well, we're in bandit country,* Verity thought. He wore the old .38 in its holster on his hip, hung from the web belt, the leather thongs dangling loose and not secured around his thigh the way he used to wear it in the War and up in North China, gunfighter-style, strapped down for a quick draw.

God, what a kid I was. Moving picture stuff.

He would soon be thirty and was not at the movies.

The North Koreans pulling out had blown up some of the docks, and there were a couple of big burned-out warehouses and some other damage, but the port was functioning. The ROKs had gotten in here too fast for the North Koreans to do a really proper job of demolition. Someone probably got shot for that. When you retreat you're supposed to blow up what you can't take along and have to leave behind, blow it up or burn it or, preferably, both. War was hell on insurance companies.

Down here by the harbor it wasn't cold. No breeze off the water, but a land wind from behind and not bad. The first big landing craft had nosed up sideways to a long pier, and when Verity arrived a gangway was already down and a couple of sergeants were shouting up at the ship. Sergeants, always shouting. Though, in fairness, Tate didn't shout much. And still got things done. Out beyond this ship was a big old liner called the *General Meigs,* and there were other craft he could see, smallish mine sweepers and a few destroyers, the rest of them LSTs or, like this one, infantry craft. There must be others still hull-down beyond the horizon.

Someone said a small coaster had hit a mine last night in the approaches, one the sweepers must have missed. Damned clever, the Russians, inventing mines you could sail over a dozen times and then, on the thirteenth pass, they blew the hell out of you. It took a curious sort of mind to come up with a notion like that, Verity concluded. He wondered if the number 13 had a sinister connotation for Russians as it did in the States.

Now there was more shouting and the first troops started down the ramps, helmeted, heavily laden with field packs and weapons and canteens and bayonets and all variety of impedimenta hung from belts, plenty of the men slung with bandoliers around their chests and over their shoulders, cloth slings carrying clips of ammo; others lugging machine guns, two men to a gun, one carrying the gun itself, the other man the tripod and the metal cans of ammunition on belts. There were other two-man crews carrying the small mortars, the .60s, one man per tube, the other with the heavy metal plate it rested on.

"I ain't never getting on a fucking ship again!" he heard one Marine sing out. They were pale, and some of them looked drawn. You get the runs for ten days, you look pale; you look drawn. Otherwise, they looked pretty much like all the Marines he'd ever seen, some clean-shaven and baby-faced like kids' bottoms; others hairy and tough; craggy men like Tate and gnomes like Izzo; pimpled boys and top sergeants going gray, men with their helmets securely fastened with chin straps, others with their steel hats cocked back off their faces, straps a-dangle.

Hell, Verity thought, *they look like . . . Marines.*

He watched for a while; satisfied he belonged, he walked slowly back up the hill of the town away from the docks in the noon sun. Some of the men were being trucked to the outskirts and others were marching, and suddenly Wonsan was how he had expected to find it, full of Marines and sergeants calling out and people with lists and men shouting hello to other men they knew, men off other ships. It was everything but a liberty town with bars and girls. That's what they needed, a couple of gin mills, a couple of local girls, and a jukebox, and this could be Oceanside, California.

They had all the Marines they needed. They might be pale and staggering and unsteady from their long voyage, but they were finally here and there were plenty of them. It was hard to imagine that what was left of the North Koreans could handle this bunch. But you never knew about the Chinese. And Verity remembered the "Japs," small and skinny and wearing eyeglasses, and how in the beginning the Marines had laughed, contemptuous of them. *And how swiftly we learned.*

He watched the first units marching through the port and through the town itself and out into the countryside beyond, where big tents were already going up and toilets being dug.

Then he was on his way to report to General Smith's G-2, a full colonel who was the division's intelligence officer.

"What do you have so far?" the colonel asked.

"Numbers of three regular Chinese infantry divisions, the Eighty-sixth, Sixty-third, and Fortieth."

"On this side of the Yalu?"

"Can't tell that without triangulation, sir, but the signal's pretty strong and the content of the traffic seems to indicate they're in Korea and no longer in China."

"What's the content tell you?" he asked.

"That they're on the move, Colonel. Lots of info going back and forth about kilometers marched that day and whether the supply train is keeping up with them and conditions of roads and bridges. Plus some chat about the need to move only at night to avoid aerial reconnaissance. It all hangs together."

"What do we know about those three CCF divisions? First-line troops?"

"Don't know that yet, sir. But if they're regular CCF units, they could be pretty good. They'll know how to fight."

Verity found himself in the odd position of defending Chinese intervention. After the G-2 left, other men on the staff asked questions.

"Why would they be coming? What makes this their fight?"

"Well, it's their backyard. Used to be, anyway."

"Korea? I thought it was the Japs ran this place."

"They did, after they beat the Russians in 1904."

"The Russians?"

"Yeah. China was forced to cede Korea and lots more up in this part of the world to Russia. Eighteen fifty-eight, Treaty of Algun, whatever that was. The rest of the area went to Russia at the Peking Treaty two years later. China was accustomed to being pushed around by all its neighbors back then."

"No more, babee!" one of Smith's staff officers remarked, drawing a laugh. There was a hearsay respect for the Chinese soldiers.

Another officer looked quizzically at Verity. "Tom, how do you know all this shit?"

"Didn't you know?" he asked innocently.

"Know what?" several voices asked.

"I'm native-born Chinese. . . ."

It took two days for the Marine Division, nearly twenty thousand men, to pass through Wonsan and out into the country, where they dug latrines and did all the things Marines on the march have done for two centuries. There hadn't been much fighting here, and except for the port, the town was nearly unscarred. Locals stood on the sidewalks to watch the Marines pass in their yellow canvas leggings and bent under huge backpacks and weapons. The Koreans looked exactly like the Koreans farther south, probably because they were the same people, divided only by an invisible line and a political philosophy. Verity had no Korean, but he knew some Japanese and tried that, to middling effect. He got very little response to his Chinese even though here at Wonsan they were little more than two hundred miles from the Yalu and the border.

I can smell China, he told himself, and indeed he thought he could.

Was it a smell wafting over a couple of hundred miles? Or was it vast China itself moving south, coming closer?

He shivered. From cold, as the sun fell, not because of the Chinese. The nights were getting cooler. He wondered if he'd brought enough cold weather gear and if the Marine Corps were going to issue some. And he wasn't the only Marine wondering about that.

Then Verity shrugged. It was one of those things over which he had no control. The tanks and trucks and personnel carriers and the guns, .105s and even eight-inchers, and all the other rolling stock were coming off the ships down at the port and rolling, clanking, gears whining through the narrow streets of Wonsan, big tanks nearly touching buildings on both sides, they were so wide. Hundreds of vehicles moving through the town and out into the country, ready to start the offensive north. With all this, and considering the beating the North Koreans took at Inchon and in the fighting at Seoul, it ought to be a walkover.

The Hotel San Regis was on the rue Jean Goujon, close to wonderful bars with slim girls who chain-smoked cigarettes and young men who believed in communism, especially over a *fin,* but doted on American films dubbed in French. Elizabeth and Tom had a fifth-floor room in back, a large room, with a small balcony.

"You really should draw the drapes, Elizabeth."

"Oh?"

"Or put on a robe. Or a nightgown."

"But the air is so—"

"I know, and *voyeur* is a French word."

She made a face. "Tommie, don't be so stuffy. Looking's fun. So is being looked at."

He lay on the bed looking up at her, smoking a cigarette, and watching how she moved, and he stopped arguing.

He saw Miss Higgins once more before they went north.

"It's you. I forget your name. But you live in the countryside and don't take my newspaper."

"Not important. Any big stories this week?"

"Bob Hope. So far, he's still the big story."

"That's pretty big," Verity said, meaning it. Compared to a movie star with his own radio show, what were any of them, even MacArthur?

Maggie Higgins was wearing a dress, under an open trench coat.

The night was chilly. He wondered how much of a wardrobe she traveled with. Did someone carry it? Someone change typewriter ribbons for her?

"Tell me your name again."

She could be imperious.

"Verity. Tom Verity."

"Yes. I should have remembered."

"Among all these soldiers and Marines? Why?"

She shrugged. "Why don't you give me a story?" she said. "About going north."

"I'm only a captain. They don't tell me much." He was tempted to say, "Ask your more exalted sources." They said she knew MacArthur. That she was a "pet."

"The best stories come from enlisted men, from platoon leaders and company grade officers. No one knows war the way they do. No one else tells the truth."

"You sound . . . I dunno, cynical."

Maggie Higgins laughed, looking younger than she was. "Me, the last of the romantics?"

He grinned back at her.

"Tell me what you do when you're not listening to radios and dance bands at the St. Francis Hotel or sitting out in the country purposely not reading my column."

"I'm a teacher. At Georgetown."

"What do you teach, anything exotic? I'll try to put a line in my next story. Your family can see it."

He thought it was still a good idea to lie about the Chinese business, so he said, "General studies."

"Oh," she said, disappointed.

Maggie Higgins was forever recruiting heroes. Or creating them in her dispatches. Heroes were what made her stories sing. Real, live American heroes. Maybe this Marine captain would be one.

Feeling him out, she said, "But radio isn't very glamorous."

Verity had worked up a line and decided to use it.

"We also serve who only sit and listen."

Well, she thought, *he has wit.* She liked him.

Verity inhaled her scent. There was something of the excitement about her that he would always associate with Elizabeth. Not quite it but the suggestion of it.

Then, before either of them could say more, an enlisted man came up, a bit awkward and unwashed, but when Verity saw him he went over immediately to hear what he had to say.

Then Verity returned to Marguerite Higgins. "I've got to leave," he told her. "I'm sorry. There's something I have to do."

"You don't really. Other people can tune radios—"

"Yes," he said, shook her hand briskly, and wheeled.

The enlisted man had been Gunny Tate, who had been tuning radios and had come across a sudden flood of Chinese traffic that he thought might mean something.

"You were right, Gunny," Verity said.

He'd barely cleared the door in departing before Maggie Higgins had been taken up by a flyboy major who was telling her marvelous stories of himself.

Elizabeth, Verity thought, would have liked her.

Or hated her.

CHAPTER FIVE

*Pale hills by moonlight, covered in snow . . . Vermont looked
much like this along Route 7, with small, well-lighted towns. . . .
Except that here the towns were dark and called Sudong and
Chinhung-ni and Koto-ri and Hagaru. . . . The difference was at
Stowe, . . . there was no one waiting to kill you.*

The first snows weren't real snow. North Korea wasn't the
Arctic. The October snows fell wet and heavy, turning the
country white but enduring only on the hills, above two
thousand feet. In the valleys the stubble of the rice paddies still
showed through and on the roofs of huts it melted from the heat
inside. On the roads, gravel and earth, the trucks rolled north, sliding sideways a bit on the wet snow, then mud instead of snow, and
just as slippery. He remembered driving with his father in China
years before in one of their GM pickup trucks and how the road
seemed almost to melt beneath you, remembered New England
during college winters and ski trips to North Conway and Pico
Peak, where the bald tires of undergraduate cars made it icier.

But even this early snow, which wouldn't last, wet and heavy,
building up on the helmets and rucksacks and bent shoulders of
the Marines at march, cutting visibility, spinning under the
wheels of trucks and jeeps and the heavy, clanking tank treads,
was . . . inconvenient.

And an omen of worse yet to come. It was, after all, still October, only autumn.

There had been cold nights and mornings with frost, but when he and Gunnery Sergeant Tate and their driver drove out of Wonsan to find the leading Marine regiment and join up with it, a warm sun shone. They'd been warned to keep watch for retreating North Korean units. Just because they were retreating didn't mean they were harmless. A North Korean regiment brushed against one of Puller's companies in the night and killed twenty-five Marines in a firefight. If three men in a jeep ran into an enemy regiment. . . . And with both armies moving so fast now, the North Koreans falling back, the UN people advancing, no front as such existed; it was all fluid, shifting, difficult to define, hard to find. Verity sat up front with Izzo, while Tate and the radio lounged about in the backseat.

"Comfortable back there, Gunny?"

"Very posh, Captain, very pleasant."

Verity wondered where in his travels Tate had picked up *posh.* The sergeant had the usual BAR cradled loosely, a cigar in his mouth. Cigars, Bob Hope, Maggie Higgins, not a shot fired at them yet, this war could be a lot worse.

The country north of Wonsan changed again. Off to the right was the Sea of Japan, and from the heights of ground they could still see it occasionally in the distance, see the odd ship out there, American warships screening X Corps's right flank. On October 20 General Willoughby, the one who didn't like Marines, had declared the war as good as over. From Far East Command in Japan he issued an intelligence summary. "Organized resistance on any large scale has ceased to be an enemy capability. . . . North Korean military and political headquarters may have fled to Manchuria . . . the enemy's field units have dissipated to a point of ineffectiveness."

The North Koreans, he admitted, showed no signs of surrendering and continued to fight "small-scale delaying actions."

Verity had been shown the text by a Marine intelligence officer who said, "In Tokyo they're making plans for the victory parade. They say Third Cavalry will lead it, wearing their yellow neckerchiefs—"

"The Third Cav is a hundred miles away from here, pushing north fast."

"Right, Captain. That's the 'Alice in Wonderland' aspect of all this."

It was as if they were fighting one war on the ground, the real war, and another at Far East Command and in Willoughby's and MacArthur's heads, an imaginary war of wishful thinking.

The roads here in North Korea were much worse than in the South—not battle damage, just maintenance. The few main roads were intelligently laid and well ballasted; that was the Japanese, as efficient as Mussolini with his on-time trains. Of course they'd worked a lot of Koreans to death doing it, both North and South. The roads also grew worse as the jeep climbed. The higher the elevation, the more winter's snow, the greater the temperature differentials between night and midday, expansion and contraction to split and crack the macadam or even the simply oiled dirt and rock of more primitive rural roads. The air grew cooler as well. And just before 4:00 P.M. Verity and his men actually drove through another brief flurry of snow.

Verity remembered snow in late September in Manchuria. In New England, for that matter.

They came out again to sunshine. The driver took both sun and snow with a certain equanimity. Captain Verity reminded himself to ask Tate, when they were alone, just why in the end they'd kept Izzo. Not that Verity didn't trust Tate's judgment, but he was curious.

They came up against and stalled for a time behind other Marine units. There was no shoulder onto which you could pull out to race past. But neither he nor Tate was impatient. If the Chinese were up there, they'd been there for ten thousand years and there were plenty of them and they weren't going to go away.

"Plenty of time, Captain. Can't hurry tomorrow."

That was Gunny Tate. Verity was starting to realize how fortunate he was to have drawn a man like this, competent, cool. He didn't need a drama queen. The driver wasn't nearly as important, but so far Izzo, too, had been OK.

It was cooler still as the road climbed. Verity looked at the map.

"Four thousand feet, this pass," he said. "You can feel it."

"Indeed you can, Captain," Tate said. He could feel the air cooling. And thinning.

They were getting higher and there were plenty of hills ahead, that they could see, that were lots higher. Tate was glad he'd bribed a supply sergeant with a bottle of Haig to draw some cold weather gear. Credit this Verity for having the scotch and for telling him to scout around for heavier clothing. Captain Verity had good sense. Tate'd looked him up. Gunnery and master sergeants had ways; they looked up their officers. If a man were going to issue an order that might kill you, you deserved to know more than his name, rank, and serial number.

Gunnery sergeants took care of each other.

Verity was always aware he was being measured. Marines did that. On Guadalcanal he'd been measured as a kid enlisted man; on Okinawa as a young officer. He was being measured now, much as he'd be arrogant enough to measure Oliver P. Smith. And as Smith, in all likelihood, was measuring Ned Almond and General MacArthur. The process of natural selection, Verity concluded, as if Darwin himself had donned uniform and been called up for service in the war.

Gen. Oliver Smith had nearly eight hundred officers in his division and knew most of them. The regulars, that is—the reserves, those who'd been called up in June or July or even later, well, they were something else. The few dozen he'd met and talked with were educated college and university men. They were Marines, of course, with most of them having fought the Japanese.

But after that, in '45 and '46, they'd gone home to be schooled. To start careers, marry, and raise families. A few of them to make fortunes. Now, five years later, they were back.

Educated young men, properly reared and properly brought up.

Killing and being killed. And, once again, becoming so damned good at both.

Verity continued to monitor the radio. There was plenty of Chinese to listen to. He wrote it up at the end of each day and handed it in to General Smith's people, who might make more sense of it than Verity did, since they knew some of the codes and he just knew Chinese. But there sure was plenty of traffic. There was something going on up there. He had new numbers now, new CCF divisions? That was his analysis.

On October 14, large units of the Chinese Communist army began infiltrating into North Korea, and on the following day MacArthur and President Truman met on Wake Island. Truman expressed concern about the Chinese, but MacArthur assured him they were not a factor. On October 17, ROK troops captured the port city of Hungnam, fifty miles north along the coast from Wonsan, and pushed on against almost no resistance to Iwon, one hundred miles away. October 19, the North Korean capital, Pyongyang, fell to the U. S. First Cavalry and ROKs. Did that mean it was over?

Then, ominously, on October 25, near Unsan to the west, a Chinese attack took place. A prisoner reported there were very large numbers of Chinese troops in the area. He was not believed. And on the very next day an ROK reconnaissance outfit reached the Yalu River in the west near Chosan. The Yalu was the border with China. And it was on that day and over the following two days that the First Marine Division had finally come ashore at Wonsan.

There were plenty of Smiths in the Marine Corps of course, even several Generals Smith, one of them named "Howlin' Mad" Smith, who, during the Big War, had some difficulty with the American army, and they didn't like him nor he them. But the Smith of concern to Tom Verity was Gen. Oliver Smith, commanding officer of the First Marine Division. General Smith reported to an army general, Ned Almond, who commanded X Corps, and both Almond and the Eighth Army had to check with MacArthur in Tokyo to do anything very significant. So here was one army divided in two, with each half required to consult someone hundreds of miles away in another country before putting on any sort of big show. It was to Gen. Oliver Smith, who was not at all happy with these arrangements, that Verity had been told to report.

"Sit down, Captain, while I read this."

Smith read through the brief letter from Headquarters Marine Corps.

"So you're to attach yourself to my staff as an expert of sorts."

"I'm not much of an expert on anything, General. But I speak and understand Chinese. I was born there, grew up there, and I teach Chinese history in college back home."

"And you listen to the radio and translate Chinese for us. Question prisoners. Attempt to assess Chinese participation."

"That's pretty much it, yessir."

Smith sat down now, too. "OK, Verity. I'm sending Litzenberg's Seventh and Murray's Fifth north toward Hungnam. I'm keeping Puller and the First here in Wonsan for now. The old Quantico school solution: two regiments up, one back."

Verity smothered a smile. He could have completed the line: "Two up, one back, take the high ground, and don't piss in the stream, boys; we'll be drinking that water tomorrow."

Smith read his thoughts. Then he sobered, leaning forward toward Verity.

"Captain, we already know there are Chinese in North Korea. Question is, how many and how serious? Bodies have been brought in. You know what General Willoughby said? 'Another goddamned Marine lie.' General MacArthur's intelligence chief says we're lying. I've been ordered to send the division north against a defeated North Korean army and mop up the remnants. But I say, 'General, what about the Chinese up there?' and he says, 'Smith, there are no Chinese.' "

Oliver Smith had no histrionics. He wasn't MacArthur, wasn't even Chesty Puller. Very quietly he said, "My impression of your job, Captain, isn't to convince me of anything. Or Headquarters Marine Corps. It's to convince that bastard Willoughby and his boss. I want unit names and numbers and the names of ranking Chinese officers, that sort of specific information. Not just, well, there are a couple of hundred Chinese encamped at such-and-such. You understand? Specifics that Tokyo will believe. Give me those and you've done the job."

"Aye-aye, sir."

"Follow Litzenberg and Murray. Whichever goes deeper into enemy territory, stick with him. The closer you get to the Chinese, the better. It'll make your job easier."

Verity may have made a face.

"Well, you know what I mean, Captain. *Easy* may not be the right adjective, is all."

He was dismissed then, but Smith did shake his hand. Verity wondered if that was a good omen or a bad.

When he emerged from Smith's HQ, it was into a stiff breeze from the north. Verity had never been to Korea before, but he knew the country just a few hundred miles from here, in North China, Manchuria. The wind came out of Siberia, and that was what made the cold so bad. Behind that wind were five thousand miles of plain and steppe and frozen lakes and snowdrifted forest; behind that wind was Siberia, ice box to the world. On the first cold morning in Wonsan, Captain Verity wondered if anyone else, MacArthur or Oliver Smith, even suspected what was coming, and he thought about starting a diary, a personal account, strictly unofficial. There were rules against diaries, in case you were captured.

But he was writing daily letters to Kate.

She couldn't read yet, but in a lovingly irrational way he wanted to tell her where he was and the places and things he was seeing and that he was OK and missed her and sent love. Madame would translate. She was intelligent and would understand.

"Letter to your wife, Verity?" another officer might ask.

"Yeah."

In a way it was. Kate was what he had left of Elizabeth, and explanations were still painful.

Sometimes as they traveled north the column moved by night and as they drove, if there was no snow and the wind was down, it was very nearly pleasant.

Verity could see the pale hills by moonlight, covered in snow but not threatening. Vermont looked much like this along Route 7, with small, well-lighted towns every ten or twelve miles. Except that here the towns were dark and called Sudong and Chinhung-ni and Koto-ri and Hagaru.

He recalled driving north once with Elizabeth on Route 7 toward a ski vacation at Stowe and rooms at the Green Mountain Inn. They were in the little MG, cramped close together, and she snuggled next to him in the cold and he tossed a casual arm around her shoulder as they drove, the road straight and reasonably flat and the pavement dry, and she became playful, shifting slightly so that his hand fell to her breast and she responded, turning to kiss him quickly and just once, so as not to hamper his driving, and then rested a mittened hand on his thigh.

"Dammit, Elizabeth, cool it. I'm trying to stay on the road."

She laughed. And then he laughed and hugged her tighter with his free arm and she snuggled even closer as they sped north.

The difference was at Stowe, when you finally got there, there was no one waiting to kill you.

After Wonsan, their next stop was another port, Hungnam, about fifty miles north.

When he wasn't listening to the radio, Verity wandered through Hungnam, needing the exercise and wanting to get the feel of Korea. Except for the port, Hungnam wasn't much of a town.

"I've seen better neighborhoods around Camden," Izzo said sourly.

"And I've seen worse," Tate remarked, a country-bred man uneasy with cities, who had fought in the Pusan perimeter, Pusan where the Marines sang:

"Old Pusan U.
Old Pusan U.
She asked me what my school was.
I said, 'Old Pusan U.' "

"That's pretty good, Gunny," Verity, who enjoyed a good ditty, said.

"Why, thank you, Captain." Tate had a singing voice and he knew it.

"What was it like at Pusan?" Verity asked. "Pretty wild?"

"Yessir. Before things got stabilized when the Marine brigade came in, it was chaos and then some. They was still talking when I got there about the army Thirty-Fourth Regiment. They were there all dug in and the North Koreans appeared and they just got up and left. Didn't fire a shot. The new colonel they brought in, I forget his name, arrived from Europe wearing an overseas cap and low shoes and not even owning a side arm. It was the Thirty-fourth Regiment that left General Dean up in the air with no flank for a couple of miles, General Dean who later got captured out there carrying a rifle and playing private. That's who screwed up down there on the Naktong and in the perimeter."

"Hills?"

"Yessir, but not like these, not so high. And hot. Hot as hell. And the smells coming up out of the villages and the paddies and the vegetable patches. I don't know about the rice paddies, but they fertilize their fruits and vegetables with shit, human waste. They keep it in what they call honey pots."

That, at least, both Tate and Verity realized, was like China.

CHAPTER SIX

There was some of Nathan Bedford Forrest in most of the Marine generals and colonels . . . all of them professional killers. Forrest had been one of Lee's generals. Even Forrest's fellow Southern generals were afraid of him. If you crossed Forrest, he would kill you.

And now, as the division saddled up to move north, word came from the States to Smith: Chesty Puller was finally a general.

When they notified Puller of the star his officers gathered to congratulate him.

Puller was fifty-two years old, not young for a brigadier. Blame politics for that. Or Puller himself, for being a damned difficult man. Over drinks there was some grousing, some laughter, much genuine pleasure, warmth, and love and admiration.

One officer, in drink, remarked that Custer, another flamboyant, was a brigadier at twenty-three and a major general at twenty-five.

"Yes," said Puller, contemptuous of the army, "and at thirty-seven Custer was dead and mutilated by squaws."

Around him Marine officers nodded in agreement. Better a late star and to live to fifty-two.

With a hard campaign ahead of them, men sorted out the priorities.

* * *

It was an odd-looking column of Marines that went north, piebald and eccentric.

Some winter clothing had arrived and been parceled out. Overcoats, windproof trousers to be tugged on over kersey pants. Long johns. Felt-lined hats with earmuffs. Scarves. Heavy socks. New gloves. Mittens.

Not enough of any of them. There were even rarer novelties, better lines of merchandise, but only for the fortunate. There were new boots, thermal in design, proof against not only subzero temperatures but also immersion and sweat, shiny black boots, swiftly nicknamed, "Mickey Mouse." There were down parkas no one, save an alpinist, had ever seen before.

Yet several thousand men, veterans of the Pusan perimeter and the Naktong River campaign in the heat of August, were still clad in field jackets and fatigues, no gloves or long johns or earmuffs or windproof trousers.

The effect was so colorfully wrong, driving top sergeants and old professionals like Puller to frustration and near tears, turning enlisted rebels giddy with unaccustomed freedom, that the Marines themselves were confused. They wanted liberty; they were muddled by license.

A goddamned vaudeville show! So went the official howl.

Rarely had there been such a dog's breakfast of uniforms. Lee's men, perhaps, after Antietam. Or Coxey's Army, or the bonus marchers demanding veterans' benefits from Herbert Hoover's Washington. Or the homespun and leather and tanned skins of the farmers and hunters and bargemen and trappers who went north under Benedict Arnold to Saratoga to defeat "Gentleman Johnny Burgoyne" and the splendid royal army with which he was to split Washington's rebels and divide New England from Virginia and the rest of the South.

But if the uniform code was being sadly neglected, other things were not. As they marched north, Murray and Litzenberg had patrols ranging far out front and flank patrols high above on the ridges and hillsides, a thousand feet or so higher than the road and the column itself, rifle platoon-size patrols moving fast, staying up

with the column or even ahead, and guarding its flanks against
ambush and attack. You had to have discipline to get men to climb
that high and that fast on steep slopes with snow and then to keep
up and keep watch.

Please do not think of Oliver Smith, for all his pipe smoking and
courtesy, or of these Marine colonels, his battalion and regimental
commanders, as kindly, avuncular, courtly, and graciously aging
old gentlemen. Some of them were those excellent things, of
course, but all of them were professional killers, employed in a
hard trade: tenacious, cunning, resourceful, cold, cynical, and
tough, not the kind of men who waited patiently for the Chinese to
come and kill them.

There was some of Nathan Bedford Forrest in most of them.
Forrest had been one of Lee's generals, a cavalryman capable of
killing enemy soldiers at close or long range, with his regimental
artillery at a mile's distance or face-to-face-with sabre and revolver.
Even Forrest's fellow Southern generals were afraid of him. If you
crossed Forrest, he would kill you. Toward the end of a battle he
once raged at his men, urging them to finish off a beaten federal
corps: "I did not come here to make half a job of it. I mean to have
them all." By that, Forrest's men understood, he meant, "I mean to
kill them all."

It was said Forrest was disappointed when Union troops surrendered and at Fort Pillow he killed prisoners. Nathan Forrest was not
a nice man. Oliver Smith's division contained men of equivalent
ferocity. Not all, of course, but many. And many who had already
killed.

Tate had killed people, one of them a Japanese prison guard,
others down on the Naktong in August's heat. Izzo had killed on
the Islands during the War. Maybe again in Korea; he was vague
about that. Verity, too, had killed.

It was the work Marine infantrymen did.

*   *   *

Headquarters in Hungnam was a stone building two stories high with a tiled roof and a sort of center portico with chintzy pillars that attempted to convey grandeur. Windows had been shot out or blown by near hits, but otherwise the place was sound, and it was here Oliver Smith called his staff together, mostly colonels and majors, all armed, shoulder holsters mostly, which seemed this year's style. One officer standing near Smith bore an iron face, as Boswell once said of an attorney, another barked an alehouse laugh, most were bluff and ruddy, but that was being outdoors and in the wind and, Tom supposed, aboard ship.

It was five years since Verity had met with men like these in number; he was more accustomed today to the commons room with its tweeds and pipes.

General Smith, long-faced, white-haired, and still wearing the old yellow canvas leggings, could have been himself, except for the Colt. 45, an academic, perhaps a tenured professor of Thomistic philosophy. And it turned out his divisional HQ had been a Jesuit secondary school.

"The Jesuits seem to be long gone," Smith's operations officer remarked, "so we must pray for ourselves."

"I work for the Jesuits," Verity said, "at Georgetown University."

"Oh?" The ops officer was not sufficiently interested to explore that opening further. "Well," he said, "here's General Smith."

They all stood, not snapping to attention but simply getting up, perhaps a dozen men in the room. Oliver Smith had seen a lot of war, and he motioned them to be seated.

"Thanks for coming, gentlemen."

There was a sort of high stool, and Smith slid it under one buttock and perched there, rather as a schoolteacher might have done, then calling on one officer after another to brief the meeting and himself. There was an evident confusion.

"The objective isn't all that clear. General Almond seems to be sending the First Marine Division in three disparate directions," the ops officer said. He was a full colonel and a bit of a schoolteacher himself. Using a pointer and an acetate overlay on a small-scale map of eastern North Korea, he lectured them a bit.

"The division is to proceed northwest to Hagaru-ri, at the near or southernmost end of the Chosin Reservoir. At Hagaru we are to split up, with a right wing moving northeast toward the Fukien Reservoir, about twenty miles away. Based on Hagaru, the rest of the division is to move northwest to Yudam-ni, a village twelve or thirteen miles away on the high ground west of the Chosin. And from Yudam-ni, we divide again, dispatching a column due west to cross the Taebaek Mountain Range to make contact, vaguely out there [he motioned with a languorous hand], with Eighth Army's right flank."

The colonel paused.

"No one seems to know just how far away and where the Eighth Army might be."

Smith nodded. "Thank you, Colonel." He made no comment on the apparent confusion in General Almond's orders but permitted a moment or two of grousing by the others. This was standard procedure. Senior Marine officers had opinions and enjoyed airing them. Verity was, except for several staff NCOs, the lowest-ranked man in the room and offered nothing. Until Smith said: "This is Captain Verity. Headquarters Marine Corps sent him over. He speaks several Chinese dialects fluently. He's been listening to Chinese radio traffic."

He then paused. "I might also say the captain fought on the 'Canal as an enlisted man and on Okinawa as a rifle platoon leader."

This last, with no editorial comment, was clearly intended by Smith to tell his officers, "This is not just another Washington charm boy."

"Captain?"

Verity had been sitting on a wooden crate. He got up now. *I talk better on my feet,* he told himself.

"Thank you, General. I am not an intelligence specialist. Because I was born and raised in China and I now teach Chinese lit and history in an American college I'm here, pretty simply, to listen to Chinese radio traffic. And, if it comes to that, to talk to Chinese POWs."

He paused, wondering how far his own hunches and biases should be indulged. So he went ahead and told the truth.

"I think the Chinese are coming in. The father north we go, the more Chinese I hear. But that's reasonable. We're getting closer to the Chinese border. What has me interested is that I'm hearing numbers of Chinese corps and divisions that Headquarters Marine Corps provided me. And, on a personal note, I'm hearing the names, or at least similar names, of officers I knew in China five years ago."

This was a curveball. A full colonel jumped up.

"Wait a minute. You *knew* these guys? You went back to China?"

"Yes, Colonel. I left there at age fifteen. I went back in '45 after the surrender and served as a company commander in North China into mid-'46. Because I could speak the language I also did a lot of liaison with Chinese Communist Forces in the Tientsin-Tsingtao area. There were regular Chinese army detachments; there were the Communists; there were plenty of bandits and local warlords. After seven years of fighting the Japanese and being occupied, it was a chaotic place. The Marines tried to keep the railroad open and missionaries from getting their heads chopped off, and I did some of the go-between haggling and dickering."

They were all listening to him now with varying degrees of fascination. The division might be about to fight the Chinese army and here was a guy who'd been there and knew some of them.

Sometimes Elizabeth would ask him about the War.

"Did you shoot people, Tommie?"

"Oh, you know," he said, sloughing it off.

"No, I don't," Elizabeth said, characteristically blunt, crisp. "I don't know *anything* about war."

"Well, there's a lot of waiting around. Standing in lines. Getting up early and getting pretty dirty. And then every once in awhile there's a lot of shooting. If you're lucky, it doesn't last too long and you don't get shot."

If he thought that would satisfy Elizabeth, he was wrong.

"I know you never got shot," she said, "because I know your body. No unnecessary holes anywhere."

He grinned. *I'd hope not.*

She went solemn. "Did you shoot other people? The Japanese?"

"Yes. On Guadalcanal. By the time I got to Okinawa I was an officer, and officers don't go around shooting people unless things go very wrong."

She shook her head. "I can't see you shooting people, Tommie. Or having them shoot at you. It's just, well, it's beyond my experience, beyond imagining."

"That's what war is, Elizabeth, beyond most of us."

Then she cheered up. "Well, that's all over. No one's ever going to have to go to war again, are they?"

"Of course not," he said.

"Now, Verity," General Smith said, when they were alone, beckoning Tom to a camp stool closer to the stove, "tell me about this fellow Lin Po and whether you think he could be commanding over there."

It wasn't that simple, Verity thought before speaking, *not as if Lee called Longstreet in the night before Gettysburg to brief him about Meade.*

"It's Lin Piao, sir. And there's another name, Peng Teh-huai. Not quite clear as yet which man is senior." He'd scoured memory for Peng's full name.

Smith asked Verity to spell both names, and the general wrote them down as if wanting to get his adversaries down on paper.

"Go on, Captain. You knew them both?"

"I knew Peng. Or a gent by that name. I've heard of Lin but never met him."

"But you met Peng."

"Yessir, in North China, the winter of '45–'46. I was responsible for railroad security between Tientsin and Tsingtao. It was much too long a stretch for one company to patrol, so I concentrated my people at a town halfway along the right-of-way, sent reinforced squads to accompany trains, and tried to maintain contact with local Chinese forces—"

"These Nationalists or Communists?"

"Some of each. Plus a few local warlords with freelance armies of their own. Early in '46 the United States proposed a cease-fire between Chiang and Mao and General Marshall was actually flown out to Nanking to chair armistice talks. The talks didn't get anywhere, but the Reds agreed to the cease-fire anyway because they knew they were outgunned and would be until they could collect and service weapons the Japanese army left behind when it surrendered in September."

"And Lin and Peng, were they involved in the peace process?"

"They might have been, at times. The talks dragged on for a year. I got to know Peng meanwhile up north. He was one of the local people in authority I went to, trying to keep it cool along the railroad and keep Marines from being killed. Despite the cease-fire there were occasional brushes between the Reds and Chiang's regular army; there were the warlords raising odd hell; there were even reports up in the hills of rogue bands of Japanese infantry refusing to come in and lay down weapons. So it was a busy time. You tried to figure out who gave the orders to each of these distinct groups. Peng seemed to be the leading Red in our congressional district."

Smith gave a thin smile. "Tell me about him," he said. "What sort of fellow he was and what you remember."

Verity was twenty-five years old again and back home in China and he and Peng Teh-huai were drinking coffee in a depot café along the Tientsin–Tsingtao main line on a February morning with snow. There was steam on the windows, and neither was anxious to leave the cozy table and hot coffee. Verity was in uniform and Peng in a sort of overall with a shapeless quilted parka and furred hood hung on a wall peg behind him. Verity rubbed reddened hands together.

"Hate to be a Marine out there today on a flatcar behind a machine gun."

"Hate to be out there in the snow waiting for a Marine flatcar to come along," Peng said.

"Wouldn't it be nice if they'd leave it to you and me to settle things," Verity said, "both being reasonable men."

"Far too sensible a solution, Tom," the Communist officer said. "How would the old men justify their souls?"

Verity found nothing strange about Communists discussing the soul. The Chinese were Chinese first and everything else second, even believers in dialectical atheism and the *Communist Manifesto*. Besides, theoretical debate was harmless, since both men understood nothing was to be settled, not at conference tables.

"I just hope we're the hell out of here before you and Chiang get started again," Verity said. He meant it. Caught between two armies of a million men each was no place for a single Marine division.

"I also," said Peng. "I'd hate to fight the United States Marine Corps in any serious way." He meant it as well; he knew what they'd done against the Japanese. His men had been fighting in unserious ways much of the fall and winter. No one took it amiss. It was expected that trains would be derailed and locomotives occasionally shot up and that Marines on flatcars behind sandbags would fire back.

"Cost of doing business," was how the Marines put it. Men who'd fought their way across the Pacific and defeated Japan were not likely to go all sweaty over a few bandits or irregular troops raising hell. It cut the boredom, enabled them to forget the lousy weather and not yet having been rotated home.

That didn't mean men didn't die. Nor did Verity and Peng travel alone.

Verity's jeep, parked outside, carried a mounted .50-caliber machine gun, while his driver and company runner now sat smoking and talking and drinking coffee at a table near the door from which they could watch the station platform and beyond up the road that paralleled the narrow-gauge track. Peng had four men. They waited for him outside.

Gamesmanship, Verity thought. *His men stay out in the snow. Ergo, they've gained a little face over us.*

Peng would have agreed to this. There was another reason. He was more at risk from Chiang's Nationalists than was the American. Verity might be killed by accident during a railroad ambush; Peng would be a target of immense opportunity. Still only thirty, he ran this province for Mao Tse-tung.

Verity told General Smith all this and more, whatever he

recalled of Peng, plus an assessment of his leadership philosophy, just how aggressive or cautious he might be in a fight.

"He'd go out and get you, General. That's how he was five years ago. He went after a guy."

Smith smiled. "Good," he said. Oliver Smith liked a soldier who fought, who came out at you instead of just skulking about, nibbling at the edges. And in a set-piece battle Smith knew a Marine division could outgun the Chinese. *If only,* he thought, *they'll give us a set-piece battle.*

As General Smith told Verity, "I hate those cagey fellas tap-dancing and shadow-boxing that frustrate you into doing something silly and then they turn right around and bite off your head. I like a gent who slugs it out in the center of the ring."

"Yessir," said Verity, a bit out of his depth with all this divisional big-picture stuff.

Dear Kate,

I met the general. His name is Oliver Smith and he is very tall and smokes a pipe. So there is always a cloud of smoke around his head.

He asked me a lot of questions about China, where I grew up, and about some Chinese gentlemen I used to know who might be coming to visit us one day soon.

I told him everything I knew and he just puffed and more smoke came out.

Isn't that a funny way for a general to behave?

All love,
Poppy
xxx ooo

The real hills would begin at Sudong.

"The radio pick up better on high ground, Gunny?"

"Yessir, certainly should. Radio waves being directional, you get a tall building or a hill in between and it cuts the signal."

Verity studied the map. Sudong, situated in a high valley, was the next serious town beyond Hamhung, about thirty-seven miles away. The South Koreans were said to be in control at Sudong.

And a lot farther north than that. Trouble was, no one with sense trusted the South Koreans. Not that they lied, men said, just exaggerated. Or were mistaken. All in the constructive spirit of encouraging their gallant allies, the Americans, of course. A ROK told you what he thought you wanted to hear, whatever the reality.

The drive to Sudong took four hours. That was the quality of the road rather than weather or the enemy. They saw no enemy, only plenty of ROK troops lazing about and civilians, alternately sullen and wide-eyed with wonder, and the weather was splendid, maybe sixty degrees and sunny. Izzo drove in a T-shirt and Verity hatless to get some sun. Only Tate, the professional, remained tightly buttoned up. Alongside, paralleling the road, ran the narrow-gauge railroad. Verity knew narrow-gauge from China, two feet, six inches between the rails. Along here the rails were already rusting and weeds grew between the wooden ties, the railroad's normal schedules being somewhat and understandably disrupted.

They were getting very little on the radio that was intelligible, so it got Tate talking. Which was rare, Izzo being the talker among them.

"I'm from the part of Kansas where Quantrill's Raiders rode in the Civil War, Frank and Jesse James and them. They still got plaques up in town squares and county seats, memorializing 'Bloody Kansas.' "

Verity, from Yale, was a bit vague as to just which side Quantrill had been on.

"No confusion about that in Kansas, Captain. 'William Clarke Quantrill, Confederate raider.' That's how the Yankees put it. The South, well, they felt different, thought of him and remember him as a great man." Tate paused. "Burned a lot of towns, Quantrill did, hanged a lot of men. He probably would have done well in the Marine Corps. If we still rode horseback."

"Horses? *We* had horses? Like John Wayne?"

"Just watch the road, Izzo," Tate said mildly.

He'd been reading up on the Civil War, Tate said, until Korea interrupted.

"I got through tenth grade and then joined the Marine Corps," he said. "Family was short of money; the Depression was on. I joined up at seventeen in 1937. Been in thirteen years, going on thirty. Shanghai with the old Fourth Marines was where I picked up a little Chinese."

"No shit, Gunny, so that's how you could *parlez* Chink."

"Shut up, Izzo. Just watch—"

"I know, 'watch the road.' "

Tate had spent nearly four years in a succession of Japanese prison camps.

"Curious to think of now, considering where we are and what we're doing, but the Korean guards were the worst. The Japs didn't treat them very well, and so the Koreans treated us worse. We were even lower than the Chinese who worked around the camps. It was barnyard pecking order all the way, and we were the lowest, the Marines and later on whatever fliers they caught, some sailors off torpedoed ships, a few soldiers from God knows where, some Brits, and even a couple of French and Aussies and one South African with a blond beard. He died early of something. I forget what."

The Chinese, Tate said, while ill-handled, were still civilians and went home at night to wives and children, hearth and hut.

"We stayed behind the wire."

Some of the Fourth Marines and other Americans were shipped to prison camps in Japan itself. There was a crude system to it. The Japanese needed certain categories of laborer, coal miners for one, steel puddlers for another, and such men were sent to Japan, usually to be worked to death.

"But you see, Captain, we didn't know that at the time. There were these big arguments, debates really, about whether to tell them you were a coal miner or something else they seemed to want or to hide the fact. One school said you'd be better fed, better treated, because they needed you. The other said, 'Stay here; it's bad, but we're alive. Who knows what it's like back there?' " He screwed up his face in a half-smile. "Didn't really matter all that much; most of us died one place or t'other."

He sounded sufficiently thoughtful that Verity didn't say anything and even Mouse Izzo was quiet. Then Tate continued:

"It did matter once, whether you stayed or went. They pulled out fifteen hundred or two thousand Yanks at one time late in '44 when the War was going bad for the Japs and good for us and crammed them into an old tramp, the *Maru* something, to take them back to Japan, to repair bomb damage, that's what was said, and the *Maru* something was halfway up the Formosa Strait when it was torpedoed by a U. S. sub. The sub didn't know it was carrying prisoners, of course. A dozen or so Americans were on deck when it hit, hauling water and chow back down to the hold to the others. They got off. A few of them survived the War, and I met one of them a few years ago at Camp Lejeune. He said none of the two thousand below got out. They were chained and the Japanese didn't have time, or didn't care to bother, to unleash them. He said even in the water, swimming around and looking for something to hang on to, he could hear the men still on the *Maru* something and the sound they made chained below. He said it wasn't like men at all, that sound. . . ."

It was, recalled Tate's friend, more like animals howling.

"I don't want to be a POW again, Captain," Tate said, "not ever."

There were low hills just north of Sudong, and after Verity checked in with ROK officers and was assured the area was quiet, he and Tate and Izzo set up the radio and a pyramidal tent and the rest of their gear on a hilltop and did some listening that evening and into the night until about midnight. They didn't get much. Toward dawn, maybe 5:00 A.M., there was a big storm swept through, thunder and lightning and heavy rain for an hour or so, more like a summer storm than October.

In the morning the whole country seemed cleaner and fresher, the air sweet.

"Well, that wasn't so bad," Verity said. The tent hadn't leaked very much at all.

"Glorioso," Izzo agreed.

Tate looked at the sky. "I dunno," he said. "Back home in autumn, just before the real cold, there's generally one last good thunderstorm, clearing things out."

Verity looked around then, too. Not a cloud.

"But this ain't Kansas and I may be wrong," Tate said.

"Sure, Gunny," Izzo said. "Even a gunny can be wrong."

"Izzo, just strike the tent and load the jeep."

Verity's orders were to spend just the one night in Sudong and report back to Division. Smith didn't like to have Marine officers out too far ahead and relying on ROKs.

Fine with me, Verity thought.

Besides, maybe Tate was right and the weather would be coming off cold.

Ned Almond had his prejudices. He didn't like black troops or trust them. He'd commanded a black unit in Italy during the War, when the American army was still segregated, and had lacked confidence in blacks ever since. At one point while ordering troop dispositions in X Corps, Almond said that a black 155mm howitzer battalion and several other black units should be "bivouacked behind the lines and left there."

Nor did he like Marines very much.

But the Marines were what he had to work with and, he conceded with reluctance, they were probably the best he had. He ordered them to move out of Hungnam and Hamhung toward the reservoir no later than November 1. And to move fast.

It was Oliver Smith to whom Almond issued these orders.

CHAPTER SEVEN

"If you as much as smell *Chinese cooking," General Smith*
instructed Captain Verity, "get back here and tell me."

Homer Litzenberg, the colonel commanding the Seventh
Marine Regiment, was so aggressive a decidedly corny
nickname had adhered: Blitzin' Litzenberg. No one used
it in his presence, although his troops enjoyed it. It gave them
something to amuse themselves when the Old Man wasn't listening.

Now Litzenberg's commanding officer, Gen. Oliver Smith,
called Litzenberg aside to tell him his Seventh Marines would lead
the march north toward the reservoir and Hagaru-ri and on to
Yudam-ni to relieve the ROK forces there and to spearhead whatever farther move north or west the entire Marine division would
be ordered to make.

Said Smith, when the two men were alone: "Colonel, I don't
want you to 'blitz' your way north. Not this time."

Litzenberg nodded but looked, and was, confused. Smith wasn't
confused at all. But he was aware he was doing a very subversive
thing, something that for a Marine general officer was almost without precedent. He was coldly and knowingly setting out to disobey
Ned Almond's order.

Smith went on now with Litzenberg.

"Homer, I don't like the way this division is being used and where it's being sent. General Almond's ordered an advance to the Chosin and beyond without a secure left flank. There is nothing out there to our left but a range of mountains with no roads across them. And on the other side of those mountains it's another twenty, maybe forty or fifty miles to the right flank of Eighth Army. I think it's a mistake by General Almond and by General MacArthur to send two distinct and widely separated wings of this army north in winter conditions against what may be a major element of the Chinese Communist army. I've told Almond that. He told me those were the orders and to proceed."

Smith looked grim now and Litzenberg leaned forward, not wanting to miss any of the subtleties of his own orders, on which his own professional competence would be judged. Such things were important to career military men. He wanted desperately not to misunderstand any of what Smith was telling him.

"Yes, sir?" Litzenberg said, aware that more was coming.

Smith, too, was now tensed and leaning toward his subordinate. He knew how important it was that Litzenberg understand yet how impossible it was to reduce his instructions to paper. A written document instructing the colonel to disobey X Corps orders direct from Ned Almond would be prima facie evidence of insubordination that could easily have Smith, perhaps both of them, up on charges, facing a General Court-Martial.

"I smell something bad out there, Colonel, and I wouldn't take it amiss if you went north at somewhat less than flank speed." Oliver Smith was worried about Litzenberg's Seventh Marines and about sending Marines along a narrow mountain road with real winter coming on and, perhaps, a Chinese army waiting.

Litzenberg was no happier.

His regiment jumped off on November 1. The day before, the ROK II Corps had come under heavy attack from regular Chinese Communist Forces, the first such major encounter with the Chinese. The Chinese attack was a long way off to the west near Kanu-ri but confirmed there were heavy forces in the war and not just a few Chinese "volunteers," as Willoughby kept insisting.

Litzenberg moved out of Hamhung heading north but not in a rush, throwing out patrols on each flank and far ahead of the leading battalion and not moving a yard until the patrols signaled the way was clear. There was snow on the ground, and on the single road that would now become the Main Supply Route (MSR) for the entire division, the snow was being packed and polished into ice by treads and wheels and men's boots.

Still, it wasn't snow and ice or even Litzenberg's official "caution" that slowed the advance. It was the enemy.

At Sudong, regimental-sized Chinese Communist Forces attacked and for a time cut off two rifle battalions of Litzenberg's three. It was more than a firefight, the toughest fighting the Marines had been in since taking Seoul. Air strikes were called in, the Eleventh Marines artillery was brought up, and still it took two days to secure Sudong. Then a company of North Korean tanks—and where the hell did they come from?—came out firing and cutting up the lead rifle company before the heavier, bigger-gunned Marine tanks could be brought up. Another day and night went to the taking of Funchilin Pass, nearly five thousand feet high and deep in snow.

On November 7, after a week giving battle, the Chinese abruptly broke off and seemed just to melt into the hills.

Litzenberg didn't understand it, and back at headquarters neither did Smith. Verity was still there, still monitoring, and had been due to drive north to accompany Litzenberg when the fighting at Sudong broke out and the road was cut.

"We got lucky, Gunny," Izzo remarked. "We could of been up there with my old buddies in the Seventh getting shot."

Tate gave Izzo a sour look but knew he was right. It looked as if there was going to be plenty of fighting to go around before this was all over, and a prudent man didn't rush things.

The battle at Sudong surprised everyone. Hadn't Verity and Tate driven up there just days earlier to have a look-see and found the place solidly in South Korean hands? Where had the South Koreans fled? Why had the Chinese attacked so ferociously and then broken off?

This Peng is a chess player, Oliver Smith told himself. Worrying.

And hadn't Verity assured him the man would fight in the center of the ring? Well, maybe he would yet; maybe all this so far was just the preliminaries, the four-round bouts before the main event.

In Tokyo General Willoughby had finally admitted there were Chinese troops in North Korea, still insisting they were "volunteers."

"Yeah," responded cynics at headquarters when sure they were out of hearing, "about a million volunteers."

There were little signs of panic.

Starting October 25 when the ROK Sixth Division was hit near Unsan, Chinese pressure had built. On November 1 the army's First Cavalry Division was attacked. On the second, the Marines at Sudong. A few days later Australians had to fight off attacks so fierce they ran short of ammunition and were reduced to wielding bayonets. MacArthur demanded Washington order bombing of the Yalu bridges to cut off Chinese supplies and reinforcements.

Suddenly it looked as if "the boys" might not be home for Christmas, after all.

Yet in other sectors of North Korea, Allied patrols had reached the Yalu, meeting almost no resistance, while along the east coast ROKs sprinted north more than one hundred miles ahead of the Marines still getting under way at Hungnam.

Anyone looking at a map could see that MacArthur's two armies were spread out over a terrible range of hostile country, so much so that by November 7 MacArthur himself was ordering all units to slow down and consolidate gains.

Then, unaccountably, the Chinese fell back and vanished. By November 14 MacArthur was again preening. The Chinese, he said, had made their little demonstration and gone home. Either that, or they'd run out of steam.

The General had again been proven right.

"Come up with me, Verity," one of Smith's staff said. "We've got some bodies." They were from the fighting at Sudong, from the Chinese attack on the Seventh Marines.

Verity told Tate to keep the radio watch and followed the staff major. Izzo, he assumed, was out stealing things.

General Smith had a big tent with a stove going, and it was warm enough you could shed your gloves and open your parka. It was also warm enough to thaw the dead, and so now the staff and a handful of other officers were led out around back behind the general's tent to where nine or ten Chinese bodies had been lined up for their inspection.

"I always like to see stiffs," Verity heard one officer whisper to another. "Talk all you want about body counts. I like to see the bodies. That way you know, you really know."

"You're right," the other murmured, deferential in the presence of Oliver Smith.

"Well now," General Smith said, "they won't be the last, but these certainly are the first."

"Yessir," the murmurs went, rather pleased.

Smith turned to an intelligence officer who had, apparently, already examined the dead.

"Marsh, what can you tell?"

"Well, sir, from the little service record books we've been able to examine, one of these men, still a private soldier, has been in the army and fighting much of the time since 1937. He . . ."

Since '37? Marine officers looked at one another.

". . . was drafted in '37 by Chiang Kai-shek, fought the Japanese for eight years until VJ Day in '45, then started fighting the Communists again in '47, was still fighting when Chiang bugged out to Formosa—"

"Colonel, we say of our gallant ally Generalissimo Chiang that he and his forces evacuated to Formosa, rather than 'bugged out.' "

"Right you are, General. So when they 'evacuated,' this fellow was left behind and after a few weeks was conscripted into the CCF. Same uniform, they just added a red star on his hat. So he's been in the army thirteen years and he's still a private and until yesterday he was still fighting. . . ."

Verity stared down at the row of dead. He wondered which of them was the long-suffering private. Hard to tell, even for Verity, who knew the Chinese and had some notion of how the men aged. Women, well, they aged even faster. Functions of the social structure.

The intelligence officer lectured briefly. The dead men, "the stiffs," as the Marines had it, wore layers of uniform, all cotton, none of them proof against the cold they'd all already sampled, on both sides of the line, and knew would get worse.

As the dead were picked over for the delectation of Smith's staff, Verity thought, irrationally he knew, of Elizabeth, dead and cold in the ground. A more dignified death, of course, but no less cold, no less dead. Oh, how he loved her, how he missed her.

"As you can see, gentlemen," the intelligence man went on, "the outer clothing is dun or khaki on one side, white on the other, the camouflage potential being obvious. We might ourselves one day consider . . ."

General Smith, tall and taciturn, moved his feet impatiently. He didn't want this turning into a headquarters lecture or a seminar for the Marine Corps Schools at Quantico.

The lecturing officer was not stupid. He caught the gesture.

". . . and under this padded winter uniform, the usual cotton summer suit, plus any sweaters or extra shirts available. On the feet, sneakers. One or two pairs of cotton socks. We are finding the occasional Chinese soldier dead of wounds. But already suffering, and rather badly, of frostbite."

Several of the staff officers knelt to look more closely at the bodies, to finger cloth, like bespoke tailors or the operators of a quality funeral parlor.

The mountains slumped down toward the road, in places hanging over it. Even at noon there was shadow. Shadow and shade, a gloom, a darkness, over the snow and the land. That was the doing of the slope, the steep vertical incline, so severe it was difficult to understand how even dwarf trees grew on such gradients and clung. There was the single road, snaking more than a hundred miles through these mountains from the Sea of Japan to the frontier of China—a narrow road of dirt and gravel, not constructed so much as carved into the slopes and clinging there.

It was along this road the two armies would march: the Chinese and the Marines.

In a way, between Peng and Oliver Smith it was what in the Old West they called a walkdown, the rival gunmen walking down the dusty western street toward each other, guns holstered but ready. One night as they sat over a courtesy fire, Verity asked Tate if there was validity in the analogy.

"Well," said Tate, the student of Captain Quantrill, "there's no Calamity Jane. But there are two men very handy with guns, competent men, at opposite ends of the MSR. Which ain't too dusty. But otherwise is available for killing people."

Izzo threw up his hands.

"With all due respect, Captain, if a couple of guys in South Philly start shooting each other, not only does the police department arrive, but there are calls for the federals and the state police, maybe for committees of vigilantes. Yet when you got a couple of drunken cowboys shooting guys in Texas or Arizona or someplace, they're frigging Gary Cooper and Duke Wayne."

Tate told Izzo he didn't understand history, but Verity thought there was an argument to be made.

In the words of Mouse Izzo, "This place looks like frigging Switzerland."

Izzo had never seen Switzerland. But he was about right.

From Hungnam on the coast of the Sea of Japan to the southern tip of the Chosin Reservoir was nearly seventy miles. Soon after you left Hungnam, the port, and its twin inland city, Hamhung, you could see the real mountains ahead and yet still, at the hairpin turns, you could look back at the sea in the distance.

"Glorioso, Captain," Izzo said, very impressed, "even better than the Poconos."

"Praise indeed, for I have seen the Poconos," Verity replied, enjoying the moment.

Smith released him from headquarters with instructions to drive north and catch up to Litzenberg, monitoring the radio all the way. Where were the Chinese? Where had they gone after the fight at Sudong?

"If you as much as *smell* Chinese cooking, Verity, get back here and tell me. I want to know what your chum Peng is up to."

"Yessir."

As Izzo drove north, the sun dimmed, a sort of yellow veil coming between it and the earth. And it got colder with the wind up. By two in the afternoon they could no longer see either the sea behind or the distant mountains ahead. Then the snow began to fall, heavy snow, heavy and wet, coating everything.

"Oh, shit," Izzo said, no longer admiring the landscape.

It was the first half of November.

Gen. Oliver Smith was not happy. His First Marine Division had reached Hagaru-ri, at the southern end of the reservoir. To the northwest, two of his three rifle regiments, the Fifth and Seventh, would soon be based on Yudam-ni, north of Hagaru. The other infantry regiment, General Puller's First Marines, was still far to the south, having been sent off on the equivalent of a wild-goose chase, waiting to be relieved by the Third Army Division so it could rejoin Smith and the other Marine regiments to re-form the division as a whole. Smith did not like the way X Corps had broken up his division or what Generals MacArthur and Almond were telling him to do.

More fundamentally, Smith didn't like MacArthur and didn't much like Ned Almond, who more and more took on his master's (MacArthur's) posturing and protective coloration. There were army generals who felt the same as Smith did, but their careers depended on MacArthur's favor. The Marines had never liked MacArthur (calling him Dugout Doug), and as a Marine general Smith could get away with a lot more backtalk. Sass, his grandmother used to call it.

*   *   *

Oliver Smith, wreathed in pipe smoke, sat at a table in the old Jesuit schoolhouse at Hungnam that served as divisional HQ with his ops officer, his intelligence chief, and four or five other members of the division staff.

"Captain Verity, sir," a duty officer announced.

"Send him in."

When Verity came in, blinking in the gloom after the bright sunlight of the long jeep trip south, Smith welcomed him, told him to pull up a chair, get out of his coat, and light up if he wished. Verity always worried when encountering such high-level urbanity, and he was instinctively on guard.

"Yessir, thank you, General."

Smith made the brief introductions. "Now, tell us what you've got."

"Yessir." Verity looked down at his sheaf of notes. Began to read.

"Gentlemen, I've identified by number the Forty-second, the Twentieth, the Twenty-seventh, and the Twenty-sixth CCF Armies. The Forty-second seems to have three infantry divisions, I've got the numbers when you wish, and the other three armies have four divisions each. By my count there are at least six of these divisions already in the general area or a day's march from the Chosin Reservoir. The other nine divisions seem to be a farther north. How far, I don't know."

One of the staff officers said, "Four entire armies? Surely that can't be."

The G-2, Smith's intelligence officer, a gloomy man, explained, "Their armies are more like our corps. What we call an army the Chinese call a field army."

"But still," Smith said, "elements of four armies, with six divisions identified?"

"Yessir," Verity stated. "The divisions I've listened to are the One-twenty-fourth, the Fifty-eighth, the Sixtieth, the Eighty-ninth, the Eightieth." That made only five, but no one protested.

The ops officer spoke up now.

"We've known about the One-twenty-fourth. The Seventh

Marines came up against them at Sudong November second. Then the One-twenty-fourth broke off and went back up into the hills November sixth or seventh."

So at least one of my identifications proved out, Verity thought, exhaling relief. He was glad he didn't do this sort of thing for a living.

"Their infantry divisions," the G-2 told them, "average about ten-thousand men. So if the captain's correct, they've got at least sixty-thousand men close to the Chosin. We've got a division of twenty-thousand Marines and there's probably another twenty-thousand Army and ROKs in the neighborhood."

"So it's our forty to their sixty," someone put in.

"Unless those other nine divisions show up," Smith remarked, sounding oddly cheerful at the possibility.

There was some detailed questioning of Verity, and he tried to respond accurately and, at the end, turned over all his notes.

General Smith nodded at him. "Thank you, Captain. You can rejoin your attached unit now. Or drive back in the morning, which might be a better idea, considering the road and the hour. I'll expect immediate reports from you regarding any change in the enemy order of battle. Especially if those nine other divisions come onstage. You understand?"

"Yessir."

He and Izzo and Tate were billeted in tents for the night, fed a hot meal, and asked, "What's it like up north?"

"Glorioso," Izzo told the headquarters enlisted men. "We live like frigging kings."

The next day, after receiving yet another communication from Ned Almond urging him to prepare his entire division for a "sprint" north, Oliver Smith sat down to write his November 15 personal letter to the commandant of the Marine Corps, General Cates, at Henderson Hall, Arlington, Virginia.

It was a letter no army general could or would have written:

> So far our MSR north of Hamhung has not been molested,
> but there is evidence this situation will not continue. . . .

Someone in high authority will have to make up his mind as to what is our goal. My mission is still to advance to the border (with China). The Eighth Army, eighty miles to the southwest, will not attack until the twentieth. Manifestly, we should not push on without regard to the Eighth Army. We should simply get further out on a limb. If the Eighth Army push does not go, the decision will have to be made as to what to do next. I believe a winter campaign in the mountains of North Korea is too much to ask of the American soldier or Marine, and I doubt the feasibility of supplying troops in this area during winter or providing for the evacuation of sick and wounded . . .

Smith told Cates in detail what he was doing, using engineers to improve the road for tanks and heavy vehicles, ordering airstrips built and the like, a steady, measured advance securing its MSR as it went along, rather than the headlong dash Almond was ordering. He was not pessimistic, Smith assured Cates, but he admitted concern over "the prospect of stringing out a Marine division along a single mountain road for one hundred twenty air miles from Hamhung to the border."

On that same day, the Seventh Marines entered Hagaru-ri, the sizable town at the southernmost shore of the Chosin Reservoir. That was where Verity and Tate and Izzo were heading, driving in a jeep with the top down. The temperature November 15 was four below zero, Fahrenheit.

It was also on November 15 Captain Verity turned thirty years old.

"My birthday, Gunny."

"By God, sir, that's fine," Tate said, who was a year older.

There were no celebrations or observances of Verity's birthday, none at all, and the war went on.

Izzo, too, was notified. "Yessir," he said vaguely, "and the best of many returns."

Izzo was twenty-eight and his good wishes had not come out

precisely as intended, but Verity appreciated them nonetheless, and when Izzo and Tate told him their ages Verity thought, *We are all getting old,* then said so aloud.

"And I hope we get frigging older, sir," Izzo observed with considerable fervor.

Now the cold closed down, seizing the land, the mountains, and the men in its metallic grip—a category and dimension of cold few of these men had ever felt bar those of the northern plains states, the Dakotas, Alaska, or men from interior Maine and Vermont north of Burlington.

There had been, early in the month, a freakish spell, a thaw following the early snows and hard frosts. On November 3 a Major Lupton reported having permitted the men of his command, marching south of Sudong, to fall out and bathe in a mountain stream. Temperatures were in the fifties, and the sun shone and men stripped to their skivvies, cavorting loudly.

"Considerable grabass," the major noted amiably.

Two nights later the glass fell below zero for the first time. And kept right on falling. Ten below. Twenty. Twenty-two below Fahrenheit.

"Those thermometers don't go that low."

Some did; some didn't. After a point it became academic. Machinery froze; weapons jammed; rations were inedible; men slowed.

There still remained five weeks of calendar autumn, but already the long, hard winter had taken the Taebaek Mountains and the high tableland and the winding, narrow road into its frozen grasp, not to relinquish it until April or later.

"Be dead by then. Or, better, home."

That was the conventional wisdom in these first days of the really terrible cold, when men were still capable of humor. And of prodigies of invention.

"Wild Root Crème Oil! That's the stuff. Gets the bolt action working no matter how cold. Hell of a lot better than gun oil."

Twenty-five below now. For the first time, the division was counting more casualties from the cold and frostbite than from wounds.

It wasn't only the Marines who were short of winter clothing or equipment designed to work in this weather. In the west, the Army's IX Corps attacked north, its objective the Yalu River. Ninth Corps was not considered, even by its own officers, to be a very good outfit, but it went anyway.

As they moved out, it was reported, in one line company all but 12 of 129 men discarded their steel helmets in favor of pile caps. Only 2 men of the 129 had bayonets. Half the men carried entrenching tools; they averaged only one hand grenade per man and sixteen to thirty rounds of ammunition per rifle and carbine.

In a brisk firefight you might fire off sixteen or even thirty rounds in the first minute and a half.

And these were American soldiers about to attack in bad weather in hostile country over mountains and to drive everything before them to the borders of China. Those were MacArthur's orders.

She loved singing "Sur le Pont" and hearing Poppy sing it to her.

But Kate was, for her age, intellectually curious.

"Do you know other songs?" she inquired of her father.

"Why, yes, I do. Though I'm not much of a singer."

"Oh," she protested, and meant it, "but you sing so nice and loud."

Tom Verity thanked his daughter, rather gravely, and, encouraged by her compliment, did actually sing a few songs he knew and liked and which did not demand much of a voice: "Dixie" . . . "The Music Goes Down and Round" . . . and "Waltzing Matilda."

"I learned that one in Australia, a long time ago," and he explained to her what a "swagman" was, and a "billabong."

Naturally, being a Yale man, though never a Whiffenpoof, he tried her out on their song, "poor little lambs who have lost their way" and all that. But only the repetitive "baa . . . baa . . .

baa . . ." caught at her attention. Whether she liked a song or not, Kate heard him out, patient and desirous of learning.

Then, she would say, "You know, Poppy, I think 'Sur le Pont' is still best."

He laughed at that and she laughed and then they sang "Sur le Pont" all over again. Loudly, and in French.

The railroad that paralleled the mountain road would soon pinch out. Then they would have only the road, dirt and gravel, a cliff towering above them on one side, a chasm falling off sharply on the other.

"Don't drive on the shoulder," Izzo muttered to himself from behind the wheel.

On the higher passes through the mountains, engineer battalions were already at work with 'dozers, grading and trying, where there was elbow room, to widen the road. The big tanks, the Pershings, were too wide to negotiate the tighter bends, and only a handful of the smaller Shermans had as yet gone north toward Hagaru and the reservoir. The remaining North Koreans might still have some of those big T-3 Russian tanks up there, and you didn't want to fight those with old Shermans. No one knew what armor the Chinese might have.

When the three men rolled into the railhead of Chinhung-ni with its small frame houses dusted with snow, smoke rising from tin chimneys, the big, sagging dun tents, the piles and stacks and scatter of crates and sacks and rolls of wire and other freight just dumped there on the frozen ground, with a background of steep, snowy hills and sparse forest, men moving and lugging stuff, bundled and earmuffed, it reminded Verity of grainy old sepia photos of the Klondike in the time of the gold rush. He asked Tate if it didn't.

"Well, I guess, Captain," Tate said, considering the proposition.

Izzo was more enthusiastic. "Jeez, suppose there was gold here, Skipper." He looked ready to grab a pan and seek out the nearest pebbled stream, staking claims as he went.

Tate regarded Izzo with a certain degree of admiration. "Izzo, no wonder you're good at selling cars."

"The best, Gunny. You see a sales opportunity, you grab it."

"Carpe diem." Verity felt he should toss in.

"Yessir," Izzo said. "And you, too, Gunny; whatever the captain said goes double for me."

Tate just cleared his throat. Izzo took the broad hint.

"Anything you want done now, Gunny? Just say the word."

"Yes, Izzo, find us a house with a roof and at least three walls and without too many lice or other bugs."

Izzo was eager to please. In dealing with gunnery sergeants, this was good practice. Neither could he resist the huckster's snappy retort.

"Wall-to-wall carpeting?"

"Izzz-zohhh!"

It took the Mouse less than an hour.

"A light colonel had his eye on it, Captain, but I hinted strongly it was for General Smith himself. Sort of."

He'd even found a few chunks of wood and some straw and gotten a fire started. Verity once might have felt guilty about having a roof and a fire while other men huddled out of the wind in open fields, squatting or lying on frozen ground with only a bit of canvas for shelter. Not now. Cold did that to men, reducing them to clever, self-absorbed animals ready to do anything for warmth, almost anything to survive.

Elizabeth had always liked November.

"It's your birthday and Election Day, which is fun of a different sort, and then there's Thanksgiving and big football games and the country is lovely with foliage on the turn and maybe the first snow flurries and that's wonderful as well."

She wouldn't like November here quite that much, Verity thought.

"And I can wear the new fall clothes . . . ," she had added, occasionally the practical woman. Fall. Autumn.

This is fall, he realized. Winter was still a month ahead. December 21 or 22, something like that. North Korea was still in November, two-thirds of the way through autumn, and they were already losing men to frostbite.

And Elizabeth was a year dead.

The snow fell, whipped by the wind, and Verity shrugged deeper into his old down parka, shoulders hunched against the cold, shivering, wondering if calendars had gone mad or if he were simply a man confused by war.

The snow fell and in the narrow valleys where streams rushed through the bottoms the swift water slowed, grew mushy, and froze hard.

CHAPTER EIGHT

There were things Verity didn't like about the Marine Corps,
never had, but he enjoyed seeing good troops march. Before
battles. After a bad fight, troops didn't walk the same.

Koto-ri didn't mean anything to any of them.

"Just another little half-assed Korean town."

Now they were coming up on Koto-ri and the mountains were higher, and the road steeper and narrower, the weather
colder. Far behind them was Hungnam. That was the sea, naval
ships standing offshore, an airstrip, port facilities and warehouses
and buildings almost Western in their cunning sophistication,
some with indoor plumbing. And an ocean view. It was comforting
to be able to see blue water when you were a Marine heading off
into high mountains with winter coming to fight a campaign
against the largest army in Asia. Hungnam was safety; Hungnam
was home.

Tom Verity had always liked mountains. He was a skier, not
the skier Elizabeth was, lacking her grace and style, but he could
get down the hill. He liked the silence of the chairlift going up
through the woods and then, briefly, swaying over the rocks at
timberline, looking down at rabbit and deer hoofmarks and imagining there might still be a black bear down there in sleep or a
bobcat prowling.

Now?

Izzo, for his part, had become excited.

"Look at them Alps!"

Tate prudently snuggled deeper into his parka but otherwise did not seem intimidated.

There was still one pass to get over before Koto-ri, the Funchilin, on some maps thirty-two hundred feet high. By alpine standards, despite Izzo's enthusiasm, this was nothing. But here in North Korea with the wind coming out of Manchuria and from the vast ice box of Siberia beyond, the November snow was already piled deep and drifting in the pass.

Verity thought, *I wonder what it's like in true winter.*

Thinking that way, he shuddered, involuntarily, his shoulders contracting and jerking upward, his neck vanishing into the parka. Tate, seated behind him with the radio, noticed. And Verity knew he had.

"Sorry, Gunny. Stupid of me."

"Nosir, it's cold. It surely is."

Izzo, intent on the winding road and its slick surface, didn't know what the two men were talking about.

Tate, shrugging off Captain Verity's shudder, did not forget it. Sure it was cold. He felt it; they all did. Verity's behavior was nothing more than a matter of temperatures. Tate hoped that's what it was.

They rolled into Koto-ri by early afternoon, the radio chattering Chinese, some of it clear, some staticky and distant. Tate wished he knew the dialect and what the hell they were talking about. Verity, who took notes, didn't say all that much.

Ahead of them, north of Koto-ri, were more mountains, higher still, massive, and looming.

"Reservoir's up there, Captain," Izzo said, consulting his map, "another ten miles, I'd say. Over them mountains."

"Right, Izzo," Verity replied, trying to reestablish authority and to communicate calm.

In the War, Tom Verity never considered himself a hero. But he'd been cool and efficient under fire, under stress, and in some fairly dicey situations. He was often afraid; most sensible men were. But they had functioned, done the job, killed the Japanese, and won the War. Even while being scared.

This was a situation of another dimension entirely.

And he knew why. In World War II he was in his twenties and had no child. If he had been killed back then, it would have been sad for him, worse for his parents. If he was killed in Korea, who would care for Kate?

It was that which made the difference. And which frightened him in an entirely other way. Husbands and fathers he concluded, had no business going to war. Combat was for the young and unencumbered. Not for responsible people on whom children they loved relied.

Well, that was stupid. Verity was hardly the only man in the Marine Corps who had a kid.

Which didn't make things any better or relieve his anxieties. He'd been shaken badly and he knew it.

They drove slowly past working parties of Marines erecting tents and trying, without apparent success, to dig latrines in the frigid earth, and could already see frozen turds here and there on the ground. But that was OK; they would soon be covered by snow.

Verity was relieved that his pen was still working. Maybe ink did freeze; it hadn't frozen yet.

"Dear Kate," he wrote.

Madame would read the letter to his daughter. It really didn't matter so much the words as the spirit of the thing. He assumed sensitivity on the part of Madame.

"There are wonderful mountains and snow, Kate. Quite cold, but we have big warm coats and boots. There are many strange people here and I will tell you all about them one day soon. Someone saw a brown bear that bumped into a tent in the night. You never heard such shouting. The poor bear was scared away. Do you and Madame do your French every day?

I hope so. For when I come home we will have to plan our trip to Paris. I love you, my darling."

He really did think about their Paris trip. Surely the small bar of the Ritz on the rue Cambon side could arrange a chicken sandwich and a glass of milk.

"I'll have a martini and you some milk and perhaps Dalí in his flowing cape and hat will come in. Or Hemingway."

He would explain to her then who Hemingway and Dalí were. And about martinis. And other inside information about Paris all three-year-old Americans should know. It was healthier thinking about Paris and the Ritz bar and Hemingway than brooding about the reality of where he was and the great hills and this cold that had begun to frighten him.

They weren't at Koto-ri long; it made no impression. Later, it would.

"Move it; move it; move it."

Litzenberg was still ahead of them, by now having passed through Hagaru heading northwest for Yudam-ni around the shores of the big lake. Hagaru was a good-sized town with ware-houses and two-story buildings and an actual grid of paved streets in a decent-sized valley.

This is the place, Izzo told himself. *We can do business here.*

The Marines were already building an airstrip. Hagaru was the one place north of Sudong and Chinhung-ni flat enough for a real airstrip that could take big cargo planes. Smith was counting on Hagaru. Without telling anyone, he was already planning to fall back on Hagaru if things got sticky up there at Yudam-ni or beyond. Hagaru could be defended, supplied. He was less sanguine about Yudam-ni.

Verity and his two men drew hot rations from the engineer bat-talion hacking out the airstrip and ate sitting on the warm hood of the jeep, watching the engineers work. It was interesting to see, especially if you didn't have to do it. The ground was so hard-frozen the pans of the bulldozers could only scrape an inch or two deep at every pass, and then pneumatic drills had to be brought up to crack the frozen earth from the pans so the 'dozers could go back and scrape again.

"I don't think I want to grow up to become an engineer," Tate remarked.

"No, Gunny. Looks too much like work."

Nor were they long at Hagaru.

"Colonel Litzenterg's at Yudam-ni, sir," Verity was told. "That's Seventh Marine headquarters now."

"Not Hagaru? We were told they were here."

"Not no more, Captain. They went north."

Now they were closing on the Toktong Pass, at four thousand feet the highest ground traveled by road. Higher still, of course, and looming above the narrow road, the steep hills to either side.

Narrower and steeper. Verity recalled an early line from Dickens, a wintry London just before Christmas, "foggier yet and colder."

Well, we don't have the fog, Captain Verity thought. That was about all they'd been spared, and glad of it.

They had the cold and they had the first snows and there were Chinese up there ahead somewhere and they had this damned narrow mountain road, claustrophobic as the Baltimore city tunnel, where the mountains on both sides squeezed the road and sometimes shut it down completely with slides of stone and rock and earth, and now snow, so that 'dozers had to be brought up to push the way clear again.

"They maintain the streets better in Philly, Captain," Izzo remarked, "where the commissioner is the mayor's brother-in-law."

Tate, riding in back with the big radio, kept looking up, swinging back this way and that, watching for rockslides. Izzo had all he could do to keep the jeep solidly on the road and provide a running patter without the distractions of looking up.

"Here's some Chinese, Captain!" Tate would sing out, screwing the volume up higher so Verity in the front seat could hear.

"Yeah."

Sometimes Verity waved Izzo out of the line of traffic grinding slowly north so they could cut the motor and perch by the side of the road without having to listen over the sound of the engine.

Most of the Marines marched north. It wasn't that tough. Not yet. The pace was slow. Litzenberg saw to that, and what his orders didn't do the hills did. By now the men were in good shape again after the diarrhea and nausea of shipboard and as they moved past Verity's jeep were still in good humor, sporting and calling out: "Take a crap for me, pal! I ain't got time to stop!"

Izzo told them to go frig themselves. But good-naturedly. Verity, listening to the radio, taking the occasional note, liked watching the men marching past, weapons slung, rucksacks full, canteens and knives and bayonets and cartridge belts a-jangle, helmets kicked back off their faces, the men's noses and cheeks red with cold but pleasantly so. When there was sun the cold was brisk, stiffening, not hurtful. There were things he didn't like about the Marine Corps, never had, but he enjoyed seeing good troops march. Before battles. After a bad fight, troops didn't walk the same.

In all fairness, MacArthur did not fight the war entirely from his palace in Tokyo. On November 24, against the advice of his officers, he ordered his transport plane to fly north over enemy lines to scout out the ground between his armies and the Yalu.

"An endless expanse of utterly barren countryside," the General reported, "jagged hills, yawning crevices, and the black waters of the Yalu locked in the silent grip of snow and ice. It was a merciless wasteland."

Into which he had ordered Eighth Army and X Corps.

On his return to Tokyo, MacArthur promptly issued a detailed communiqué regarding future operations. Seldom had any general so recklessly revealed his hand, and both Peng and Lin Piao received accurate translations of the communiqué within twenty four hours.

Oh, yes. General MacArthur was awarded a Distinguished Flying Cross for his sight-seeing flight.

*   *   *

The army's Seventh Division, moving north toward Hagaru to relieve the Fifth Marines for the offensive to jump off from Yudam-ni, was already suffering severe frost-bite injuries and some deaths from the cold on November 24, nearly four weeks before the start of calendar winter. Along the MSR the division dropped off two-man MP posts to watch and secure the mountain road, the posts several miles apart. Now word came in of truck convoys coming through and finding MPs dead in the morning, dead from the cold if they'd tried to get through the night without a fire, dead of bullet wounds and bayonets by the ashes of a fire if they'd lighted one. One convoy, traveling by night, had to pull over to revive men who'd simply fainted from cold and could not be brought around by other men in the truck pressing against them and massaging them. An artilleryman reported the convoy was stopped, men ordered out to cut brush with their bayonets, and a fire built using spare gasoline. At which point, the fainted men regained consciousness.

"I really think they would have died without them fires," the artilleryman said.

The night of November 24, the Seventh Division headquarters, situated in a valley near Pungsam, reported a temperature of thirty-six degrees below zero Fahrenheit. No one knew how cold it got in the hills above.

On the approach march to the Chosin and then the left turn toward Yudam-ni, Verity monitored the radio and took notes, new names, new divisional numbers. Not that there was any question the Chinese were in. Hardly that after Sudong and what happened over in Eighth Army. They had the hard evidence of bodies, and not even that bastard Willoughby could ignore the dead.

Now there were two questions: Had the Chinese pulled back to the border after those early fights, satisfied that they'd made their demonstration and bucked up the North Koreans? And if they hadn't pulled back and were still close, lying low and waiting, how many of them were there, who led them, and what had they planned?

This, largely, was Verity's job. Whenever Verity heard a new unit number or some other fragment of what might be significant (and probably wasn't, given his lack of intelligence training), he passed it on, sending Izzo back or ahead in the jeep to wherever higher-echelon headquarters seemed to be in the long, accordioning reptile of a column. Sometimes Izzo came back with thanks to Verity. Often he was turned away with scant courtesy.

"They say they know all this frigging stuff, Captain," the Mouse complained, a man sore put upon. "They say they know there's a million Chinks out there."

"OK, Izzo. We'll try again tomorrow."

Chinks. People among whom he'd been born, his friends and tutors and neighbors. And now his enemies.

A million of them. Well, he hadn't counted that many, but it was possible. They had the men. And China was just a river away, across the Yalu. Some of the unit numbers he identified were familiar to him, units from Peng's old Chinese Eighth Route Army, in '45 and early '46. It was almost like a reunion weekend with fellow alumni. But when he mentioned this to Tate, only half-serious, he got a look.

"Yessir," Tate said, an eyebrow figuratively raised.

"Forget it, Gunny," Verity said. He'd forgotten just how literal Marine gunnery sergeants could be. Well, it was precise, literal work they did, the good ones, men like Tate. Very precise, very literal.

"Yessir," Tate said, precise and literal.

But wasn't Verity the same? A matter of degree. Here they were flanked and trailed and hunted and quite possibly surrounded by Chinese divisions, maybe a quarter of a million men, maybe half a million, if not the million of Mouse Izzo's rumor mill. And what was Verity doing? Listening to the radio to determine which Chinese were in the war; their names, ranks, and serial numbers.

Marines ought to make good academics, cutting through vague generalizations to get to the heart of things, to the essence, to where truth resides.

A bracket of mortar shells came in then, hitting frozen ground on either side of them, and Tate and Verity both swung quickly into the jeep. Izzo already had the motor running, and they pulled away, spinning wheels on the frozen snow and hard brown earth. The march to Yudam-ni was still getting organized, and a single jeep and three men, traveling on their own, could still cut in and out of traffic and move when they had to.

"Frigging mortars," Izzo muttered. He didn't mind rifle fire or even artillery; he didn't like mortars, the way they came straight down at you, following you right into holes. Or jeeps.

The radio crackled now as they drove.

"Chinese?" Tate prompted.

"Chinese," Verity said, "another dialect," and again began taking notes. Unlike Izzo, he was cool about mortars, always had been.

Izzo looked back at Verity, over his shoulder. "Frigging Chinks," he said, slightly resentful, as if Captain Verity were to blame for them. Jesus, he could be in Philly, selling cars. Instead, he was here, driving a jeep on a mountain road in cold weather while frigging Chinks tried to kill him. Or maybe it was raggedy-ass North Koreans. Didn't really matter, did it, just who was firing mortars, not if they frigging hit you.

Verity looked at Izzo and grinned. Izzo grinned back, but deferentially. You never knew with officers. It didn't pay to get them on your case, and what did a grin cost?

Behind them another mortar crashed in now and then, but that was hardly their concern now. In a war, you move on to the next hand. You deal with new cards.

As the Marines drove farther north, deeper into bandit country, the risk of ambush grated and rasped and men turned edgy. Jumpy.

They argued endlessly, Which was the worst duty? To have the point? Or flank patrol?

You know how it is being there on the point, the mines and the machine guns and the odd sniper and the serious ambushes waiting. And it is always the point man, the very first Marine of the twenty thousand yet to come, who first pads cautiously into view.

But never cautious enough. And when the point man dies, the infantry always asks why they didn't send a tank first, instead?

But flank patrols? Man, in country like this, there was no serious debate; in mountains like these, flank patrol was the worst.

Imagine it. You are tired already, with cold feet and carrying a fifty pound pack and a BAR along the frozen, windswept road, and suddenly the platoon sergeant calls out, "All right, you people, this here squad is now going on flank patrol and ascend this here hill to that ridgeline up there and from that vantage point you will ensure the safety and integrity and so forth of the entire battalion!"

Or regiment, or division. It depended on how large a vision the sergeant possessed.

So you cursed and spit (a disappointing crackle of frozen saliva) and hitched your fucking pack higher and began to climb. Sometimes there was a gentle slope, fifteen or twenty degrees, and if only you didn't slide back so much, it wasn't bad. Sometimes it was so steep, snow slid from the shelving rock and the men crawled, hand and knee like alpinists, fingers alert for handholds, cracks and fissures and crevices, or a runt pine, anything to cling to with frozen fingers. But they were not alpinists. They lugged weapons and heavy belts of ammo and huge packs and rations and sleeping bags. They might be up here on the ridgelines a thousand feet above the road on flank patrol for a day and a night, even two nights. They needed rations to live; without the sleeping bags they would die of the cold.

And sometimes, on the ridgelines, they collided with other flank patrols, sent out by the retreating North Koreans or the advancing Chinese, and exhausted, frozen men fell upon each other in a chill rage and did themselves to death.

Below, on the road, Verity and the others heard the sound of firing and kept moving north, glad they were here and not up there on the ridges on flank patrol.

Tate, with his fondness for military history, was having walking, waking nightmares about Custer and the Seventh Cavalry as he and Captain Verity and driver Izzo made their way slowly north through Hagaru and then beyond it to Yudam-ni. Even the numbers seemed ominous, the Seventh Cavalry under Custer and the Seventh Marines, to which they were attached. He kept all this to himself, not wanting to spook Izzo or worry Verity. But he could not help brooding on Custer's approach march through southern Montana toward the Little Bighorn and ten thousand waiting Crow and Cheyenne and Sioux.

They'd been cocky, too, Custer's men, his Irishmen and the veterans of Shiloh and hard men from the borders, confident they could whip any hostiles out there, sure of themselves and their regiment and of "the Boy General" who led them. Smelling the offal fertilizing the small farms and the firs and other needled trees and the distant cooking smoke of the villages of conquered North Korea, Tate wondered if the Seventh Cavalry had enjoyed their ride toward death, if they'd stopped to smell the freshly trampled grass under the hooves, the prairie ripe in the sun, the beautiful country, to savor the look of far mountains.

Tate trusted his officers, General Smith and Colonel Litzenberg and Murray and old Chesty Puller. But he expected the men of the doomed Seventh Cavalry had trusted Reno and Tom Custer and Benteen and Yellowhair himself, George Armstrong Custer.

Walking beside the jeep, Tate looked across to Verity, ambling along the gravel road, chewing comfortably on an unlit cigar. It was on his tongue to ask Verity what he thought. He bit off the question, saying nothing except, to himself, are we, too, walking into a trap?

Verity, hardly as comfortable as he looked, was wondering the same thing, wondering if they were, just how he would handle it.

While Tate, who had been a prisoner before in Asia, angrily rejected the idea of ever being one again.

Maybe the wind was worse than the snow or the cold.

"It comes out of Siberia," Tate said. "Not a hundred fifty miles from here to Siberia."

"That's Russia, ain't it?" Izzo said.

"That's Russia," Tate agreed.

Izzo laughed. "Hell, we finish off these Chinamen, we go a hundred fifty miles north and start up with the Russkis."

"Sure, Izzo, sure."

Verity didn't really think they need go looking for further difficulties.

When the wind came it scoured the road clear of loose, dry new snow and left it a glistening, ribbed, shining, rutted ribbon of ice off which the sun, when it shone, bounced, blinding the men and reflecting off Izzo's mirrored glasses like theatrical spotlights. The ice was steel-hard, even in the sun, at those temperatures, and the deeply cut rubber tread of snow tires spun helplessly on the up-inclines and ran madly out of control on the way down, so that men were drafted into service as draft animals might have been, pushing the skidding trucks uphill and hanging onto them, feet planted and skidding on the way down.

"You men, get on that there truck; grab hold; pull!"

The sergeants drove them. But who drove the sergeants? Men with frozen feet shuffled obediently to push or heave against a fender, a bumper, the tailgate of a laboring, careening truck.

Even tracked vehicles skidded wildly.

The sergeants shouted at them, too, and the tank drivers, perched a dozen feet above in the open turrets, shouted and cursed back.

Nothing was accomplished, the tanks and motorized guns too heavy for even a dozen men to make much difference pushing up or braking down, not on the ice, not on the inclines, and every so often they lost a truck or a howitzer, memorably once a tank, or a jeep, and watched it slide and bounce away down the side of a mountain toward the ravine and frozen stream below, men leaping off at a great rate, rolling or sliding downhill on the snow until they came up against a rock or a tree and stopped with a sudden whack. Incredibly, except for a few men they lost in this way, most of the Marines crawled or climbed their way back up the slope to the road to continue the journey as pedestrians, sore and limping and cursing long and steadily against their fate.

"Does the men good to curse," Tate remarked. "Healthy to let off a little steam."

"It does," Verity agreed, and concluded that if he thought it would help him even one bit, he would let off a power of oaths.

Izzo made up for him.

*   *   *

It was an empty country.

There were few farms or anything that resembled grazing land, no orchards laid out. Once you got away from the coastal littoral and the land climbed, there wasn't much of anything, roads, villages, power lines or telephone poles, bridges, conduits. Only a few huts here and there between the towns, and the towns were nothing much, eight or ten miles apart. No central market town as you might expect. The hills were formally called the T'aebaeksan Range, and there were traces here of hunters and little else.

Was it climate denuded the place, the cold and wind out of Siberia and Manchuria, or that the soil was barren? There was no lack of water, and plentiful water usually meant people. Or had the Japanese in their forty years of occupation shifted population elsewhere? Or just killed them?

Tom Verity was accustomed to another Asia, a-teem with people, so many there was never sufficient land or water or timber or food. Or anything. In the Asia he knew, China, they killed off girl children to hold down the size of families and blunt famine. They weren't supposed to, but they did. Japan, too, was overcrowded. He knew that from books. And don't even talk of India or Burma or Siam or French Indochina or the East Indies.

In all the vast continent only Tibet and Mongolia were as empty as North Korea. Only here and in such places was the country left over to the wind and the snow and the cold. And to men who used these places as killing grounds.

Yudam-ni sat in a bowl ringed by seven-thousand-foot mountains.

Verity reported to Colonel Fleet, who had the point battalion of the regiment.

"We're the meat on the end of the stick, Captain," Fleet said. "They've got us out here poking at the Chinese just to see who bites. We might just get eaten."

"I was told to join the lead battalion, Colonel. The closer I can get, the better radio reception."

Fleet was a lieutenant colonel, a regular, a dry, slender man nearing forty who had few illusions.

"That's fine. Just don't get too far out. I can't spare people to bring you back if you hit trouble."

"Colonel, I'm staying right here with battalion headquarters if it's OK with you. I have absolutely no heroic tendencies."

Fleet permitted himself a small smile. The two men understood each other.

It was snowing again and they sat on camp stools inside Fleet's tent. A stinking oil stove made the interior smoky but relatively warm. Verity was glad for a chance to thaw.

"If you can give me the general situation, Colonel, it'll help me make more sense of what I'm hearing of the Chinese traffic."

"Sure. This regiment is just west and farthest north of anyone in the First Marine Division. And my battalion is the point. My job is to probe north looking for Chinese, just patrols. They've got orders to scram back home the minute they encounter Chinese. Grab a prisoner if they can, but come home. I've got other patrols out sidling west. They're supposed to contact elements of Eighth Army, if and when. Trouble is there's a spine of mountains running between us and Eighth Army. A dozen men moving light can get across those mountains. But you're not going to move trucks and artillery and such over those mountains. Not in this snow. So the whole business of maintaining contact with Eighth Army is just slightly surreal. In case of trouble X Corps can't do a damned thing for the Eighth Army and Eighth Army can't do a damned thing for X Corps, which means the Marines. Clear?"

"Yes." Verity liked plain speaking, and except for that "surreal" line, Fleet spoke plain. He also permitted himself a jab at MacArthur.

"For the life of me, and it may literally come down to that, I can't understand what the hell General MacArthur was thinking about when he divided this army in high mountains where the two elements of the army can't possibly support each other."

"I don't understand it, either. But my orders deal only with developing intelligence on how many Chinese may be out there and just what they're going to do."

"You got a cigarette, Captain?"

"You're welcome to a cigar." Verity pulled one out and the colonel was really grinning now.

"I keep trying to stop smoking to please my wife. She thinks it's bad for me. Up where we are right now I say the hell with that. Up here everything's bad for me." An enlisted man came in and asked if the two officers wanted coffee. As they sat drinking it, steaming hot and bitter black, Fleet said, "Funny, but coffee always smells better to me than it tastes."

"Yeah."

"And speaking of that," Fleet went on, "the first time you smell Chinese food, Captain, pull back."

General Smith had told Verity the same thing. He wondered who wrote their lines. Maybe Bob Hope, back at Wonsan, one hundred miles and a century ago.

This was a good group of officers. You could tell that right away. A bad one stood out, not so much in what he did or who he was but in how the others sort of edged away from him, not wanting to catch whatever it was.

Up in North China it had been like that, too, Verity remembered. A good group. And there was Schiftler, the bad apple. No one could really put a finger on why except he was pious and smarmy and somehow slick. But Verity remembered how drunk everyone got that first night after Schiftler was sent home. Happy drunk. They didn't even mind that they were marooned up in North China in winter fighting bandits while that bastard Schiftler was heading back to the States.

"Hell," someone remarked, "we got lucky. Feel sorry for America."

Here in Korea so far, they all seemed to be OK, and Verity had not yet smelled a bad one among them.

Izzo was a master at scrounging and Tate carried the gravitas of a gunnery sergeant, and between them they confiscated a small house.

"Only a few bugs, Captain," Izzo said enthusiastically, "and they're all dead, froze. I've seen lots worse."

They parked the jeep out front and installed the radio inside. The house had one room and no running water or toilet, but there was a sort of combination fireplace and oven and they got a fire going. Except for the dead bugs, it was pretty cushy. There were majors, even colonels, sleeping under canvas, and Captain Verity had this house. And with a fire.

"I could frigging get used to this, Gunny," Izzo admitted, "if we could pick up the Eagles game on the radio Sunday."

Instead, they picked up more Chinese.

"What do you make of it, Verity?" General Smith asked. He'd flown in to Yudam-ni by chopper from Hagaru for an officers' meeting. Verity gave his report, drew certain conclusions, tried as best he could to answer Smith's questions.

"It's all very strange," the general said.

It was that. It was the quiet that worried them; an army as big as the Chinese ought to make noise. They certainly had for a time there:

In late October the Chinese entered the war in large numbers and with extraordinary ferocity. Forty miles from the Chinese border, a ROK battalion of the Sixth Division encountered a large detachment of Chinese and was routed. The next morning the Chinese fell upon a regiment of ROKs, which promptly abandoned all its vehicles and three artillery batteries. On the twenty-eighth, in the same area, another ROK regiment was committed. U. S. air cover supported the regiment during an all-day fight. Once night screened the Chinese from air attack, they smashed the ROKs. Of 3,500 officers and men in the regiment, 875 escaped. By the next day an entire ROK Corps had been driven back forty miles. And it wasn't just the ROKs. The American First Cavalry Division, near Unsan, was to have its turn. To the din of brass bugles and whistles and truck-mounted rocket fire, the Chinese attacked. All day long on November 1 the lines bent and swayed and held. But by November 5 one entire American battalion had ceased to exist. All along the line the Chinese attacked. By the end of the first week of November the UN drive to the Yalu had been halted or driven back almost everywhere.

Then, and this was the strange thing, the Chinese just melted into the hills.

"Any new theories on that, Verity?" Oliver Smith asked.

"No, sir. Not one."

"MacArthur continues to think they came in to make a political point, to sound a warning, and having done so, they've gone back home."

There was some discussion of that. On November 2 the Chinese announced over their own radio that the men in Korea were "volunteers."

"You don't buy that, Verity," Smith said.

"No, sir. The division and regimental and corps numbers we've gotten so far are all regular army. Organized as divisions and corps. So if these are 'volunteers,' they 'volunteered' unanimously and in volume."

"Maybe they just ran short of ammo and food and pulled back to regroup."

It was agreed that was possible.

The division's intelligence officer read from a report. It was considered odd that while North Korean troops routinely shot wounded POWs through the head rather than burden themselves with enemy casualties, the Chinese were reported to have provided medical attention to ROK and American wounded. It was clinically primitive, but it was as good as the treatment their own wounded were getting.

"That sounds like regular Chinese army stuff, General," Verity offered, "not ad hoc, not what you'd expect of a bunch of volunteers."

"I agree on that."

Smith wasn't windy, whatever else he was.

Ned Almond entertained his generals, hosting a Thanksgiving dinner at Hungnam. Linen tablecloths and napkins, silverware, good china, saltshakers, and pepper mills. Every appointment but finger bowls.

MacArthur flew over and presided. The Mikado. Maggie Higgins was there and some of the other media pets. MacArthur said grace and piously asked the blessing. His intelligence chief, Willoughby, was very smooth, urbane.

Almond spoke ripely of a last, triumphant drive north to the Yalu. And to China.

Gen. Oliver Smith, of the Marines, whose division was extended over thirty miles of snow-covered mountains and who had six CCF divisions in his neighborhood, lacked appetite and left early, pleading an early dusk and a long drive.

"Of course, General," Almond said, "and my compliments to your command."

In the jeep heading back north from Hungnam, Smith thought how he despised Willoughby, who continued to insist the main Chinese weight was to be found in the west, opposing Eighth Army. Over dinner he had said, "There's nothing opposite you, Smith, but a screen. You'll brush them aside. A skirmish line will do it."

Oliver Smith sank his head deep into the collar of his parka against the chill as the jeep sped north, a driver, a general, and two bodyguards with automatic weapons celebrating the Pilgrims' first harvest in Massachusetts Colony.

Thanksgiving Day was cold and clear at Yudam-ni, and Verity and Tate took turns sitting in the jeep tuning the radio and watching Marines play touch football on a patch of flat ground. Where they got a football wasn't quite clear, but they played with vigor and much shouting, and the occasional cry of foul for leaving your feet to throw a block.

"In 1916 on the Somme," Tate said, "when the English went over the top, someone tossed out a soccer ball and they kicked it toward the German trenches."

"They get there?"

"No, sir. They attacked at dawn walking into the sun and lost sixty thousand men killed and wounded that first morning."

"Well," Verity said, "there'll never be another war like that. Men won't allow it to happen; men just won't do it, not like that. Not ever again."

He'd read that somewhere. Now where the hell . . . ? Then, he remembered.

"Scott Fitzgerald wrote that," Verity said. "Or something close. When Dick Diver took them on a guided tour of the old battlefields in *Tender is the Night.* . . ."

"Yes, sir," Tate said, not entirely sure just who "Dick Diver" might have been. It was Tate's experience that men would always do stupid things. In wars or not. It was their nature.

When the football game was over, a padre drove up and said mass with an altar cloth spread over the hood of his jeep. Maybe a hundred men attended. The priest wore incongrous red earmuffs throughout and his vestments flapped loudly in the wind, but Verity wished, not for the first time, that he had a religion he believed in and practiced. It seemed a comfort to men who did.

"You pray, Gunny?"

"Yessir, I surely do. Always have. Don't get much to church, but I'm a great one for praying. Helped get me through the prison camp, I believe. Men stronger and healthier than me died who had no belief in anything bigger than themselves. Makes you think."

By Captain Verity's reckoning from radio traffic and the unit numbers and commanders' names he fed into G-2, the First Marine Division now received back from Almond's corps headquarters this estimate: "There are eleven Chinese Communist Forces divisions in your area."

That was November 24. Two days later the Marines got this updated message: "There are now fourteen CCF divisions in your area." General Willoughby over Thanksgiving dinner had told Smith he faced only a Chinese "screen."

Oliver Smith looked around at his staff, at the stunned look on even hardened faces.

"For what we are about to receive," he said quietly, "let us be duly grateful."

The following day the count of CCF divisions surrounding the Marines had risen to sixteen. Nothing Verity heard suggested this was exaggeration.

*   *   *

They had fashioned a campfire somehow, which was a feat, considering the scarcity of trees, and Colonel Fleet, who was in a mood to chat, and Verity sat warming by it while other men hunkered deep in sleeping bags laid directly on the snow or, the fortunate ones, on pneumatic mattresses inflated by mouth and providing a luxurious insulation.

Colonel Fleet was talking. About the Corps, which surly enlisted men sometimes called the Crotch, but for which Fleet manifested a fierce love. Verity had heard words like these before, much of it grandiose crap. But when Colonel Fleet said them, there was a difference.

"We're a ferocious little confraternity, we Marines. A violent priesthood. You aren't simply enrolled but ordained. If I ever become commandant, which is hardly likely, along with those first gleaming gold bars every new second lieutenant will be anointed with holy oils and prayed over, while superior officers wash his feet, symbolic of Jesus with his apostles just before he died. Incense rising and choirs chanting."

"Yes, well . . . ," Verity said, a bit ashamed to know so little of religion. He agreed the Corps was a magnificent body of fighting men, but a lot of bullshit went along with it. Though not, he hastened to correct himself, that Fleet was talking bullshit. The colonel took Captain Verity's silence for encouragement. This was at Yudam-ni, with Verity temporarily on Fleet's staff.

"Read the New Testament, Verity, especially the Gospels. Matthew, Mark, Luke, and John. You could be reading the *Guidebook for Marines*. . . ."

He was a southerner, a VMI man like Puller, like so many of them in the Corps, and had an easy grace. "We could have done worse than hooking up with this outfit," Verity told Tate in the morning, and the gunny agreed.

"They have a good feel to them, Captain, and it ought to be cushy once we get to know them."

They never got to know some of them.

CHAPTER NINE

The first Marines off the hill had a couple of Chinese prisoners,
small, glum-looking men in their padded cotton suits. One of
them had no left arm, and the side of his uniform was rusty
with dried blood. "Sumbitch won't die," one of the Marines
accompanying him said in wonder. "Must of been the cold
stopped the bleeding."

It was November 26 that Eighth Army, as military historian
Joseph Goulden would later write, began falling apart. There
was one startling victory in a sea of defeats, routs, flights, and
panic. The five-thousand-man Turkish Brigade, in Korea only a
few days and without orientation or acclimation, with no South
Korean interpreters or American advisers and guides, was rushed
into action by a desperate Gen. Walton "Johnny" Walker. ROK
regiments were throwing down their weapons and running, entire
regiments, not just a few men here and a platoon there, leaving
adjacent. American units with their flanks in the air and the Chinese coming on. The American Second Division seemed especially
imperiled, and it was to its flank that they hurriedly ordered the
Turks, with their reputation for ferocity and martial ardor.

It worked. Meeting the onrushing Chinese face-to-face, the
Turks not only held their ground and turned back the enemy with
bayonets; they also captured hundreds of Chinese prisoners. The
Second Division rushed its interpreter, a South Korean lieutenant,
to question the Chinese POWs. The "Chinese" turned out to be
South Koreans, survivors of a ROK regiment attempting to flee

south, survivors then mowed down by the ferocious Turks. All the dead and captured "Chinese" were South Korean allies of the Turkish Brigade.

There was a sort of retribution the very next day when the Turks encountered authentic Chinese and were themselves nearly wiped out. It took only a day for the proud Turk Brigade to be smashed. That's how fast the Chinese were moving and how good they were.

"No one ever accused Almond of being lazy. Or lacking guts."

No, thought Oliver Smith, *or of having good sense.*

It was morning at Hagaru, November 27, and Almond had ridden a jeep sixty miles north from Hungnam to see Smith as his Marines jumped off from Yudam-ni toward the west to link up with Johnny Walker's hotly involved Eighth Army. It was the second day of the renewed CCF attack, and Eighth Army was already in travail. That's why the Marine offensive was crucial, so it might relieve Eighth Army by drawing off major Chinese units.

Fourteen or fifteen miles to the north, as Smith and Almond conferred, the Fifth Marines under Murray moved out on the attack. It was zero degrees Fahrenheit, with heavily falling and wind-whipped snow that blinded the advancing infantrymen as well as grounding the planes and masking the artillery forward observers. One rifle company commander reported: "Canteens burst; plasma and rations freeze solid; mortar base plates crack in the cold; carbines and most BARs are inoperable. Only the machine guns and rifles are working."

In sixteen hours of tough fighting the regiment had gained only fifteen hundred yards and suffered heavy casualties. And they were still within the town limits of Yudam-ni, where they had started.

Not even Smith realized it, but they were fortunate not to have advanced farther. That night the CCF attacked in overwhelming force on both shores of the reservoir, against the Fifth and Seventh Marines in the west and MacLean's regimental task force on the other bank in the east.

The night attack surprised Smith, surprised them all. He expected the Chinese to break off and take a breath after fighting all day. They didn't.

Verity had not fired a shot in anger at another man in five years. Okinawa, the summer of '45. Despite what he told Elizabeth, he had shot plenty then and always in anger. Then a few times, less angry, up in North China, sometimes to frighten off or impress and not always to kill. That was the winter of '45–'46. So for almost five years no shooting, nothing. Not unless you counted that one time a man he knew on the Eastern Shore had several of them come up for the goose shooting on Chesapeake Bay. Verity could handle a shotgun, but he lacked bird-shooting experience and kept missing the goose, shooting fore or aft of the bird as it flew in and then over them as they shot from the blind. He didn't know how fast a goose really flew so could not lead properly with the shotgun.

But he knew how to lead a man. He knew how fast a man moved and precisely how far out front of him to aim.

Nor had he been shot at in anger (is there any other way?) for five years. Be fair about it: everything was a trade-off. Yet you never forgot the sound, the whine of the ricochet, the delayed, distant crack of a weapon, the sound that reaches you after the bullet is past, the extremely odd realization that someone you don't know and have never met just attempted to end your life, and the blissful knowledge that you have, and literally, dodged the bullet.

Now, in late November of 1950, he again was exchanging shots.

There were ranging shots first, from the 61mm mortars, and overhead fire by machine guns, long-range and ineffective. Then there were rifle shots, scattered and then steadier, more intense. The sound came mostly from the east, from the shores of the big lake. Was that it? Were the Chinese coming across the lake? Trouble was, it was snowing, hard, dry, wind-driven snow, cutting visibility almost to nothing.

"Let's get ready, Gunny!" Verity shouted. "We could be in the middle of this!"

"Aye-aye, sir."

How do you fight as an infantryman in snow so heavy you can't see fifty yards ahead? They didn't teach you that at the Marine Corps Schools, Quantico, Virginia, where all Marine officers are trained before they are sent out to command.

Verity wished there had been such lessons.

In snow this heavy the attacking Chinese could be among you before you knew it. That's when their burp guns worked to good effect, in close. The Marines, with their superior rifles, had the advantage at a distance, two or three hundred yards, even more.

In the snow of the Chosin in November, you might not be able to see thirty yards.

Not now when during a blizzard the Chinese army launched its attack on the village of Yudam-ni. Now, having fought all day, without backing off for food or rest or rearming, they were counter-attacking, challenging the Marines on their own ground.

These are good troops, Gunny Tate thought. *This is not the minor leagues we are playing in.*

In Washington, as elsewhere, the Christmas decorations had gone up at commercial enterprises at Thanksgiving. Kate, seeing the coverage on television, asked to be taken downtown to observe the wonders.

Madame was unsure. What would Mr. Verity have done? The mother, as she understood it, was a Jew. Just how was the child being raised?

In the end, acting *in loco parentis* (and wanting to see the stores herself), she took Kate to Garfinckel's and to Woodward & Lothrop and to any number of lesser stores and shops where they enjoyed the holiday windows and the Christmas displays and encountered, dizzyingly, any number of Santa Clauses, even a few who actually looked the part.

Kate wondered if they also decorated stores in *Koree,* using the French pronunciation.

"Korea," Madame corrected her, giving the pronunciation in English. She assumed they did.

"And are there many Santas there as well?"

"I think so."

"Why were there so many Santas?" Kate wondered, and wished Poppy were here so she could ask him.

*   *   *

"Cowboys and Indians, Gunny! Cowboys and Indians!"

Tate knew that for once, Izzo wasn't just shooting off his mouth.

The Chinese had broken into the town itself after smashing through the perimeter from the east.

"They must of come across the lake on the frigging ice!" Izzo shouted.

He and Verity and Tate sheltered behind the jeep outside their hut, firing at the bulky padded Chinese coming at them in the squalls of snow. Then, abruptly, the snow thinned and the shooting was pretty good. There were already five or six Chinese down within a few yards of the jeep lying there on the snow-covered street. One of them was still crawling around and screaming and Verity thought about firing at him to finish him off, but he had only the .38 Smith & Wesson and not that many cartridges he could afford to be charitable. The Chinese broke off then, and the small-arms fire fell off and stilled.

I should have drawn a rifle, he thought. *That was stupid.* Anyway, in a firefight there were always plenty of rifles lying around later that you could pick up.

A few yards off, one of the big Pershing tanks was firing its cannon at distant targets in the hills, and Verity could feel the concussion and recoil of the big gun through his groin and belly and chest where he lay prone on the hard snow. Funny, though, he wasn't cold. Once a firefight began, you forgot the cold. All of Litzenberg's rifle companies were up in the hills, defending in depth as the Marines always tried to do if they had the manpower. That left the actual defense of the town itself, once the Chinese got through the hills or breached the road, to "casuals" like Verity and what he had come to think of as his "merry little band," and to clerk/typists, truck drivers, engineers, radiomen, staff officers, corpsmen, the handful of tankers, artillerymen, and other assorted and unlikely front-line troops. Everyone but the Catholic chaplain.

"They even got a squad of South Korean policemen," Izzo had reported before the breakthrough.

The police, and God knows what they were doing a hundred miles up in North Korea in their blue uniforms (one even had a pair of handcuffs in his belt) and smart, peaked caps, defended what was apparently the village hall, a building about as impressive as a one-car garage.

Yudam-ni sat surrounded by hills on all sides except to the east where it met the shoreline of the Chosin Reservoir, and the fighting in the hills began late in the afternoon, as the western hills and the town and its little valley slipped into gloom and then full night. You could hear the firing in the village of course, and then the artillery joined in, firing at the Chinese positions in the hills as called in to the fire control center by forward observers up there with the rifle companies. If you are anywhere near a 155 howitzer when it goes off, you know the sound, and the ache and ringing you carry for hours after in your ears and head. This wasn't really tank country and the tanks were there just to punch through on the road north or, if the regiment was pulled back, on the road south, but Litzenberg was using the tanks as mobile artillery and they, too, fired into the hills. The flash lighted up the sky, and Verity instinctively looked away whenever one fired, to retain night vision. It was the rods and cones in your eye that adjusted to darkness and enabled you to see. He remembered that from Hotchkiss and freshman biology. But could not recall which were the rods and which were the cones. He thought of asking Tate, who seemed to possess an enormous valise of trivial knowledge, but did not.

The snow no longer fell.

"Captain!" Izzo cried. "Here they frigging come again!"

Verity blinked his eyes clear, checked to see the .38 was loaded, and knelt next to Izzo behind the engine of their jeep, still marginally warm from being run one hour on, one off, to keep from freezing. He could see the Chinese, coming at them across the lake and up a gentle slope. Then a burst of burp gun slugs whipped past and he ducked. Behind and around them mortars were crashing in, small ones, 61s probably, the kind a single infantryman could backpack in. That was just about the biggest artillery the Chinese had, not much more than a supercharged hand grenade, and thank God for it. A hundred yards away was regimental headquarters, set up in a big pyramidal tent. A squad of Chinese was headed for the tent.

"Jesus," Verity said, half-aloud. There was no evident Marine presence around the tent, no screen of infantry, no sentries. Litzenberg and his staff couldn't be asleep. Not with all this racket. They . . .

Just then a lone figure broke from the tent, sprinting across the snow, and then another. Litzenberg's staff was coming out. There were shots, fired by both sides, and the first Marine, a staff major, fell, twisting. The other sprinted past him and the firing picked up. One of the Chinese knelt by the fallen officer, and Verity wondered, *What the hell?* . . .

Two more people emerged, firing, from the tent, and the kneeling Chinese fell across the major's body. He'd been trying to strip his boots and had died for it.

Izzo, who was proud of his marksmanship, had an M-1 and was stolidly squeezing off single shots, focused and methodical, only becoming excited when he hit.

"You seen me drop that one, Gunny? Oh, man, it was glorioso! Took him right through the chest."

Even with a damnfool pistol it wasn't difficult shooting, Verity knew. The only problem: running out of cartridges.

This wave of Chinese coming off the lake finally broke and ran, leaving their dead. But you still had plenty of fighting other places in the village. It was behind and to their left and right, and Tate, with the big BAR, kept swiveling to see, not wanting someone to come up on them sudden, not the way the headquarters tent seemed to have been surprised. A light colonel came by, checking them for info and if they were set for ammo. He was the one that told them it was a staff major who'd been shot coming out of the tent, the one who almost lost his boots.

"Funny," the colonel remarked. "I threw a quick look at the Chink that was taking his boots and they wouldn't have fit at all. The major had big feet."

Well now, Verity thought, *isn't that interesting?*

It was how men talked right after a firefight, saying silly, banal things, telling corny, pointless yarns, just out of nerves. It was still being alive and perhaps surprised by the fact that got men nattering on as the light colonel had.

Tate sent Izzo to scout around a bit for a rifle for the captain, and in a few minutes Izzo came back with two.

"This looks like a nice clean weapon, Captain. The action works just fine. I got some clips for you, too."

He'd taken one rifle off a dead Marine; the other was just out there in the snow with blood all around, as if a wounded had been carried off and his weapon left.

"Personally," Izzo said thoughtfully, "I like to keep a weapon private, you know, what with so many guys thaw out the action in the morning pissin' on 'em. But that weapon I gave you looks pretty clean. Leastways, I didn't smell no piss on there."

Verity thanked him for his concern.

The Chinese came back twice more that night and there was a lot of shooting and some people hit, but it wasn't all that bad. Verity hated to think what it would have been if the snowstorm kept up. Then the Chinese could have gotten right up all over them in the village, and who knew what the hell would have happened then?

He didn't like to imagine.

In the hills around Yudam-ni where Litzenberg and Murray had their rifle companies, the fighting was bad, nothing like these little skirmishes in the town. Really bad. On Hill 1240, Dog Company of the Second Battalion Seventh Marines began the night with almost two hundred men and six officers, under command of Capt. Milton Hull. By dawn there was only Captain Hull and sixteen men, barely a squad left out of a company, and them just hanging on. In daylight a relief platoon from the Fifth Marines, commanded by Lt. Harold Dawe, came up to the remnants of Dog Company, and between what was left of Dawe's men and Hull's squad they took back Hill 1240, sweeping the last Chinese in front of them. But by eleven in the morning the Chinese counterattacked with two battalions supported by heavy mortar fire.

That did it for Dog Company; it just ceased to exist as a unit.

A couple of dozen Dog Company Marines drifted in eventually, most of them walking wounded. The rest were still up there, they said, on 1240, dead or taken.

"Chinks came through firing and bayoneting and we ran out of ammo. They took some of us, tied their hands behind, and pushed 'em along with bayonets."

In this cold a man with tied hands wouldn't have hands very long.

Other men, Dog Company reported, had been stripped of their boondocker field shoes and their shoepacs and gloves and barefoot in the snow, driven north by their captors. Other men were just missing from Dog Company and would never be found.

Colonel Litzenberg had been a Marine nearly twenty years and couldn't ever remember a regimental commander's losing an entire rifle company in one fight. Not the whole damned company, officers and men both. And this was the first night of fighting at Yudam-ni, not the last.

Not by a damn sight.

At Hagaru, fourteen miles south of Yudam-ni, cut off by fighting at the Toktong Pass, and isolated from Puller in the south at Kotori, where the road had been, at least for the moment, severed, Gen. Oliver Smith raged.

"Idiots! Blind, stubborn idiots!" Was it stupidity or pride or just what?

In the west, Eighth Army, hammered savagely by the Chinese, was falling back across an eighty-mile front with huge gaps where ROK units and some army units had been overwhelmed or just bugged out, and Johnny Walker was screaming for help. Here in the east two of Smith's three Marine rifle regiments were surrounded and under heavy attack at Yudam-ni, while his third regiment, Puller's, had no way of reaching them. The MSR on which all three regiments desperately depended had been cut in half a dozen places. Verity and the pilots reported new Chinese units arriving at the Chosin by the hour.

And Smith was still under orders from Almond and Tokyo to attack? To send the Fifth and Seventh Marines into the mountains west of the reservoir, on foot, in a blizzard, to march forty miles to relieve Eighth Army?

There was a possibility they could not even hang on to Yudam-ni under this pressure, never mind go over to the offense. What the hell was Almond thinking and where was MacArthur? Did they know or care what was happening up ahead at Yudam-ni to the Fifth and Seventh Marines?

As dawn broke in the eastern sky, turning black into gray and then something brighter, the Chinese again disappeared.

"They just sink into the ground," a Marine complained, exasperated.

"They carry bed sheets. We brung in bodies and seen 'em. In daytime they lie down in the snow and pull the bedsheets over them."

"Just like their momma was tuckin' 'em in."

Whatever, they were gone.

That next night, November 27–28, it was as if God and the Chinese had entered into conspiracy.

With the Seventh Marine's surviving rifle companies strung like beads on the necklace of hills girdling Yudam-ni, the temperature fell to twenty below zero Fahrenheit. The Marines on watch in the hills had no foxholes, no trenches. There were eight inches of hard frost in the earth no entrenching tool could penetrate. It was like digging into a big-city sidewalk. Later, at Hagaru, Item Company of the First Marines would demonstrate ingenuity by fashioning shaped charges of C-3 explosive inside empty ration cans and blowing down through the frostline so that holes could be shoveled out and the excess earth used to fill sandbags.

The Seventh Marines fought all that night without foxholes, without sandbags.

It was full light by seven, and the Marines came down the slopes slowly, like ghosts, through the gray morning and a light snow. There was no wind and you could hear them come, leather creaking, metal on metal, shoepacs and boots slipping and gripping, a few words, the odd shout. There were almost no curses. Men were too tired to curse. What was also strange, most of them had bayonets fixed to their rifles.

But no one ever actually uses a bayonet, Verity thought. Bayonets were a joke out of John Wayne movies, useless things fit for opening cans and making noise. If they had bayonets fixed there must have been some fighting up there; when you fix bayonets you are damned near finished, or so the wisdom went.

The first Marines off the hill had a couple of Chinese prisoners, small, glum-looking men bulky in their padded cotton suits. One of them had no left arm, and the side of his uniform was rusty with dried blood. "Sumbitch won't die," one of the Marines accompanying him said in wonder. "Must of been the cold stopped the bleeding."

They had brought him in as a curiosity, for their fellows to see. The other Chinese, well, they might get some intelligence out of them.

Also coming along now, with a couple of Marines leading them, two Marines trussed up in makeshift straitjackets, their parkas reversed with the sleeves tied snug behind. They weren't prisoners, just men who'd broken up there, who'd cracked during the fight.

"They're shook," someone said, "just shook."

That was the new word, *shook*. Once it had been *shellshock*. Then *battle fatigue*. Now it was *shook*. Each war brings its own vocabulary.

Some Marines didn't buy: "Gutless bastards."

The trussed-up Marines vanished into the maw of the camp and were not spoken of again.

Verity and Tate got to question the prisoners, including the man without an arm, who proved unaccountably cheerful and willing to chat while a corpsman cauterized the stump. Assisting them, or perhaps just getting in the way, was a smart-as-shellac young intelligence major sent up by G-2 at Division, an Annapolis trade-school man who kept showing his class ring.

"What is this fellow speaking now, Verity?"

"It's a dialect of Cantonese, Major. He's from down south, near Hong Kong, a province called Haiku. A fisherman, once, but he's been in the army a long time."

The major nodded solemnly. "I wish I had some Chinese," he said. "But at the Academy I took three years of French."

"Oh, good. French. Well," Verity said.

Tate looked away. It didn't do for gunnery sergeants to make sport of Academy majors even when they were fools.

The one-armed prisoner and three others Verity interrogated told much the same story. They were from the Forty-second Division CCF; they'd crossed into North Korea a month ago and had been hiding ever since. They were short of food and now of ammo, and there was a lot of frostbite.

"Feet mostly, he says," Verity told Colonel Fleet. "Their sneakers are no damned good. And they've got only one pair of socks. When the socks go, they're barefoot inside the sneakers."

Fleet himself already had frostbitten toes, and he shuddered sympathetically.

"It's surprising how much Chinese troops know, Colonel," Verity said. "Right down to platoon level they've been pretty well briefed on the mission and their adjoining units and they know they're fighting Americans. Though they don't seem tremendously impressed by our being Marines. They thought we were an army division."

"Bastards," Fleet muttered. And was suddenly much less sympathetic about their goddamned frozen feet.

Fleet's battalion was up in the hills, three rifle companies scattered over three hills, linked only by radio and company runners and by sound-powered phone where they'd been able to lay wire. Now, as the morning filled, the casualty and ammo reports began to come in. One of his companies had lost forty men, fifteen of them dead or missing, the others wounded. Another had gotten off light. Eight men were dead, three missing, a dozen wounded in the third. By noon Colonel Fleet was off himself on foot, chugging uphill, wanting to visit with each of the three companies before dark fell, when the Chinese, it was assumed by everyone, would come again. The early snow flurries had ended, and in the brilliant blue sky you could see the vapor trails of the bombers high up heading farther north to bomb Chinese supply routes, the Yalu bridges. The tactical air support, carrier planes, and land-based fighters flying out of Kimpo and the other South Korean fields came in low over and over again, occasionally dropping napalm on a ridgeline or squeezing off machine-gun and cannon fire at likely targets.

"They can't see a frigging thing, Captain," Izzo remarked idly. "They're just firing for show."

They probably were. But it was good to know they were there. And if it was simply show, it would still have an effort on the Chinese in the hills waiting for night. Verity had been strafed on the 'Canal by Japanese Zeros and had not enjoyed the experience. If only they could get close air support during snowfall or by night.

When the Chinese would come again.

No one really gauged how bad the cold would be. Not even Puller.

They were short of winter parkas in the First Marines, and as they set out from Hungnam on the march north toward the reservoir, in reasonably temperate weather, Puller rashly gave his parka away, to an enlisted man who didn't have one.

As he joined the convoy, Puller disclosed that he wore cotton underwear, wool underwear over that, a wool sweater and shirt, green wool trousers, then a pair of waterproof trousers, a fleecy woolen vest, and fleece-lined trousers and a field jacket.

"How the hell I'm going to walk is a mystery," he told people, "but by God, I won't freeze."

He was wrong about that.

By two in the afternoon his jeep had reached Koto-ri and Puller was shivering so violently he could spoon up only a bean or two from a can of rations heated on the engine. By now it was snowing and twenty-five degrees below zero here on the plateau. Puller's driver and radioman and aide saw how bad he was and quickly got a tent erected, sealing in the canvas skirts with logs and then pouring water over the logs that froze instantly, and setting up a pot-bellied stove inside for the Old Man. Most Marines bivouacked outdoors at Koto-ri, sleeping bags their only shelter.

"That damned wind came right out of the heart of Manchuria," Puller said. "I believe Genghis Khan was right. . . . Nobody can win a winter campaign in the land of the Mongols."

Winter was officially still a month off, and the campaign had hardly begun.

CHAPTER TEN

*Less than five miles from Hagaru, Faith was killed. . . . His men,
singly or in small, leaderless bands, were chivied and hunted like
animals by the victorious Chinese chasing at their heels.*

Captain Verity suspected, and with reason, that a new
hand had been dealt. For him. And perhaps for his child.
The time of monitoring the radio and passing on unit
identification numbers to a general officer, the time of questioning
Chinese POWs, including those lacking a left arm, and telling a
colonel like Fleet what he'd learned that might be of value to his
battalion, the time of playing at war, was over.

They had promised Verity that he wasn't being sent to Korea to
command troops and fight as an infantryman. "We've got plenty
of rifle company commanders, Verity."

Oh, yeah.

Verity hadn't been lied to by that smooth headquarters colonel
back there on a hot day in Virginia; he understood that. But the
ground rules had changed. The war had changed. His role had
changed.

So had his chances of going home after a lousy month or six
weeks. He was here; the Chinese were here; the First Marine Division was surrounded.

"Oh, Kate, I tried to make everything right for you. I asked for compassionate and I thought I had it. We'd already planned our Christmas. And I've failed you. I won't be keeping my promises to you. To your mother. To myself. . . ."

MacArthur said "the boys" might be home for Christmas. He lied. Verity had told his daughter they'd see the bridges of Paris. Together.

Now they wouldn't. Not this year. Not this Christmas. He'd lied to his child. Now it was coming down to something more basic than Christmas. Would Tom Verity ever see Kate again?

"Sur le Pont d'Avignon . . ."

Until the previous night, when they fought in town and beat back the Chinese, Thomas Verity hadn't been in a firefight for five years, and then it had been against the Japanese, swift and clever, courageous and desperate, most competently supported by artillery and tanks and planes. Now it was Chinese infantrymen with no artillery at all beyond mortars, no tanks, no aviation.

Thank God for small favors.

The Marines held a low ridgeline a mile outside of the town, a ridge that despite no great height dominated the supply route. Verity and Tate and Izzo wouldn't be freelancing anymore, fighting on their own. The three of them, along with spare artillerymen and company runners and truck drivers and other casuals, had been drafted into a makeshift rifle company to beef up the thin line. There had already been two attacks on the ridge, and Chinese bodies littered the slope, one or two still moving weakly, helplessly, but ignored. Other bodies had been dragged uphill to where the Marines lay in the snow. They couldn't dig in, they had no sandbags, and the Chinese bodies functioned as primitive cover for the prone riflemen, who rested their rifle barrels on the torsos or heads of the dead to steady them.

"Chop suey sandbags," one Marine said, laughing, as Verity moved past to take his place, filling a gap in the line.

He shuddered reflexively, not able to help himself. Then, because it made sense and it no longer mattered to the Chinese and might save his own life, he got back up and slipped and slid a dozen yards downhill to claim his own corpse, grabbing it by the ankle and dragging it back up.

"Tate, you and Izzo get one, too!" he called out. Day before yesterday he had been advising the general; now he was dealing in carcasses. It was still light but going gray fast, and soon the night would close down and the Chinese would come again. These bodies were from last night. Verity remembered the stench of the dead on Okinawa, on Guadalcanal, American bodies and Japanese. Both stank and sometimes, when a man had to dig in close, he would gag and retch, just from the smell. The dead in the Korean cold did not smell. They just lay there, stiff and waxy-looking. But they were just as dead.

Now, the Marines waited. The hard part of that was the cold. You lay on your stomach on the snow, not moving about much to maintain sound discipline, but that didn't mean you didn't shiver. Verity cradled the M-1 rifle at first, roughly sighting it over the Chinese body and down the slope up which the Chinese would come. He wanted to take advantage of the last light to read terrain, to pick out and register the ground, the draws and little dips through which the Chinese might come, taking brief shelter before they burst out to sprint toward the Marines. If they could sprint. No one moved very fast coming uphill over snow and ice. Even under fire, when men moved quicker than they were able to.

Verity settled in, trying not to shiver too much. On both sides of him Marine enlisted men did the same. Tate was perhaps ten yards away; he'd lost track of Izzo. There was a moon and it came early, just after seven. That was good. A clear night with moonlight on the snow was good. You had visibility. When your eyes adjusted to the light you could see almost as well as by day. If the Chinese came tonight it would not be easy for them. Verity found himself feeling pretty good. If it weren't so damned cold. He wouldn't like to have fought Japanese in weather like this, not with your fingers stiff and hands shaking and eyes tearing while you tried to sight a rifle.

At 10:00 P.M. they came.

First there was incoming, forty or fifty mortar shells crashing down on the ridge, mostly light mortars, Verity thought, a few heavies, maybe .82mm stuff, and not very effective despite the Marines' lack of shelter. Too diffuse, all up and down the line on the forward slope and behind them on the reverse. Somewhere off to the left a man was screaming, so they had hit somebody. Otherwise, as Tate might say, it was pretty cushy. The mortar concentration lasted only a few minutes, and then, way down the forward slope, they could hear the Chinese coming, blowing police whistles. That must be another way in which they retained march discipline by night. There were no bugles. From what he'd heard, Verity had expected bugles. He almost felt cheated, there being no bugles. Nor were there Mongolian ponies. The Chinese used them, too. But not tonight. Tonight it was just infantrymen coming heavily up the hill toward them over the snow and in the moonlight.

These were familiar-looking figures to Verity, having grown up among them, small, compact men, most of them, but bulky in the padded cotton uniforms worn against the cold. Rotund, a bit like that French tire commercial of the Michelin man composed entirely of inflated tires, and moving very slowly uphill because of the slope and the footing and the weight of the weapons and ammo and the padded uniforms. Along the Marine line, no one fired. A lieutenant was in charge, and he was somewhere behind them toward the center of the line so his orders would carry by voice or could be passed along. Verity wasn't playing captain now; he was just another rifleman, just another body thrown in to hold the line and keep the Chinese from taking yet another ridgeline from which they could cut the MSR, sever the lifeline, block the way out.

Now he could see individual faces coming uphill toward him in the moonlight.

"Fire at will!"

The lieutenant's voice sounded high and a little scared. Or maybe he was just cold.

Verity's rifle was sighted in on a tallish man coming straight for him, moving slow like the rest of them and with his mouth open, as if to draw in more breath against the exertion and the slope of the hill and the cold. Oddly, he looked a bit like a man who had worked at their place when Verity was a kid. That man would be very old now. He fired and the man fell. Verity didn't know this weapon, and it may well have been another shot that dropped the Chinese with the open mouth. It didn't matter, did it? He swung the weapon a few ticks right and sighted in on another Chinese, short and chunky. This one fell, too. Now the firing was constant all along the line, but the Chinese kept coming, some of them firing burp guns from the hip, others just intent on getting there. One Chinese stopped to throw a grenade. Then, when he attempted to launch another, he was hit in the face and fell backward. Verity could see the blood spurting from his chin. That's how good the visibility was by moonlight off snow. But the first grenade had gotten somebody and off to his right there were sounds of a man rolling around on the ground, yelling. None of what he yelled made sense.

Then there were no more Chinese coming and the few left standing were running away, downhill.

"Cease fire!" the lieutenant called. He didn't sound nervous anymore.

Verity rolled over and propped himself on an elbow. Tate gave him a half-salute from down the line. He still didn't know where Izzo was. Funny, he wasn't cold now. It was good they had a moon. If the Chinese came up that slope in fog or falling snow or on a dark night, it would be a close thing indeed.

The Chinese weren't finished. They came up twice more that night to much the same result. After the second attack the lieutenant sent a working party halfway down the slope to pull bodies away and clear fields of fire. There were so many bodies now the oncoming Chinese were using them as cover, their own dead, much as the Marines did up here.

In the morning there were no more live Chinese to be seen barring a few wounded thrashing about or crying out. The lieutenant, who looked about seventeen years old, a skinny kid, conducted a body count. Two hundred eleven Chinese. The Marines had lost three dead, fourteen wounded, only a few of them bad.

"Boy, they kept coming, didn't they?" Tate said.

He was very calm.

"You OK?" Verity asked.

Tate nodded. "They only got one guy anywhere near me. Artilleryman. That's what happens when you let artillerymen get in firefights like proper infantrymen. Get themselves killed."

At 8:00 A.M., the casual platoon was mustered on the hillside, including Izzo, also unhurt, glad the night was over. Verity hoped they wouldn't have to do this again tonight.

"Hut, hut!" Tate called as they marched back into Yudam-ni, not really trying to keep anyone in step, just to remind them who they were.

Marines.

For two days there were no new orders from Tokyo, no responses to General Smith's call for guidance.

"It's as if they're in a panic. They're frozen. They don't know what to do because suddenly they realize they could lose their army."

So concluded senior Marine officers and others on the ground.

An aide thought MacArthur was starting to crack. They swapped stories about him, floated theories.

"The Old Man's expecting the Republicans to nominate him for president as the last American hero. And now he's been suckered by the Chinese and screwed by Truman and his army is surrounded and maybe falling apart."

Another recalled MacArthur's early penchant for drama and self-pity as army Chief of Staff way back in the thirties. His aide then, Lt. Thomas Jefferson Davis, did a memoir in which he remembered long conversations with MacArthur as he sat there, revolver in hand. And one train ride through the South.

"We are nearing the area where my father won his medal of honor, Davis. I've done everything I can in army and life. As we pass over the Tennessee River bridge, I intend to jump from the train. This is where my life ends, Davis."

The lieutenant, who had been through this sort of thing before, told his commanding officer, "General, would you hurry up and get it over with so I can get back to sleep?"

In the corridors of Far East HQ in the Dai Ichi building in

Tokyo officers now recalled such yarns and repeated them with furtive whispers.

They fought like that, up on the line as riflemen, for a second night. In the morning, there was rare sun, a real dawn, cold but clear. The Chinese had died pretty quickly. It was all very efficient. The gunfire killed you or the cold did. A badly hit man didn't last long. Not when he lay on the snow on the side of the hill and the glass was at ten or fifteen below zero Fahrenheit. Blood froze on the snow like cherry topping on a vanilla sundae. Because he was still an officer, Tom Verity asked Tate how Izzo had done.

"From what I saw, Captain, he was doing OK."

"Sure, he'll be OK," Verity said. He was less sure about himself. Last night had been bad. He didn't know how many nights like that he could take. The fighting, the cold, and no sleep—they ganged up on a man, sapping his will. Lying in the snow all night without shelter while crazy Chinese came at you firing burp guns and yelling, that was something. He tried to recall if he'd ever been this frightened, either on the 'Canal or Okinawa. He didn't think so. But on the 'Canal he was twenty-one; on Okinawa, twenty-four. And there hadn't been the cold. There'd been the Japanese and that was bad enough. But you weren't trembling with cold the whole time you were trying to fire back and hold steady and not get killed. Verity realized in all the excitement, he hadn't even thought of Kate.

He wanted to say something about this to Gunny Tate but didn't. An officer doesn't whine or seek guidance from men serving under him.

Instead, he looked around. Up and down the ragged line Marines were getting stiffly to their feet, eighteen and twenty-year-olds moving creakily, like old men. The cold did that, too. It was seven o'clock and full light of morning. No wind, thank God. The cold alone could kill you; the wind only sped the process. Overhead were the morning vapor trails of the carrier jets, crisscrossing the front and the MSR. It was the jets and the artillery spotters that sent the Chinese to ground at first light, not the Marine infantry.

Verity got up feeling like a man in his fifties, say, even older. He was just thirty. Tate was moving along the line, checking things out and taking names. That was what gunnery sergeants did.

I can learn something from Gunny Tate, Verity thought, not for the first time, and tried to focus his mind on why he was here and what they were going to do next. If you had a problem to ponder and try to solve, you didn't fall into an apathy that could drain and eventually kill you.

"Captain, I swear, what a night, what a frigging night!"

It was Izzo, small and spare and moving as he always did, furtive and gliding and not like old men. He was a hard case.

"You all right, Izzo?"

"Yessir." Now he had a BAR instead of a rifle. Well, in a firefight you ran short of men before weapons. The BAR was nearly as tall as Izzo was. The Mouse. A good name for him, rodentlike and rapacious, a survivor.

By ten a fresh company came up the hill from the road and passed through what was left of this bunch and settled in. They couldn't dig in any more than Verity and his people had. Verity and Tate and Izzo walked back downhill to the road to the town. The jeep was still there, off to the side, unhit. So, too, the big radio. Izzo tried to get a fire going without fuel.

"Turn it on, Tate; see if we can get anything."

"Yessir." Tate played with dials and the aerial. Verity didn't even know what he hoped to hear. There was static and lots of English traffic and some Chinese. Not that much. Maybe they were sleeping off the night before over there, too. Tate sent Izzo off to find out if there was any hot chow coming up and where the warming tents were, if there were any warming tents. Without a fire, their hut was colder than outside. It was better now with the sun up and moving around, but everyone was still cold. Verity thought some fingers were frostbitten, and he was sure about Tate's nose.

"Well, Captain," the gunny said, "they say if it doesn't turn black, it isn't a total loss."

"Try to rig something, a bandanna or something, Gunny. That's a pretty fine nose, and I'd hate to see you lose it."

Tate grinned. Verity was feeling better already. They had coffee now, cooked on the jeep engine block. Funny how sunlight and hot coffee got a man on his feet again. And Tate did have a good nose, sizable and straight, and without the frozen snot dripping from the nostrils as so many men did.

"Personally, Captain, I find it disgusting," Izzo had remarked a few days earlier. "I mean, however bad things get, I want to tell them, blow your frigging nose once in awhile! Jesus, we need this and the Chinks, too?"

Izzo did have his sensibilities.

Now a runner came along the road, red-faced and cheery.

"Captain Verity?"

"That's me."

"Regimental commander wants you, sir."

Izzo brightened. He hadn't found hot chow or a warming tent.

"Maybe they're gonna fly us out to Japan, Captain, you and me and the gunny; we got all this valuable intelligence."

"I doubt it. Anyway, get the jeep turned around. May as well ride in style."

Captain Verity was feeling a lot better. Except for some artillery fire, outgoing from the Marines onto the Chinese hills, and occasional jets coming in loud and low, it was quiet. The sun climbed higher, the sky clean and pale blue. The temperature was way above zero now, maybe fifteen, twenty degrees. *Yeah, this was a lot better,* Verity thought.

Then he glanced at his watch. Almost noon. In five hours it would be dark again and the Chinese would come back. The day went too fast; the night came too soon.

"OK, Izzo, let's get moving," Tate said, climbing in back with the radio and the two BARs they had now collected.

"Yeah," Verity said, "let's move it." So they moved it and at regiment they had Verity question prisoners. It wasn't too bad. In daylight nothing was as bad.

Once upon a time, Gen. Oliver Smith mused, war was a more courtly affair, and armies went over to winter quarters. They erected tents and dug proper latrines and drilled some but mainly stayed indoors out of the snow and the cold, enjoying the fire and smoking pipes and honing bayonets and oiling and cleaning rifles. That was how soldiers were supposed to spend the cold months and not out there fighting a full war on the hills and ridgelines with men on both sides freezing to death and professional general officers reduced to wearing side arms day and night in case hostilities broke out right there at divisional HQ.

It was, Smith thought, not appropriate at all. And you could blame that damned MacArthur.

Although, in all fairness, the fault might go back in time a few years. To when Washington totally ignored tradition and niceties by crossing the Delaware in a blizzard on Christmas Eve to attack the Brits and the Hessians over their pipes and rum.

That, too, was a hell of a thing. And Smith, while admiring Washington's initiative, still considered the entire affair a bit unseemly.

God never meant honest soldiers to fight winter wars. Not here, not anywhere. And that, Oliver Smith concluded, was the truth.

General Almond's chopper was expected, and Oliver Smith stood at the margin of the Haguru airstrip waiting for him to come in, turning his back against the wind of the rotor blades and the dust and the snow and pebbles whipped up.

"Good to see you, General," Smith said, saluting.

"Thank you, Oliver." It was Almond's second trip in three days to see Smith.

Haig was with Almond, Alexander Haig, his sleek young aide, a man they said would one day wear stars.

When they were inside the small factory building Smith used as HQ, he told Almond right away what Murray and Litzenberg thought.

"My two regimental commanders up at Yudam-ni want to abandon the offensive and go over to the defense. Right now. Murray fought one whole day just trying to get out of town. Made maybe fifteen hundred yards. And this was still on the flat ground, not even trying to get up the hills. Last two nights, we've been under attack. The place is swarming with Chinese. Litzenberg's brought in the dead from three CCF divisions so far."

"And you, General, what do you want?" Almond asked, stiffening and formal.

"I agree with Murray and Litzenberg. I want to go over to the defense, dig in, and see what we've got out there."

Almond, obviously unhappy, wound up the meeting swiftly.

"I want to get up to see MacLean before dark," he said. There was a brief handshake and he was out of there.

But Oliver Smith had what he wanted. Almond hadn't ordered him to resume the advance west toward Eighth Army.

Maybe they could still save the First Marine Division.

On leaving the Marines at Hagaru, Ned Almond and Alexander Haig flew by chopper to visit Colonel MacLean, whose regimental task force had been badly battered the preceding day on the opposite, eastern shore of the reservoir. MacLean confidently expected to be told to pull back to regroup at Haguru. Instead, with less than a regiment left and severely hurt, Almond unaccountably told MacLean to resume his march north, largely unsupported by any other UN force, the Marines being separated from MacLean by the width of the Chosin. When MacLean looked puzzled, Almond said, "We're still attacking and we're going all the way to the Yalu. Don't let a bunch of Chinese laundrymen stop you. . . ."

On this same day, November 28, and without Almond's knowledge, from his office in the Dai Ichi building in Tokyo, MacArthur signaled Washington that the Chinese army had intervened in great force, that this had suddenly become an entirely new war, and that "I am going over to the defense." But he didn't yet tell General Almond.

MacLean, a good soldier, gave orders to renew the advance north on the morning of the twenty-ninth. Almond had not given him any options. MacLean was army and Almond did not feel compelled to be diplomatic, as he had been with the Marine, Oliver Smith.

What would happen to Task Force MacLean shocked and even frightened Ray Murray and Homer Litzenberg. They, too, were colonels commanding infantry regiments. Allan D. MacLean, it was said, was an excellent officer, and his regiment, the Thirty-first Infantry, though not Marines but army, was a good one except for its attached reinforcing ROK troops. MacLean had been specially chosen by Ned Almond to drive North to the Yalu, around the right shore of the reservoir, in hopes of getting to the Chinese border before the Marines. Murray and Litzenberg knew you did not send a mediocre officer on such missions. Not even Almond would do that.

Murray, especially, knew how close his Fifth Marines had come to a disaster of their own, having been ordered to drive west from the reservoir through the mountains to link up with Eighth Army, forty or fifty miles away and in disarray and worse. If the Chinese had been more subtle, Murray thought with a very palpable shudder, permitting the Fifth Marines to get six or eight miles into the hills before coming down on them, Colonel Murray, like MacLean, might have lost his regiment.

And his life.

MacLean had one rifle battalion and a battalion of field artillery at Sinhung-ni, about ten or twelve miles north of Hagaru. He was killed or wandered off or was captured, no one was quite sure at the moment, during the second day's fighting. Lt. Col. Don Faith, with a battalion of the Thirty-second Infantry, fought his way north to Sinhung to assist and bulk up Task Force MacLean, only to discover MacLean was gone, and what was left of both units now became Task Force Faith. There was no longer any question of pushing north to the Yalu past these "Chinese laundrymen," but of trying to get what was left of the regimental combat team disengaged and back to Hagaru, where they might regroup. Faith took command of all three battalions and set up a defense perimeter against the encircling Chinese. He had already had five hundred casualties out of an initial thirty-two hundred men and could only be supplied by air. On the twenty-ninth, General Hodes sent a company from the Thirty-first Infantry, supported by a couple of tanks, north to link up with Faith, an inadequate effort the Chinese easily turned back. On December 1, fearing his position would soon be overwhelmed, Faith destroyed his howitzers and, with his wounded, began a fighting retreat south toward Hagaru, supported by close-in air support. Less than five miles from Hagaru, Faith was killed. And his column of frozen, exhausted men, short of officers and senior noncoms, began to break up. By late that night some six hundred and seventy stragglers had come through the barbed wire and the minefields into Hagaru, where the Marines rushed them into warming tents to save their lives. The others, in small, leaderless bands, wandered into the hills or down onto the frozen surface of the big lake, chivied and hunted like animals by the victorious Chinese chasing at their heels.

One of MacLean's men, James S. Sellers, reported:

We were attacking hills with less than three banana clips of ammo for our carbines and with bare bayonets. On the food side one ration of C Rations every three days. We once found some frozen potatoes and ate them raw. Everyone had dysentery. I went from 154 pounds to 118 in my time on the line. I froze my hands and feet. I fought my way into the Marines along with what was left of our outfit. I saw men fall through the ice of the reservoir and freeze to death before we could get them out and other men just lie down on the ice and freeze. I went back later with a Marine detachment to try to rescue wounded left on the east side of the reservoir. We found the trucks full of wounded had all been machine-gunned, gas poured on them, and set on fire. We found guys who had been captured, stripped of their clothes and left to freeze to death. After that on the way to Hungnam I took no prisoners. I shot them where they stood.

Marine lieutenant colonel Beall led the rescue mission young Sellers joined and found a number of missing army troops "wandering about in aimless circles on the ice, in a state of shock."

Three hundred dead were found in the machine-gunned, burned-out truck convoy. One thousand and fifty of the original 3,200 survived, only 385 of them able-bodied soldiers, who at Hagaru were quickly formed up into a provisional battalion and armed and outfitted by the Marines.

Sellers remembered: "We had been the most completely equipped winter outfit in Japan. We had to turn in all that winter equipment as we were told by the powers that be we would be home by Thanksgiving. We went into North Korea and the mountains in field jackets, summer fatigues, with ponchos and a blanket (two if you could steal one), no sleeping bags, leather glove shells with wool inserts, and combat boots. The field jackets were unlined."

Ned Almond made no apology, public or private, for sending MacLean and Faith north so poorly supplied and supported.

The Marine colonels, Litzenberg and Murray, realized that they might have met the same terrible end on the western shores of the big reservoir if Oliver Smith hadn't stood up to Almond and demanded to be allowed to go over to the defense rather than pushing farther north and deeper into the Chinese trap.

Back in Yudam-ni, they were trying to handle the wounded. There was no airstrip to fly them out; they had to do the best with what they had. And that wasn't much.

Working in a tent, occasionally pierced by rifle fire, regimental surgeon Chester M. Lessenden, a navy lieutenant commander, operated by lantern light. The wounded, waiting their turn, lay outside in the cold on straw pallets covered by tarps.

Navy corpsmen thawed frozen morphine syrettes in their mouths so that the wounded could be sedated during the surgery.

"Everything was frozen," Commander Lessenden said. "Plasma froze and the bottles broke. We couldn't change the dressings because we had to work with gloves on to keep our hands from freezing.

"We couldn't cut a man's clothes off to get at a wound because he would freeze to death. Actually, a man was better off if we left him alone. Did you ever try to stuff a wounded man into a sleeping bag?"

You couldn't blame the entire fiasco on MacArthur; Gen. Oliver Smith knew that. Much could be laid at the feet of the professional West Point careerists ambitious for a second star or fearful of losing a first, officers whose "can do" alacrity, when ordered to do things they knew they couldn't, was little more than caste-system ass-kissing. Few officers dared speak back. John S. Guthrie, commanding officer of the Seventh Infantry Regiment, was one.

Guthrie's regiment included two thousand ROKs, illiterate and untrained, swept up from the streets of Seoul and pressed into service without basic training. When difficulties in communications with its American troops and officers arose, Guthrie's commanding officer, "Shorty" Soule of the Third Infantry Division, told Colonel Guthrie, "There is no language problem. I will not *accept* a language problem."

"Yes sir, General," Guthrie responded. "There is no language problem. But we better tell that to the American GIs out there so they know."

Soule was one of several army generals who was a known drunk. Oddly enough, despite this and his mulishness, the Third Division performed creditably and "Shorty" Soule was decorated.

Gen. Oliver P. Smith's forefinger traced lightly a medium-scale map. His division was still stretched out over nearly fifty miles of narrow mountain road that had already been cut at half a dozen points by marauding Chinese troops who could, it seemed, at any time slash through at another score of places.

"There are now sixteen CCF divisions in your vicinity," X Corps had informed him. Maybe it was that which drummed sense into Ned Almond's thick head after two wasted days of moronic adherence to an implausible objective: the advance due west across mountains to link up with Eighth Army. Damned fool! Almond should have been man enough to stand up to MacArthur and tell him the thing wasn't doable. Instead, all this lickspittal bullshit. Almond could still lose his army. So could Johnny Walker over there on the other side of the hill. And how would Douglas Jesus Christ MacArthur like that?

Smith was in a tent at Hagaru with his staff and about to issue orders for a march to the sea, starting with a pullback of the leading regiments from Yudam-ni. Not a retreat, he told himself, but a march. He knew what happened even to good troops when things got bad. A retreat could become a rout, a rout become flight, flight become panic, and in the end you had a stampede. That's what had happened just the other side of the reservoir to Task Force MacLean. They had the figures now, as good as they were ever likely to have them. Maybe there were a few still out there, wandering around on the frozen lake, ducking the Chinese, hiding from patrols. They wouldn't last long, not in this cold. He thought of the dead MacLean.

Now, thanks to MacArthur and Ned Almond, Smith could lose an entire division.

"Gentlemen," he said, rapping a knuckle sharply on the map table to quiet their chat.

His orders to the staff were crisp, very specific.

"No unit moves south until it's been leapfrogged by another and until that other unit has reached its objective and secured it. I don't want two units moving simultaneously. Everything's to be orderly, step-by-step. No bunching up or milling about. If a unit is held up by Chinese resistance or terrain or a blown bridge, the unit behind it doesn't move south until the problem has been eliminated and the first unit's reached its objective. If you are not clear on this, ask me now. I want no confusion, no lack of clarity."

Marines weren't soldiers like MacLean's Task Force, but they were still men. Anyone could panic.

"One unit anchors before the unit north of it begins to move south. Got it?"

There was murmured assent. Oliver Smith was nothing if not clear. When he was sure they understood him, Smith turned the meeting over to his ops officer, the G-3, to go into details as to the order of march.

There were desperate fights just to get out of Yudam-ni and through the first hills hemming in the road. The Chinese had two entire Marine rifle regiments penned up here and much of their artillery, more than two-thirds of the whole division, and if they could keep them here, or kill them here, X Corps would collapse. During the firefight a Marine platoon surrounded by Chinese was reduced to using entrenching tools alternately as weapons, chopping at the Chinese with the steel blades, and as baseball bats, slapping back hurled grenades coming into their position much as a good singles hitter sprays base hits. It was small, ugly brawls like this, lots of them, that got them out.

Maggie Higgins somehow hitched a ride into Hagaru-ri on December 5 to meet and talk with Marines from Yudam: "They had the dazed air of men who have accepted death and then found themselves alive after all. They talked in unfinished phrases. They would start something and then stop, as if meaning was beyond any words at their command."

In New York and other places Americans read her dispatches over breakfast and wondered if she exaggerated. The newspapers often do, don't they?

You rolled a few yards forward with the wheels slipping in place or sliding sideways and then you stalled. Then you moved a few yards again and stalled. It wasn't your vehicle that wasn't working but the vehicle ahead that had skidded or broken down. Or there was fighting ahead. A firefight, even a brief one with a lone sniper or a half-dozen Chinese trying to cut the road, could bring the whole damned line of thousands of men and hundreds and hundreds of vehicles to a halt. There was no way to get around, no shoulder.

For most of the way, the road was carved into the side of the mountain, with the upper heft of the mountain looming steeply above the narrow road and the lower slope equally steep, clifflike, falling away five hundred or a thousand feet toward some ravine or streambed below.

You stayed with the road or you got the hell out of the vehicle and played mountain climber.

When they stalled for perhaps the tenth or maybe the twentieth time Verity, growing impatient, said to Izzo, "Maybe you ought to cut the engine when we get hung up like this. Save gas."

"We got plenty of gas, Captain. I got jerricans in the back that—"

"And not have the radiator boil over."

"Sir, the radiator on this vehicle ain't going to . . ."

Verity shrugged. He drove an MG around Georgetown; this bird was supposedly wheelman for a Philadelphia holdup gang.

"OK, Izzo, just an idea."

"Yessir, and I want the captain to know I appreciate it."

In other words, "Screw you, Captain Verity."

There was firing up ahead and they could see Marines in trucks in front of them standing up and craning their necks to see.

"Marines," Tate said partly in wonder and partly in disgust. "They'd pay good money to see someone else in a firefight. They hate to miss the double feature."

Occasionally a ricochet from the fighting up ahead sang its way down the line of vehicles and men ducked, instinctively, only to straighten up again right away trying to see what was going on and who was winning, the good guys or the bandits. They had, after all, a rooting interest.

"But I did think of one thing, Captain," Izzo resumed, "which I thought may be was an excellent idea."

"Yes?"

"Well, now that we're pretty sure it's Chinks up there on the hill, like you been trying to prove all this time, and now we got the bodies as evidence, thanks to you, Captain, I thought maybe to save weight and space we could sort of lose that there radio back there."

Tate growled in response before Verity could say anything. "I checked out that radio, Izzo. My name's on the requisition. Any-one shitcans that radio it's going to be me." He looked toward Verity for approval.

Verity shrugged. What the hell, Izzo had a point. With Chinese all around them, sixteen divisions' worth, there wasn't a lot more intelligence Verity and his radio were going to give the division or Gen. O. P. Smith or anyone else. But Tate was a regular who'd signed out the radio.

"We'll keep the radio, Izzo. Just drive."

"Aye-aye, sir."

That afternoon a corpsman flagged them down. "I got some wounded here, sir, and I'm trying to get one or two of them aboard vehicles."

Marines got their wounded out if they could. That was the tradition. Always had been.

Verity looked past the corpsman to where six or seven men lay on the snow just off the road. Some of them looked pretty bad, eyes staring and sunken.

"Tate?"

"Yessir, we can squeeze one back here with me and the radio, if he ain't too big."

Verity turned back to the corpsman. "OK, Doc, pick out a small one if you can."

"Yessir." Then bundled in a smallish, almost beardless young man with a leg wound. "Thank you, sir."

The wounded man was reasonably chipper. Probably glad to be out of the fighting this easy. By sundown they had two more wounded riding with them, one perched on a fender, holding on with a good arm, the other stretched crossways over the hood on his back and not looking very sprightly. That one died quickly.

"I wish there was nurses, Gunny," Izzo said. "We could make room for nurses, squeeze 'em in somehow."

"I'll squeeze you, Izzo."

That night the column secured about 11:00 P.M. and didn't roll again until seven the next morning. By then the boy with the leg wound who had seemed so chipper was dead.

"Shock. Or loss of blood. I dunno, Captain."

"OK, Gunny, tie him on somehow with the other one 'til we find someplace to turn 'em in."

Jeez, Izzo thought, *it's like driving a hearse.*

They did only four miles that next day.

In Tokyo, rainy but not cold, and even amid the imperial trappings of his Caesarite, MacArthur panicked.

On October 25 he saw the war virtually at an end. His armies, both of them, could soon be at the Yalu. The North Koreans were finished. The Chinese cowered behind the border, an enormous bluff. The General was jotting notes for his victory speech. American boys, at least some of them, would be home for Christmas. The 1952 Republican convention wouldn't be a contest; it could be a coronation.

"Jean, we're going home!" he had informed his wife.

Not five weeks later, by the last day of November, both his armies were bloodied, entire units had been smashed, at least four and perhaps six Chinese army corps had been identified in North Korea, and it looked very much as if an entirely new, and larger, war had begun.

If the General swore, he would have done so.

He got little consolation from Willoughby, his intelligence general. For years Willoughby's consolations had been welcomed. But MacArthur had the numbers of ROK and even American battalions swallowed up in the maw of the shocking surprise Chinese attack.

This was beyond mischief. MacArthur called Washington on a secure line to inquire as to the availability of nuclear weapons.

CHAPTER ELEVEN

"All right, you peepul, move out. And smartly!" It was an NCO's
voice, still crisp, the kind of NCO with the kind of voice that
would get Marines moving again even if their officers broke.

T hank God they don't have artillery."
That was Tate talking, but it could have been anyone on
the line of march south from Yudam-ni along the road
flanking the west shore of the big lake. With the rolling stock and
the bulk of the troops using the single narrow road, a few artillery
pieces could chop up the Marines at will.

But there was no Chinese artillery beyond mortars and some
shoulder-carried rockets. The Chinese were moving off-road, along
the ridgelines and in the parallel valleys and over the mountain
passes, routes only good infantrymen and mules and their small
Mongolian ponies could handle.

The Marines knew they'd gotten lucky with artillery; they had
plenty themselves. They also had a few tanks and, when the
weather cleared, plenty of air. The Chinese had thousands of tanks
but none of them here. And there were also thousands of planes,
most of them Russian, north of the Yalu. So far, so good on Chinese air: there was none.

The Marines thanked God for that, too.

As desperate as were the nightly battles when the Chinese swarmed around and over and through and sometimes swamped the Marines, dawn almost always brought respite. Unless there was heavy snow, the planes came in then off the carriers and from the airfields farther south, navy jets and Marine Corsairs and Air Force, too, and the forward observers marching and fighting with the Marines could see well enough to call in both air and artillery on the Chinese targets.

Except that the Marines were outnumbered by ten to one, the odds were otherwise in their favor.

"I feel sorry for the Chinese," Puller impishly remarked. "They're all around us."

Verity wasn't the only officer who knew the Chinese, who'd served there. Puller had as well. And the old man talked often about the past, not bragging of his exploits but dazzling in his recall of people and places and events. He told a good yarn:

"I got to Peking in '33. February. Cold there, too. There was a Marine battalion assigned to the legation, six hundred men. I'd been there a month when they gave me command of the cavalry, what they then called the Horse Marines, a fifty-man detachment mounted on Manchurian ponies. Small horses but fine. Excellent horseflesh. I'd been a rider as a child and had been riding on and off ever since. George Patton and I probably would have gotten on well, both of us riders, both of us slightly, well, unconventional."

Puller somehow had gotten a genuine field kitchen going here at Koto-ri, and the First Marines, those not actually in combat at the time, were given at least one hot meal a day.

"Don't let them eat frozen rations," he kept telling his officers. "Man eats frozen food he'll have gastrointestinal problems for a week. And you know what that means in this weather. A man with diarrhea won't make it. He won't be strong enough."

Even if you didn't have diarrhea, his officers thought, knowing from experience what it was like to sit on a wooden ammo box in a driving snow with the temperature below zero and your trousers down around your ankles, trying to have a bowel movement.

But these dinners with Puller, served before 4:00 P.M. with the darkness coming on and the Chinese moving up toward the Marine lines, were as pleasant under the circumstance as a meal could be. Sometimes they ate outdoors.

"Let the men use the warm-up tents," Puller kept saying. "Won't hurt us to eat around a fire."

If the Chinese had real artillery, gathering a regiment's staff around a fire would have been an invitation to slaughter. Puller wasn't foolhardy, for all his dash; he knew what a soldier could get away with, when you could cut a corner and when not.

"First time I ever saw Japanese troops was at Peking," he would start out, and the men around him, many of them famous Marine officers in their own right, would lean forward, wanting to hear, knowing that the story would be good. "There was this Ming shrine about twenty miles out. We drove out to see it, sightseeing, three or four officers in a closed car. In summer Peking could be one hundred and twenty degrees Fahrenheit; in winter it could be twenty below. Nothing like it in the States except maybe North Texas, the Panhandle, where they say there's nothing between Texas and the North Pole but a barbed-wire fence."

There was no organized liquor ration, and Puller was hell on drunkenness, had broken both officers and men for being drunk. But a bottle might be passed about, bourbon, usually, just enough for each man to have a drop. Bourbon was very Marine Corps, a southern drink, with so many of the senior officers, men like Puller from Virginia, men of the South, men of Dixie. One reason you never heard much of Marine heroics in the Civil War: half the Marines were on each side.

"So we drove out to the Ming Tombs. And there we'd find this battalion of Japanese also stationed in Peking. But they'd marched out in formation. They carried full gear, weapons, ammo, plus a bundle of firewood. They'd already marched maybe twenty miles, and when they got there they stacked arms and did exercises and then, finally, they broke off by twos and massaged each other's neck and shoulders. After that they cooked rice and bean powder and had a primitive meal. Then they were permitted to gaze upon the

Ming Tombs before marching back to Peking. We ate a picnic lunch and went sightseeing and drove back in the most leisurely of fashions. And the damned Japs were always marching through the gates of Peking before us.

"I knew then they would be terrible adversaries in war."

He might as well have been talking about the Chinese, who lived on nothing and marched in deep snow in sneakers and carried mortars and machine guns on their backs and could pursue all day and fight all night. Then Puller went on, finishing his little sermon: "The Marine battalion, for its part, did only one field exercise a week. And that was called off if it was too cold or too hot. Or if rain threatened."

Puller did not draw the lesson. His tone of voice did that, manifesting disapproval and disgust.

Tom was still writing letters to Kate, not daily anymore but when he could. By now it was compulsive, near obsession, and irrational. Especially since there was no postal service.

What Tom Verity wrote his daughter was an expurgated, child's version of the day's events, the landscape, the shelters in which they might fortunately bivouac, the weather, how the old jeep rattled along, nothing like their MG, not at all, but all the more dear to him for its odd wheezes and clanking.

> It has no top, Kate, even in rain or snow. Poor little jeep. Mr. Izzo, our driver, keeps it going whatever the weather, and we warm cans of food on the engine. We must try that someday with our car on a picnic. Some Campbell's chicken noodle soup? You bring two mugs and spoons and napkins and we'll heat the soup together on a cold day and then sit in the car and eat our soup and be toasty warm together.
>
> Did I tell you Mr. Izzo is very short and rather small and wears sunglasses even at night and his friends call him Mouse? Isn't that a funny name for a man?
>
> Love,
> Poppy

Since there was no postal service, he would fold each letter carefully, pressing it very flat, and jam it into an inner pocket. And he
wrote about everything but the killing.

The battalion commander, a light colonel, was crying.

"It's the wounded. What the hell do you do with the wounded?"

Verity didn't know the colonel's name. He was from one of the
other rifle regiments. It didn't matter. He could have been any of
the battalion commanders. None of them knew what to do with
the wounded. The casualty lists were themselves becoming a disaster within the larger, looming catastrophe.

We may just not make it, Verity thought, clearheaded and
almost calm. It was a possibility that had to be considered, if not
spoken aloud. Who knew what small thing it might take to send
even Marines into panic and headlong flight or surrender? The
Chinese army might really kill or capture them all.

He and the battalion commander were standing at a narrow
place in the road where snow sliding down from the hill had once
again cut the route south. They were using a tank as a snowplow,
running it back and forth, pushing at the snow and tamping it
down flat, the engine whining, the gears rasping dry, metal against
metal, since lubricating oil only froze and it was better to run
machinery dry.

"Maybe a 'dozer will come along," Verity said, not really believ-
ing it but not knowing what to say to a colonel on the brink of
breaking down.

The man brightened. "Yeah, maybe it will. We could use a
'dozer. If we had a 'dozer we could get out."

There was an edge of panic in his voice.

He was sure right about the wounded. That wasn't panic; that
was reality.

Maybe we ought to stand and fight, Verity thought. That way
they could dig in, get out of the wind and out of the line of fire,
build fires, put up warming tents, get warm. Straggling along the
mountain road like this in the cold and under fire, they were losing
men they couldn't replace, dead and wounded.

It was December 1, three weeks to go before official winter, and they were still retreating abreast of the reservoir and hadn't yet made Hagaru-ri.

"Someone said it's twenty below, Captain."

This was Tate, not a man to exaggerate.

"Feels it, Gunny."

"Yessir. Some men are saying we should've stayed at Yudam-ni. That we could have made a stand there and stopped the Chinese."

"I don't think so, Gunny. I don't think we've could have stopped them. Just too many." He wasn't that sure but an officer didn't want to convey doubt.

Tate nodded, the chiseled chin firm as ever. "I think you're right, Captain. It's just some of these boys are cold and tired and scared out here on the open road. But I think you're right. The Chinese would've overrun Yudam-ni."

It was a theoretical concern by now. Yudam-ni lay behind them and Hagaru-ri ahead, and who knew how many of them would live to get there?

And the wounded were always with them.

Verity understood why the light colonel wept. These were his men, fifteen hundred of them. Verity had no command, just Tate and Izzo and himself and one goddamned jeep, and neither Tate nor Izzo had been hit or limped on frozen feet yet. When it was your men lying there bleeding or unable to walk, that was something else; that was where you felt the terrible weight of command. It was responsibility that broke men as much as fear. The awful burden of fifteen hundred men you were losing man by man and hour by hour and with not one goddamned sensible, useful thing to do about it. At Quantico, at the Marine Corps Schools, they taught you the "school solution" to just about everything. What was the "school solution" to Marines' dying from loss of blood when it was so cold the plasma wouldn't go into solution and the tubes clogged with ice and the corpsmen couldn't change dressings with gloved, half-frozen hands rigid with cold?

Now there weren't enough warming tents even for the wounded. Men who weren't wounded could forget it; no warming tents for them. With the division on the march this way, slow and punctuated by halts as it was, they no sooner got a warming tent up and the wounded into it than they were taking it down to move another mile, a half-mile, a quarter- , a hundred and fifty yards. So when they could, they put the worst wounded inside and lay the other casualties on straw mats outside the tents on the lee side away from the wind and covered them with tarps.

"One good thing," Verity heard a surgeon say. "It's so damned cold, blood coagulates. Just wrap 'em up the best you can and don't move them around too much or drop them and maybe some of these boys will make it."

When one didn't, he was stacked like cordwood until a tank or 'dozer came along and the dead would be piled on top, as many as a tank could carry and still have a field of fire for its guns.

At Hagaru-ri, it was said, they'd carved out an airstrip. Maybe some of the wounded could get out then. Verity started to say something about this to the light colonel, but the man was crying again, tears freezing on his face, his nose running into icicles, and so Tom said nothing.

What could he say? In the War against the Japanese he'd seen officers break. Go nuts. Shoot themselves. He couldn't recall seeing a man defeated as this light colonel was. He was like the Marines coming off the hill that morning with their parkas turned backward and their sleeves tied. Someone ought to get a replacement up here. And quick. And maybe there was no replacement. And who the hell was Captain Verity to be parceling out advice when he was here reluctantly and riding as a passenger?

"All right, you peepul, move out. And smartly!" It was an NCO's voice, still crisp, still disciplined, the kind of NCO with the kind of voice that would get Marines moving again even if their officers broke.

The tank had done its work flattening the snowslide, and men got to their feet and picked up their rifles and shuffled on, a ghastly procession of tired men on a mountain road in the cold. But they were up; they were marching.

"Well," Verity said to the battalion commander.

The man shook himself, making an effort. "Yes," he said, "time to move out." He rubbed the back of a filthy mitten across his face, smearing the snot away and trying to smile.

It didn't really work. But he moved on. Maybe he was thirty-five; he looked older.

The three of them crouched low behind the jeep, sheltering from bomb fragments or the errant round. The Corsairs came in low and loud, pounding the Chinese on the hillside with aerial cannon, machine guns, and hundred-pound bombs. Then came the napalm, bouncing against the slope and exploding, a huge fireball first and then just the blackened snow and the reek of jellied gasoline you could smell down here on the road.

"Go get 'em, babee!" Izzo shouted. "Furioso!"

Boy, Verity thought, *they're good, coming in that low and through these hills and hitting the target.*

Sometimes they killed Marines. That was what close air support was. To work, it had to be close. You took the good with the bad. And tried to be philosophical.

Sons of bitches. That, too, was how the Marines thought of the aviation, not only the navy pilots but also the Air Force and even their own Marine flyboys. They were up an hour, maybe two hours a day, and when the mission was over it was back to the carriers or the airfields down south. To warm bunks with actual sheets and pillowcases, to hot showers, to bottles of Coke and hot meals on real plates, to movies and mail and a laundry that delivered clean clothes again the next morning for that day's flight.

And we'll still be here in the same filthy clothes, hungry and cold and cramping up, living in shit like animals.

That was the difference between the Marines coming back from Chosin and the fliers risking their skins to help them out.

Stories came back through the air officers assigned to the rifle battalions to control the close air support, of carrier pilots returning from raids on the Chinese hills whose planes were hit and went down in the sea between here and the ship, sometimes less than a mile away, and the pilots, unhit and unhurt, bailed out.

Sometimes it took the carrier only five or six minutes to get a rescue chopper over to where the pilot fell into the sea and he was already dead, frozen right through his flight suit and boots and thermals. Just as dead and just as board-stiff as the Marines who fell asleep along the road from the reservoir and never woke. The fliers died cleaner, is all, but that made them no less dead.

At least the Marines had the road.

Bad as it was there on the road, the Chinese up in the hills and in the parallel valleys on the Marine flanks were moving through rougher country and deeper snow and lugging everything but what the ponies carried. Sometimes the valleys turned into box canyons and the Chinese had to backtrack and go around, covering twice the ground. Marine patrols cut across their track. Word came in of entire Chinese units down in the snow, some of them already dead, others dying, a few desperately trying to get fires going and fashion shelter.

"We found one platoon, maybe thirty men. Only four or five still alive, and they couldn't move. Feet frozen, hands, and it's ten below with a foot of fresh snow."

The Marines went through the bodies for papers and left the dead and most of the living behind. There was no point trying to bring in a prisoner with frozen feet; you'd have to carry him. A man that badly frozen wasn't going to live through the night any-way. If they got one who could walk, they brought him in to be questioned, not even bothering to tie his hands.

Verity questioned the prisoners that came in to regiment. Tate monitored the radio and Izzo held a gun on the POWS while Verity talked to them.

Although Captain Verity had no formal training in military intelligence, he'd questioned civilians and the occasional deserter or bandit in North China that winter. He found it an interesting chess game, trying to assess what was truth, what a lie, and what simple confusion or boasting or lack of knowledge.

The Chinese soldiers captured here in Korea, terrified at first or reticent, talked freely once they realized they weren't going to be handled all that roughly.

"When I don't bring out the whips and pliers, they get pretty comfortable. Downright chatty."

Sometimes one of the other officers would suggest maybe the whips and the pliers might make the prisoners even more congenial. Verity laughed these officers off. And if a man, stupidly, pushed it, Verity had an effective out line: "I don't think that's such a good idea, but if you want I'll bring it up to General Smith when I report in."

"No, no, Verity, just an idea. Just a notion."

People, Verity knew, were fairly easy to bluff; that was why there were so really few good poker players. And he didn't bother to impress such officers with details of just how warlords he had known in North China had dealt with the difficult and recalcitrant, to say nothing of deserters and spies: inserting them alive into a working locomotive's furnace.

Kate Verity knew about Santa Claus. Madame called him Pere Noel. But for Kate's parents, he was simply Santa. They hadn't made a fetish out of it.

"But a child should have something to hang onto," Verity said.

Elizabeth, the natural skeptic, to his surprise agreed. "I wish I'd had Santa. Our house was so fashionably rational."

Tom, raised in China, where people still believed in ghosts and cow spirits and the year of the dragon and of the snake, was less rational, more willing to suspend critical judgment.

And so, on December 1, at kindergarten, where they began talking about the number of days until Christmas, young Kate spoke up:

"My father is taking me to Paris for Christmas. To see Pere Noel."

A dozen three- or four-year-olds looked uncomprehending.

"Oh," Kate said, "that's the name Santa Claus uses when he's in France. So the French children will know who he is."

Most of the kids nodded, solemn and impressed to have a classmate so worldly and knowledgeable.

*   *   *

It was night, a break in the shambling, slogging, awful march from Yudam-ni to Hagaru-ri, and for once they could hear no firefights on the flanks or to the rear; there seemed to be no organized fighting ahead.

"Maybe the Chinks are cold and tired as we are," Izzo said, his voice enthusiastic with hope. So much so he forgot he was not to call them Chinks; the captain didn't like it.

How could they not be cold and tired? Verity thought.

Izzo had contrived to make a small fire, scrounging a few twigs and branches somehow in this barren place, lighting them with a cup of gasoline from the jeep, and now they huddled around it, sheltering from the wind in the chill dark.

"When Lee retreated from Gettysburg," Tate began, "he had lost twenty-eight thousand men and, more than that, the loyalty of Pickett and Longstreet and others who believed Lee had destroyed the army. The line of wagons, mostly filled with wounded, just like here, stretched seventeen miles. It was raining and they moved slow, the horses and even the mules slipping and sliding. But Lee got them somehow across the Potomac on flatboats and back to Virginia. Meade didn't pursue. Lincoln, they say, went ape. It was Meade's chance to end the war right there, by following Lee and running him down in the flat country before the hills. But he didn't. No one ever explained quite why."

Verity listened, enjoying hearing a man talk who knew of what he spoke. So many speak without knowing. He knew too many men like that.

Tate resumed, "So maybe the Chinese will get tired. And they won't run us down and we'll get out."

"From your mouth to God's ear, Gunny." That was as pious as Izzo ever got, and Verity was impressed. With Izzo calling on God sincerely, and not just looking for an edge, things were looking slim.

"Let's hope so, Gunny," Verity said. He realized even Tate was no longer talking of winning but of getting out. Verity wondered how deeply that notion had taken the division in its grip. If Gunny

Tate spoke that way, in terms of trying to save the division, then it might be tight indeed. Verity still had cigars and he brought them out now. Who knew when they would have another few hours as placid as this?

"Thank you, Captain," Tate said, rolling the cigar deftly despite the mitten, but Izzo declined.

"I'm faithful to Lucky Strike, Captain. You come across a carton of Luckies, I'd be much obliged. You know the slogan, LSMFT: Lucky Strike Means Fine Tobacco." He looked pleased to have remembered the commercial's ditty.

Verity had been told by a major who seemed sure of it that up ahead, from Hagaru-ri on south, planes were supplying the column, dropping ammunition and fuel and food. Maybe there would be a carton of Luckies there for Izzo. Verity did not expect Havana cigars, though, and continued to ration himself to one per day except in moments like this, when he treated Tate and offered another to Izzo and was relieved, without saying so, when the Mouse refused.

Here the way was too narrow, too imposed upon by hills, the road running through a ravine too deep, for them to be resupplied by air. Maybe a fighter plane could get in here, flying with a desperate caution, a Corsair or something, but you couldn't fly transports. And only transports could drop supplies in any meaningful volume.

Hagaru-ri! That was where they were heading; that was where they had an airstrip, or so it was said; that was where they would find fuel and hot food and warming tents and fresh, strong reinforcing battalions. Occasionally here, on the Chosin road from Yudam-ni, men thought they heard transport planes.

"Ours!" they cried, craning necks toward the low gray sky.

But the planes were only a tease, only the cold wind howling, a haunting sound that fired false hope and then cast it down, damp and chill.

Racial integration was still a very new thing, ordered by Truman but not yet fully digested. Older officers, many but not all of them southern, would never fully swallow the idea. Puller wasn't one of them, but he had his moments. While he was still in Hungnam before the march north, his accustomed contempt for the army had been stiffened by an incident involving black troops. When reports of an army debacle filtered back into Hungnam, Puller wrote home: "An all-Negro artillery battalion, sent to the front, was delivered by an all-Negro transport battalion to its place in the front lines. On the way back by night the transport men were ambushed by six North Koreans, and the four hundred truckers ran without a fight, leaving the vehicles standing with the lights burning and the motors on. The Reds burned the trucks and hiked up the road into the rear of the artillery battalion, which they sprayed with fire and scattered. The Reds took all the guns. I saw many of the broken men who came back. It was a terrible day for our arms."

The corpsman leaned close to the wounded man.

"Cigarette, Mac?"

It was what medical care was coming to on the road south from the reservoir, a cigarette, a shot of morphine, being laid out flat on the snow instead of left broken on the road.

"Have a butt, kid?"

Most of the wounded wanted one. Everyone had a Zippo lighter. The Zippo with a windscreen worked even in the snow. The Marines would happily have given endorsements.

"Cigarette, pal?"

"I don't smoke."

He was young and the stomach wound had stopped oozing blood, so maybe he had a chance.

"Hey, it'll take your mind off stuff."

"OK then."

The corpsman lighted the Chesterfield, but the boy coughed hard on the first puff. When he'd stopped coughing he said, "My ma made me promise not to smoke till I was twenty-one."

"Oh?"

The kid died about an hour later. The corpsman had seen a lot of men die along the road, but for this one there was guilt.

" 'Cause of how he promised his ma and I lit one for him anyways."

"Hell," one of the other corpsmen said, "tough shit."

"I'll never pass another frigging faucet without stopping to take a drink."

That was Izzo. Tate didn't phrase it as cogently but, tall and lanky, felt the same way.

"It's funny," he told Verity. "I was always thirsty in summer, in the heat, at Pendleton and Parris Island and in prison camp during the War. Never thought about it in the winter until now."

"Sure, we all feel it. We're dehydrated. Chewing snow just doesn't get enough liquid into you."

The canteens, of course, were frozen. So were the jerricans and the water tanks of several hundred gallons towed behind the occasional truck or jeep. There was no way of thawing them without building fires and taking hours, and they lacked the fuel and time. So men scooped up handfuls of snow in gloved and mittened hands and munched on it, freezing their lips and tongues and mouths and tiring their jaws, and ending with a trickle of stale water down parched throats.

"I heard a guy say he laced his canteen with a couple of shots of rye whisky, Gunny," Izzo offered, "and he claimed it didn't freeze up."

"Fine, Izzo, and where's *your* bottle of Four Roses?"

"Well, jeez, I was just telling you what I heard." He rolled his eyes toward Verity, as if to demonstrate how sorely put upon he was.

Captain Verity rewarded Izzo with a bleak stare. He, too, wished for a glass of cold, clean tap water. Just one glass. Such implausible dreams kept them going as they trudged south.

On the evening of December 3, the first column of Marines from Yudam-ni reached the outskirts of Hagaru. Relative safety. But only relative.

Verity and his little band were well down the line and wouldn't get in until the following morning. Izzo scrounged up food and the news: "They said last night they marched in, just like on parade—"

"Of course they marched in," Tate growled. "They're Marines, aren't they?"

Jesus, Izzo thought, *he never eases up, does he? You'd think I wasn't a Marine, that I was a Canadian Mountie or something. . . .*

It had taken four days to cover the fourteen miles from Yudam to Hagaru. Colonel Litzenberg's Seventh Regiment had only one tank left. There was a new Chinese general in the area, Sung Shin-lun, a veteran of the famous Long March of 1934–35, and his command now consisted of twelve divisions of Chinese regulars. They fought for every one of those fourteen miles, for every hill, for every ridgeline, for every narrow place in the road. After the firefights the regimental surgeon, a naval officer, said of the Marine wounded, "It was very strange to see blood freeze before it could coagulate. Coagulated blood is dark brown, but this stuff was pinkish." And the doctors concluded that while some men froze to death, some of the wounded survived rather than bled to death untended because their blood congealed.

Verity and Tate walked beside the jeep while Izzo drove. At one point they had four wounded Marines and one dead man stowed aboard.

"I could do without the stiff, Gunny," Izzo complained.

"Just shut up, Izzo; you don't know how cushy you have it."

And it *was* cushy. Verity agreed with Tate. For all the cold and the exposure and thirst and stomach problems, at least they weren't humping up and down the hillsides to attack Chinese positions and clean them out so the column could move forward. When Col. Ray Davis's battalion fell out to assault Fox Hill and resecure the Toktong Pass with a night march through mountains and then a dawn fight, Davis reckoned his men were carrying one hundred and twenty pounds apiece, and this was on a climb through deep snow in the dark. Now, at Hagaru, a good-sized town, there were houses, barns, stores, places with walls and roofs against wind, against the falling, drifting snow. Tate didn't even bother to scout anymore for lice.

"Doesn't matter anymore if it's lousy," Verity told him, "just so long as we can get warmed."

"Aye-aye, sir."

Theirs was just a hut, nothing more, but with four walls and a door and even a broken window. It was fine. Snug. Only a little snow filtered through the chinks, and the roof was sound.

"And there's an alley right out back," Izzo enthused, "where you can shit out of the wind."

That night, exhausted but despite fatigue unable to sleep, Verity lay awake on the earthen floor in the stinking sleeping bag for a long time. Perhaps twenty minutes. Thirty. What time was it now for Kate? he wondered.

In Georgetown it was morning and people woke in warm beds to shake themselves alert before going downstairs to the door, snatching the *Washington Post* or the *Times Herald* from the doorstep, retreating discreetly then, to kitchen or bath, for steaming coffee and fresh juice or back upstairs for a leisurely bowel movement and steamy shower. Such people wore leather slippers and Brooks Brothers PJs and flannel robes of Black Watch plaid.

And not foul trousers smelling of piss and shit and wool undershirts damp with sweat, thawing now in the blessed lee of walls and roof, steam rising from their bodies, crawling into a sleeping bag stiff with filth and body fluids and, here and there, a little blood.

When Verity pulled off his socks they, too, were bloody where the soles of his feet had frozen to the wool and the skin pulled away in tatters and patches. But you had to get wet socks off your feet and pull on dry ones. Otherwise it wasn't a little skin you lost; it was your feet.

Nor in Georgetown, he realized, were people lousy. Or frostbitten. Or likely to die that day.

"We ought to write a letter to your papa, Kate."

"Yes, Madame, Poppy would like that. We must tell him that here at home it is sunny and warm. So nice."

Kate thought.

"And are there French soldiers there, too, with Poppy?"

Madame beamed.

"But of course, and gallant."

CHAPTER TWELVE

The general was wearing both a shoulder holster and an automatic shoved into the waist of his trousers. . . . That wasn't Georgie Patton bullshit with ivory-handled revolvers; this was because Oliver Smith knew Chinese soldiers might be coming through here later that night, that the general himself might be not only commanding a division of twenty thousand men but also fighting for his own life. It sobered you.

Hagaru-ri itself had not been spared during the fighting at Yudam-ni and the first leg of the march south. Once the Chinese cut the MSR south of Hagaru, cutting it in a half-dozen different places, it was obvious to both contending generals, Smith and Peng, that only Hagaru's airstrip could keep the Marines supplied and fighting until attacks were mounted to smash the Chinese roadblocks and reopen the mountain road. That was when Peng threw in his men against the perimeter hill defenses of the town and against the town itself and its airstrip.

"You can't frigging believe it!" a Marine marveled as scores of Chinese soldiers rolled dizzily downhill in the snow toward his machine gun, rolling over and over until they reached the Marine lines and instantly sprang up, firing their burp guns and hurling grenades. There was a moon and even this unorthodox tactic failed, as Chinese bodies piled up in the snow in front of the machine guns. Inside the town a large Chinese unit broke through, very close to divisional HQ, only to evaporate in an orgy of looting, ransacking warehouses in search of boots and blankets and warm clothing. Artillerymen and engineers and army troops back from the north were all thrown into the fight along with the single Marine rifle battalion holding the town. And by the time the Seventh Marines and elements of the Fifth marched in from the north, the Chinese had melted away, leaving only crimson trails in the snow and their dead.

With the airstrip again secure, the big C-47 cargo planes resumed their flights, carrying out the wounded and sick, carrying in ammo and rations and even five hundred fresh Marine reinforcements, a short battalion, and welcome. And along with them came reporters, David Douglas Duncan of *Life* and Maggie Higgins among them. Duncan would stay with the Marines the rest of the way. Miss Higgins would not.

Verity was at the airstrip, seizing the opportunity to send out letters to Kate and try to find out what was going on. Then he saw Maggie Higgins.

"Everyone's trying to get out and you fly in," he told her.

"Oh, it's you."

They were in a big warming tent erected on the margin of the airstrip. The tent was warm enough but sagged, buffeted over and over by the prop wash of the transport planes, and was lighted by Coleman lamps.

She liked his eyes and the intelligence. You encountered many things in a war but not always intelligence. She pulled out a cigarette and he patted his pockets for matches but had none, and she lit it herself, deftly, using a big, battered Zippo.

"I was vague on purpose back there at Hungnam," Verity said, not apologizing but explaining. "I'm supposed to be a Chinese language expert. It's something I teach at college. And a good reporter might interpret that as somehow significant. Now, of course, it doesn't matter. The Chinese seem to have made their intentions clear."

"A Chinese expert?" she said, sloughing off evasions. "How did that come about?"

"Born there. Lived in China until I was fifteen. My father had a business."

He smiled at her and she smiled back, as if this were the start of something and not two strangers caught up in chaos.

"And now you're an officer."

"Only a captain. A civilian, really. Two months ago I was at Georgetown lecturing on the Ming dynasty. I'm not at all important, Miss Higgins."

"And I specialize in 'important' people?" She knew the gossip about herself.

"You don't have to be defensive, Miss Higgins," Verity said mildly. "I meant nothing by it."

"OK then," she forgave him.

"How'd you get here? We're supposed to be trapped."

"Hitched a ride. I knew a pilot."

I'll bet you did, Verity thought, and disliked himself for it.

She took a few notes and chatted with other men, officers and enlisted both, and then, warmed, she went out to see what else was happening, to count the planes or the stretchers or do whatever it was newspaper reporters were supposed to do in wars. Verity shook her hand and watched her go. Her scent, whatever it was, lingered in the big tent.

Jesus, if I *can smell her,* Verity thought, she *must have smelled me.*

Marguerite Higgins had been out on the tarmac less than an hour when Chesty Puller came along.

"Is that a woman?" he demanded, knowing it was, and furious.

Puller hadn't been told of her arrival, and when he first caught sight of her she was doing interviews just off the airstrip, talking with wounded Marines on stretchers or laid out on the snow, waiting for the next plane.

"There's an active eight-holer over there!" Puller exploded.

Old-school Virginian that he was, Chesty Puller could not accept a woman in close proximity to six or eight Marines sitting on old ammo crates, trousers down around their ankles, smoking and chatting and enjoying a good bowel movement.

"I want her out of here!" General Puller ordered.

Miss Higgins, objecting vigorously, would be aboard the next plane going out. The next day her airstrip interviews with the wounded and the dying ran on page one of the *Herald Tribune.* There was no mention of the eight-holer.

Mouse Izzo, in a philosophical mode, inquired about Chesty. "Does he frigging think women don't shit?"

Verity had watched her climb into the battered C-47, moving well, her rear end surprisingly shapely considering the cold weather gear she wore.

Twenty thousand Marines were trying to get the hell out and would do just about anything for a ride, and here was this New York newspaperwoman flying in and arguing her right to stay.

Elizabeth. Elizabeth would have argued, too.

Tom Verity wondered, if his wife possessed Miss Higgins's professional skills, would she, too, have gone off alone to write about wars?

And concluded, yes, had Elizabeth been a journalist, she very well might. And would have looked good, too, in whatever she wore.

Men had different attitudes toward the war correspondents. Some gave them grudging admiration. They, after all, didn't have to be there. Others hated them. Vultures, circling over the roadside and picking at the dead, earning big money and fame by auditing the casualty rolls.

Verity had his opinion of the correspondents. They saw the war, sworn witnesses to its horror; they took notes, reported as truthfully as they could, chronicling the war. They did everything but fight it.

And why hadn't Tom Verity sent back via Miss Higgins his letters to Kate?

There were the wounded, the dead, and the missing. And then again, some men just vanished.

The sergeants were forever taking roll call, checking lists, keeping after the squad leaders and fire team corporals.

". . . Keep an accurate muster. Only way."

"Yes, S'arnt," the corporals agreed.

That's how it went down the line of command from General Smith to the last sore-assed private in the division. Someone was always supposed to know where you were. That was the standard procedure, the Marine routine, the only way you could keep the division from falling apart, becoming a mob like the army.

Still, men disappeared into the night and the snow and the cold, falling out of the line of march to take a crap and never catching up, or turning the wrong way on patrol to end up tired and cold in a box canyon where you might sit down for a few minutes in the snow to work things out in your head and rest a bit, and then . . .

Or being taken by a long shot, freakishlike, from a sniper. Those Marines, too, might never be found if they were out on the flank.

In the spring, maybe the war would be over, with Red Cross people allowed in, and somewhere up in these hills they'd find bones and teeth and know they were Marines from the belt buckles and the weapons, the metal grommets on the canvas leggings, the web gear and canteens, the tin hats and dog tags and Zippo lighters and leather wallets with photos of the kids or old Mom, the Barlow knives and eyeglass frames and religious medals, the things that didn't rot or rust away under the snow when the men died.

Things that wild animals wouldn't bother eating.

Izzo was cursing steadily, hopping around, first on one foot, then the other, next to the idling jeep.

"What the hell are you . . . ?"

"I was trying to take a leak, Captain."

"Well, go ahead."

"With all these clothes and three pairs of pants and skivvies besides, by the time I get my cock out, Captain, begging the captain's pardon, I forget what the hell I'm going to do with it."

Tate was the philosopher among them: "You know, Captain, it could be worse." Tate was heating a canteen cup of cocoa over a meager fire in the lee of the Jeep, and snow was falling. The cocoa was for drinking and the dregs for his every-other-day shave.

Verity didn't bother to answer, but Izzo, furious, spoke up for him. "Worse, Gunny? It could be worse? You shook or somethin'? Here's the captain with frozen feet, you're shaving in cocoa, and I just pissed down my pants leg because it's too cold to pull out my dick and with you things is just great? Jeeezus."

Tate ignored him. Instead, since it consoled him, he reached back in history to other wars: "Why, at Stalingrad, Captain, the Germans fought all summer and into fall to take the city and then fought all winter to hold it. Half a million Germans fighting half a million Russians in the ruins of a great city."

"That's another thing, Gunny," Izzo put in. "You come from Kansas or someplace. What do you know of cities, Gunny, not like the captain and me, who come from Washington and Philly?"

"And it was cold there, too," Tate went on, unperturbed. "I believe the first snow fell on Stalingrad in October and the Germans finally surrendered in February. Five months of winter fighting, a million men on both sides."

Izzo made a strangled noise of anger. Of disbelief. "You couldn't fight five months in this shit, Gunny, I don't care. Nazis, Commies, even Marines. Men can't do it. They'd just lie down and die first."

Some men had already begun to do just that, Verity knew, lying down at the side of the road in the snow and dying. But he didn't say anything, just watched Tate shaving in his cocoa and tried not to think about his own feet and how Mouse Izzo had just wet his pants.

They got plenty of people off the tarmac at Hagaru, the wounded and frozen and sick, plus the malingerers, but not without cost. Air Force Capt. Lillian M. Keil, a nurse, wrote of those flights in and return flights out: "We were fired upon and often had to land in slush, which was dangerous because the planes could skid. One of the nurses was killed."

Captain Keil said of the Marines who came aboard the evacuation flights out: "Their hands and feet were so frostbitten they could hardly hold a gun or walk. . . . We wore hats and gloves and flight suits with fur-lined jackets. I gave my outer clothing to the shivering GIs that came aboard."

* * *

For all the cold and the perimeter fighting and the occasional Chinese foray into the town itself, the nightly firefights, there was something almost quaint about Hagaru.

The airstrip gives us that, Verity thought. *A link to the other world beyond the hills and the Chinese. In an hour a man could be out of here. In less than an hour a Maggie Higgins could fly in. Then leave as swiftly.*

"You know what it's frigging like, Captain?"

"No, Izzo, what?"

"You ever see *Lost Horizon?*"

"Sure, Shangri-la and Margo growing old and all that."

"Remember the opening? Ronald Colman is the British ambassador or something and the warlords is killing everyone and Brits and Yanks and mandarins are trying to get out just as the warlords overrun the airport and there's only one plane going out—"

"A DC-3, as I recall."

"Right you are, sir, as always," Izzo said, the quintessential enlisted man deferring to the officer, and then, having observed the niceties, resumed his narrative. "And Mr. Colman is shouting at coolies and he's got a handgun—"

"A Webley revolver, as I recall."

"Right again, sir, a Webley." Izzo understood officers. "And there's Mr. Colman ticking off names and shoving people into the plane and whacking at the coolies. And of course all the passengers are Westerners . . . not a slant-eye among them, begging the captain's pardon."

"Go on," Verity said, chillier.

Izzo sensed the rebuke.

"Well, that's just about it, Captain. This frigging airstrip at Hagaru-ri International Airport reminds me of *Lost Horizon* with old Ronald shoving people into the DC-3 and shooting bandits and whacking at coolies and off they go with the warlords coming, bouncing along the runway as the control tower blows up and the huddled masses, like it says on the Statue of Liberty, are all panicking and running out on the tarmac and the plane lifts off just as a million Chinks—"

"I get the picture, Izzo."

Captain Verity repressed a grin. "Hagaru-ri International." That was pretty good. One dirt airstrip gouged out of the snow and the mountain hardscrabble.

Izzo wasn't easily turned off.

"And I mean millions of them. Whoever made that movie, he knew his mob scenes. They didn't burn Atlanta in *Gone with the Wind* better than *Lost Horizon* did mobs of guys in coolie suits running down the tarmac."

"So?" Verity said.

"So the only difference is, instead of Ronald Colman, we got Chesty Puller."

Tate was off with the jeep to look up fellow gunnies, to find out what they knew, and to scrounge or requisition supplies.

"What I can't find Izzo can steal," Tate said. Marines were nothing if not pragmatic.

Verity began seeing the little airstrip at Hagaru as Izzo did, through the eyes of a tired, gallant diplomat shoving people into aeroplanes (and that's how it would have been spelled back then) before the rebels got there to rape the women and behead the men and sell the children into slavery. Hagaru even had its British, real-live Brits, Marine commandos in their ridiculous berets, carrying Sten guns (or were they Bren guns?) and being polite.

"It's funny," Verity said, "even when they're cursing people out, the British sound civilized."

Gunnery Sergeant Tate hadn't seen many Brits before, only a few in prison camp, and he, too, marveled.

"Wouldn't work in the Marine Corps, Captain. No one would take a first sergeant serious if he didn't sound pissed off."

Izzo was making barter arrangements, staring at the British berets.

"I know those hats don't frigging begin to keep your ears warm, but I could use one of them hats."

Verity glanced over at the parked jeep to be sure the precious radio was still in place. To barter you had to give something up to get something, and by now he knew Izzo.

There was something else odd about the Brits. Tate saw it, too.

"They don't look whipped, Captain. Don't look like they got their ass kicked."

Well, they had, as just about everyone had, but they didn't look it. Verity knew exactly what Tate was saying. The British Royal Marine Commandos still looked like soldiers.

You couldn't say that about many of the American army outfits coming through and only a few of the ROKs.

The Marines were sore about it.

"The ROKs is just shit." You heard that over and over. Their officers ran even before the men, most of them, and when an officer stood and tried to hold his men, to keep them in position, they ran right over him, sometimes clubbing him to death as they went. Few of the ROKs had weapons; they'd been thrown away. And it was their damned country, wasn't it?

The American army wasn't that bad. But the Marines kept having to pull unwounded, able-bodied soldiers out of the queues of wounded waiting to be airlifted out. A few Marines tried that stunt, too, but only once. Some of the soldiers went back again and again. These were the men of the Seventh Army Division. Their division had been broken east of the Chosin and they were the worst. A Marine surgeon reported that if the soldiers just lay down on a stretcher and groaned they would eventually be carried to a plane. One day more than nine hundred "wounded" were flown out of Hagaru. The Marines reckoned maybe seven hundred were legitimate, the rest malingerers.

By December 5 some forty-three hundred casualties, real and imagined, had been airlifted out.

Verity was asked for dinner that night by General Smith. There were maybe a dozen officers in a big tent, and as a captain he was junior in rank. It didn't stop Oliver Smith from sounding off, having a young captain there. It was pretty comfortable inside the tent, warm, and the food, too, was hot. It was rations, but they were hot.

"Ned Almond didn't want me to build this airstrip," General Smith said. "He raised hell. 'Waste of time and effort and energy,' he told me. So I stopped telling him about the airstrip and just built it."

Smith was irate about the performance of American army troops.

"Most of them just threw away their weapons. Then they tried to sneak aboard the medical evacuation planes. And now that they're here, they refuse to put up tents or organize latrines or even feed themselves. Lazy, undisciplined mob, that's what they are. They aren't even soldiers."

Among the enlisted Marines, who saw the army troops up close, General Smith's criticism would have been taken as understatement.

Verity felt so good after a hot meal and listening to Smith blackguarding the army that when the smoking lamp was lighted after dinner he pulled out a Havana cigar and, rather showily, smoked it with enormous pleasure before the envious, all of them officers who outranked him.

"You shouldn't, Captain; you really shouldn't," Tate said when Verity got back and told the gunny.

"Well, it's one of the advantages of being a reserve, Gunny. A career man like you'd be different."

"Yessir," Tate said, enjoying the thought of lighting a cigar in front of the commanding officer of the First Marine Division. But disapproving, still, the way regulars always disapproved, at least mildly, of reservists.

The end of May, the same Saturday they ran the Kentucky Derby, was the Virginia Gold Cup in Warrenton, and Tom and Elizabeth Verity drove down for it on Friday, getting there in time for the Gold Cup Ball the night before.

"I wish you could ride, Tommie," she said. "Maybe you could take lessons."

"I'd just fall off. Or the horse would fall on me. And what does a horse weigh?"

"A thousand pounds, maybe twelve hundred."

"Well, I won't do it. And what do you care anyway?"

"If you could ride, then I could get you one of those wonderful pink coats to wear at the dance, instead of your stuffy dinner jacket."

The "pink" coats were red, as far as Verity could tell, but everyone called them pink and only men who rode in one of the local hunts were permitted to wear them and, he had to admit, they did look dashing.

The next day it was sunny and there were bookmakers taking bets and chalking them up on portable blackboards and the horses ran around for four miles jumping fences and some of them falling, and people sat on the roofs of the cars to see and the Veritys had their little MG and they met Scotty Reston of the *New York Times,* who lived nearby, and everyone drank a lot and cheered the horses and Elizabeth's nose got sunburned in the early spring sunshine and she looked very wonderful with her red nose.

They stayed in a country inn with a big bed and drove back home to Georgetown Sunday, and Elizabeth said while they drove and her hair streamed out in the wind, "Let's have another baby, Tommie."

"Just one?"

"Well, one at a time."

With the rifle companies moved up into the hills establishing a perimeter, Hagaru-ri itself was defended by an odd lot of rear-echelon people.

At Yudam-ni the last line of resistance in the town center had been a squad of South Korean policemen with two machine guns. Here the mix was somewhat better organized, not quite as droll.

"Verity, you've had a rifle platoon before, haven't you?"

"Yessir, Okinawa, long time ago."

The ops officer, a major, was a hard man. "Like riding a bike. You never forget how."

"Yeah, well, I'm supposed to be here translating Chinese radio traffic for Division. I—" He was damned if he'd volunteer. Yudam-ni had been different, a last minute desperation. He'd had little choice.

"And I'm supposed to be sitting in a warm tent drawing plans on acetate overlays, Captain. When the Chinese get inside the perimeter you and me and General Oliver himself Smith are going to be playing riflemen like that asshole General Dean down by the Naktong last summer."

Verity didn't say anything. It was an argument he couldn't win, and anyway, he saw the merit in it. At Yudam-ni he'd played rifleman; platoon leader was a promotion.

"Just point me in the right direction, Major."

The ops officer smiled. "Good. We're pulling a provisional rifle company together from truck drivers and bandsmen and radio operators and cooks and engineers and company clerks and whatever the hell else we got. You have a good NCO?"

"A gunny. Named Tate. Good man."

"Then he's your platoon sergeant. Pick out the squad leaders yourself. I wouldn't be particular whether they're sergeants or corporals or PFCs. Just pick your own and let them run with it."

"I'll pick riflemen if I can find any."

"Makes sense." The major was feeling better about this Verity already.

Last light would be around five in the afternoon. A full colonel whose name Verity never got mustered the makeshift company on the street in front of where Smith had made his divisional HQ and personal quarters as well. There were maybe one hundred and fifty enlisted men, a dozen or so officers. Above the barked orders they could hear an occasional shot echoing down from the hills. There was no snow, but the mercury was falling fast.

"Zero already," someone muttered. Zero and not yet dark.

"How do they look to you, Gunny?" Verity asked. He trusted Tate's judgment on the men more than his own. Tate was closer to combat.

Tate sort of wiggled his hand, palm down and flat. "They're Marines, Captain. About all I can say."

Bandsmen. Motor transport drivers. Clerks. And we got the Chinese army coming for dinner. That was what Tate was thinking. But Marine gunnery sergeants do not indulge themselves.

"Well, they're what we've got," Verity said, remembering fondly his platoon on Okinawa.

He reverted to his staff role during an officers' meeting called by Oliver Smith at 8:00 P.M. "We think they'll hit the perimeter about eleven tonight," the commanding general said. "We had counter-intelligence people out there all day. It's quite extraordinary. Either our people are very persuasive or the Chinese just talk too much. But that's what they said. They'll hit our rifle companies in the hills about eleven. No information as to whether they'll come through here as well."

Verity, standing in the semicircle of officers around Smith, noticed the general was wearing both a shoulder holster and an automatic shoved into the waist of his trousers.

It was weird walking back through the darkened streets of the little town toward the hut he shared with Izzo and Tate, the dry, packed snow crunching under his boots, thinking about General Smith and his two guns. That wasn't Georgie Patton bullshit with ivory-handled revolvers; this was because Smith knew Chinese soldiers might be coming through here later that night, that the general himself might be not only commanding a division of twenty thousand men but also fighting for his own life. It sobered you.

"Hey, Captain, some sergeant came by. Said I've been reassigned to some provisional platoon."

Izzo disliked being told what to do. For once, Verity humored him.

"Ignore it, Izzo. You're assigned to Gunny and me. Wherever we go, you come right along."

"That's right, Izzo, and don't be bashful." Tate delivered that line with a dry laugh. The notion of a bashful Izzo amused him.

Verity was glad the two men were still capable of resentment and humor. The Chinese army was about to come out of the hills, and they weren't concerned with the details. Verity called his three squad leaders up and deployed his platoon. That part was easy.

Hope to hell I'm as cool as they are when the shooting starts, he thought.

Verity remembered being afraid in the War but doing the work regardless. Then he was a kid. Now he was thirty; now he had sense.

Izzo took the first watch of an hour, Tate the second. Verity was to take the third, at midnight. But by eleven-fifteen everyone was awake.

The Chinese army was coming in.

At midnight, precisely, they were there. They seemed to be coming into the town from every direction.

But they can't! Verity told himself, crouching behind sandbags. There were blocking positions out there. They couldn't have gotten through *every*where.

Still, they had, blowing bugles and trilling sweet, strange music on flutes.

Why don't their lips freeze to metal? men wondered.

A terrible moonlit serenade, a nightmare scene, a lunatic's delight.

Verity had a rifle and he fired it over and over into the darkness at the looming, screaming shapes, a reasonable, rational American college professor in a war only shrinks might understand.

That night again the Chinese penetrated to Hagaru center before being thrown back. Why were they fighting so hard for this nothing place? Why were they so ready to die?

Once again, Tate and Izzo and Verity had been lucky. All round them men had been hit and gone down. Yet all three of them were there in the dawn, able to flex cold, cramped limbs and stand. It wasn't logical to think that their luck would hold.

Especially after what happened toward dawn when Marines, having beaten down yet another wave of attacking Chinese, rose up spontaneously and without orders, to run at the remaining Chinese, firing and shouting and jabbing and slashing with their bayonets and clubbing them with rifle butts as, in a manic, frenzied rush, like surf sweeping up on a beach, they drove the Chinese before them, back out of the town and up into the foothills.

Verity, swept up in madness, ran with them, then paused at last, bent retching over his rifle, attempting to catch his breath and asking himself, *Now what the hell was* that *all about?*

"And where is Poppy now, Madame?"

"In the mountains, Kate."

"The Alps?"

"Oh, no, smaller, meaner mountains. But with much snow."

The nanny had been following the war communiqués in the *Washington Post* and on the radio. Kate was provided a somewhat bowdlerized version.

"Yes, much snow. Very deep and white."

"Oh," said Captain Verity's daughter. "I hope they have sleds."

CHAPTER THIRTEEN

It was as if the five years of civilization since Okinawa had never happened, Verity had never gone back to Yale . . . , had never met Elizabeth or had a child named Kate.

Now when he saw the Marines lying stiff and dead by the side of the road . . . he walked by as casually as men pass newstands where no headline catches their eye.

Plane after plane took off from the meager airstrip of Hagaru-ri in a gust of prop-driven snow and brown earth. Another four thousand men were flown out in two days, wounded, frozen, malingerers, factotums, brass, correspondents. Thomas Verity watched them go. Tate knew what the captain was thinking but said nothing.

Izzo, less sensitive, said aloud, "Jeez, Captain, we oughta be on one of them planes, seeing that we done our job so good."

"Mouse."

"Yes, Gunny?"

"Go see if you can scrounge some gas for the jeep."

"Gunny, I already told you, they don't got—"

"Gas, Izzo. And now!"

Frigging Marine Corps!

As they continued the evacuation by air, General Smith sent for Verity. Smith's adjutant, a colonel, was there. But Smith spoke.

"Captain, you've done a fine job for us. We've had more hard intelligence on the CCF than any other division in Tenth Corps. I think more than MacArthur himself had. Some of what you brought in may have saved the Fifth Marines at Yudam-ni. Maybe the entire division. You kept bringing in Chinese unit identification numbers, names of their commanding officers. No one else was getting us that stuff in such detail. Maybe a few of the brethren around here [he permitted himself a smile] were dubious at first. But you sold them. You made us believers. Job well done, as they say, Captain. Job well done. . . ."

"Thank you, sir. My gunnery sergeant and driver shared the work and—"

"Yes, yes, give us their names. They'll be suitably recognized."

Verity felt the rebuke, stiffened, and said, "Aye-aye, sir." The tent had gone cold.

General Smith smoked a pipe. And like the odd academic Verity knew, the general used it as a prop when he found it difficult to turn a phrase or answer a pointed question. Or tell a man he'd been lied to.

"Captain, I know promises were made. You were sent here to do a listening job on radio and report your finds. You did. Magnificently."

Tom Verity saw it coming. He should have murmured the conventional, "Thank you, sir." But didn't.

"And that job is over. So you think you ought to be on one of those planes heading out. You think you're getting screwed."

This time he couldn't resist.

"Yes sir, General, that's what I think." He was remembering Christmas promises to Kate.

Oliver Smith recoiled, almost as if he'd been cursed out. Verity was not going to make this easy for him. Then, as a good general should, Smith stiffened.

The hell with you, mister. You're going to be screwed. And you're going to stand there and take it.

The general did not say any of this but went on, under control, pipe between clenched teeth, biting into the stem. Occasionally Smith lost pipes this way, biting right through. When he had to do things he hated to do and did them anyway.

"Well, I can't send out an able-bodied officer with combat experience who knows how to fight and who also speaks Chinese. Can't do it. We'll need you to interrogate prisoners and more. You might end up commanding a rifle company. A battalion, even. We're short of officers now and losing more every day. I can't put you on one of those planes, Verity. And I won't."

Tom's knees sort of sagged. *I've just heard my death sentence,* he thought.

"No, sir," he said dully, empty by now even of anger or righteous indignation.

Smith and his adjutant, the colonel, waited for Verity to say more. He wasn't going to—what good did it do?—and then, sensing a last chance, he did. "When they came for me in Washington, General, came to my house, they told me flat out from the start, 'Look, you're unique. You're the only guy we have who speaks all these dialects, who understands this stuff.' I kept saying, 'No, there are other people like me. Some of them better. I'll give you their goddamn names.' "

Verity looked up at Smith, tall, glacial. Oliver Smith had twenty thousand men in his command. And on his conscience, if generals had consciences. His face was flat and unmoved. In a giddy instant, Verity thought, *Maybe that's why they pay generals more. Because they have faces that don't show pain. Or shame.*

Immediately he regretted this. Smith was a decent man and a good officer, and he was in a hell of a difficult position. Getting Verity here hadn't been Oliver Smith's notion.

But it was Oliver Smith who now represented the Marine Corps, not that smooth colonel in Washington. It was Smith who would decide if Verity might live. Or die. Smith who could send him home or keep him here, in this frozen hell. In a silly, vagrant thought, Verity wanted to tell the general, "Look, Maggie Higgins flies in and out every day. Just let me go along with her next time. I'll brief her, tell her wonderful stories."

He said nothing. Though he meant it. He would kiss Smith's feet. Or his ass. To get out of here alive.

Smith, seeing he'd won, permitted a grim smile. "We might even need you to palaver a bit, with the Chinese, I mean."

"Palaver?" Verity wasn't thinking very crisply right now. He was thinking of Kate. And of promises of Paris, of Pere Noel.

"Yes. Palaver. In case the Chinese army decides we've surrounded them and they want to capitulate. . . ."

It was General Smith's little joke, and he waited, briefly, for a laugh.

"Yes, sir," Verity said, acknowledging the reality of his situation but not sharing in the amusement. Not one bit!

Smith, who had a temper, stood up.

"All right, Captain, you can go now."

"Aye-aye, sir."

Verity started to say something more but didn't. Smith was silent, his face set. The interview was over. Verity and the adjutant walked from the tent together.

"Verity."

"Sir?"

"You know," the colonel said, his voice hard, righteously angered that a lousy captain had annoyed the boss, "maybe you never were all that unique, Verity. Maybe the Marine Corps had three or four other men doing exactly the same job you were doing on the Chinks. And we took cross-bearings, compared their reports with yours. Ever think of *that*, Mister?"

Verity couldn't help it; his mouth fell open.

Had they been lying the whole time, right from that day in Henderson Hall? It wasn't desperate need that took him from Kate; it was a goddamned Marine lie! Or was this bastard lying *now?* Just rubbing it in because he'd given the general a hard time?

Verity's eyes began to fill and he pushed past the colonel and out. The Marine sentry saluted as he went by.

Friggin' officers, the sentry told himself, *don't bother to salute back. Friggin' staff.*

It was a lousy job pulling sentry duty at the general's tent. Dull, boring duty. Nothing ever happened. You just stood around in the cold trying to look sharp and you saluted people coming and going and acting as if important things were happening, and nothing ever did.

Right across the entire front American officers were breaking down or snarling in defiance.

At Kunu-ri in the west, in I Corps, Lt. Col. Melvin Blair, commanding the Third Battalion Twenty-fourth Infantry, fled the field. Colonel Blair blamed his black troops, claiming they said "Bugout Boogie" was their official regimental ditty.

The black soldiers said their colonel ran first and they only followed.

The commanding general of the Second Army Division, Gen. "Dutch" Keiser, was fired when his division crumbled and broke.

Giving Keiser the bad news, a staff officer assured him, "General Walker will take care of you with a job around headquarters."

"Dutch" Keiser responded, "Tell General Walker to shove his job up his ass."

Robert B. McClure, who replaced Keiser as division commander, promptly admitted to an aide that he was too old for the job and had not expected to ever again lead troops in combat.

"I can only brace myself by hitting the bottle," General McClure explained. "I'll be doing a lot of drinking."

In his first order to this famous division of fifteen thousand soldiers, McClure ordered that every man grow a beard.

A runner caught up with them just south of Hagaru past the airstrip. He was in a jeep and had been stopping every jeep he passed.

"Captain Verity?"

"Yes."

"Dispatch for you, sir."

It was very brief and from Smith: "Captain, General Puller will leave Hagaru last in line of march and his regiment will guard my rear. Please join him now. Your Chinese may be of help to him."

It was signed "Oliver Smith," no rank or wax seals or anything.

Verity felt his stomach fall. Just a few inches, but it definitely fell. He let Tate read the message and then Izzo. After all, it involved them, too.

Izzo exhaled. "And I thought we were outta here."

Tate didn't say anything. It wasn't in the nature of gunnery sergeants to show emotion at such times. Verity swallowed disappointment, resentment. The sense that generals had ways of getting back a man.

"Well, we're not 'outta here.' So let's go find Chesty Puller."

They U-turned the jeep to ride the shoulder back north, slowly, against the flow of traffic, of trucks and artillery pieces and tanks and jeeps, Marines marching in column, some soldiers doing that as well but most not, and what could even in kindness only be called mobs of South Korean soldiers slogging along, all headed south, all getting as much distance between themselves and the Chosin Reservoir as they could.

For the first time, now that he was no longer part of but facing the line of march, Verity could see the retreat for what it was, mile after mile of men.

He didn't know how far back it stretched. Beyond Hagaru, surely, up west toward the reservoir. If Puller's First Regiment was the rear guard for Smith's division, there was someone back there behind Puller, watching out for his ass. There was always, Verity concluded, someone worse off than you, some last platoon, last squad, last rifleman cagily looking over his shoulder.

Jesus, but they looked terrible, the troops coming south from the reservoir. The Marines looked bad enough, shivering and bearded, but they still marched, carried weapons, looked about them alertly. Looked for someone to kill. The army troops just walked. They'd thrown away everything, not only their rifles but also their web belts and packs and canteens and steel helmets. Not their sleeping bags. A night in the open without a bag would kill a man. Even the Seventh Division men knew that. And the ROKs looked worse than the American soldiers.

As they drove north, back from where they'd come, there were still Marines with sufficient energy to hassle them: "Hey, Cap'n, that way's Peking, y'know."

Verity grinned and waved a mittened hand. Izzo told them to go frig themselves. Tate said nothing but scanned the ridgelines on both flanks, keeping watch. He had the BAR cradled and ready. Occasionally he could see a Marine patrol up there, paralleling the line of the march, watching over its flanks so that the Chinese couldn't come in and hit them from the high ground and pinch off the road. He nudged Verity's arm, nodding toward the ridges.

"Good to see that, Captain. With all that happened and the

beating they took, they've still got people out patrolling, nice and proper."

Tate took a professional's satisfaction in good soldiering.

They were back in Hagaru-ri by about noon. A Marine lieutenant was watching a sergeant setting up three 60mm mortars on the margin of the airstrip.

"Where's Puller?"

"Back there, Captain. Maybe a mile. He's got a big tent."

Puller in a tent. That didn't sound right. Men still talked of how he gave his parka away that first night of the march north. The Puller legend wasn't yet complete, not with stories like that.

There was only one road through the town and it was impossible to miss the regimental CP, and when Verity saw a big tent he told Izzo to pull over. A sentry stopped Verity at the entrance.

"General Smith ordered me to report to General Puller."

The Marine looked at the piece of paper and saluted. Coming out of the midday light it was all gloom inside the tent, and for an instant Verity couldn't see.

Someone said, "Yes?"

"Captain Verity, reporting as ordered to General Puller." He handed over the single sheet of paper, by now smudged and starting to curl at the edges. His eyes were adjusting and he could see Puller, leaning over a sort of table, a pipe in his teeth, poking a gloved finger at a map. He looked up at Verity from under the bill of his fatigue cap.

"What do you want?"

"Captain Verity. General Smith told me to join you. I'm the guy who speaks Chinese."

"Oh, do you?" Puller was notorious for favoring old sergeants over young officers and rarely masked disdain.

The general paused, then rattled off some Chinese.

"No, I don't think it's going to rain, General," Verity responded, also in Chinese.

Puller's flat mouth broke into a grin. "Come over here, old man; tell me where you learned your Chinese. You're too young to have served there prewar. Not an old China hand."

"Nosir. I was born there. Lived in China until I was fifteen."

"What'd you do then?"

"My parents sent me to the States for school."

"What school?"

"Hotchkiss. It's in—"

"I know where it is. You attend college?"

"Yale."

"My, my, my, a Yale man among us. This regiment is twice honored. They assign us the rear guard and send us a Yale man."

Verity didn't say anything, but the other officers—there might have been eight or ten of them—laughed. They were Puller's staff; they knew the cues. He didn't and just stood there. Puller continued his little catechism.

"Regular?"

"No, General, reserve officer."

"Intelligence?"

"Nosir, 0-three-0-two." That was the military occupation specialty number for experienced infantry officer.

"Good," Puller said. He liked 0302s. "Where'd you serve? Pusan?"

"No, General, I just got here last month. I was on Guadalcanal and later Okinawa. After the war, North China for a time."

"What'd you do on the 'Canal?"

"Carried a rifle. I was just out of Parris Island boot camp."

"Good. What about Okinawa?"

"I was commissioned by then. I had a rifle platoon, then a rifle company."

Puller smiled, a real smile this time, the pipe still there.

"Verity. That means 'truth,' doesn't it? Yes, it does. I know that much Latin. Well, Captain Verity, you tell the truth and we'll get along just fine. This meeting's just about over and we're opening this tent to the troops to warm up. Come by about four for dinner, Captain. I'd like to hear more about you and China. And your adventures at Yale."

"Aye-aye, sir," Verity said.

"Too bad there won't be wine. Then we could see if it's true about your name, you know, 'in vino, veritas.' "

"Yes, sir," Verity said, a bit stupefied that Chesty Puller was making sport.

"Though from what I've noticed in a lifetime," Puller continued, "most of what you get 'in vino' is boasts and other rot."

"Yes, sir."

"Hold up here."

Chesty Puller was out of the jeep before it stopped rolling, moving quickly for a man his age and so bundled up.

A six-by truck stalled in traffic panted a few yards away. Puller looked up at the cab.

"What about these headlights, old man?"

"Well, sir . . ."

There was supposed to be night discipline, no driving with headlights.

"You have a wrench up there, a hammer, old man?"

"Yessir," the driver said, relieved Puller only wanted to borrow a tool and not make trouble. Sometimes these old officers got crazy.

"Good," Puller said, taking the wrench when it was handed down and circling briskly to the front of the truck, where he smashed first one and then the other headlight.

"Here's your wrench, old man," he said mildly, handing the tool back up.

"Yessir," the driver said, stunned.

That, too, was Puller, not taking names and numbers and writing people up, just taking direct action.

Izzo was complaining. Tate was having little of it. But he was being tolerant, trying to improve the young man's spirit, to elevate his morale.

"But being the rear guards, Gunny, that's a stinking job. Why us? Why not give it to someone else?"

"Marines have to do it, Izzo. You couldn't give an army outfit responsibility for keeping the Chinese off your ass, could you?"

"No, but there's other regiments. I think Puller puts in for these things. He sends in applications."

"Maybe. But whatever regiment pulled the duty, Captain Verity was going to go with 'em. And you and me."

"Yeah," Izzo said, glum.

"Anyway, cheer up. It's an honor to be rear guards. Remember Marshal Ney?"

"Which side's he on?"

"He was Napoléon's best general. French. Marshal Ney was always up front, always leading the old charge. And then, later on, when Napoléon lost the occasional away game, they put Marshal Ney and his men in the back there as the rear guard. It was Ney fought his way all the way back from Moscow in winter and saved the army."

"Jesus," Izzo said, "wasn't he the fortunate one. Just like frigging us."

No one swaggered anymore; no one strutted.

It was Guadalcanal after the bad fighting at the Tenaru River in the fever months that Verity first saw Marines lose their swagger. It struck him Marines at the 'Canal shuffled along like the unemployed from the Dearborn auto plants that he saw lined up at the soup kitchens of 1938.

Now, in the dreadful miles along that road south from Chosin, the Marines had again lost it, that small, defining swagger.

Occasionally a Marine would look into the rearview mirror of a truck and not recognize the face he saw there. Some officers tried to get their men to shave. Puller was one of those.

"If there's a little hot coffee left in the canteen cup in the morning, use that. Just as good as shaving cream and hot towels, everything but the shoe shine and the lilac water." Gunny Tate agreed. But he was a gunnery sergeant and an exception.

Most men didn't shave. Their skin was red and chapped and pocked with blackheads and angry pimples and caked with soot from the fires, when they had them, and their eyes were sunken from lack of sleep and from staring at the snow by day and through the blackness of the night. Maybe it was better they didn't shave. Hair helped flesh keep from freezing and hid the filth and grime and skin eruptions.

In the cold, it was difficult to urinate. The testicles drew up into the body to retain warmth and the penis shriveled and shrank, and when a man stepped to the side of the road it was tough to find his cock inside all the layers of stinking clothes and when he did and pulled it out, the urine didn't always come right away, not in the cold, and when it finally did, the way the penis was shrunken and the balls drawn up, he usually pissed all over himself, as poor Izzo had done, inside his trousers and down the front of them outside, so you always knew when a man had just taken a leak, from the yellow stains and the scum of yellow ice down his leg.

You were always pissing on yourself, no matter how soldierly and neat you tried to be.

Men died.

Verity was surprised to realize he wasn't shocked. It was as if the five years of civilization since Okinawa had never happened, he had never gone back to Yale to graduate, hadn't studied at Harvard, had never met Elizabeth or had a child named Kate.

Now when he saw the Marines lying stiff and dead by the side of the road after a minor skirmish to clear a roadblock, he walked by them as casually as men pass newsstands where no headline catches their eye.

Tate remarked on it.

"When they're froze like this, it's different, Captain. This summer on the Naktong down there it was hot as hell. Inchon and Seoul, it sure wasn't cold. The dead stink; they swell up; they look . . . dead. I never saw dead men on ice before except at funerals back home. It's like the mortician came in with the rouge and the pancake makeup and tidied them up a bit. I know they're dead; they just don't look like dead Marines used to look. . . ."

Verity knew what he meant. There were no maggots working at the dead, no flies buzzing, no slimy things coming right up out of the earth to take possession. Dead was dead. But still . . .

Izzo took a more pragmatic tack.

"Seems a shame to bury good parkas, Captain. And I seen a stiff back there with them new thermal boots."

Verity shook his head. "We're not going to strip our own dead, Izzo."

Word came down that except for drivers, all able-bodied men were to walk out to the sea.

"Suits me," said Tate, who, like Verity, was already walking. You didn't get as cold that way. And with ice and snow and the road surfaces and the inevitable breakdowns, it was no strain keeping up. Verity, who had a good map, reckoned on average they were moving at about a quarter-mile an hour.

"At that rate, Captain," Tate said, "figuring sixty-eight from Yudam-ni and that we march twelve hours a day, we're going to be out here for about three weeks."

"Jesus," Izzo said, "I can't take three weeks of this frigging stuff."

"Cheer up, Izzo," Verity said. "Think of the gas mileage you're getting."

He didn't know quite why, but Verity seemed to have thrown off the depression of a few days earlier, at what Smith had done to him. Maybe it was because they were a few miles, another couple of days, closer to the sea.

If we can just get to Hamhung, he thought. *If we can get there, we're OK. We get there, we live.* Staying alive was becoming an obsession, a full-time job, and not only with Tom Verity.

Men were saved by their sleeping bags and sometimes died because of them. The standard-issue down bag, ironically coffin-shaped, could keep a man alive lying in the snow all night without a fire or tent in temperatures below zero. It was better if he had a rubber air mattress underneath, but the bag kept him alive.

The rule was you zipped the bag all the way up, right under your chin. This wasn't some arcane Marine fetish for uniformity and neatness; it was how the bag was designed, so that when zipped all the way it could be burst open instantly in an emergency by the man inside shoving upward with both arms. If it was zipped only part the way up, one hand had to be extended to the outside to unzip the bag all the way down. That took time; it could also take your life.

That first night of November 27 when the Chinese came up on Hill 1240 and other hills against the Seventh Marines, men died in their bags before they ever had a chance to get out and fight. On the morning of the twenty-eighth in one platoon they found five Marines still in their bags on the ridgeline, dead of bullet wounds or bayonet thrusts.

"They really are coffins," Marines complained. "I'm sitting up tonight. Hell with it."

"Sure," the NCOs said sourly. "That's awful smart. By two in the morning you'll be dead of cold and the Chinks won't be able to do nothing to you."

"Well, I . . ."

"Zip the bag like you was told and you might live through another night and not freeze either. If you're lucky."

There were the Chinese. There was the cold. One as inexorable, as unforgiving, as deadly, as the other.

Wolfe wrote about "Time and the River," "the Web and the Rock." If he lived, Verity thought he might turn to literary composition. "Of the Chinese and the Cold." It was a splendid title. Good as Thomas Wolfe's. If only he could fashion a plot. How jealous would his colleagues in the commons room be with their "publish or perish" mind-set. There was consolation in such fantasies.

On still nights without cloud and with all this snow cover, the earth's heat simply oozed away at dark into the unfathomable depths of the void. How far out did it go? How distant was the Milky Way?

The Chinese were more easily measured. They were only men. And the cold killed them as it did Marines.

"Little bastards, ain't they?" an enlisted man remarked on seeing his first Chinese dead and prisoners. Well, the Japanese were little, too, and bastards. They learned that soon enough. Verity supposed the Mongols had been small, cavalrymen on ponies. But Genghis Khan did all right. So did Attila and his Huns. Were they little bastards as well?

But you could fight men. That was a trade the Marines knew. Be stronger, more clever, cagier, better armed, and you won. They'd won against the Japs; there was no reason they couldn't defeat the Chinese. They might even have taken old Genghis and the Mongols, Attila and his boys on horseback. Being well armed and clever didn't help much against the cold. When you got right down to it, there wasn't a hell of a lot anyone could do up here in these mountains in cold like this. You built fires and found shelter or you died.

Colonel Santee was a regular, and something of a classicist.

"It is not unknown," Santee was fond of informing people, "for a regular Marine officer to be widely and even deeply schooled in matters academic beyond the science and art of war."

He was a light colonel now and commanded a battalion. Verity enjoyed him; others thought him a bore and parodied his pompous language.

"The present situation," Santee was going on now in a warming tent large enough for a platoon, "reminds me of nothing more or less than Xenophon and the ten thousand. The parallels are inescapable. All one need do is ponder."

"That's what I do best, Colonel, ponder. I ponder all the time."

This was Major Peal, a Georgia cracker and somewhat dense. He could be ignored. The rest were too pleased to be inside and warm to spoil the moment with argument.

"And just who was Xenophon and who played the ten thousand?" someone else asked.

Verity was vague on the details. Greeks, he recalled, and at war with Persia. Beyond that, little. So he listened to Santee.

"It seems that about 360 or 365 B.C. a mercenary army, employed by Athens, or it may have been Sparta, I tend to confuse the city-states on occasion, invaded Persia, intent on seizing power from Cyrus the Great. The army numbered about ten thousand troops and was led by Xenophon, not only a soldier but a poet. And a good one. But with Xenophon and the lads well inside Persia, and doing nicely, Cyrus sprung a trap. Very much like what old Mao did up here—"

"Well, that's a hell of a yarn, Santee. Might make a movie, too, if you could get John Wayne or someone to play whatsisname—"

"Xenophon. With an X," Santee responded, not at all annoyed. He was accustomed to being ragged. "And you're right about its cinematic possibilities. But more to the point, consider the similarities in Xenophon's account, which he entitled, incidentally, the 'Anabasis,' which means—"

"Oh, for chrissakes," someone muttered near one of the space heaters, and Santee caught the note of impatience.

". . . not that it matters," he went on. "What is striking is how Xenophon and his ten thousand got out of Persia, fighting rear guard actions all the way, leapfrogging units, bulling through roadblocks and ambushes, fighting off a Persian army many times their size and doing it in enemy territory, all the while heading for the sea, the Aegean, in their case. Remarkably like what we're attempting to do here."

"Attempting?" It was marvelous how objective a scholar could be, Verity thought, as if their predicament were for Santee simply an abstraction in a book and not a life-and-death matter.

Some enlisted men and senior NCOs had gathered round, enjoying listening to officers insulting each other.

"And how'd the mercenaries make out, Colonel? They ever get to the sea?"

Santee looked blissful. "Why, yes, they did, and gazed again on the Aegean and ancient Hellas, which as you know is Greek for, well, for . . . Greece."

"Oh, Jesus, who wound him up?"

Let them argue. Verity didn't give a damn. He was in a warming tent. He didn't even mind the pain of frozen joints, of knuckles and toes thawing. When they were frozen, the pain was dull; when you warmed, it was like hot needles. But he didn't mind.

Oh, God, let me stay here and not have to go out again in the cold, he thought.

*   *   *

Then he remembered Tate and Izzo, who were still with the jeep, and he tugged on mittens and hat and parka tight around him and went reluctantly to the entrance of the tent and into the snow, back to his men.

"Captain, what do you know of the Donner party?"

Verity, numb, did not understand. "The what party?"

"The Donner party. You know, the people who froze to death in the Donner Pass trying to get to California for the gold rush or something."

"Oh, yeah," Verity said. He didn't remember much.

"Didn't they eat one another?" Tate asked.

Izzo couldn't resist: "Jesus, Captain, with all respect, I don't think we frigging need that!"

"Sorry, Izzo."

Tate was sorry, too, that he had brought it up. "Forget it, Izzo, it was a long time ago. Not modern times like this."

"Well, I frigging hope so. Eating people! We don't need that shit."

The snow fell more heavily and the road was once again blocked.

"Well, Tom, and how are you keeping?"

This was Mack, whom he knew from Okinawa and North China and now had a battalion.

"Cold, like everyone else, Mack. But OK. You?"

"I wish we were out of here, Tom. I don't like this narrow road. There's a scary feeling to it that we'd better hurry up or be left behind."

"I know what you mean."

"And why are you here, a staff grandee of some sort? You ought to be back at Hungnam having a bourbon and branch water and waiting for the poor infantry."

"I'm here because I was sent."

"Not a volunteer?"

"Mack, when did I ever volunteer?"

The trucks and the jeeps and the occasional tank moved slowly past and the men, on their frozen feet, even slower. There were Marines hanging onto every tank, every truck, and there were jeeps with six or seven men piled aboard. These were supposed to be the worst cases of frostbite, but how did you know? There were no corpsmen to check, and even if there were, how could you pry the boots off a man to examine his feet out here in the cold, and even if you could, how did you get the boots back on those swollen feet? Anyone who could was hitching a ride, even a few officers, though Litzenberg and Murray and, most quotably, Puller, had told their officers to walk. They'd changed orders again; now the men could ride. Not the able-bodied officers.

"As long as there's a Marine walking, my officers walk," Puller growled, biting down on a stubby unlit pipe.

Puller himself walked, fifty-two years old.

Steep hills and ridgelines bordered the road, giving it that claustrophobic feeling Mack had talked about. And to guard their flanks the Marines had to put men up there, on the ridgelines and patrolling the hills. Else the road could be shut down by a few Chinese with a mortar and a couple of machine guns, else the column could be ambushed. It was hard enough slogging along the frozen road from Hagaru-ri; being sent out to patrol the ridgelines a thousand feet higher was asking what some men could no longer do.

"I lost a patrol yesterday, Tom. Sent them out on the flank, maybe fifteen hundred feet up. They ran into some Chinks. We could hear the firefight. Then it was over. It had taken them four hours to climb up there through deep snow and there was no way I was going to send another squad, another platoon. I'd just lose them, too. Nice boy, the patrol leader I sent. Big, husky kid from Connecticut. Said he loved the look of this country, reminded him of New England. Well, he's part of it now, that or a prisoner."

"I wouldn't like to be a prisoner, Mack."

"Nor I, Tom. But I don't brood on it."

Mack was a southerner, but he seemed to take the cold pretty well and moved as if his feet were still OK.

But as the van of his battalion passed, three more tanks came by, the treads clanking metallic and crunching in the snow, and there were no Marines riding on these, only bodies, stacked crossways and lashed on with rope, maybe a half-dozen to each tank.

As they passed, Verity heard a Marine remark, very flat and not emotional, "At least they're trying to get the stiffs out. I'd like them to get me out if I was a stiff and not just leave me here."

"Shit, you wouldn't know the difference, pal."

Verity listened to their conversation and that of other Marines and then got started himself. You chilled pretty fast when you stopped moving.

There was no entertainment. Beyond talk. Or shooting China-men. Over smokes or at the fire, sometimes in the jeep when the column stalled, Izzo would get Tate talking about home, about Kansas, but being careful not to tell him again how foolish a name Engine was for a town.

"Jesse James? Was he still alive when you was a kid, Gunny?"

"Long dead. Him and brother Frank both, and Quantrill as well."

"I seen the movie. Tyrone Power was Jesse and Henry Fonda was Frank."

"Yes," Tate said, "not historically very accurate."

"But they shot him, Jesse, didn't they? Or was that just Holly-wood?"

"No, a man named Bob Ford shot Jesse. Shot him in the back. Never would have taken him in a fair fight. Jesse was hiding out. Called himself Howard. They wrote a poem about it."

"No shit?"

Tate regarded Izzo disdainfully. "Yes, they did, an actual poem. It ends like this: 'And that dirty little coward; Shot poor Mister Howard.' "

Izzo shook his head. "They don't write poems about holdup men in Philly. Not that I know of. Kind of a shame, you know, see-ing as how some of them was also outstanding personalities, much like the James boys, if you can believe the movies and like that."

"You can't, Izzo. But take it from me, Jesse and Frank and Quantrill . . ."

He didn't say more, reckoning it was wasted on his audience.

CHAPTER FOURTEEN

*"To a Chinese soldier," Oliver Smith remarked, "a wound . . .
was a death sentence. He was left to die of exposure."*

*The Marines could hear the Chinese . . . dying, could hear the
cries of the Chinese wounded, cries which died away as they froze
to death.*

Only from the air could you see the whole retreat. Only
the carrier pilots coming in over the frozen mountains
from the sea could appreciate it as spectacle, the long line
of men and guns and vehicles moving south out of Hagaru and up
over the passes and across the half-blown bridges and through the
narrow places where the Chinese set their ambushes and their
blocking positions; only the fliers could see the entire battle unfold.
Thousands of Marines and all their goods plus God knows how
many army troops and ROKs and Brits and all the flotsam and jet-
sam, all headed south, all trying to get out of the hills and the cold
and reach the sea, and only the fliers, dodging in and out of snow
squalls and trying not to collide with mountains, knew how long
and ragged a column it was and how narrow the road.

And how close behind them came the Chinese.

Gen. Oliver Smith could feel their weight, knew how near they
were. And he didn't like the way the Chinese kept coming, taking
their losses and still coming. Good troops. Very good troops. If
they had big guns and some air it would be a narrow thing
indeed.

Narrow enough as it was.

No good thinking of the numbers, thinking like this. The men would sense it; men could smell fear. Just let them smell it on him, Oliver Smith realized, and his fear would take hold of them.

He could lose this division.

That was the scary thing. Scarier even than the numbers. No general had ever *lost* a Marine division. Well, he'd been a Marine officer for a long time and he wasn't going to start now getting all sweaty and upset the troops.

General Smith pulled out a pipe and rapped it into his palm, shaking the dottle free. A pipe calmed a man; that was what the tobacco advertising always said.

A drowsy Verity looked over to his left through the swirling snow to see Tate attempting to lift some sort of bundle from a drift beside the road.

"Gunny, leave it. No room on the jeep now."

"It's a Marine, Captain."

"Dead?"

"Soon will be if I can't get the son of a bitch on his feet."

Verity wearily got out of the jeep, swinging his frozen feet out first and then not sure if they'd yet reached the ground. Loss of feeling. He was riding again only for that.

"Don't get too far ahead of us, Izzo."

"Nosir, Captain." Izzo knew what Verity was thinking. If he and Tate fell too far behind they might never catch up; they might be the ones left sitting on the snowdrifts, nodding off and falling into a sleep from which they would never wake.

Together, Tate and Verity got the man to his feet.

"Just wanna sleep," he murmured, not really arguing but registering a small protest, as young children do when awakened in the night.

Verity shook his head. "OK, lay him across the hood. Maybe the engine heat will keep him alive. Tie him on with his web belt."

Behind them a truck driver honked his horn and swore.

"Move it the hell out, you bastards."

The dead and the dying had become an inconvenience, an annoyance.

Verity and his men weren't the only ones tidying up as they went. Puller had a big command car, twice the size of his original jeep. It was open to the sky, as was everything else, but it had a big engine that blew a little heat in along the floor, thawing his feet so he could get out and walk some more. He had his own three men along and two more, wounded. Now they paused beside a limping man. "You OK, lad?"

"I'm from Loosiana, General. I never seed snow before."

"Well, son, I'm from Virginia, myself," Puller said, "but that's what being in the Marine Corps does for a young man, shows him the world and the glory of it."

"Yessir," the Marine said, not quite sure just how great a consolation this was and nursing sore feet.

"Indeed," Puller said, warming somewhat to the task, "there are tours of duty so breathtaking a man should turn back his pay. Although," he added, more thoughtful, "there are also hardship posts. Among which our present assignment might well qualify."

"I surely think it might, General, by your leave, sir."

Plenty of them had never seen snow before. From Camp Pendleton you could see snow on the Santa Ana Mountains or, just a bit off, the San Jacintos. But seeing snow in the distance was like picture postcards. This snow was real; this was cold; this chilled and intimidated men who gradually and grudgingly began to realize it could kill them.

Maybe the men of Valley Forge had endured cold. But they weren't on the march; they were in winter quarters. The Marines were on the march, fighting a dozen times a day and sleeping out nights, when they weren't attacking or being attacked.

The Chinese were killing them. So was the cold.

Not only the Marines were dying, the cold being an impartial killer, making few distinctions.

The CCF Twenty-sixth Army reported: "The troops were hungry. They ate cold food. They were unable to maintain the physical strength for combat. The wounded could not be evacuated . . ."

The Twentieth Chinese Army: "The troops did not have enough food, they did not have enough houses to live in, they could not stand the bitter cold ... when the fighters bivouacked in snow-covered ground during combat, their feet, socks and hands were frozen together in one ice ball; they could not unscrew the caps on the hand grenades; the fuses would not ignite; the hands were not supple; the mortar tubes shrank on account of the cold; seventy percent of the shells failed to detonate; skin from the hands was stuck on the shell and mortar tubes ..."

"To a Chinese soldier," Oliver Smith remarked, "a wound ... was a death sentence. He was left to die of exposure."

The Marines could hear the Chinese around them dying, could hear the cries of the Chinese wounded, cries which died away as they froze to death.

It was only early December, two weeks to go until winter, and Col. Ray Davis's thermometer reported that nighttime temperatures fell to twenty-four below zero. And the men were living aboveground, most without tents, without fires. . . .

Another bridge had been blown or another ambush sprung, and once again the long double line of men shuffled to a halt. Captain Verity had been walking alongside the jeep, forcing himself to keep his feet moving. Now a captain he knew by sight but whose name he had forgotten came up and sat down next to him on the crusted snow just off the road at the base of the hill.

"Verity?"

"Yes. How you doing?"

"Not good. I lost my company back there three nights ago. Puller relieved me."

"Hey, I'm sorry."

"My fault. Puller did what he had to do. It's just I keep seeing that company, how good it was, how they looked coming over the seawall at Inchon, working house-to-house in Seoul. When was that, Verity?"

"September, I guess. Yeah, September."

"And now it's December. Two months and a fine rifle company's lost and a lot of good men dead."

"Yeah." Verity didn't know what to say except to agree with the man. He tugged a cigar from a pocket and stuck it in his mouth. It was really just half a cigar, smoked down, with the mouth end frozen and with no more taste than an icicle. The other officer saw this and pulled out a pack of cigarettes and a Zippo lighter, but his hands were too numbed to get a cigarette to light.

"Aw, to hell," he said. Verity could see tears on his cheeks, frozen solid, and he didn't know if the man was crying now or his tears derived from earlier griefs.

Verity got the man's cigarette going and, grateful, the captain's words just came out, like snow thawing, swiftly rushing.

"I told Puller I couldn't send out another flank patrol up those damned ridges. I lost an eleven-man squad up there six days ago, maybe seven. Then a couple days later I lost nine more men. I sent them up there and they just never came back. We heard firing, but they wouldn't let me stop and go looking for them. 'You're holding up the column,' they told me.

"So the next day I refused. Just wouldn't do it. Hell with it, let 'em run me up. I couldn't send another dozen Marines up there, Tom, just couldn't. I know I'm wrong, but it's how I am."

He pulled at the cigarette, and as it came away from his lips the paper stuck and pulled away skin and a trickle of blood ran down his chin. The captain didn't seem to notice, and the blood soon froze. His executive officer was dead, killed at Yudam-ni. They'd given his company to one of the rifle platoon leaders.

"Nice kid, boy from the Jersey shore. I hope he does OK. It was a good company I had."

The captain looked into Verity's face, trying to make him understand.

"I'm pretty good myself, Tom. Used to be. That's over now, I guess."

I guess it is, Verity thought but did not say.

Izzo maintained sanity. By doing calculations.

"I figured it out, Gunny."

"What, Izzo?"

"Our rate of speed."

To the usual ambushes and mechanical breakdowns and skid-ding accidents were now added small snowslides, hardly real ava-lanches but sufficient to block the narrow road, and force the sergeants to resume shouting for men to wield entrenching tools and clear the way.

"One quarter-mile an hour, Gunny. Just like Captain Verity cal-culated himself. What do you think of that? It takes us four hours to go one mile."

Tate wasn't paying attention. He was thinking how much faster they could clear the snow if they had real shovels, broad-bladed aluminum snow shovels like they had leaning on porches back home. It would be odd to insist that along with all their other weapons and equipment a Marine division inventory snow shov-els. Odd, but it would make sense.

"Gunny?"

"Shut up, Izzo; I'm thinking. About shovels."

"Jeez. . . ."

Verity had been listening to Izzo, agreeing with him. A quarter-mile an hour? Why, if a man had the endurance and was suffi-ciently determined, he could crawl at that pace and keep up. Maybe that's how it would end for them, crawling out.

He didn't care. Captain Verity would crawl; he'd squirm on his goddamned belly, pulling himself along on his knuckles if he had to. Anything to get out.

Anything.

Captain Verity was hardly alone in having nightmares.

Sergeant Tate's were different, is all; didn't mean they didn't scare him.

Tate's derived from his having been in the Fourth Marines at Shanghai. In the clubby intimacy of the Marine Corps, you didn't have to say much more. Marines all knew what had happened to the men of the Fourth Regiment at Shanghai, understood why, in a very special way, they hated the Japs. Verity didn't much like the

Japanese, either. But he'd been privileged to fight them, kill them. Tate had been their prisoner.

Ten days before Pearl Harbor the detachment at Shanghai was issued a "war warning" and went over to a combat footing, a thousand of them (804 men more precisely) surrounded by a million Japs. Most of them were boarded November 27 onto the *S. S. President Harrison* to ship out to the Philippines. One small detachment including Tate and a few Marines manning garrisons upcountry and in Peking were to follow soonest. Except that war broke out first. There was talk of setting up a hedgehog defense in the town, talk of fighting their way upcountry to join up with Chiang, talk of getting away by sea in junks and small boats by night. In the end the Marines stacked arms and marched out in surrender. All those other options were but failed dreams.

In all the horrors of the next four years Tate remembered most shockingly that first terrible moment as they stood in perfect formation to be inspected by their new captors, when the bandy-legged little Jap officer came strutting along and slapped a Marine captain's face. Later there was worse.

Of all the pain of imprisonment maybe shame was worst.

Sergeant Tate tried hard to keep that in mind when the Japanese starved and beat and worked him near death and laughed at this tall American in his misery.

Bastards!

He'd rather die fighting the Chinese than ever again be taken.

It was odd, even callous, but when Elizabeth died giving birth and the child died, too, Tom had wept and mourned and raged only for her. Not for the child.

After all, in a way, it was the child that had killed her. A boy.

Later, but only later, Tom felt guilt when he looked at Kate and tried to imagine how his son might have looked. The son he ignored in his first grief. And later mourned.

Now, on the march south from the Chosin, he was thinking not only of Kate but of his dead boy whom he had never gotten to know. And had resented.

And now, too late, had grown to love. To think of as, "my son, *our* son."

The snow crunched underfoot, loud as saltine crackers. Verity walked as often as he could, alongside Izzo's jeep. His feet were frozen and he had an irrational dread of losing them. A strange country. There was plenty of snow on the flanking hills, and it lay deep and packed here on the road. But there weren't that many snowstorms. It was as if the snow had fallen and then slacked off, leaving itself to the terrible cold to congeal and conserve until spring. Walking on the crunching snow was better than sitting on the slow-creeping jeep, even absent Puller's orders. It kept the blood moving, almost raised a small sweat, and forcibly drove blood into the extremities of fingers and toes, earlobes and nose.

Gunnery Sergeant Tate felt the cold as much as Verity did. But he was handling it better.

"Gunny, keep an eye on me. Don't let me start to shake. If I ever start shaking, I may never stop."

Tom meant that, literally.

Occasionally, as they trudged slowly along the mountain road, a man fell out, not from fatigue or illness but from sniper fire. A single shot.

"We ought to have people up there, Captain," Tate said disapprovingly, looking toward the ridgelines, standing out white and stark against the sky. Until today, or maybe yesterday, Marines still worked the ridgelines. No more.

Verity knew Tate was right. The ridgelines paralleled the road a thousand feet higher. What a marvelous bit of high ground. The Marines preached that: "Take the high ground." But exhaustion and ambush and just plain inertia discouraged officers from sending flanking patrols to the ridgelines. In this weather, in deep snow, it might take a handful of men hours to climb six or eight hundred feet, and by the time they got to the ridgelines there might be a hundred or five hundred Chinese infantrymen waiting. The few patrols that reached the ridges were either exhausted or swiftly killed. Right or wrong, Marine officers on the right-of-way had largely stopped sending men into the high ridges unless ordered by Higher Echelon.

I know it's wrong, Verity thought, *but would I have the strength to drive them up there, to insist that they go, order them up, and then live with myself when they never came back? Five years ago, on Okinawa, I would have driven them up. With a pistol if need be. It's this damned cold that dulls the mind and congeals spirit and freezes men's hearts, as well as toes and fingers.*

"Sloppy," he said aloud, critical of himself, "half-assed."

Chesty Puller would still have officers brought up before a court for not throwing out flank patrols, especially on higher ground. But they weren't all "Chesty."

"Captain!" Izzo shouted from behind the wheel, more aggravated than alarmed.

"Yes?"

"Something going on up ahead."

Tate climbed up on the hood of the jeep, tallest of the three. Up there where the road narrowed between hills there seemed to be something.

"Can't tell what. Lot of milling around, Captain."

Verity had a map out, trying to unfold it in the wind and hold it steady in the cold.

"The map shows a bridge. Maybe that's it."

"Oh, shit," Izzo groaned. "Maybe they blew the frigging bridge."

Captain Verity no longer wrote letters to his daughter. He wanted to; there was so much he had to say. But his fingers could not hold the pen. The earliest unmailed letters had been neatly folded and secreted in inside pockets deep in layers of stinking wool close to his chest. Later letters, folded more crudely, the writing not nearly as crisp, were shoved into outer pockets easier to reach, the pages wadded and balled up. And although Verity did not know it, the ink had begun to smudge and run, courtesy of the sweat of exertion and the melting snow filtering through cloth or driven by the wind.

He still planned to mail Kate her letters. If they ever reached a place with such civilized conceits as a Fleet Post Office. And if he did not die on the road from the reservoir.

"Cut off! We're cut off! They blew the damned bridge!"

So blazed the word up and down the line of march in minutes. When it came to gossip, Marines were worse than hairdressers.

They all knew the bridge that the rumor said was blown. They'd marched across it going north, a one-lane structure less than fifty feet across, spanning a steep ravine. Now it was blown. Oh, shit.

Infantry troops might scramble down the slope of the ravine and wade the stream at the bottom and climb up the other side. With the ice it would be tricky, but they could do it, carrying packs and weapons. There was no way trucks or tanks could do it, no way they could get the wounded across. You couldn't carry wounded men down and then up frozen slopes like that. There weren't enough choppers in the Pacific to lift them across. And the Chinese up there on the high ground would shoot down the choppers.

Maybe the story of the bridge was all bullshit. Just a rumor. That possibility now sped up and down the line. The brass knew better.

"It's gone," General Smith was assured. "They blew it late yesterday afternoon. Laid it in the ravine as neat as you'd want. Nice, tidy job."

This was an engineer officer reporting. Engineers admired competence, even in disasters. Oliver Smith listened carefully. Then he said, "OK, now let's get ourselves a new bridge."

Astonishingly, there were such things as "new bridges." Steel spans barely wide enough to suit a tank's treads, thirty feet in length. Thirty? The ravine was forty feet at least! No problem, you bolt two twenty-four foot lengths of bridge together, end to end.

For once, the army had them, steel treadway bridge sections, twenty-four feet long, heavy but not so that they couldn't be dropped by air. Bigger parachutes were hurriedly flown over from Japan. The rear-guard Marines from the reservoir came south with their engineers; other Marines and army engineers came north to meet Puller's people at the blown bridge and to go to work.

The cargo planes came in as low as they could and dropped four lengths of treadway. Two survived.

"Two is plenty!" the engineers exulted.

The steel spans were trucked the half-mile or so to the ravine and eased out into space, engineers performing high-wire acrobatics, while from the near hills Chinese snipers added to the entertainment, trying to pick off individual engineers swinging out over the void. That demanded a response and the forward air controllers called in a napalm drop on the hills above the road by the ravine. Now all the Chinese were firing, trying to bring down a plane while, south of the broken bridge, Marine howitzers joined in, targeting the hills. By the time the last bridge bolts had been secured, a full-blown, rather brisk firefight was under way.

Now the first trucks ventured out onto the new bridge, moving slow. The treadway spans creaked and bent.

And held.

Up ahead, with the Fifth and Seventh Marines, Oliver Smith breathed more easily. Puller would get out now, too. Wouldn't have to leave his wounded and guns and vehicles behind. On such slender threads as bridges dropped by air, do men, and armies, live or perish.

They'd come through Koto-ri on the way north to the reservoir, and now they were coming through it again, a mere village between peaks, nothing compared to that thriving metropolis Hagaru. There wasn't an airstrip long enough to take much more than OYs, small observation planes, two-seaters. Piper Cubs without the bright paint. This was plateau country, a remote steppe ringed by mountains.

It served now as headquarters for Chesty Puller's First Regiment, acting as rear guard for the First Division and the entire X Corps.

It was the last flat place in the road for fifty miles, until they reached the coastal plain.

His officers came to Puller with the report.

"We have just enough trucks and other rolling stock to get the wounded out, General. Not the dead."

And there was no way to bring in cargo planes.

Marines who'd come down the terrible road from Yudam-ni and Hagaru looked around now at Koto-ri and shrugged.

"This place ain't much."

Had they asked Puller, he might have agreed. At Koto-ri there wasn't enough of anything. For the living or the dead.

Like Patton, Puller was an educated man. He'd read deeply and widely in history and recalled his Shakespeare, *Henry V.*

"You know," he remarked one evening to his officers, "all anyone remembers of Henry the Fifth is the fight at Agincourt, the night visits he made to the troops, incognito and cloaked. And then the great speech just before the battle, 'we happy few, we band of brothers,' and all that about, Crispin's Day."

His officers nodded, even those who hadn't the slightest notion of what Chesty was talking about, who Henry was. Then Puller went on.

"They forget what came just before. After Henry took Honfleur, he deputizes loyal officers to handle things there and tells them, 'With winter coming on, we will go to quarters at Calais.' "

Chesty Puller looked around him and met looks of appalling blankness.

Ah, well, men don't read anymore, Puller thought. And then said, aloud but half to himself, "Calais was the French port closest to England that rather reminds me of our Hungnam, gentlemen, though with distinctions in the architecture and other things."

"Sir?"

"Nothing," Puller said. "Just thinking out loud, old man."

Hungnam meant the sea; it meant safety. Even Chesty was thinking that way now.

There were only a couple of warming tents and huts still standing and little firewood to burn and no fuel to waste, and men lined up in patient, shivering queues, long lines in the wind and snow, much in the way homeless, idle men lined up during the depression for soup or a flophouse cot. And those had been vagrants and rummies or men simply down on their luck. These men queueing up at Koto-ri were the officers and men of the United States Marine Corps, with its distinguished and famous history.

Verity, who took his turn standing in the line, remembered Detroit in the late thirties, before the war economy kicked in, when workers laid off by the auto factories shuffled along broke and without hope, trying to sell apples no one wanted, and few could afford, what his father and the editorials and politicians called hard times.

Izzo, who had joined the warming queue an hour or more before Captain Verity, now emerged, oddly glowing, almost cherubic.

"Captain, this ain't much of a town. I seen small towns before but never one without no gas station. Not until now. But there ain't a mansion on the Main Line in Philly that stacks up against this here warming tent. Not for cash nor credit."

"Maybe after the war you could come back, Izzo. Open a car dealership."

"Water buffalo's more like it, sir." He moved away toward where they'd left the jeep to relieve Tate for his turn in the queue.

Another twenty men were allowed inside, and Verity shuffled ahead, closer to the tent, a bearded, unkempt figure with icicles hanging from his matted hair and upper lip. He knew how he looked, like a bum at a soup kitchen. It didn't matter. All that mattered was that he would soon get out of the cold.

And once you'd been inside for a few minutes and the steam started to rise from the men and their layers of muffled, stained, discolored clothes, you caught the smell, the reeking stench.

Near Verity a man retched and threw up, the vomit thin, as sour as bile.

"We do have ourselves a time in the Crotch, don't we?" someone remarked, drawing a rough laugh.

What the hell else could you do? It was laugh or lie down in your own filth and die.

Then Verity's thirty minutes in the charnel house were up. He passed Tate coming in as he went out.

"Nice and warm, Gunny," Verity said, "cushy."

"Good to hear, sir."

Tate looked frozen and Verity concluded there was no point in ruining his day. He'd smell the place soon enough.

Chesty Puller didn't have to use the communal tent. He was a general officer and they had a pyramidal tent for him, and it was to this tent he now summoned his staff. Specifically to consider the dead, whose bodies were stacked like cardwood behind the big warmup tent.

It wasn't snowing. But across the brief flats of Koto-ri and down the circling hills and through the coulees and little runs where streams ran in the summer, snow blew off the ground horizontally across ice and hard-packed brown earth tough as cement and scoured clear of snow by the awful wind. Up the road from them a respectable mile or three north was the Chinese army, trailing the Marine column, specifically trailing Puller's rear guard, ready to pounce but wary, so often and so terribly bloodied in the fights of the last ten days.

December 8. The Feast of the Immaculate Conception. It wouldn't be winter for two more weeks.

"You can't dig graves, General," Puller was told.

Puller hated to be told a thing couldn't be done. But the heavy equipment, the big 'dozers and front-loaders, had already gone south or been blown up to deprive the Chinese. That was what rear guards did, got out what they could and burned and blew up the remainder. It took a certain destructive streak to be a successful rear guard. They called it scorched earth; that was what it had been called since Ney's time. Perhaps since Xenophon's.

"I won't leave the dead to the wild dogs."

That was Puller. He wouldn't abandon his wounded; he wouldn't betray the dead. Nor to the Chinese. Nor to dogs or whatever else hunted foul-breathed in these damned mountains.

Verity had served under and with fine men, good Marines, had commanded some and more than a few. Was there ever a better gunny than this Tate? He'd been sure of Tate almost from the first, when they met at Kimpo Airfield. But Mouse Izzo? He'd had his doubts about the Mouse. So had Gunny Tate. And with reason. But Izzo, too, had turned out fine. Maybe better than fine.

CHAPTER FIFTEEN

"Where's your lieutenant?" Puller inquired.

"Got killed, Colonel. I took the platoon."

"Good for you, Sergeant. That's what God made sergeants for, since getting killed is what lieutenants do best. Having been a lieutenant once myself, I can testify to that."

"Yes sir, Colonel," the sergeant said, while around him men grinned.

Then, in all the lengthy chronicle of horror during the march out, the most terrible thing happened.

Puller buried his dead.

For all the hardness and the stiff back, Chesty Puller was nurturing and loving, jealous of men's lives in his care. And that was why he did what he did in the snow at Koto-ri.

"Come now, old man," Puller said to his executive officer, the man who would command the regiment if Chesty fell. "You know it must be done."

There was no way to carry the bodies out. And you couldn't just leave them behind. It was one reason Marines fought so well, knowing if they took a hit, they wouldn't be left where they fell.

At last count there were 117 dead at Koto-ri, mostly Marines, a few army troops and British Royal Marine Commandos, a couple ROKs, all of them laid out now in the open, shrouded only by snow.

"Fly them out?" someone asked. A stupid question. They couldn't even fly their wounded out of here, not as they'd done from the big strip at Hagaru.

"We'll bury them here," Puller said. When Puller said things like that, those were orders.

The small bulldozers they still had were put to work and had been digging now for two hours, and one of them had already broken its steel pan. Just snapped it in the cold. And the little earth and rock and ice the remaining 'dozers scraped up had to be chipped off the pans with pneumatic drills. It had been twenty-five degrees below zero Fahrenheit at dawn; had not warmed up much since.

"General, if we had some shaped charges, we could dig holes with them."

Puller brightened. The demolitions officer was hustled up.

"Not a one, sir. No real need for shaped charges unless you're going up against fortified positions, bunkers and pillboxes and the like."

Puller never indulged his temper when a man told the truth.

"All right, that's good sense. Should have thought of it myself, old man. Thanks for your time."

Other schemes were briefly floated and rejected, as empty as Ponzi's promises. Puller, impatient with failure and intolerant in general, grew restless.

"Colonel?" Some couldn't break habits or get used to Chesty's new rank.

"Yes, old man?"

It was a master sergeant, one of Puller's favorites, leathered and gnarled.

"They got root cellars under some of these huts, Colonel. Below the frost line, to store potatoes, turnips, and such."

Puller brightened, the corners of his flat, turned-down mouth lifting and widening in a gorgeous smile.

"Now that, by God, is creative thinking." And not by some paint-fresh young officer but by an enlisted man with a little time on him. "Knock down the huts and blow the cellars out. Large and deep as you need."

"Yessir."

It didn't take any time at all for the bulldozers to flatten the flimsy village huts of stucco and wood and straw and to clear the ground all about and for working parties of Marines to empty and tidy up a bit the blown root cellars beneath.

The bodies handled easily, the 117 of them, stiff as telephone poles, neat, too, with no bodily fluids running or leaking out, not in this cold, just as if they'd been gutted and embalmed by the finest morticians at Campbell's of Madison Avenue. It had begun to snow again, and in the early afternoon, the light was already fading. Puller wanted to get out of Koto-ri by tomorrow's dawn at the latest, what with the Chinese again cutting the road south and edging closer to his rear from the north, but impatient as he was, Chesty wasn't going to rush the dead.

A funeral detachment was rounded up, Verity and his men among them, and mustered in the wind on the snowy field surrounding the place where the huts had been and where the root cellars gaped brown and open, not yet drifted over. The surviving officer of the Royal Marine Commandos and several of the officers from army units were fetched. There was even a ROK major they'd corralled somewhere.

"We'll have a squad of riflemen," Puller told one of his staff.

"Yessir."

Then Marines, four to a body, came up and laid the dead in, side by side, each laid flat, not just tumbled in, as straight as frozen limbs would permit. When they were all in their graves, the several hundred men on the field of Koto-ri were called to attention.

"Fire!"

A dozen rifles fired into the air. Then again. Then once more.

There was no bugler to play taps. A bugler couldn't put his lips to metal in this cold without their freezing to the mouthpiece.

Verity stood between Tate and Izzo in the snow, saluting. He felt bad about looking so cruddy. At a Marine funeral an officer ought to be smart.

"Fill 'em in!" the engineer officer shouted, and the bulldozers came up again, lowering their steel pans to shove frozen earth and rock and ice blasted out from the cellars atop the Marines laid out below the snowy ground. Puller had the tanks roll up then, clanking and creaking, motors screaming in low gear, headlights on, making cones of light through the falling snow, and then, two or three abreast, the tanks ran back and forth slowly over the graves, grinding frozen earth flat beneath the treads, sealing in the dead under their steel tracks.

Less than a year before, Verity had watched the first gentle spadeful of soft Maryland earth fall atop the box that held Elizabeth Jeffs Verity and the smaller box that held their son. Now a hundred Marines were being buried crudely, grotesquely, and he found himself thinking instead of a tall young woman he loved, dead for reasons he did not yet understand and perhaps never would.

"Captain?"

It was Tate. The burial field was emptying. Even Puller was gone. Verity and a few others, lost as he in their own thoughts, remained, masked by the snow.

"Captain," Tate said again, taking him lightly by the arm.

"There's a warm-up tent over here without a line, Captain. Let's get us in there a few minutes; maybe you could puff a cigar."

Verity was shivering, part cold, part the burial service, part memory.

"I'm OK, Gunny. Fine."

"Yessir, but *I'm* cold as hell, so let's just get over there for a bit."

Verity went with him, understanding he was being led but not objecting more. He went and silently thanked Tate for the generosity of spirit that provided warmth as much as the reeking, smoky oil stove blazing away in the center of the little tent. Izzo was already there, but Verity didn't even see him. Nor did he want a cigar, not this once, but as he warmed his hands over the red belly of the stove, Captain Verity said, sounding himself again, "Gunny, when it comes my time, you get me back to Hungnam somehow, back to the sea. Get me out of here somehow, understand. Whatever happens, I won't be buried here."

"Nosir," Tate said. Then Izzo joined in.

"Yes sir, Captain," Izzo said, "and you do the same for me, sir, for me and Gunny, just as we'll do for you. . . ."

"You run your mouth too much, Izzo," Tate said, but gently.

I guess we're all a bit shook, Verity concluded, all of them who'd watched Puller burying his dead at Koto-ri, aware how close a thing it was that others were laid out in root cellars and not themselves.

And knowing that by tomorrow, they might be.

Captain Verity could still see the tanks coming across the field with their headlights in the snow, the bogeys grinding and treads squeaking oilless in the cold, could still hear the tanks running back and forth over the dead.

Gunny Tate could not recall having seen Marines look this bad. Not since the camps where the Japanese starved and beat them and men went nearly naked in their rags.

He did not think he would ever see Marines look like this without being defeated. When men were whipped in battle, you expected them to slump and shuffle and stare at you with vacant eyes and then, quickly, look away in furtive, embarrassed glances. Some of these Marines were starting to look and behave like that and they *hadn't* been whipped. At least, not yet they hadn't.

And it scared Tate, how Captain Verity was at the graves.

They were up and moving at dawn the next morning, ready to resume the march south, and none too early. The Chinese were all around them in the hills, and there was only the single road out, a road easily cut.

Tate knew how easily this rear guard could still be bottled up and maybe even taken. *God save me from another prison camp,* he prayed. Gunny Tate did not think he could take being a POW again.

Captain Verity knew he was being irrational. He also knew every man had his own wild, special fear. His funk. The thing that breaks him.

I'll be left behind. I'll die here and be left behind and Puller will bury me as he did his own men, the dead of his regiment, under the ice and frozen rock, to be ground under by tanks and 'dozers into the cold earth of North Korea, ten thousand miles from home, without monument or cross or name.

They passed the place of the dead now again in their jeep as they began the evacuation of Koto-ri and the next leg of the retreat toward Funchilin Pass.

"Just hold up here a minute, Izzo," Verity ordered. The driver, not knowing why, slowed to stop and then, when a truck tailgating close behind gave him a klaxon, cursed and pulled off to the shoulder.

"Yessir," he said, a bit sulky and not wanting to stay at Koto-ri one moment longer than absolutely necessary.

Verity looked out at the field where yesterday they had buried 117 men. Snow had fallen heavily in the night, and there was only a flat place in the snow. Tate knew why they'd paused and sat there, silent and patient. Verity continued to look across the field.

"Deliver me from the valley of the shadow of death," Verity murmured to himself. Not quite a prayer, for he did not pray, but a mute, desperate cry for help, the old psalm vaguely remembered. Then, inhaling deeply, feeling the cold sear his lungs, he turned briskly back to the road ahead, staring toward the high pass and the road south.

"OK, Izzo, let's move it." He sounded angry, sore at something.

"Aye-aye, sir."

Jesus, you'd think it was me slowing us up and not him, the driver thought. *Maybe he's going mental. And who could blame anyone for going mental in this shit?*

Verity turned again to look back, but there was nothing to see, only the long line of trucks and tanks and big guns and jeeps and marching men. The burial field was back there, he knew, unholy and unconsecrated, by now just another flat place between the hills.

New snow began to fall, drawing a dull veil over everything as Koto-ri disappeared behind them.

"Can't you get a move on, Izzo?" Verity demanded, not entirely reasonable.

"Trying my best, Captain," the driver said.

Tate knew what was bothering Captain Verity was not Mouse Izzo's driving.

"Well, get it going then," Tate said, shouldering his share of Izzo's resentment to help Verity, whatever it was that was eating at him.

"OK, Gunny, oh-frigging-kay."

Izzo noisily shifted gears in a dumb show of acceleration. All three of them knew it was only for effect, since the trucks in front of them weren't going to move any faster no matter what Verity feared or Izzo wanted.

No letters had arrived at the house on P Street for weeks, and Madame invented many credible reasons for this.

"The plane could not take off with all the snow, Kate."

"Oh."

Madame read the American newspapers and knew, vaguely, the truth. That an American army was trapped by the Chinese and the cold and that Kate's father was one of them. It was not a truth for which three-year-old girls were prepared.

"Madame, we haven't sung 'Sur le pont d'Avignon' yet this week."

"No, we haven't."

And so they sang, finishing very loudly, "On la danse, tout en coup!"

"There one dances, all at once!"

Madame prayed Mr. Verity would soon be home to sing to his daughter. Now her prayer changed.

She prayed he would just *get* home.

After each night of fighting their way south, Oliver Smith counseled in the morning with his staff.

A rifle company commander whose two hundred men had been badly hurt and now numbered, of effectives, fewer than a hundred reported to Smith, telling him what it was like up there in the hills and on the ridgelines where rifle companies fought battalions and sometimes regiments of Chinese troops.

"Good troops, too, General. They keep coming."

"*How* do they come, Captain?" This was Smith's command, his division; he had to know the Chinese as well as they knew themselves. Or they would defeat him.

"They tease you in the middle and then come from both flanks. In waves. Like we did in the Pacific, on the Islands, hitting the beach in waves. Except here there's no beach. Just the ridgelines and the hills, and they keep coming. And when they get there, them that's left . . ."

"Yes, Captain," Smith said, gentle and not pushing, knowing the story would come and knowing this man had lost half his company.

". . . then it's hand-to-hand, rifle butts and knives, beating their brains out, spearing and clubbing and strangling . . . smothering them in the snow facedown and nailing them to the ground with bayonets. . . ." He shook his head, wondering if he really remembered all this or was fantasizing. "You never saw anything like it, General. It must have been the way men fought a thousand years ago."

"And yesterday," Smith remarked, half to himself, and the captain, who neither heard nor understood, said nothing.

Smith stood now.

"Well, Captain, thank you for coming in. Good report, Captain. Does you credit."

One day bled into another, each night into the next.

Izzo contrived hot meals by wiring cans of C-ration ham and limas to the jeep's manifold so they heated as they drove. Verity had little appetite but ate anyway. To fast was to die. The cold drained body heat. Men pared lean, wire-thin, by the summer fighting at Pusan and those days of runs and seasickness aboard ship now lost another ten or twenty pounds they could not afford, eyes sunken deep behind hollowed cheeks.

Verity's anus bled intermittently, rubbed raw from cold toilet paper and diarrhea. Tate, Verity knew from how he walked, was the same.

Some men just shit in their trousers as they marched. Verity resisted for days before joining them.

It only stinks for a while, he realized. Then it froze. But before it froze there were a few moments when it was pleasantly moist and warming, like a soothing poultice. But only for a time. Then it solidified into a lump of frozen shit down around the bottom of your trousers where they tucked into boot tops or canvas leggings.

What the hell, Verity thought.

He wasn't the only man too weak and too cold or whose hands were too frozen to go through the whole damned rigamarole of dropping gun belts and packs and opening parkas to get at the several pairs of pants everyone wore and the two sets of yellowed, odorous underpants inside, to open themselves bare to the wind and the snow.

So they shambled along, a stinking, rotten, tired column of freezing men who, for no rational reason, continued to behave not as a mob but as an army, still dangerous, still capable of fighting back and killing its enemies, not just in defense, but in attack and pursuit, running the Chinese to death in the low hills bordering the terrible road south toward the sea.

While Izzo by miracles of improvisation produced the odd hot meal, you needed a vehicle's engine for that. The marching infantry lived pretty much off dried rations, crackers and candy bars and cheese. The pork and beans and ham and limas were frozen solid in their little cans and soon thrown away as useless weight. For miles behind the column starving Korean refugees, trailing the army but afraid to approach too close, scavanged discarded tins from the snow, some of them exploded by cold.

The Marines wore their canteens inside their shirts against their bellies to keep the water liquid and drinkable. This gave slim young men the bulbous look of the old and obese, of women late in pregnancy. Or suggested the distended bellies of starving children in some sub-Saharan famine area.

Some of the men could still urinate normally. A simpler anatomical function performed swiftly by the side of the road into snowdrifts, only complicated by the wind that required a man to piss to leeward and not to windward. Desperately seeking a jocular note, men passed the word: "Don't eat yellow snow."

Men with cramp were another category entirely. The cramp came from eating frozen food, and to relieve the pain as best they could men walked stooped over, bent almost in two from the waist. For some reason, that seemed to dull pain. Tate, well over six feet, had been taken by cramp and was no longer anywhere near as tall as Captain Verity.

What could the corpsmen do, the few doctors that they did have? Prescribe bed rest? A week in a warm climate?

Such things existed in other worlds, miles and years from here.

And the corpsmen themselves, the occasional doctors passing through, they, too, were sick and frostbitten and, from time to time, fell off to the side of the road to sleep awhile. And did not wake.

This was how it was on the line of march, along the narrow mountain road.

It was worse on the ridges where the rifle companies fought the Chinese to keep the way open. On the road, at night, Marines like Verity could at least sleep, unless they were rousted out and formed into irregular ad hoc skirmish lines, officers and men and corpsmen and truck drivers and chaplain's aides alike, to beat back a Chinese attack that had broken through the thin ranks of riflemen above. When they could sleep, Tate rigged ponchos and shelter halves from jeep to ground, weighting down their hems with chunks of frozen snow and with rock, pissing on the canvas edges to seal them with ice against the cold, creating a sort of lean-to that cut the wind and under which three men in their sleeping bags huddled and hugged together, sharing body heat. *God knows, we stink,* Verity thought, though he could no longer smell himself, not through nostrils clogged with green snot. What must it be like for the riflemen up there in the hills who couldn't steal even a few hours of sleep in their bags but must be up and about, patrolling and manning the perimeter and fighting off the midnight assaults by the Chinese before, at dawn, resuming the march south?

Verity could not imagine and did not believe he would have been capable of doing their work. Not anymore, not at his age.

That he was only thirty suggested no irony, none at all. At thirty on the march from the reservoir, you were an old man.

"Captain, you know what I think. I think—"

"Shut up, Izzo. I know what you think."

"Yessir, but—"

Tate's patience was also limited. "And you won't argue with the officer in command."

"No, Gunny," Izzo sulked. Jesus, you couldn't say frigging nothing no more. . . .

Something kept them going. Maybe that they were Marines. Maybe it was Puller.

"Come on, lads. Pick 'em up; lay 'em down. Only thirty miles now to Chinhung. Only thirty more."

"Yessir, Colonel."

Puller was over fifty and if he could do it, young men told themselves . . .

"Move along; keep moving. Saddle up and keep it going."

He was a general now, at last and much delayed by politics, but he'd not yet been confirmed by the Senate and so to himself and to some of the troops he was still "Colonel." As he would always be, though not in his hearing, "Chesty."

"Move it; keep it moving. Only twenty-nine miles to Chinhung."

Men pinned fragile hopes on Chinhung. It was nothing but a wide place in the road, but as they focused on it more and more it became El Dorado, a city of infinite possibilities with its tall spires and golden pavements, perfumed and sweet with plants and decorative lakes and exotic flowers. The reality of Chinhung and why Puller kept its image shining before them was that it was a railhead. Here the narrow-gauge track to Hungnam and the sea swung back to parallel their mountain road. From Chinhung wounded men and the frostbitten could ride to the coast in trains. Freight cars, flat-cars, boxcars, hanging on locomotives, none of it mattered. If they could reach Chinhung, they were safe.

"That's the way, lad, another few days and we'll be in Chin-hung. Just twenty-eight miles now. Just twenty-eight more."

What Puller did not tell them and what he knew was more than just a possibility was that when they got to Chinhung, if they got there, the rail lines would have been cut by the Chinese and they would have to walk, fighting all the way, to the sea.

If so, they'd walk then, Puller rather reasonably concluded, not a man to agonize over things that might not happen.

"Hurry them along there, Sergeant; keep them moving. Only twenty-seven miles to Chinhung-ni."

"Yessir, Colonel."

"Where's your lieutenant?"

"Got killed, Colonel. I took the platoon."

"Good for you, Sergeant. That's what God made sergeants for, since getting killed is what lieutenants do best. Having been a lieu-tenant once myself, I can testify to that."

"Yessir, colonel," the sergeant said, while around him men grinned.

Their lieutenant was a replacement who'd flown into Hagaru-ri early in the retreat, and they hadn't gotten to know him well enough to mourn.

"Well, keep 'em moving, Sergeant." Then, louder, "You men keep up with the sergeant here. He'll get you to Chinhung-ni. You just keep up with him and don't loiter." As he limped off, back to his car, the men gave him a little cheer.

Puller kept at them, kept after them, goading and encouraging and humoring and telling them forever, "Move it; move it; keep it moving."

There must have been men like Puller with Ney as the Grande Armée retreated in the snow from Moscow and through the Polish marshes and did not fall apart. When men are scared and cold and hungry and sick and there is a powerful and persistent foe nipping at their heels and killing stragglers and setting ambushes, it is easy for armies to fall apart.

Bodies lay here and there in the dirty snow by the side of the road like trash waiting to be collected. Sensitive men had dragged them there or lifted them from the narrow road itself. They did not want the trucks and tanks to crush and grind over the bodies. Even dead, Marines deserved better than that. Some of the dead died of wounds, others of cold, still others of pneumonia or dysentery or hemorrhagic fever or other ills. It didn't matter. They were all dead, laid out stiff and cold, young men now gone.

When a truck came past that still had room and men strong enough, the bodies were picked up and stacked, head to foot, foot to head. It was the best they could do, trying to take the dead home.

If you could just stay in the sleeping bag, the cold could be tolerated. These down bags, Verity thought, whoever makes them was no Harry the Hat Lev. Mr. Lev was a garment manufacturer who was all over the papers back in the States for cheating the military by delivering shoddy goods, raincoats that didn't shed rain and hats that fell apart and trousers short in the inseam. Maybe Harry the Hat Lev also made these damned shoepacs. He certainly hadn't sewn up the wonderful down sleeping bags that kept them alive.

Verity had long since stopped writing letters to Kate. The ball-point pen no longer functioned. The stub of a pencil Izzo gave him was less satisfactory. But mostly it was that his writing hand knotted up in the cold and the paper wouldn't hold still and he trembled when he wrote. Hen scratchings, wasn't that what people used to call bad penmanship? That Kate couldn't read what he wrote even when it was impeccably Palmer method didn't matter; he wanted always to send her whatever was the best in him.

We have a social contract, Verity thought, *and it cuts both ways.*

He dreamed a lot in the sleeping bag. Odd dreams, some of them very precisely focused on the war and where they were, on the cold and the hills and the killing. Other dreams, shapeless as Rorschach tests, peaceful and escapist. He liked those. Then sometimes he dreamed of other wars.

Those were weird dreams. Very odd.

Waterloo. He was there, first with Wellington the night before as his officers danced the gavotte and charmed the Belgian ladies, and then with Napoléon at breakfast where they drank from crystal stemware and wielded silver cutlery at a table with the finest linen cloths and napery, officers and princes who by that evening would be dead, with their faces in the Belgian mud.

He was at Gettysburg, where, the afternoon and evening before the battle, West Point classmates climbed one another's hills under flags of truce and were passed through sentry lines to say hello and inquire after wives and to wish each other well on the morrow. Verity liked that, the cordiality and camaraderie.

"Pray shoot first, *messieurs les Françaises*" . . . "*Mais non, gentlemen of England, *vous tirez d'abord.*"

That was the Plains of Abraham, where both generals, Montcalm and Wolfe, died in the very first minutes under the opening volleys after their exchange of pleasantries.

Once in a dream he rode alongside Custer at that terrible moment when the Seventh Cavalry had gone too far into the ravines of the Little Bighorn where ten thousand Sioux waited and the troopers looked around, before even a single shot had been fired, and, seeing the massed horsemen and serried tepees stretching beyond them to the horizon, knew they were dead men. Tate, too, had that dream, or something like it.

Oddly, Verity never dreamed of his own War, against the Japanese. That was too real for dreams. It lacked the charm of distance and the centuries.

The division still tried to erect warming tents along the road. But they made such a splendid target for the mortars. Squeeze six or eight Marines into one tent and hit it with an .82mm mortar and six or eight Marines died. The men knew this yet continued to queue up.

"You freeze to death out here. What's the difference?"

Whenever it was his turn and a warming tent had room, Verity squeezed inside. It didn't happen often. The jeep would approach a warming tent being erected, and by the time it was ready to take them in the column had moved a hundred yards, two-hundred, and the jeep had to roll on and past.

"Stop holding up the column, fer chrissakes!"

It was a good thing he didn't dream about Napoléon's retreat from Moscow, when the Grande Armée almost disintegrated. That also was too real for dreams, and they were already living nightmares.

Company E of the First Medical Battalion estimated that from November 14 through December 9 they had treated thirty-eight hundred casualties. They couldn't be more precise because on the night of December 11 the building they were using burned down after a field stove exploded, and paper records were destroyed.

Corpsman Jay C. Smout recalled that when his medical company was evacuating casualties from the airstrip at Hagaru, they set up a primitive sort of triage to determine how badly frostbitten people were and who should go and who was fit to stay: "The division surgeon's own frostbitten feet served as diagnostic model. Marines with injury worse than his were sent to the airstrip for evacuation. Marines with frostbite less severe than his were sent back to their units."

To fight and freeze some more.

CHAPTER SIXTEEN

*They caught up with the doctor, resting . . . on his haunches in the
snow to the side of the road, back bent, eyes staring.*

"Better get up, Doc!" Tate called.

*The surgeon lifted his head. It seemed to take considerable
effort.*

"Yes, yes. I'll be along."

*His voice was empty and unconvincing, and Tate suspected he
would not get up but would die there.*

A freak shot. One in a million."

That was Tate's read on it.

The night of December 11, with the Marine convoys
lurching south, the Chinese played one final trump card, ambushing the trucks at Sudong. Instead of their usual tactic of bursting
from snow-clogged mountain defiles to descend suddenly on the
MSR from above, this time the Chinese infiltrated the town to
materialize out of the scatter of huts and shops and small factories,
firing burp guns and tossing grenades and shooting lead truck drivers through their windshields to stall the column. Tate, walking
alongside the jeep, dived off the road to return fire from an icy
ditch. Izzo, braking the jeep to a careering halt, and Verity, nursing
his feet, scrambled to join him.

"Jesus!" Izzo panted. "After all we been through, to get it frigging now!"

Verity was thinking the same thing and maybe Tate, too, but the
gunny growled, "There isn't *any* good time to get killed, you miserable little Mouse."

"No, Gunny, there ain't," Izzo said amiably, seeing the logic.

By morning the Chinese, those they hadn't killed, vanished back into the Sudong hills, and the convoy, in daylight, was again moving south at a prudent two miles an hour when Verity felt a thud high up on his back, as if punched there by a powerful fist.

"Gunny!"

Tate, walking alongside, turned. "Yessir?" Then he saw Verity's face.

"I think I'm hit, Gunny."

Izzo, hearing him, punched the gas, pulling out of the line of vehicles and speeding ahead to a wider stretch of road where he could pull off. He was out of the jeep almost before it came to a stop, sprinting to the passenger side to help. Tate was even faster.

"I'll take care of the captain, Izzo. Grab that BAR and scope them hills. If there's one sniper up there maybe there's more."

"Aye-aye, Gunny."

Izzo was as crisp as Tate. He crouched low a few yards off the road, the BAR swiveling slowly back and forth. And ready. The Mouse, too, was still dangerous, could still kill you.

"It doesn't hurt much, Gunny," Verity said. "Maybe a spent shot. From a long way off."

"Yes, sir, I'll get under this parka of yours and take a look. Probably you're right. A spent shot."

They were very nearly right.

The shot had been a long one, not quite at random but thrown out there at the rolling column of trucks and tanks and jeeps rather than at a single man. It had been fired by a Springfield '03, an American rifle captured by the CCF from Chiang Kai-shek's army in 1949. An American rifle first used in World War One and still accurate, it was capable of killing Americans. Or anyone else. The Chinese soldier who fired it, lying atop a low ridge and braced against boulders, was a thousand and seventy-five yards away when he squeezed it off, a final, despairing gesture from a man whose unit, a company of the Forty-second CCF Division, had been badly punished in the hand-to-hand fighting the night before at Sudong.

He never knew he hit Verity. Or anyone. The shot was near its extreme range and in another two hundred yards or so would have fallen harmlessly to ground. Instead, it caught Thomas Verity where his left shoulder blade and spine came together.

As Tate gingerly pulled away the layers of clothing, hands so stiff with cold a simple button was a challenge, Verity turned his head toward the sergeant.

"I don't think it even broke skin, Gunny. Doesn't feel bad. I'm warming up back there."

By now Tate had peeled back the parka and pulled away the two sweaters and a wool shirt and a wool undershirt and had his hands on the captain's T-shirt. It was wet. That was the warmth Verity felt. Blood. His own blood.

The wound was small and neat. Sometimes the Chinese, the Marines as well, used a pocketknife or bayonet to gouge a deep cross into the soft lead point of a bullet so that when it hit a man it splayed out, creating a much bigger wound. Dum-dum bullets, they were called. They were supposed to be illegal, Geneva Convention rules, but everyone did them, both sides. Not this bullet. At nearly eleven hundred yards it was flying true, spinning and not whirling erratically, and it had entered Verity's shoulder or upper back as cleanly as a bullet could.

"Break skin?" Verity asked, almost clinically curious and quite calm.

"Yes, sir, a bit. But a nice clean wound, far as I can see. Medium-caliber, probably a thirty-ought something. No bigger'n that, for sure."

"How's he doin', Gunny?"

"Just keep watching the ridgelines, Izzo, and leave the medicine to me."

Jesus, I just asked.

Trucks rolled past and jeeps and the occasional tracked big gun, and snow began again to fall as Tate poured iodine into the wound and then, clumsily, stuck a gauze pad onto Verity's upper body and began to stuff him back into the parka.

"Sorry if it hurts, sir. I've got morphine if you think you need it."

"Doesn't hurt, Tate. You can have my business anytime. Give

testimonials. Dr. Kildare couldn't have done better. Don't feel a thing."

That was what bothered Gunny Tate.

Verity should at least have winced and probably should have cursed him out when he used the iodine.

It wasn't normal that he didn't hurt.

A small, triumphant thrill ran through the column, starting at the head, the word being passed north.

"We've won! We've won! We're out!"

They were out of the trap, saved. That was what passed back from the point. Men moved with surprising quickness off the road to scramble up hillsides, seeking height and a vantage point.

"Is that the sea? The damned sea out there? Oh, babee!"

"The sea? They can see it, the sea?"

Izzo slowed the jeep and then came to a halt, had to, the truck in front of them stopped so that a Marine could climb atop the cab on tiptoes.

"Can you see anything, Gunny?" Verity asked. Tate was still the tallest of them, unless the cramp was at him.

"Just the line of trucks, and I don't think anyone can see the sea yet, Captain. I think they're just imagining."

Up ahead there was a V-shaped gap in the hills. Verity couldn't see beyond that, and he knew Tate was probably right, while wishing him mistaken.

Men continued to shout that they were out, that they'd won, that the sea was just ahead, and then, picking up momentum slowly, the column again began to move, accordionlike, along the road south. Verity kept looking, but even after they'd passed through the V of the hills, he still couldn't see the Sea of Japan.

Not that he couldn't imagine it, toy boats out there, white against the blue-green water, flat and welcoming, the distant surface smooth as billiard tables.

Izzo kept them moving, but it was slow. Still, they were getting close. What was it Henry V called for at Agincourt, after they'd beaten the French?

Te Deums. Glory to God. *If there was a God,* Verity suggested, *He'd gotten them out. Who else could?*

In Tokyo, MacArthur, confidence restored, had resumed issuing sunny communiqués and meeting with the press.

"The First Marine Division has cleared Chinhung-ni and is intact, men, guns, and vehicles, and is heading south. The first elements of the division should reach the Hamhung-Hungnam area by midnight December eleventh to the twelfth. They are coming out as a division and with their wounded and their dead."

Delicately, there was no mention of men buried at places like Yudam-ni or Koto-ri.

No mention, either, of minor scraps and small ambushes and snipers harassing the tail end of the column near Sudong.

"Good news for a change, Jean," the General told his wife.

He might still get out of this thing with his reputation intact.

Tate found a navy surgeon on the road, another tired figure bent under his pack, looking frozen, but walking out.

"You could look at him, Doctor."

The surgeon did, briefly. Barely bothering to pull back Verity's parka.

"Bleeding's stopped," he said. "Just don't bounce him around too much and get it started again."

This was what medical science had come to on the road from Chosin.

"Could you take a look at his back? Where he got hit?"

"Stripping him out here would freeze tissue, Sergeant. It's shock kills a man, not just the wound. Besides," he said, "my fingers are frozen. I can't do an examination. Fingers won't move."

He gave Tate a clumsy gloved pat on the arm and shuffled off ahead of them, their jeep again stalled in this line of march. Two hours later, maybe three, they caught up with the doctor, resting with a couple of Marines on his haunches in the snow to the side of the road, back bent, eyes staring.

"Better get up, Doc!" Tate called.

The surgeon lifted his head. It seemed to take considerable effort.

"Yes, yes, I'll be along."

His voice was empty and unconvincing, and Tate suspected he would not get up but would die there.

To Captain Verity, who dozed fitfully, it was like a ballroom, everything a-whirl, loud music and light, stage snow falling, his head spinning, crystal and frost, a manic and deadly *Nutcracker Suite,* with Chinese dancers. Too many Chinese dancers. And no Sugar Plum Fairy.

Kate had never seen *Nutcracker.* Elizabeth had wanted to take her last year, but they decided that, at two, she was too young and might be frightened.

Fat chance. This kid was Elizabeth's. And (afterthought and no false modesty about it) his.

"Captain?" Tate asked, having heard Verity say something.

"Nothing, Gunny, just a night at the ballet, Tchaikovsky and all that. . . ."

"Yessir."

Tate waited a few moments until Verity had calmed and then slid a hand over his forehead, lightly, to see if there was fever.

Both hand and head were too cold to tell.

Verity pondered past and future, yesterday and tomorrow. Today, and now, held little meaning.

His feet didn't hurt. That was how freezing took you. And the bullet in his back provided distraction. He was no longer removing his boots once a day to change from wet socks to dry. There was little point and he disliked seeing the blackened toes and the black moving up the instep, hated the stink of himself and the rotting flesh. And the last time he'd taken off the boots, three or four days ago, it had taken nearly an hour to get them back on, the leather stiff and unyielding. No man could walk barefoot or in socks. To lose your boots, to be unable to pull them on again, meant you stayed here by the side of the road to die. Or lie there helpless until the Chinese came and did the job for you.

The Chinese were still close. They kept on the tail of the Marine column. The rear guards were always fighting; the Chinese forced that on them, keeping up the pressure. It was Mao's guerrilla strategy at its most basic: when the enemy attacks, retreat; when the enemy retreats, pursue. The Chinese were as cold and tired and hungry as the Marines were and had taken far heavier casualties, yet they kept coming. Verity wondered who led them, if it really was Peng. It was too bad he didn't know, wasn't sure.

I'd like to see old Peng once more, Verity thought, *before he kills me. Share a coffee and have a chat.*

Now they could see the lights of Hamhung.

"Eight miles, maybe ten," Izzo said. "We got it made, Captain."

Verity was riding, of course. He didn't feel guilty about that, because he could no longer walk. Jesus, he hoped he wasn't going to lose the feet. To go through all this and then come home to Kate and not be able to walk down to the C. & O. Canal to see the barges and the donkeys and then carry her back, that would be hard. His feet worried him more than the gunshot.

By now they were under the navy's guns. There was one battleship out there, firing sixteen-inch guns, projectiles that weighed two thousand pounds and landed twenty-five miles away. There were cruisers with eight-inch guns and a lot of destroyers. In the War they had called destroyers tin cans. Verity wondered if they still did that or if the military was more deferential this time. It didn't matter. Under the umbrella of the navy guns the division could pause and rest and shelter. MacArthur was not going to lose his army after all. They were nearly there.

The road south broadened as they neared the twin cities of Hamhung/Hungnam, the way rural roads do as they approach market towns or turnpikes do in the shadow of great cities. There was even paving now, in places, and the jeep ran more smoothly, jouncing only in the potholes.

"Like a Cadillac, Captain," Izzo said smugly, "a frigging Caddy, and I drove plenty of them."

A Cadillac? Well, not quite. But it had gotten them to Hamhung. Or nearly there. And he was trying like hell to drive smooth. For the captain's sake.

It was odd, Izzo thought, that the captain didn't even wince when he hit a pothole, jouncing the jeep. It should hurt like hell. But Verity wasn't saying a word, wasn't even groaning.

There were other things not explicable.

This truth occurred to Thomas Verity as he sat, still and cramped, very cold but not hurting all that much, by Izzo's side in the slow-moving jeep.

Not explicable how ordinary men could work and walk and shit and eat and sleep and survive wounds in such weather at these temperatures without shelter of any sort, even at night, and still fight, still kill the other guy. When was the last time he or Tate or Izzo had even entered a warming tent to thaw? Three days? More? And for some of the riflemen up there on the ridgelines it might have been a week. Maybe Eskimos could live in this, burrowing into snow in their furs, rolling up fetal-like to leech off the body's own heat. But no one was coming to kill the Eskimos in their holes.

Also strange, with Koto-ri days and miles behind them, the smoke of rifles long since drifted away over the graves, but Verity still heard the grinding metal-against-metal of the tank bogeys, the gears screaming, the crunch of the tracks, could see again the yellow cones of tank headlights through the falling snow as they rolled back and forth, back and forth, over the root cellars of Koto-ri, the Marines' cemetery.

"Gunny!" he shouted in panic, voice strangled.

"Yes, sir?"

Tate was there instantly, and solicitous.

"Get me out, Gunny. Don't let Puller . . ."

Tate saw the fear in his face. And understood, without the words being said.

"Yes sir, we'll get you out, skipper. Just be easy about it, sir. Count on Izzo and me."

"Yes," Verity said, sitting back, calmed and easier about things, not as fearful.

Then, suspecting he might be dying and wanting finally to understand the inexplicable, he said, "Gunny, one other thing."

"Yessir?"

"I can't feel my feet, Gunny."

"That's the cold, sir," Tate responded, knowing that it wasn't.

Nor could Verity understand where Elizabeth came from. How she was here in Korea and alive.

There, all in white, on a sun-bleached court, she lunged, long-legged, long-armed, for a tennis ball just out of reach.

"Your shot, Tommie," she pouted, sweat-slick and golden.

"*My* shot?" She was forever poaching in doubles and then blaming him. Damned nerve!

"*Your* shot, Tommie," she insisted. My, but Elizabeth could be firm.

He stretched out his racquet for the ball as her call echoed, her voice different now. No longer chiding, but shocked.

"You're shot, Tommie."

"Yes," he said, "I am."

And he ran toward her in the hot sun, laughing at their private joke.

Izzo was talking to the captain. Or rather, *at* Verity, next to him in the front seat.

"Shut up, Izzo," Tate ordered.

"I'm just talking, Gunny. Trying to take the captain's mind off of his own troubles. It's a consolation, y'know, when you hear of people worse off than you."

"The captain don't want to hear your tale of woe, Izzo. An officer don't want to know a damned thing about your private life. You been in the Corps long enough to know he don't."

"Sure, Gunny. But considering all we been through, me and you and the captain, you make exceptions. Right?"

Since Verity was asleep or unconscious or both and taking no notice of Izzo or his accounts, Tate felt the question was reasonable.

"OK, Izzo," he said.

"Why, thanks, Gunny. What I was about to say to the captain was a kind of confession, you know, like us Catholics do Saturday afternoon to the priest. 'Bless me, Faddah, for I have sinned. . . .' "

Tate said nothing. He was out of his depth when Catholics got started on the sacraments.

". . . so I just wanted the captain to know that I was sorry for bullshitting him all this time and I wanted to—"

"What the hell kind of religion is that? Telling the captain, or telling a priest, you were 'bullshitting' him? Catholics talk like that in church?"

Izzo ignored the question. "I wanted to let the captain know I never was a wheelman. Never ran with a stickup gang. I stole a car once, hot-wired and heisted it. And got caught. That was when they gave me the choice. The Corps or six months inside reform school." He paused. "God knows why I didn't just frigging go inside."

"So you were only bragging what a big, important gangster you were?"

"Well, yeah. Guy as small as me, he makes himself bigger, y'know? I never even held a gun 'til boot camp. I was just looking for an edge back there in Philly, looking for a little respect from the guys. To be well thought of."

"And telling him you drove for stickup men would make the captain think highly of you?"

"Yeah. I only wish now that he's shot that I told the captain the truth. That I was just a wild kid trying to sound dangerous."

Verity still wasn't listening. Not that Tate could see. The jeep moved ahead, slowly, Izzo nursing the wheel with his usual competence. So Tate said, "You're well thought of here, Izzo."

The driver's head swiveled. "Why, Gunny. That's something. Coming from you and all. . . ."

"You did OK, Izzo. No one can say you didn't."

"You mean that?"

"I do. And I know the captain thinks so, too."

Izzo shook his head. "No shit."

Behind them someone shouted from the cab of a six-by, "Move the hell out, you peepul!"

Izzo gunned the motor, and their jeep moved another dozen yards south along the mountain road.

CHAPTER SEVENTEEN

Time magazine put it this way: "The running fight of the Marines and two battalions of the Army's 7th Infantry Division from Hagaru to Hamhung, forty miles by air but sixty miles over the icy, twisting mountainous road, was a battle unparalleled in U. S. military history. It had some aspects of Bataan, some of Anzio, some of Dunkirk, some of Valley Forge, some of the 'Retreat of the 10,000' (401–400 B.C.) as described in Xenophon's 'Anabasis.' "

He's dead, Gunny."

"Yes, he is, Izzo."

The driver pulled off his pile hat and then, more significantly and deferential, removed his shades, blinking his eyes in the unaccustomed light.

Tate reached over to straighten Verity's cap, gone just slightly askew. The captain ought to look right, the gunnery sergeant thought, coming into town and all. A shame he didn't have a clean uniform laid away they could get him into, tidy him up a bit.

Then, seeing that Izzo was still just sitting there, as trucks and jeeps and a Sherman tank rolled by, heading into Hamhung:

"All right, Izzo, not making money sitting here. Let's get rolling."

But the words, so familiar, were gentle. Not the usual bark.

"Right, Gunny."

Izzo replaced the glasses after rubbing a chapped, dirty fist into his eyes.

The engine kicked in and the little car moved ahead.

*　*　*

Kate Verity ran to the window.

"The first snow!"

And it was. Georgetown's first of the season.

Madame came at her excited call and joined in exclamation at the beauty and wonder of it.

"Oh, I wish Poppy could see it. He loves snow, too. And we could get out the sled and he could pull me."

"We shall get out the sled, Kate, and I will pull you and then you will pull me. We will take turns."

"Oh, yes," the child said, clapping hands and, for the moment and in the joy of a first snow, forgetting her father.

The three of them came down out of the hills nearing Hamhung, and the road was smoother, mostly paved and downhill. There was plenty of traffic, enough to draw MPs urging drivers along and giving hand signals, irritating people and throwing their weight around.

"MPs," Izzo said, disgusted.

The traffic was trucks and jeeps and occasionally a tank or even a big gun, a 105 or a 155 howitzer being towed along. Marines rode on the tanks, hitching rides, and the trucks were filled and so were the jeeps. Almost no one walked now. There were a few new dead, men freshly killed at Sudong or along the road in ambush and men who had died of cold or old wounds, over the last few days, their bodies stacked in the trucks, occasionally tied snug across the hood of a jeep. It was all very neat and antiseptic.

"Cold storage," Izzo said.

They'd shed their own bodies north of here, at the rail depot of Chinhung-ni, including one without an arm. Izzo had been glad to get rid of that one. "I like to keep a tidy vehicle," he told Tate, even though, in all fairness, the stump's coagulated blood hadn't made that much of a mess.

They carried only one body now, Verity's, and they had him up in the front seat, slumped over slightly as if napping during the drive.

"It looks nicer, Gunny, than having the captain stretched out like just another stiff, you know what I mean?"

"I surely do, Izzo. He looks fine, sitting there like that."

This wasn't just a concern for Captain Verity's appearance. Tate and Izzo had been having it out even before they came down from the last of the hills onto the coastal flats and while Hamhung was still only a smudge of smoke on the horizon. The sea was beyond that and they knew it was there, but they couldn't see it. Not yet.

"I don't want to turn him in with the rest of the stiffs, Gunny. Let's take the captain right into Hungnam down by the port so they'll be sure to get him aboard ship and the hell out, so they can't plant him here."

"Izzo, they got regulations. There's MPs all the way from here on in, you know that, directing units and checking off numbers. We're back, Izzo: this ain't the war no more. It's garrison duty and you do what they damn well tell you to do. We could get away with stuff up there fighting in the hills. Not here."

As he spoke, Tate realized something terrible, that already he missed the war.

"Morgue's up ahead. Turn left in about three hundred yards."

That was another MP, waving them along.

Now Izzo became urgent.

"Look, Gunny, we keep the captain, see, and take him right into Hungnam. We leave him here who the hell knows what happens when the Chinks get here . . . ?"

"He doesn't like you calling 'em Chinks, Izzo. The captain is very particular about that and you know it."

"OK, sorry. But them Chinese ain't maybe eighteen hours behind us and coming quick. These army troops I see manning the perimeter around here couldn't stop Steve Van Buren and the Philadelphia Eagles, never mind we got a dozen Chinese divisions coming."

"So what?"

"So, I don't want Captain Verity left here in Hamhung, dead and unable to help himself none, when the army is bugging out and him feeling the way he did about being buried in Korea." The words tumbled out until, winded, Izzo paused. Then, more slowly, "So I think we just drive into Hungnam with the captain and see that he's properly treated, as befits a man like him."

Tate inhaled. He remembered Verity at Koto-ri, how the captain had looked and what he had said, about "no one needs tank treads mashing him under, dead or alive, Gunny."

"Nosir," Tate had said, very much in agreement.

After a bit, thinking it was the least they could do, Tate said crisply, "OK, Izzo, we take the captain into Hungnam."

As the troops poured through the market town of Hamhung and into the port of Hungnam, secure now under the naval guns and the close air support, all those jets screaming overhead and low, and freed of the narrow mountain road where the Chinese had hemmed them in, the whole attitude changed.

Time magazine put it this way: "The running fight of the Marines and two battalions of the Army's 7th Infantry Division from Hagaru to Hamhung, forty miles by air but sixty miles over the icy, twisting mountainous road, was a battle unparalleled in U. S. military history. It had some aspects of Bataan, some of Anzio, some of Dunkirk, some of Valley Forge, some of the 'Retreat of the 10,000' (401–400 B.C.) as described in Xenophon's 'Anabasis.' "

"Glorioso!" Izzo said, rubbing his hands. "I got a plan."

Tate was sure he had. He always did. By now he knew Izzo's mind, shrewd and warped.

"Go ahead, talk."

"OK," Izzo said. "First of all, before he gets frozen too hard, Gunny, let's you and me fix the captain up a bit, wedge him straight up in the seat but more lifelike, so he'll be riding with me, his faithful driver, and you, the gunny, in back with the radio. Everything proper. That way none of these rear-echelon pogues will be telling us where to take him and what to do with him. They'll be too busy snapping off salutes and saying 'yessir' and 'nosir' and clicking their frigging heels."

Tate thought about it for a time. Gunnery sergeants are not paid for rashness and are noted for the judicial pause. That's how they got all those stripes and how, one day, if they live long enough and sufficient top sergeants are killed or retire, they might one day make top sergeant their own selves. So Tate meditated.

"Gunny . . . ," Izzo urged, impatient and risking retribution.

"OK, Izzo, we'll try it your way."

Once he said that, Tate felt better. They would take Verity into the port, where Graves Registration would get him aboard ship. For the gunny, weights had been removed.

But rearranging Verity's frozen corpse into a naturally lifelike pose wasn't as easy as Izzo suggested, the captain's right leg taking on a will of its own, refusing to bend at the knee so he could sit up straight.

They wrestled with it, both of them, pushing and pulling. No good. Izzo threw up his hands in frustration.

"If you gotta break his damned leg, Gunny, break it. He ain't feeling it."

"I don't like to do that, Izzo."

"Here, gimme the BAR. I'll whack him with the stock. That ought to frigging do it."

Tate imagined the sound of dead bone splintering and, revolted, gave one great final shove.

"Good! He's in," Izzo enthused.

They replaced Verity's helmet snug over his cap and tidied up his parka a bit and propped his head at an angle that was almost jaunty. Izzo even breathed on his silver captain's bars and polished them with a dirty sleeve.

"If we had a pipe or something, he could almost be MacArthur his frigging self, Gunny," Izzo said, very excited.

"Well, he's got a few cigars left."

Tate knew he, too, was becoming giddy. Snow had begun to fall again, and it was getting colder. Izzo tugged a Havana from the breast pocket of Verity's dungaree jacket inside the parka and tried to shove it into his mouth, but the face was frozen now, not from cold alone but in death, the mouth taking on the hideous grin of rictus mortis, and he could not pry the teeth apart even a little.

"Forget the cigar, Izzo," Tate ordered, "and let's move out or we'll all be dead."

"Aye-aye, Gunny," Izzo said, climbing in behind the wheel and patting Verity on the left knee. "We're taking you home, Captain. They ain't gonna bury you here."

As the snow came down heavier, he drove slowly back onto the road, maneuvering the jeep dexterously into a gap between marching men, bouncing slightly as the tires jounced over the rutted, frozen surface of the dirt road.

There were lots of MPs now, officious and loud, shouting instructions, but they came through Hamhung in good order with a silent Captain Verity taking the salute.

"Walking wounded turn left here. Nonwalking, drop 'em right here and we got people will pick 'em up. Stiffs, straight ahead half a mile. They got a morgue; make a hard right."

The MPs liked giving instructions, and neither Tate nor Izzo took it well, Tate because of his five stripes and gunnery sergeant's sense of dignity and propriety and Izzo because he didn't like policemen, military or otherwise.

"Frig you," he muttered under his breath.

"Just shut up, Izzo, and drive slow. We'll get the captain somewhere we can find officers who knew him."

"That's the ticket, Gunny." Izzo brightened. "Glad you thought of that. I wondered what we was going to do if we got him this far."

"Well, that's why they pay me gunny's wages, Izzo, and you get two-striper's."

"I knew it must be something like that," Izzo said, a bit sulky at the reproof.

There was one sticky moment when traffic slowed at the turnoff to the morgue, where trucks were adding their dead to a line of corpses on the ground, as Graves Registration men scrutinized dog tags and compiled lists.

"There's a job you couldn't pay me to do, graves reg.," Izzo said. "I knew a fat guy in high school, Murphy, he wanted to become an undertaker. Funny guy, too, and smart. Never could understand it."

"Let's just get out of here," Tate said, more prudent and a bit nervous now, their jeep idling in the traffic with Verity sitting there, very still. The snow had thinned again, and you could see better now. Could see too well.

One of the graves reg. men looked up: "You got another stiff there or that guy's asleep?"

Tate gave him a hard look, a gunnery sergeant's look.

"That 'guy' is Captain Thomas Verity and he's asleep. We had some fighting back there up the road a bit. Or hadn't you heard?"

"Sure, Gunny, sure."

Tate had ticked the five stripes on his sleeves with a mittened hand, casually, as if by accident.

The graves man knew it was no accident and bent swiftly to his work as Izzo gunned the jeep and pulled slowly away.

"Pull over when you get a break in the traffic, Izzo."

There were actual jams now, here on the outskirts of Hungnam, plenty of army vehicles, trucks and jeeps and such, servicing the perimeter troops and installations, and the Marine trucks and tanks and guns coming south from the reservoir.

"OK," Izzo said, looking for an opening.

When they parked, Tate got out and began to build a fire.

"We're going to tidy up a bit before going into town, Izzo, look a little soldierly."

Izzo looked down at himself. "My pants stink of shit and piss and the rest just stinks of me and you want me soldierly? Why don't we get into town first? Maybe they got a Turkish bath."

"And we'll start with a clean shave," the gunny said, "soon as I get some water heated."

Exasperated, Izzo demanded, "And are we gonna shave the frigging captain, too?"

Tate looked at him. "You know, Izzo, we just might. I hadn't thought of it, but yes, we might."

And Gunnery Sergeant Tate mulled another idea, as well, relying on chaos and panic at the port of Hungnam. He was reasonably sure they were going to find the frightened bustle and impatience of a forced evacuation ("Sweet Jesus! Don't leave me behind!"), the mingling of broken units and stragglers and deserters and the malingerers. With construction gangs throwing up temporary, jury-rigged shelters in counterpoint to the work of

demolition parties. It was a situation made for bungling and brawl-
ing, officers gone mad, disobedience by surly enlisted men, frenzy
and drunkenness, looting and panic, brutal and licentious soldiery
all about and run amok.

In confusion a determined man can usually do and get what he
wants. In such confusion they just might smuggle Verity through.

Soldiers manned the perimeter, men of the Seventh Army Division. "About time they did something," Marines remarked, unchar-
itable. Marine MPs managed the few roads, waving Marine
vehicles through and down toward the port, directed Marines
walking in. Marines gave them the finger and moved on, saving
their abuse for soldiers. Now the press was here. Not just David
Douglas Duncan, an old Marine from the War who had walked
back from Hagaru with the division (as a man should!), but new
people no one had seen before. These new correspondents hurried
about conscientiously, as if sheer industry would make up for their
not having been there during the bad times. There were rumors
James Michener was there, that Ed Murrow of CBS was on his way
to do a "Christmas in Korea" report for TV. As their jeep moved
slowly into the town along the clogged main road in the wake of
trucks and tanks and tracked howitzers, Izzo saw Marguerite Higgins standing off to the side, leaning elegantly against a truck
fender, wearing a fur-hooded parka that was decidedly nonissue,
notebook in hand, interviewing Marines as they slogged past, a few
who recalled her from early in the fighting or up at the airstrip of
Hagaru, calling out, brash and familiar, "Hey, Maggie, it's me!"

"Sure, Marine, give me your name. I'll get it in the paper if I can."

The correspondents were there to record salvation.

"Crows," one Marine called them, "hangin' around, lookin' for
carcasses at the side of the road."

Puller thought they were more like professional mourners,
people paid to attend funerals and keen at wakes.

Others thought the reporters were just doing a job. And for a few
of them, like Duncan, who had marched with them, the Marines
demonstrated not just tolerance but affection.

Maggie Higgins, chic in her parka, had a jeep and driver supplied by Almond. She was taking notes, scribbling fast, shouting to

Marines as they passed, asking their names, their units. Izzo, whose eyesight was phenomenal when it came to loot or women, had seen her a long way off.

"Hey, Gunny, it's Maggie Higgins. You remember, her and the captain, they knew each other."

Tate, painfully aware of the dead Verity propped up next to Izzo, hissed orders.

"Just shut up, Izzo. No waving or nothing. We drive by like she wasn't even there. No eyes-right, no stunts. You get me?"

"OK, OK, OK, Gunny, Jeez."

"Just keep driving. We don't need to be noticed. Not by her, not by reporters, not by nobody."

"OK, Gunny, OK!"

Jeez, the way they jumped all over you for nothing.

Miss Higgins stayed there for more than an hour, talking to men she remembered or who remembered her, recognizing a few, faking it with others.

Some senior officers, colonels, she knew. They snapped off salutes as they went by. To have come seventy miles down that road from Yudam-ni and still be alive, you had to feel pretty good. You had to be glad to see anyone you knew from before, not just an attractive woman. Being an attractive woman made it better, of course.

Marguerite Higgins might have remembered Tom Verity if she saw him. Perhaps not his name. But she might have remembered.

The jeep bearing the dead Verity rolled past and she didn't even look, either at the vehicle or at the officer sitting stiffly next to the freshly clean-shaven driver.

"Hey, Maggie! Put my name in the paper, huh?"

"Sure, Marine, what's your name? What's your hometown?"

Men yelled back and she took notes. A few would find their way into print. Most of them she would toss away.

For hours the Marines trudged down the road into Hungnam, men reprieved by the governor, granted a new trial.

"Wave and look happy! Wave and look happy!"

That was from the press photographers there at Hungnam down by the port, standing by the side of the road, looking for the good shot for tomorrow's front page.

"Wave and look happy!"

Some of the grimy, tired Marines did just that. Others just slogged silently past. And one called back.

"Fuck you and the horse you rode in on!"

Peng and Lin, the senior generals in the field, had smashed Eighth Army and sent it reeling back hundred of miles and would shortly cross into South Korea and take Seoul. Again. In the East, X Corps had been battered and bloodied and forced to evacuate by sea. Two great Western armies had been defeated. Remarkable feats for a Chinese force without air or big guns and moving on foot through deep snow in winter mountains.

But Lin and Peng had committed the unforgivable sin, of defeating an enemy army while failing to destroy it.

This was noted in Peking, and eventually the two victorious generals would be returned to China, where, having embraced this dialectic or that, having backed one party faction or another, Lin and Peng fell into Mao Tse-tung's disfavor and were stripped of honors.

Then they were fastened to wooden posts and shot.

"It's a drive in the country, Gunny," Izzo enthused, "a day at the Jersey Shore."

It was, too. Hungnam was full of replacements and broken units and Marines and soldiers and even sailors off the ships, and thousands of North Korean refugees wanting to get away, and plenty of ROK troops that had just bugged out without asking anyone's permission, and a corral holding a couple thousand Chinese and North Korean prisoners, and too much traffic, with engineers wiring explosives to warehouses and docks and the town hall and just about everything else, for when the word came down to blow it all. Choppers circled overhead, landed, and rose again, ferrying staff officers and the badly wounded out to the ships. Higher up, the white vapor trails of the jets streaked the December sky.

They were through the town and down in the dock area and on the beach before they knew it. Which was where Izzo pulled over, slamming on the brake hard, tossing Verity's body forward and Tate damned near out of the backseat.

"Izzo!" the gunny said menacingly.

"Gunny, it's the most fabuloso idea ever. Look at them LSTs pulled up on the beach with their ramps down and trucks and tanks and jeeps going aboard. The whole First Marine Division is leaving town, twenty thousand of us. Why, all we got to do is drive right down there with Captain Verity and we—"

"We're turning in the body, Izzo. We're not smuggling bodies aboard naval vessels."

"Gunny, this ain't a body. It's Captain Verity."

"Don't tell me about Captain Verity, you Mouse you! There are rules and regulations—"

"He's dead, Gunny. He's frigging dead. There's some sort of statute of limitations when you're dead? I never heard that, not even in *Rocks & Shoals.*"

Rocks & Shoals was what Marines called their official book of regulations.

There were seven LSTs lined up abreast where the surf came up lazily onto the sand as if it were too cold even for the sea to make much of a fuss.

Queues of six-by trucks and jeeps and tanks and armored personnel carriers and tracked howitzers were lined up, quite neatly, along the waterfront and then down onto the sand. Here at the water's edge, there was very little snow, just a bit drifted gray and dirty against the tin sheds and piers and warehouses and other structures of the port. The hills, inland beyond the town, were completely white.

"Well, Gunny?" Izzo said.

"You're getting shook, Izzo. Just don't get shook."

"Shook? Shook? Me frigging shook?" There was an uncharacteristic nerviness in his voice.

He was at the wheel of the jeep and Tate was behind him, next to the radio, with the BARs and their sleeping bags and packs. Up front, next to Izzo, Captain Verity, upright and frozen, dead eyes open and staring.

"Well, well?" Izzo asked. He wished they'd closed the captain's damned eyes. They were creepy.

"Just put a sock in it, Izzo." There was a finality in Tate's flat tone. But he was the whole time watching the beach, and thinking.

As the trucks and tanks and jeeps ground slowly in low gear toward the steel-gridded ramps of the big landing craft and then up and in, disappearing into the great, dark ship's maws, MPs kept tally, working with clipboards to take down vehicle serial numbers and keep the traffic moving. There was no sense of urgency here at the beach, simply efficiency. But the MPs were there at each ramp. Watching.

Tate suffered the curse of indiscriminate memory, his historian's mind retaining trivial facts of little use, and now as he watched the MPs and the lines of vehicles crossing the beach and being waved aboard landing ships, a nagging recall began to take hold.

"Gunny, you know what I—"

"Shut up, Izzo!"

Tate was thinking faster now. The Cid! When he was killed in battle, didn't his wife or somebody put him back dead on his horse and tie him on, the sword in his hand, trot him out in his armor, so that when the Moors saw him they were astonished and fell back in disarray and Valencia, or someplace, was saved for Christianity and the king?

Turning now to Izzo, sulking and silent, Tate addressed him scornfully. "Don't you know anything, you ignorant little man? Didn't you ever hear of El Cid?"

Izzo stared at him. They were all a bit nuts coming down from the reservoir, but Tate? The gunny?

"Sid who? Gunny, you frigging lost me."

"Old boyhood hero of mine, Izzo. Spanish gent. Good soldier."

"Yes, sir," Izzo said, brightening, "like you and Captain Verity are heroes of mine. Always will be, too." Pause. "What regiment was this Sid in?"

Tate didn't reply. He was too busy puzzling the thing out. If there was some way they could disguise Verity, mask his death, they, too, might might be able to confound the Moors.

"The MPs, Izzo. That's the problem. MPs are policemen, Izzo; they're cops."

Izzo shuddered slightly; the police were an irritating memory.

"Hell, Gunny. I know they're cops and you're a gunny. I'm a frigging driver. The captain . . . well, he's a frigging captain. On the staff and all."

"The captain, Izzo, is dead."

"Hell, I know he's dead. And I remember how he felt about being left behind and buried by a 'dozer. We both know that."

"We surely do, Izzo." Tate was still thinking. And while he thought, he watched the MPs, nothing which of them seemed alert and nosy, which more languid, in his inspection.

"You see, what I think—"

"Shut up, Izzo."

Boy, he could be stiff, Izzo thought. *As if the whole thing were my fault. . . .*

Tate knew he was being unfair. Truth was, he didn't know what to do. He leaned forward, looking at Verity's face. The dead eyes bothered him. Then!

"Izzo, give me your sunglasses."

"My shades? You want my shades?"

"Izzo, we don't need a debate every time I want you to do something. Whatever you call them, just damned well do it!"

"All right, Gunny," Izzo said sulkily, injured. "I won't ask. Just take my personal property like it was nothing but—"

Tate examined the glasses, breathing on the lenses and then polishing them against the bandanna tied across his frozen nose. His nose hurt. Here at the water's edge the temperatures were higher, so the frozen tissue was thawing. Rotting. And it hurt. While it was still frozen there was only a dull ache. Now it was like a bad burn.

"Jesus, Gunny," Izzo said, "it's getting warmer. We don't want him . . . you know . . . melting or something."

"No, we don't want that." Tate was almost gentle and Izzo silently forgave him.

Now Tate reached around Verity's shoulders very carefully and placed the sunglasses on his face, delicately inserting the wire legs under the earflaps and helmet behind the captain's ears.

He then looked at Verity's face, three-quartered, from behind.

"Mmmmm."

"What?" Izzo demanded. "WHAT?"

"How does he look now, Izzo? Can't see the eyes now, can you?"

Mouse Izzo turned now to examine Verity, full face on. He came from a family of barbers and beauticians, those were his bloodlines, and he scrutinized the dead man intensely for a moment or two.

"Gunny, I gotta say he looks pretty good. For a dead man, you couldn't do better."

Tate grunted assent, not listening, really. The Marine Corps had plenty of rules about live people, but beyond the regulations laid out for proper military funerals, he couldn't think of a one about the dead.

So he grilled Izzo further. The little bastard had a nimble mind, and there may have been things occurred to him that Tate hadn't himself thought of.

"What happens if we get him aboard?" Tate inquired.

"I dunno, Gunny, but we got to get him aboard. That I'm sure of."

Next to him Captain Verity sat quietly, the dead eyes no longer staring.

"Gunny, you know the captain never would of let you down. Or me. For instance, if you were getting captured he would of shot you. He said he would and I know he meant it."

"Thanks," said Gunnery Sergeant Tate, understandably sour.

But Izzo was encouraged. Eagerly he went on.

"I would of myself, Gunny, knowing how strong you feel about not getting captured again. That's how I feel about you. That's how I feel about Captain Verity and not leaving him behind to get buried."

Tate, trying to touch all bases, said, "And what do you think the navy will do when they realize they've got a dead man on board?"

"The navy never had anyone frigging die before, Gunny? I guess they'll lay him out proper. A ship the size of an LST, they gotta have a reefer. They can put him in there with the sides of beef and bacon and such, I guess. What the hell do I know? I'm a frigging wheelman."

And how much do I know? Tate repeated silently. *I'm a gunnery sergeant of Marines, not a mortician.*

* * *

In Washington, Truman and Secretary of State Dean Acheson and other great men in high office, were somewhat confounded by the successful march of the Marines to the sea. Of course they wanted them out. No president, no American, wanted another Bataan, with U. S. troops defeated, encircled, rounded up, captured, and put on display. A defeat like that would only encourage Stalin and Communist movements from France to Italy to Central America and Southeast Asia and beyond. Truman himself might not have survived such a national humiliation.

But there was still MacArthur. That son of a bitch!

If they could have buried MacArthur and saved American honor, no one would have hesitated.

Harry Truman, over bourbons with Clark Clifford and his cronies, gave reluctant tribute. He'd assailed the Marines as possessing a public relations apparatus superior to that of the Soviet Union. Now the Marines might just have saved his ass. And he acknowledged as much.

Had they also salvaged MacArthur? Mr. Truman, with bourbon or without, was determined they would not. He'd had enough of the general.

While Izzo cajoled, Tate was watching the speed with which trucks hit the ramp, the distance between MPs, and how closely they checked off vehicle numbers on their clipboards, how closely they scrutinized driver and passengers, if any.

Izzo started to wheedle again but saw something in Tate's face and shut up. After a moment the gunnery sergeant turned to him.

"OK, Izzo, we go."

A few moments later, they were rolling, very slowly, sliding in between a two-and-a-half-ton truck and a battered armored personnel carrier that had seen brighter days.

"Stay at their speed until I tell you, Izzo."

"Aye-aye, Gunny."

Up and down the beach, Marines waded into the Sea of Japan to board ships small and large that would carry them away from Korea. Next month, next spring, perhaps, they would be back, fighting again. But for this moment they were men who had lived through the terrible autumn, fought the cold and the Chinese, and not died.

Miracle enough.

Tate watched them queue up and stamp their feet in the sand and then, when the infantry craft were ready, shuffle ahead, heavy-laden, to board ship and leave. People had to understand their slowness: their feet were frozen.

The LSTs only took vehicles. Tanks and trucks and tracked guns and personnel carriers and ambulances.

And jeeps, caked with mud and pierced by shell fragments and driven by surly little men who were sure something was being put over on them.

"What the fug y'mean, what am I doing?" Izzo cried at the first dubious MP. His legitimate outrage was more than impressive. And he kept the jeep moving.

" 'Zackly what I mean, buddy."

"Yeah, sure." That was the extent of Izzo's response. Tate looked into the MP's eyes balefully. Captain Verity, up front, stared straight ahead, stern and cold behind his silvered glasses.

The entire division; twenty thousand men less the dead and missing, was being taken out. To fight again. No one looked too closely at heroes.

Except this one MP.

"Something wrong with this officer?" he asked Tate. "He sick or something?" He leaned toward the jeep.

Tate gave him his best gunnery sergeant glare, and then, crisp and sure, he said, "Captain Verity, back from the reservoir, with dispatches for the general!"

The MP hesitated, still looking into Verity's face, and then, after a moment that to Izzo seemed an hour, stepped back to snap off a salute.

"Yes sir, Captain."

"Hit it, Izzo," Tate said, jaw set and eyes glacial.

The jeep leaped forward in the sand, wheels spinning, sending up spumes of grit and beach, racing down to the water's edge, where it cut deftly in front of a huge Pershing tank and hit the steel ramp hard and loud.

"Hey, you!" the tanker shouted from his perch a dozen feet above them, to which Izzo responded with a loud, discordant squawk of the horn and an echo of Tate: "Captain Verity with dispatches for the General!"

The jeep bounced buoyantly up the ramp, its tires burning rubber on the metal grating, before vanishing into the darkness of the ship's hold, followed by the big Pershing, the final vehicle this LST could hold.

"Move it! Move it!" the MPs shouted as they waved off the next vehicles and directed them down the beach to another LST, as the heavy ramp creaked and groaned upward on its cables, sealing in the Pershing tank and the little jeep carrying Izzo and Tate and Captain Verity out of Korea.

"You see that jeep cut in there ahead of the tank? Three Marines?"

"Ferget it," the MP sergeant growled.

"But, Sarge . . ."

"They're crazy, them guys who was up there."

"Crazy?"

"Sure, all them from the reservoir. Crazy or froze or dead. Or all three. Be grateful they didn't take a shot at you."

The MP, disappointed, like a traffic cop without a ticket to write, started to argue. The sergeant cut him off.

"Let it go. You'd be crazy, too, you was up there."

Within minutes, its powerful engines in reverse, churning up sand and mud and silt, the ship bearing the body of Captain Verity slid laboriously off the beach at Hungnam and out into deeper waters, where it would turn and set course to sail south on the evening tide.

"Glorioso, Mouse," Tate muttered. "That was glorioso. . . ."

"Why, thanks, Gunny. Nice of you to—"

"Now, just shut up."

Jesus, this was some gunny.

"Jean," the General said, hearty and bluff, "I wouldn't be surprised if we were going home at last."

"Home? Douglas, what a glorious thought."

She was southern, with a soft voice full of charm but also very genuine enthusiasm for her man.

"Yes, Truman will recall me. I sense it coming."

"But you saved the army, Douglas. No one else could have."

"And might have won," he agreed, "had the president and the Joint Chiefs possessed vision. And the will."

She was too excited by the thought of home to be pensive. Their lives had taken on the curious rigidity and internal logic of the Druid Circle. And now, to break out, to see America again . . .

"Just think of it, home." She was thinking, too, of their son. When her General remained silent, she said, hoping to arouse him, "And think of how the country will celebrate your return. How the people will call for you. Oh, what a dazzling moment it will be."

"Yes, Jean, home is of all destinations sweetest."

But in his heart the General knew America did not elect as president men who evacuated armies and retreated.

At Hungnam they dug a hasty cemetery and buried there the men from the reservoir who'd died on the road south and been carried in by truck or on the tanks or the narrow-gauge railroad. When the ceremony ended, Chesty Puller broke away from the formation of senior offices and went up to the line of Marines who'd fired the rifle salute over the bodies, thanking them for volunteering for this small, last service.

Then he wrote his wife: "Darling: With the help of the Almighty and no other unit or person, my regiment is on the beach at Hungnam and will be aboard ship before the day is over."

This was December 13. Puller himself boarded the transport *General Collins* on the next day and would play poker all night with officers and enlisted men both.

Kate Verity, in a velvet-collared coat, white knee socks, and Mary Janes, stood quietly to one side with her nanny outside the church while all these tall people consoled one another.

They buried Tom Verity next to his wife in a Maryland churchyard of no particular religious denomination but of great beauty, and snowless in the mild winter.

A few days later, in Christmas week, with wreaths still hung and the crèche decorated, the Jesuits held a memorial service at Holy Trinity, a church in Georgetown just off university property and, like the college, a Jesuit institution.

From Henderson Hall came two Marine officers in dress blues, with all the medals, properly grim and concerned and attentive, saying the right things and standing erect at appropriate moments. Neither of them had ever met Captain Verity; they knew little of him or how he'd died and had come to mourn on official orders to do so.

Georgetown's students were home on Christmas break and the church was largely empty, but some faculty and Elizabeth's sister from Philadelphia, attended, and Mr. and Mrs. Verity, the parents, older and grayer, very much so, had flown in from Grosse Pointe. A Jesuit spoke, the tone and the words well chosen, and then one of the officers, and there were several hymns from the organ, tunes Verity would not have recognized.

It was a fine service (the Jesuits did such things well), and Izzo and Gunny Tate in likelihood would have enjoyed it, seeing what the captain meant to them and Izzo being Catholic and Tate, a career noncommissioned officer, partial to ritual and rite, but they hadn't been notified or invited. In the muddle of evacuation and later in the refit and reinforcement of the division both men had been reassigned, and nothing was ever put down in writing of their services to Captain Verity. So commissioned officers who didn't know Tom Verity attended in their place.

When the ceremony was ended and they all filed out into the bright winter sun, blinking after the proper gloom of the church, Elizabeth's sister and the elder Veritys stopped to thank the priest. They weren't Catholic, but they had manners. As they spoke, Kate Verity, in a velvet-collared coat, white knee socks, and Mary Janes, stood quietly to one side with her nanny outside the church while all these tall people consoled one another. The child thought carefully about what she had seen and heard inside and remembered how the lighted candles danced, trying to understand some of what these strange men had said about her father, and why none of them was the "Mouse" of her daddy's letters, and who drove their "poor little jeep" and wore sunglasses, even at night, and she also wondered why they played such odd songs, instead of one of those her father sang. Like "Sur le pont d'Avignon."

Then she tugged at the nanny's hand and inquired, politely but wanting very much to know, "Madame?"

"Yes, Kate?"

"And who will take me now to France to see the bridges?"

AFTERWORD

I've been asked by several people who read this novel in pre-publication if the fictional Thomas Verity was inspired by my rifle company commander in the Taebaek Mountains of North Korea, Captain John H. Chafee of Rhode Island, who would later become governor of his state, Secretary of the Navy, and a United States senator. Yes, he was. My portrait of Verity draws on Chafee's education at Yale and Harvard, his combat experiences on Guadalcanal and Okinawa and service in North China, and on his gallantry, his gentleness, his love of family and of country and of the Marine Corps. In those matters, and in none of Verity's flaws, the story owes much to Captain Chafee, who also died in the autumn, on October 24, 1999.